SOMEBODY'S DAUGHTER

DAUGHTER

ROCHELLE B. WEINSTEIN

USA TODAY BESTSELLING AUTHOR

PRAISE FOR ROCHELLE B. WEINSTEIN

"Weinstein has given us a wonderful tale of life and its distractions. She gives us characters that are flawed and yet lovable . . . You will find yourself affected to the very core by the depth of her work."

—*Blogcritics* on *Where We Fall*

"Compelling . . . *What We Leave Behind*'s twists and turns generate real tension, and Weinstein renders Jessica's feelings with enough complexity that her ultimate decision carries emotional weight."

—*Kirkus Reviews* on *What We Leave Behind*

"Each word of *What We Leave Behind* invokes raw emotion as we are brought deeper into the soul of a woman that can be any of us. This moving story will echo strongly with any woman who has had to face love and loss, life and death, and everything in between."

—*Long Island Woman* on *What We Leave Behind*

"A heart-wrenching tale of loss, loyalty, and the will to overcome . . . Weinstein explores the difficult facets of grief that are often too painful to recognize, the solipsism of mourning, the selfishness of regret, and the guilt of moving on . . . Ultimately, this novel full of mourning has a large, aching heart full of sympathy and potential, and will keep the reader listening for signs of restored life."

—*Kirkus Reviews* on *The Mourning After*

"Weinstein hooked me with her first novel, and *The Mourning After* has made me a fan for life. She has that rare ability to hook you from chapter one, keep you turning the pages and then continuing to think about the characters long after you have put the book down."

—James Grippando, *New York Times* bestselling author, on *The Mourning After*

SOMEBODY'S DAUGHTER

ALSO BY ROCHELLE B. WEINSTEIN

What We Leave Behind
The Mourning After
Where We Fall

SOMEBODY'S DAUGHTER

ROCHELLE B. WEINSTEIN

Published by Lake Union Publishing, Seattle

www.apub.com

Amazon, the Amazon logo, and Lake Union Publishing are trademarks of Amazon.com, Inc., or its affiliates.

ISBN-13: 9781503949256
ISBN-10: 1503949257

Cover design by Damon Freeman

Printed in the United States of America

For anyone who has ever made a mistake. And for those who have judged and been judged.

CHAPTER 1

"Excuse me," my husband whispers in my ear, shimmying up alongside me at our double vanity and teasing me with his eyes. "Do I know you?"

His dark, messy hair grazes my cheek, and a fresh line of stubble tickles my neck. Our bodies fit together in the bathroom mirror, and I smile at our little game. "Not now, Bobby." Though I'm pleased after nearly twenty years of marriage he still likes to play.

We hear their laughter before they enter, and soon our girls fill the small space. They scoot in front of the mirror admiring their identical faces, while matching Ross Hotel bathrobes frost us all in white.

"Mom, where's my dress?"

Zoe's face is panic-stricken, and I pass the garment bag in her direction. "Here. I had it steamed for you."

"Do you like these earrings?" Lily asks, holding large diamonds up to her ears, the ones Bobby's mother gave me for college graduation.

"Hand them over," I say, extending my palm.

Disappointment clouds her face.

Bobby watches us in amusement and cozies up to me again. "Happy *birth* day."

I sink into him and let the sentiment soothe me. "Their turning fifteen means we're getting older, too."

"You're not getting older, honey. You're getting better."

I wince at my reflection and pull on the strands that nip my shoulders. "I shouldn't have cut my hair."

His lips find my forehead, and he nuzzles me. "I like it. And I like you."

The girls roll their eyes and nudge us aside. Excitement covers their faces, and I reflect on the years that took us by surprise. Tonight's party has them growing up before my eyes. Literally. And armed with thick layers of hair and the weapons to make it straight, they're part *See what we've created*, and another part *What have we done?*

Bobby catches me staring and drops a hand on my shoulder. It slides down my back.

"You're not half bad for a mom of teenagers."

"Funny," I laugh, elbowing him in the ribs. "I'll always be younger than you. Even if it's a couple of months."

I watch Bobby tease the girls while recounting the day they were born and how he almost fainted in the delivery room. It gives me time to observe the subtle differences. To the outside world, the girls are genetic clones: matching brown hair that sweeps past their shoulders, fair skin dotted with freckles, full lips, and crystal blue eyes they inherited from their grandparents. Only those closest to them know the real differences. Zoe's nose is slightly broader. Lily's freckles a shade lighter. Zoe is a leftie. Lily uses her right hand. Lily's eyes are a pinch brighter. Zoe's are tinged in a subtle gray. There are deeper differences, too.

"I told you girls," I say, interrupting his story. "Women are the stronger sex." Bobby's dark eyes lock on mine, and I swipe my fingers across the shadow lining his jaw. "You're shaving that, right?"

"Yes, dear." He smiles, running his hand through his thick brown hair. "I think I spotted some gray." He bends over to show me, which interests the girls.

I've been going gray since college. I don't feel sorry for him at forty-one with a few strands of silver. Lily lets go of the flatiron and pulls at the single hairs.

"Don't do that," Zoe laughs. "He'll grow ten more."

Lily's eyes are doubtful. "That is so not true. Don't believe everything you hear."

"Ouch," he says to Lily as she pulls. "That hurts!"

His arm comes around Lily, and he draws her close, but she's quick to pull back. "Daddy," she says with a half smile. "You're messing up my hair."

He throws his arms up in the air. "I need sons."

I've studied his contradictions for years, the tenacious real estate mogul who can't say no to his daughters or wife.

He dips his hand inside the top drawer, pulls out a razor, and waves it in the air. "You ready, Zoe?"

It was a game they played when Zoe was little. She'd complain when his beard scratched her face, and when she was five, he handed her the first razor. With patience and love, he showed her how to hold it in her small hand, lather on the shaving cream, and gently stroke the side of his face. She basked in the attention and affection, taking pride in "cleaning Daddy's face." There were nicks and scratches over the years, but he never minded, and it became their special ritual.

"Daddy." She smiles at him. "I'm too old for that."

His face falls.

"How come you never let me do it?" Lily asks through a face full of makeup I'm not quite sure how she learned to apply. Her pale-blue eyes are shaded in a smoky sex appeal that makes her way too pretty.

"You hate blood," her sister reminds her.

I watch Zoe while she lines her eyes—the long lashes, the curve of her nose. She has her father's eyebrows—thick with an enviable arch. Lily glosses her lips for the fifth time and smacks them together in a way that makes me shudder.

"Daddy, we need some privacy," Zoe says in all seriousness.

"This is my bathroom," he pouts.

"The lighting's better in here," Lily chimes in, which is nonsense since our entire penthouse on the beach has floor-to-ceiling windows that make every room bright and airy.

Zoe feels sorry for him. She folds into his arms, and he plants a kiss on her forehead and both cheeks. It's their practice, usually reserved for before bed, and she doesn't back away. Her freckled skin turns a soft pink. "At least one of them likes having me around."

I link my arm into his and guide him out the door. "I like having you around."

He flops on the bed and follows my robe as it falls to the floor. It was a lot easier to undress in front of him when we were younger, two teenagers with a beach as our blanket, before time and gravity made their mark. After nineteen years of marriage, he's seen the changes, what pregnancy's done to my hips and breasts.

He watches, doing everything in his power not to be fresh while the girls are within earshot. He likes what he sees, I can tell, but I'm not always comfortable in this changed body of mine, even when he tells me it's just right. I slip inside the black dress thrown across the bed. It's lace with a silk camisole underneath, and I turn around for him to zip me up.

He stands and kisses the base of my neck. I close my eyes, and the feel of him against me takes me somewhere else. To our upcoming interview with *Ocean Drive* magazine. I've been rehearsing what I'll say about his accomplishments, how we manage to live in the hotel we own, and how we first fell in love. The long history frames us. It began on the crystal shore—innocent and playful. Then it became steamy and hot. Classic Miami.

I'm back in the present. Twenty-five teenagers are about to join us for a birthday dinner downstairs. I remember what we were doing at fifteen, and I tense.

"Is everything set with security? Do they have the guest list?" I ask.

"Emma," he says, reaching for my hand. "The staff has everything under control. Relax."

I turn my gaze upward, a well of emotions clamoring to come out. "It's our girls, Bobby. I want tonight to be special for them. Because you know what happens . . . they become these people we don't recognize . . . then they hate us and cut us out of their lives. You watch. One minute they're sweet and innocent, and the next they're . . . that's what teenagers do. And then they go to college. And it's all over."

He appraises me with his eyes. "I love how you love them . . . how you worry. Tonight's going to be perfect . . . nothing to worry about."

The pair waltzes out of the bathroom, and he stops. The reverie comes to an end. He lets go of my hand, and I'm not sure if his expression is appreciation or shock. It's astonishing in itself to bring two babies into the world at once, but when dimpled bodies become lengthy curves, and childlike innocence channels a rare sophistication, it's tough to wrap your head around. So we just stare.

"What do you think?" Lily asks, striking a pose.

"Where are the rest of your clothes?" Bobby asks.

Lily's black dress hangs dangerously low, accentuating her newly sprouted cleavage. The skirt rests high above her knee. Her long, toned lacrosse legs rise from spike-heeled sandals I believe are mine.

"I told you he was going to freak," Zoe mumbles to her sister.

"Everything's going to be perfect . . ." I remind Bobby.

Zoe's draped in a more conservative black dress. Her stick-straight hair is pulled back in a long ponytail. Her shoes are a comfortable height. But their faces. Good God. Images of braces and baby fat float through my brain. *Who are these young women, and what did they do with my little girls?* A parenting quote comes to mind that I'd recently liked on Instagram: "The days are long, but the years are short." The words are so truthful I might cry.

"Dad," says Lily in an adult tone I don't recognize. "You have to get ready. We can't be late."

"If the Olsen twins could get out of my way, I'd make myself presentable," he says.

Lily smiles while Zoe, my curious one, turns to him in question. "What would our names have been if we were boys?"

"Daddy liked—" I begin.

"Anything but Monty," he interrupts. "You would never be a Monty."

I'm mouthing the names Zachary and Luke when I freeze. *What?* The name rolls off his tongue without a shred of contempt, though I know it's there.

"Ew." Lily scowls. "Why would that even be an option?"

My body tenses. I flatten the already smooth fabric of my dress, the shame of that name coursing through my fingers. *It doesn't mean anything,* I tell myself. I inhale and exhale deeply. *He doesn't know.*

His eyes turn to me, their dazzling brown unaware that they've just pushed me, that my unsteady legs may fall. I suck in my breath and admire the girls, his handsome face. It wasn't long ago I was an actress. It's a pastime I still miss. Hence, our game. *Excuse me, do I know you?* Sometimes I'm a European painter, other times a schoolteacher. It's lighthearted fun, and Bobby loves seeing the different sides of me. *I can do this.* I pretend what he says doesn't matter. I pretend it means nothing that he remembers the long-ago name. I pretend that because we've been happily married all these years, a name can't uproot me. But it does. And I close my eyes and pretend harder.

I'll push the name far to the back of my mind, where it's stayed all these years. I have to. It's the only option.

Then I open my eyes and smile.

The elevator chimes and whisks us downstairs. I fix Bobby's collar and straighten his navy blazer. The girls fidget in their dresses and stare at their reflections in the mirror. They're snapping selfies and chattering about someone's "story."

I'm always proud to walk through our sleek white lobby together. The Ross is retro glam with an earthy simplicity, a space that feels less like a hotel and more like a cozy living room. The familiar scent of lime basil and mandarin fills the air, and I breathe it in. Bobby works hard and maintains a superior hotel. It shows in our staff and the pleased guests who pass us by. Some offer hugs and greet the girls with birthday wishes, while others shake Bobby's hand and remark on the recent Heat game. The girls are gracious about the attention we receive. They know everyone by name and are careful to look them in the eye when they speak. I am thankful they've tucked their phones away.

While I don't have a formal position in-house, Bobby boasts I'm the epicenter. He maintains, "I may be the boss, but you hold the heart." All things pump through me. I see to it that the guests leave here happy and eager to return. That our staff is treated with respect. That no detail is overlooked. It's not the job I had intended, not since abandoning my acting dreams, but the Ross satisfies me. I consider the hotel our third daughter, and I relish watching her grow. I spot Alberto and Luz up ahead. The burly man, our GM, grabs me in a tight hug. His Paco Rabanne tickles my nose like it has for many years. Luz, with her frosty silver hair, moves in for a squeeze. She's petite, like me, and our shoulders touch.

"Quince años." Alberto's deep voice and thick fingers come down on the girls. They let him hug them. They always do. "Let's hope your driving skills are better than your tricycle skills."

The hotel keeps our best memories alive, and we laugh. Lily steering her bike into the pool is a favorite.

"Poppy Berto, are you going to tell that story at my wedding?" Lily asks.

"God willing," he says, and his arm falls around Bobby's shoulder. "Your parents would be proud of these young ladies. *Preciosa!*"

When we step through the ballroom doors, we are greeted by a burst of lively teenagers. They bounce around the room to Drake and

Katy Perry and nosh on sliders and sushi. The centerpieces I worked tirelessly on with our event manager, Tara, are perfect. Crystal vases brim with lavender, lilacs, and pale-blue hydrangeas, and the girls and boys drape themselves around the long table, snapping pictures with their cell phones.

The years wash over me. It hits with a gentle force. I try not to think about how quickly time changes things. How fast Bobby and I went from being innocent kids to hovering on the brink of adulthood. Jonny, his brother and our head of marketing and PR, sidles up next to me.

"I don't remember fourteen or fifteen looking anything like this," he says.

"It's crazy," I agree, while a foreboding chill dances on my skin.

The celebration of time does nothing to keep Bobby's words from echoing in my ear. *Monty.* My reaction spilled out of me, but I managed to rein it in. He had no idea what that name did to me. What it could do to us. And though I don't want to think about it tonight, I see how these girls are dressed. I see the phones curled in their hands like appendages. The poses. And the boys who stare at them hungrily. I know we are on a new course, a new stage of raising teenagers. I don't know if I'm ready.

"Man, would I get into trouble growing up in these times." Jonny's candor breaks apart my thoughts. I focus on his full lips and the burst of blue from his eyes. He is a prettier version of Bobby. Too good-looking, if you ask me.

We planned the party exclusively for the girls and their friends, plus the longtime employees who make our family larger. Alberto and Luz. Our pool manager, Kinsley, who is engaged to our head of housekeeping, Elle. There's Sandra and Tara and Heather. Tabitha, Bobby's secretary. They see to it that our hotel comes to life each day, a lively bunch with a tender hand in raising our kids.

I pause to glance at the girls and their cast of friends. Lily sits at the helm of the table, poised and radiant, a glossy smile framing gleaming white teeth. One of her arms motions in the air as she tells a story that has them all rapt. The other extends along the back of a chair filled by Bradley Blackwell. His grandparents were Bobby's parents' close friends. The girls' best friends are scattered between the two of them. Skinny Grace Howard is talking on her cell phone. Her honey complexion accentuates her hazel eyes and highlighted hair. Shelby Moore is fixing her blonde tresses while she talks to the new girl, Ava something-I-can't-remember.

Zoe is less animated, planted at the other end of the table with Chelsea Bloom, the pale brunette beauty on one side and Raquel Cohen from the school debate team on the other. Lily teases her sister regularly about the *nerds*, but it's a harmless joke, one Zoe responds to by referring to Lily's lacrosse friends as *beasts*.

Bobby summons me to our table for a champagne toast. I hold my glass of water, but he insists it's bad luck. "One sip."

I don't want a sip. He knows this, but I hold the flute up anyway. I catch Kinsley's shiny blue eyes, and Elle beams at me. She's a clone of the famous model. Legs that go on for miles. Long, golden-blonde hair.

"I'm a lucky man," Bobby tells the staff, "having you all here with us tonight. Celebrating the girls. They're fortunate to have an extended family in you. Thank you for being here with us. And to my wife . . . the one who makes it all happen. Day after day. To my Emma. The love of my life. I can assure you that everything good about the girls comes from her."

The glasses clink, and the sound reminds me of spring. "One sip, Em, for good luck," he persists. I pretend to take a drink, and Bobby smiles.

Two cakes come out, one for each twin, and the speeches from the girls' friends follow with ripples of laughter and praise. Chelsea, Grace, and Shelby feature a video highlighting the passage of years, and Bobby whispers in my ear, "Where did the time go?"

Uncle Jonny entertains with stories of mistaken identities and practical jokes until Bobby gets up. He makes his way toward the baby grand, and I admire the way he's maintained his youth. He runs his hands across the keys, and the gentle trickle dances through the air. He's always loved that piano and how the keys come to life beneath his fingertips.

I fell in love with him on that bench, and the memory wraps around me. Banging the keys at ten. Billy Joel. A kiss. First my forehead, then my cheek. Chopin. Pressing me against the piano, lowering the lights and locking the doors. My backside against the keys, a tempered wail. Him grabbing my face, my hair, and making love to me right there against the Steinway. I would never hear Beethoven again without feeling his touch.

The song he's playing is one of the girls' favorites, a song he used to play when they were babies. *Sing out. Be free. Live high. Live low.* He isn't Adam Levine, but he can silence a room of teenagers with his voice.

When he's done, I join him. We thank everyone for coming and shamefully boast about the kind, honorable girls we've raised. Bobby speaks for the two of us. "We wish you a life of joy and beauty. One that makes you grateful and whole."

Lily dances onto the stage. Zoe follows, her steps practiced and slow. The attention quiets her. They fall into our arms while the room erupts with cheers and applause. I know I shouldn't get emotional, but I'm overwhelmed by love and the prospect of our girls growing up and away from us. If only I can hold on to them a little longer, but they are quick to get back to their friends. Their wings are hard for me to miss. When I return to the table, Luz joins me, and the older woman's arm wraps around my shoulder.

"Emma dear, a mother's job is to teach her children not to need her anymore. The hardest part of that job is accepting success. Now run to the *baño* and clean up *su cara linda.*"

CHAPTER 2

Luz's words echo through me. I almost don't make it to the bathroom before bursting into tears, and when I do, I seek refuge in a stall, latching the door behind me. Our toilet paper is the soft, plush kind, so I grab a few squares to wipe my nose and blot my eyes, and I eventually take a seat. Bobby's back on the piano, and Chelsea's silky voice filters through the door.

I hear the girls before I see them. Their laughter and chunky heels echo against the marble floors. If I peer through the crack in the door, I can see them fingering their hair and reapplying lipstick. Ava what's-her-name stares at her reflection in the mirror and asks Shelby if she prefers the red shade to the pink. Shelby seems torn about her response, afraid to give the wrong answer.

"Cool party," begins Ava, lining her green eyes with a chalky pencil. "No one at my old school owns a hotel."

"Lily and Zoe are great." Shelby's smoothing out her blonde tresses. Her off-the-shoulder dress is flowing black silk. "You'd never know they own this place. They're always nice."

I settle back and listen to their exchange. Their innocent banter buoys the residual melancholy. I'm trying not to eavesdrop while I jot down notes in my phone about upgrades, one being individual bathrooms instead of impersonal stalls.

"It's cool they included me," says Ava. "It's hard switching schools."

A series of beeps follow, and the girls are silenced. "Oh my God," says Ava. "Are you on this group text?"

A few seconds pass and Shelby answers, "No. I'm not."

Ava sounds surprised. "It's a blocked number. Are you sure?"

"I'm sure. Why? What is it?"

Ava hesitates. "This is crazy."

I'm typing into my phone, recording my vision for contemporary doors that match the modern chrome fixtures and ivory marble.

"What is it?" Shelby asks again.

"I think this is one of the twins," says Ava.

The mention of twins momentarily halts my fingers, but I quickly regain traction. There are lots of twins in Miami.

"Ava, you're scaring me. What is it?"

I lean forward and eye the girls through the crack: Shelby with her curious blue eyes, Ava holding the phone in two hands.

"Were you at the party last weekend?" asks Ava.

"Yeah," replies Shelby.

"Looks like it got a little wild."

One of our girls was at a party last weekend. I'm being ridiculous, but my heart makes that tiny thump inside my chest that sounds louder than it is.

"What is it?" Shelby begs.

"Here. Press 'Play.'"

I strain my neck to hear the muffled sounds. It's a recording. A video? It's hard to make out the hushed words.

"Oh my God," Shelby shrieks. "How could she do that?"

I am on my feet. Shelby tosses the phone at Ava. Her blue fingernails cover her open mouth, as if they can wipe out whatever it is she just saw. I'm straining to see and hear. *One of the twins?* My mother mind sabotages rational thought. *No. It can't be.*

Shelby's round eyes are full of surprise. "Oh my God. You have to delete it," she begs.

I slowly inhale, letting dread in and then breathing it out.

"This is bad," Ava says. "Do you know how fast these things get around the Internet?"

"We have to do something," Shelby says, panicking. "She's one of my best friends. She'd die if she knew this was going around."

"You can't tell her tonight!" Ava replies. "But if I got it, other people got it, too."

I remind myself these are teenage girls. They get dramatic. They get carried away. *Don't get carried away, Emma.*

Shelby bites at her freshly painted lips. "What do we do? Why would she do this?" She sounds like she's about to cry. "Why would she let someone film her?"

I do my best to block out the worst of the visuals, but according to these girls, a twin, possibly my daughter, is doing something "crazy" on a video. Something so crazy she would die knowing it was being sent around. *No.* I repeat it again. *It can't be,* but the loop inside my brain asks, *What the hell is on that phone?*

Ava bobs her head to the side. Her long black hair falls down her shoulders and lands on the top of her strapless dress. "Maybe the lacrosse girls are fast on and off the field."

Efforts to calm myself are quashed by the word *lacrosse.* Lily is on lacrosse. But she didn't go to any party. Dark thoughts pile up, a reel of dreadful scenarios I can't slow down. Maybe they're confused. All the girls look alike. Same hair. Same outfits.

That's when I hear Shelby. "That's not Lily, Ava. It's Zoe."

I freeze. *Zoe?* No. It's not possible. Whatever it is they're looking at, they've misread. *Fast* meant things our girls didn't do. For God's sake, they're in ninth grade.

The bathroom door closes behind them, and my legs buckle. *Fast. Zoe.* I place my palms on the walls for support. I'm forced to sit. What the hell is on that video? Kids today exaggerate. It's probably nothing. But my body knows it's not. I'm claustrophobic; my long-awaited exhale dissolves into the air. My heart beats, but I'm not sure I can move. *Fast.* The word sucks me of life. Zoe is the furthest thing from fast. That's why she's on the debate team.

Sounds of music and laughter filter through the space beneath the door as I try to push the apprehension away. A faucet drips. I'm dizzy, a whirl of uncertainty nipping at my brain.

Shaky hands guide me out of the stall. The clicking sound of the latch startles me, but no more than what I've just heard. I creep over to the vanity and grab hold of the surface. *Breathe, Em, breathe. You have no idea what the girls were looking at.* But there's a rebuttal running around my head like that of a broken record. *Zoe. Fast.*

I clamp my eyes shut. *Excuse me, do I know you?*

I'm imagining things. Someone's playing a silly trick. Yes, an idiotic, teenage prank. Ava is confused, and it sounds worse than it probably is. The bathroom door squeaks open, and I hide my face and wash my hands.

"Mom, what are you doing?" It's Lily. "Daddy's looking all over for you."

I'm wobbly. Unsure. Whatever's on that phone hasn't reached her yet. "Lily," I release into the air.

Her eyes narrow in on mine. "Are you all right?"

I dry my hands on one of our lush towels so I don't have to face her. "You know I get sentimental."

Her shoes click on the floor, and when she's near, she throws her arms around me. "Tonight was perfect. Thank you to you and Daddy."

Closing my eyes, I hug her and inhale her fresh, clean scent. When I open them, her barely there dress reflects in the mirror. I want to cover her with my body. *It's all a mistake.* I hold her longer than usual and stroke her hair until she pulls away.

"Let's go," she says.

But I stall, my feet drilled to the floor. I don't want to go out there. "Are you sure you're okay?" she asks again.

My response is part whisper, part refusal, and rolls like rubble off my tongue. "I'm fine."

She walks me back to the table, our arms threaded together. When she finds her girlfriends, she unleashes my arm, and I stare around the room. It's changed. Hazy, like someone pulled a plug. Fear boils in my belly, making it impossible to breathe. Crashing waves drag me under the surface.

I spot Bobby surrounded by a group of parents picking up their kids. Drew and Lisa Howard, Grace's parents, find me through the crowd and smother me in an embrace. Our families raised the girls together, and it's easier to dissolve in their warm welcome than feel the gnawing in my gut.

"Are you sure Grace doesn't want to stay?" I ask Lisa.

"It's the sleeping-out thing," she replies. "Maybe this year she'll get over it."

We say our goodbyes, and I convince myself everything is fine. Then I berate myself for not approaching the girls and demanding answers. But Zoe and Lily would kill me for interfering with their friends. Parental rule number six: stay out of their business. I'm impatient and distracted. I fight the urge to make this a bigger deal than it is. Should I question them? Do I tell Bobby? The rest of the goodbyes are a blur.

Nearby, the girls recap their night with Chelsea and Shelby. I study their faces to see if the video has made its way to their phones, but the waiters are clearing tables, blocking my view, and Bobby leads me to the dance floor.

"You okay?" he whispers to the top of my head, pulling me close. "I asked them to play this."

Hearing the strum of one of our favorite songs, I nod. It was the one that told me if I got lost, I'd find him. I was lost once before. He was far, far away. And now he feels farther than ever. His embrace is strong. *Solo tú,* we say. Only you. I shut out the memories—I'm good at that. It keeps them from interfering with what I'd heard. And I convince myself there's no connection between bad luck and that name.

Bobby's nearness has always been a source of strength and comfort. I should tell him what I heard, but I'm already feeling overreactive. Even so, he could make it go away. He'd make sense of what makes no sense. He'd say I was too emotional when it comes to the girls. He is far more pragmatic, though tender. He'd say, "Come on, Em, teenage drama. I'm sure it's nothing." And I'd agree with him, the worry flowing into the ocean, all a big mistake.

Instead, I keep it to myself a while longer, letting him hold me tighter, falling into his comfortable rhythm.

"Should we sneak outside and fool around?" He laughs, reminding me of the probability the girls were conceived on a deck chair by the pool.

I tighten my grip. He can't see inside me. He can't see the worry clawing to come out.

"They're a nice group. Good kids," he says, pulling me closer. And when I don't respond, he asks, "Are you listening to me?"

I hear him, but I'm somewhere else. I'm terrified something very bad is about to happen. Call it mother's intuition, paranoia, whatever it is, I can't sit with it alone. I stop moving. "Remember last weekend when Zoe went to that party? Lily was sick?"

"Uh huh."

"Something happened."

His arms drop to his sides, and he cocks his head. "What do you mean?"

"Mom, we're going upstairs," interrupts Lily, who moves in for a hug. Zoe and her friends follow. I squeeze Zoe harder than usual, afraid to let go.

"Love you," she whispers, and I stare deep into her eyes, searching for an explanation. An answer.

"I love you more."

When the door closes, I take a seat at the empty table. Bobby sits beside me, his brown eyes holding mine. Waiters scatter around, clearing tables and breaking down chairs. Their noises jab at me.

"Could you give us a moment alone?" he says to the staff before facing me. "What is it, Em?"

"I don't know," I begin. "Something happened at that party." His jacket hangs from a chair, and I throw it over my shoulders. My hands shake. There's worry in his eyes. "It's probably nothing," I say. "It has to be nothing."

"Emma," he says, "did something happen with the girls?"

Jagged words rush from my throat. "I was in the bathroom. Shelby and Ava were talking about something *crazy* on one of their phones that was being sent around." I don't face him. I focus on the flowers on the table. The beautiful hues of lilac and blue. "They said it was one of the twins. At a party last weekend. They said she was *fast*." I pause. The rest doesn't want to come out. "They said it was Zoe."

"Did you see what it was?" he asks matter-of-factly.

"No."

He stares everywhere but at me. "That could mean a lot of things. It could be anything."

"Did you hear me? Ava said *fast*. She said she was fast on and off the field."

"Lily?" he asks, confused.

"I thought the same thing, but Shelby corrected her. She said, 'That's not Lily. That's Zoe.'" I stop to catch my breath, and then I panic. "Zoe! What could she have been doing that made them freak out like that? They said it's going to get around!"

He's pulling me toward him, but the worry remains. "C'mon, Em, I'm sure it's nothing."

"How can you say that?" My voice is shaky. "I'm telling you what I heard. I'm telling you what those girls in the bathroom were saying!

Whatever's on that video . . . it doesn't sound good. You know how fast this stuff gets around."

He's always been the strong one. "There's no possible way Zoe got herself into trouble. Maybe Lily, but not my Zoe." He's rubbing his freshly shaven chin when he says this.

"Is that supposed to make me feel better?"

"Let's talk to the girls," he suggests. He eyes the half-empty glasses on the table for the one he can guzzle. "If something happened with one of them, they'd tell us. Or they'd tell on each other. You're worrying for nothing. Whatever it is, I'm sure it's a big misunderstanding."

I hold on to what he's saying. He makes perfect sense. Logical. But not everything is as it seems. It never is. People hide parts of themselves. Masters of denial. He rests his lips on my forehead, and I press into him. "Maybe you're right . . ."

"I usually am," he laughs.

"She said she'd never even kissed a boy. We were getting our nails done. Two weeks ago." It's a mother-daughter moment I need to bring to life.

He stands up and squeezes my shoulders. "We'll take care of it. Don't worry."

We make our way to the elevator past the throng of guests enjoying the Saturday-night bar. Festive voices blend with the music but do little to pluck me from my troubled mood.

Bobby stares at me in the mirrored walls. "You know how girls are. They exaggerate. This is probably some joke. Some game. For all we know, Zoe's kissing a boy in that video. She's fifteen. It's normal." Then he gathers me in his arms. "We were teenagers once."

The memory slides down my back and presses on another nerve. The elevator doors open and we separate.

"I'll talk to her tomorrow," he says.

His hand rests on my back as he leads me to our bedroom. The girls' laughter floats through the air and swaths me in false comfort as I undress. My movements are stilted, slow, painful motions awaiting an aftershock. What I'd heard has broken me. My body is unable to take the punch.

I am beneath the covers, neither awake nor asleep, when he curls around me. "Tonight was terrific, Em. Don't worry so much."

My voice is empty and flat. "I'm scared."

"There's nothing to be scared of. Trust the girls."

Emotions bite at me. The name. The bathroom. This birthday. I burst out, "We're losing them. Their lives are full with debate and lacrosse and their friends . . . soon they'll be driving . . ."

"Em," he interrupts, "they'll always need their mom."

"And I love being their mom."

He spoons me, and the nagging doubts dissipate. "Maybe I need to go to back to the stage," I say. "Theater might be good for me." Until the doubts crawl back. "Except they need me more than ever . . ."

"Everything's going to be fine," he whispers as he drifts to sleep, snoring in my ear.

My mind spins and whirls. A looping spiral I can't slow down. It's his fault. He mentioned Monty. He resurrected the name from the dead. He reminded me of what I'd done. It collides with this video and whatever Zoe did on it. I try, but sleep eludes me. I wrestle with barging into their room and asking Zoe point blank, but her friends are there, so I put the idea to rest. Opening and closing my eyes returns a sense of control, but I grow tired of the weary motion and settle for darkness. I lie in his arms long after the whispers and laughter fade from down the hall.

The light of a full moon glares at me. I blame it for what comes next. At once, I rise up and toss the sheets aside. I tell myself I'm just checking on the girls. Their door is closed, but I push through. I trip over bags and clothes and shoes. Shelby and Chelsea share a blow-up bed on the floor. They're all peacefully asleep.

They're fine. Go back to your room. Turn around and leave.

I know I shouldn't be doing this. My heart blares it's a mistake, but I can't help myself. I find what I'm searching for: a phone. I don't know whose it is, and I don't care. I'm only grateful that it isn't locked. I tiptoe out the door, careful not to make a sound.

While the phone powers up, I know there's time to reconsider, to walk away, to save myself from being the mother who snoops on her kids. The bright light burns my eyes, but I don't stop. I'm searching and scrolling, checking e-mails and texts for anything with a video attachment. I see the group chat. It came in a little while ago. A blocked number. I press "Play."

The video's grainy, but there she is.

Zoe. It's definitely Zoe. Bile burns my throat. She's on her knees. I can make out her face and a hand against her shoulder. The hand of a boy who's standing in front of her. The stifled sounds I had overheard in the bathroom are now uncomfortably clear.

My daughter is giving a blow job.

The phone slips from my hand and slams on the hard floor. It takes with it my breath. I panic, and a flood of adrenaline soaks my veins. I stare at the screen as it screams to me: *"Don't stop. It feels good."* I don't touch it. I don't want to see her face. But the sounds are loud, and I can't risk waking Bobby or the girls. I'll be caught, and they'll be pissed. Shaking, I grab the phone and fumble with the buttons. The noises mingle with my revulsion. The phone powers down, and I make the few steps to the door.

Only I walk smack into Zoe in the hall. And she's crying.

CHAPTER 3

"Mommy," she whimpers.

My heart drops.

"That's me." She's hyperventilating. "That's me you're watching . . ."

The phone is a wall between us. It keeps me from throwing my arms around her. I want to slap her, too, but her eyes call out to me. *Oh my God, Mommy. Make it go away.* I want to. I want to unsee what I just saw, but there's no way. The images are burned to memory.

Love and pain collide inside my heart. Shame pools around us. She shakes, her cries deep and animal-like. Words come out as sobs. "Don't hate me."

I hug her hard and whisper in her ear, "I could never hate you." Though I'm afraid my mix of reactions is sneaking through.

Zoe steps back. In a split second my daughter is someone else. Her eyes are heavy with regret, her cheeks a dull white. My arm comes around her, and I guide her down the hall to the guest bedroom. My fast pace is fueled by indescribable fear. Yet it feels like the longest walk of my life. Bobby's steady breathing fills the air as we pass our bedroom. If it could only silence the pounding of my heart. I close the door. The need to protect him is strong. My overreaction will become his reaction. I have no idea what this will do to him.

She collapses on the bed. It's an ungodly hour, but I'm wide awake. The phone is in my hand, and she grabs it.

"Zoe, don't."

She swats my fingers away and powers it up. She knows exactly where to go. The glint highlights her agony. I see the shock. The shame. It splatters across her face. "I can't . . . I can't . . . oh my God . . . who sent this? How did everybody get it?"

The rest I can't follow. Garbled sounds mix with a bone-chilling helplessness. A sliver of nausea climbs through my body. I don't know what to say. I don't how to help. She buries herself under the covers, and I get in beside her. The phone falls to the floor, and neither of us pick it up.

"How did this happen?" I ask. It comes out rational and calm, but it's desperate and ruffled.

The glimmering night sky shines through the windows. We don't need to turn on the light to see the pain between us. Her body's rounded in a ball, shaking with each whimper. The sounds escalate.

"I didn't know I was being filmed."

Zoe on her knees flashes before my eyes. I seal them tight to shut it off, but the image haunts my internal screen. Was she naked?

"Why were you snooping through our phones?" she asks.

It would hurt worse to tell her the truth. My arms loosen around her—from weakness, not a loss of affection, so I grip harder and let the question fade into the sheets. "Did somebody force you to do that?"

"I want to die," she whimpers, pressing a fist into the pillow.

I swallow the ache and rub my hand up and down her back. The steady motion keeps me from lashing out at her.

Her lip quivers as she talks. "I didn't mean for it to happen . . . there was a party . . . I'm so stupid . . ."

"Tell me," I say, every instinct in my body shouting to be heard. "Tell me, so I can help you."

"You saw it yourself," she says. "Oh my God, this is so embarrassing."

Shame is a dirty, dark secret that knees you in the stomach again and again and again. When you're your own worst enemy, sharing the grime with someone else—especially your mother—is tough. I give her time to collect her thoughts, because I honestly don't know what to say.

When she finally starts, it's in a whisper. "Last weekend . . . I was so excited to go to that party . . . Lily was home sick . . . do you remember?"

I didn't want Zoe to go without her. I liked when they were paired and looking out for each other. It was a party with older kids. I had every right to be nervous.

"You said it was okay . . ."

Bobby and I were in the kitchen when she came to say goodbye. The blue of her shirt brought out the color of her eyes. Her skinny jeans accentuated parts of her that made me take a second glance. Her friends were meeting her downstairs. Chelsea, Shelby, and Grace. Bobby told her how pretty she looked. And when the elevator doors shut, I'll never forget, he said, "She looks so much like you."

The tears spill from her eyes, and I grab the tissue box next to the bed.

"I thought it would be different . . . we do everything together . . . but then it happened so fast. One minute I was hanging out, and the next I was somewhere else . . . with him."

"Zoe, who's the boy?"

"Price." She wipes her nose. "He's new. He's in our grade."

"Do you know anything else about him?"

She shrugs.

Seeds of something evil plant themselves inside my head. Zoe was fourteen a week ago. She's still really young. And there are other concerns. "Zoe." I pause. "Think. Did he do this to you? Did he force you?"

Her voice is normally husky, but her cries make it worse. "Everyone's gonna see it. They're gonna make fun of me."

"Zoe!" I'm shrieking. "Did he force you?" Because it's the only thing that makes sense.

"I can't believe this." She rocks back and forth. "How can I go back to school?"

Something is growing inside me. It's destroying any semblance of patience. "Zoe, you need to listen to me."

She turns away and covers her eyes. "Mom, please, you don't understand. You just don't."

I try to pry her fingers away from her face. "Then explain it to me."

"He didn't force me," she snaps. "It just happened." She yanks her hand away.

"What does that mean, Zoe?"

She doesn't respond.

"Answer me."

Quiet.

I'm back in my Chicago bedroom listening to my mom tell someone on the phone how my father cheated. *Sex makes you think you have something special, but without feelings, without respect, you've got nothing.* I take a deep inhale. "It doesn't 'just happen' . . ." *Sex is for those you love who love you back.* "Zoe, I don't understand."

She cries while I sit with hypocrisy so pungent I can't finish the sentence. She did this. She wanted this. And I know what they say about girls like that.

"Nobody would've ever known about it," she argues. "It wasn't a big deal! Now it's on everyone's phones! *That's* a big deal."

"What did you say?"

"Please, Mom. Just stop."

I'm in her face. "No big deal? Is that what you think? You think giving a blow job to a boy you hardly know isn't a big deal? You're *fourteen*, Zoe . . ."

"Fifteen. And everybody's doing it. That's what kids do."

Words can sometimes slap you where it hurts. That's what hers do to me. When it's your little girl, you try to protect her, to keep her innocent for as long as you can. But when I think about the flagrant way she describes this reckless behavior, the anger creeps up my body.

"Do you know how ridiculous that sounds? You're young. Way too young. Did you think you'd get attention that way? Did you think this boy would like you? C'mon, Zoe. Do you have any idea how valuable your reputation is?" I'm shaming her, and I'm judging her; I'm doing to her what I once did to myself.

She curls into herself. "This is why kids lie to their parents."

We were once her age, Bobby and me, sprawled across a span of beach, palm trees fanning around us. We took things slowly. It didn't just *happen*, as Zoe proclaims. My mind travels on the crazy train and stops at my next fear. "Were you drinking? He could've slipped something in your drink. He could've taken advantage of you . . . been the one to film you."

Zoe focuses on everything but my face. "I don't remember every detail, but he didn't force me to do anything."

It's a flimsy voice I don't recognize, and it heightens my anxiety. Pity and a twinge of fury fill my heart.

"Stop looking at me like that," she snaps.

"You were drinking." It's not a question. And when she doesn't respond, I know. That she chooses to keep this part from me is mildly ironic. She's turned on her side, and I lean over, watching her, her eyes closed. The cold air that slithers down and around my body is like a vise, squeezing. "I want this boy's number. His parents need to know."

She shoots up, her eyes ablaze. "No, Mom! You can't do that!"

"The hell I can't!"

She recoils, and for the first time in her life she acts afraid of me. My chest is heaving, my face hot. I see her hand lying limp on the bedspread next to mine, but I can't bring myself to touch it.

"I'm calling his parents, Zoe. He could've put something in your drink." That's what I want to believe. What I need to believe. "You don't know anything about him." My eyes throb, and I worry I will burst into sobs.

But I can't do that. This is about Zoe. I push back the feelings and face her, taking her shoulders in my hands and trying not to shake her. Her hair is scattered and unruly. The leftover makeup from the party has left her with raccoon eyes.

"Where were the parents?" I ask. "You told me the parents would be home. It's one of the reasons I let you go."

"I didn't know they weren't going to be there!" she cries.

"How can I trust you, Zoe?"

Her eyes are steeped in sorrow. "I'm telling you the truth."

"Why am I hearing it a week later? Why didn't you tell me?"

She pouts and starts to chew on a fingernail. "I didn't know someone was going to video me. It was nobody's business."

My stomach knots when I ask, "How long have you been drinking? Was this the first time?"

"You're more upset about what I did than about someone videoing me and sending it around."

"I'm upset about all of it!" I shout. "The drinking, the lack of supervision, your judgment, the video. I'm trying to help you. I'm trying to understand, but you're not explaining yourself. How much did you drink? Who drove you to Grace's house? And where was Lisa? God dammit, Zoe, I trusted you!"

The faint light paints her face and makes her hopeless and small. Our bodies are near, but we do not touch. She's hysterical when she screams at me, "It's not my fault!" She rolls over and pulls the sheets over her head. "Make it go away."

I'm not sure if she means the dim light shining on her face or something else. I'm afraid to blink. Life can change in an instant. Drinking. Sex. Hours ago none of these things were an issue. I should go wake up Bobby, but I'm crippled. This would kill him. When I was faced with sobering truths, I chose door number two. To lie. And my excuse was to protect him. But Zoe's so young. Much younger than I was. And even though she's covered in Victoria's Secret Pink pajamas with a splatter of childish hearts, her decisions remind me she's no longer a child. I study her body for a sign, something that signifies a change, a missing piece, a code that would break down why she would let this happen. I shudder when I think, *She's just like me.*

"You're making this more than it is." Her voice is muffled, an echo under the sheet.

"How do you expect me to react? Last time we talked, you hadn't even kissed a boy. We were far away from drinking and blow jobs."

The words taste awful. Regret unwinds. Flashes of conversation unravel—lectures on alcohol, taking pride in your body, boundaries, and the meaning of *no*. Bobby made it very clear when he had said, "No doesn't mean yes. It doesn't mean maybe, and it doesn't mean someone has the right to push you into yes. No means no. Period." So much for doing everything right. What did it matter, when my daughter spits back at me about the alcohol she drank and tells me it's *no big deal* to do things with a boy she doesn't really know?

She pops her head out. "I'm sorry." Her eyes are so tired and sad I slide next to her and gather her into my arms. Maybe if I hold her close she won't slip away. "I don't need a lecture."

"I'm going to lecture, and there will be repercussions. What business do you have drinking at your age? Your father's going to raise holy hell, so you'd better prepare yourself."

The lone tear that slides down her face takes my heart with it. She stutters when she speaks. "For one single minute in my boring universe I was having fun." She stops. It's hard to watch someone so gifted in language trip over a sentence. "I wasn't . . . I wasn't worried about what people were thinking. I wasn't being compared to anyone."

The wound that stretches across her face lands deep in my abdomen. Her pain is my pain, and I don't know how to make it go away. "Do you really feel that way? You're happier to be drunk and . . . doing that?"

"Mom, you don't get it."

"I get it, Zoe. I know what it's like to lose yourself. I know about temptation. Trust me."

Her lithe body curls into my belly like long ago. She raises her voice and sinks her head when she says, "I don't know what I feel."

I'm remembering a time when I was free and it, too, "felt good." But I'm not that young girl. I'm her mother. And I whisper into her hair and hug her hard. "Alcohol does that to people, Zoe. It impairs judgment and confuses you. And it's not how you get a boy to like you."

"Do we have to tell Daddy?" Her tender voice takes on a childlike tone, and it chills me to the very core. "He's going to ground me for life."

"We don't keep things from your father." And I notice how my fingers are crossed, fending off the hypocrisy.

This is how it will go down. Bobby will scream. Then he'll mandate punishments: no phone, no sleepovers, no parties, no social life whatsoever. Then he'll question me. He'll ask if I had *the talk* with her. He'll ask if I knew about the boy and kept it a secret from him, *the private mother-daughter language*, he calls it. Then he'll break down, and his eyes will well up. Just when they're about to brim over, he'll wipe them away. And like that, he'll cross out what Zoe did. Because he can't stand to see his daughter as anything but his innocent little girl.

This hits right at the heart of my worst fears—for Zoe and for myself. Because for the coup de grâce, he'll exact revenge on the boy and his parents and whoever videoed them. He'll make it his personal cause to destroy all their lives.

I return to Zoe's sorrow. I take her fingers into my palm. "We're going to figure this out."

She pulls the blanket tighter. My head swells with worry. It spreads through years and generations and crosses lines I hadn't had to cross before. Bobby and I discussed these things all the time. Truth benders. Parents who smoked weed regularly but forbid their kids the same. The ones who claimed they were virgins when they married. I could lose myself in the white lies that divided adults from their spawn, the distinction that created firm rules. But I'd never had to answer the question about my past or how it might impact my own daughters. I'd never had to figure out how far in our new viral world a video had gone, who was watching it, and how we could stop it. Not to mention the personal scrutiny: How could I have failed so miserably at teaching my daughter to respect herself properly? Could she get a disease? Would she outgrow her reputation?

"Mom." Her fragile voice pulls me out of my spell. "I don't want this video to get out. I don't want them to call me a slut."

Every emotion I've tried to conceal comes trickling out. I catch my eyes in the mirror and they're more black than gray.

"Did you hear me?" she asks.

I take her hand and squeeze. We'd been hearing these stories for some time now. The dangers of social media. A video here. A photograph there. It was happening all around us. But I, in this moment, can't grasp that it's happening to my child, to my Zoe. So I squeeze tighter. For her. For me. For us. And I make a promise many parents have made before me, one I don't know that I can keep: "I won't let that happen. Ever."

CHAPTER 4

Morning comes in a shade of gray that matches my mood. I've given up on sleep, so I pick the cell phone off the floor, return it to the girls' bedroom, and climb back in bed beside Zoe. Her actions hijack my mind, spinning it wildly out of control. They've pushed a button I can't ignore. A memory so deeply buried its sharp edges stab at me.

She's asleep, her slender body tangled in the sheets. I get up, stretch my legs, and stare out the glass doors as the clouds sweep across the sky. I used to enjoy this time of day. The quiet calm before the beach comes alive. Despite the sun's efforts, the day is pale and unpromising. Downstairs, staff members sweep away the water on the pool deck, and I watch their rhythmic motions in a daze.

"Emma?" Bobby comes up behind me smelling of sleep. "What's going on?"

He leans in to greet me, though I pull back, motioning to Zoe asleep in the bed.

"We need to talk," I say.

Before we reach our room, I hear Lily's feet slap against the floor, and the punctuated sound means she turned on her phone and she's pissed.

"Did you see this?" she blares, shoving her phone in my face. Her hands are perched on her hips, an admission of utter shock. "Half the city thinks that's *me* in that video!"

Bobby's eyes dig into mine. "What the hell is that?"

Not like this. Not here in the hallway. Fear rises in my belly, and I can't stop what happens next. I snatch the phone from her fingers. The sounds, the images, they burn like fire.

"Emma, is that what I think it is?" he asks.

"It's Zoe!" Lily yells. "I wasn't even at the party. This is what sucks about being a twin."

I grab her by the shoulders and force her to look at me. "Calm down. I already know. Your sister's been up half the night, devastated."

Bobby stands over us, combing his fingers nervously through his hair. "Somebody tell me what's going on. Now."

"I told her not to go that party!" Lily yells.

"Emma." His unyielding tone stretches across the hall.

Chelsea and Shelby slink out of the apartment with their volleyball bags strung over their shoulders. They hide their faces from us, and when I know they're gone, I head to our bedroom with Bobby and Lily close behind.

Bobby's eyes smolder with questions. "Emma, what the hell's on that phone?"

The dread seeps into my veins. How can I tell him this?

"You do not want to know," Lily blurts.

"Lily," I say, "can you give your father and me a minute?"

She storms out of the room, but not before yelling, "This is humiliating!"

Bobby doesn't get nervous. He runs a successful real estate company with multiple properties and has rarely, if ever, let his guard down. The worry in his eyes is hard to miss. He is backed into a corner, and his arms cross his chest. I don't want to replay what I saw. "Last night. It's true. What the girls in the bathroom were talking about. Zoe's in trouble."

"Say it," he says. "What did she do?"

"Bobby, you need to promise me you're not going to do anything stupid. She's really upset." I can't face him. Horror straps itself to my chest, making it hard to breathe. I stare at our ketubah instead. The framed document that holds our Jewish marital vows. "There's a video. It's bad."

"How bad?"

My body stiffens. He comes closer, his eyes penetrating my defenses. "Is she having sex?"

And a fresh wave of panic crashes into me, because I had forgotten to ask. *How could I have forgotten to ask?* I answer no, but the single word is not convincing, and he glares at me. I can't find it in myself to utter what will crush him. "Remember your mom's birthday dinner at the Forge?"

"Which one? She had lots of birthdays there."

"You don't remember?"

God, he's handsome staring down at me. I wish I didn't have to tell him. I wish I didn't have to remind him of when we were young and reckless and falling in love, because it so varied from what our daughter did. His desperate plea urges me on. "The white dress. We snuck off into the bathroom."

"Wait." His voice hardens and he pauses. "Please tell me my daughter wasn't videoed giving a blow job." His face is stricken. A vein in his neck pulses.

"I can't do that."

Color drains from his cheeks, and he deflates. My arms come around him, and I feel the hurt through his bare chest. He can't speak. Instead, he buries his face on the top of my head, rubbing his cheek in my hair.

When he speaks, his voice cracks. "She wouldn't do this."

Excuse me, do I know you?

I hug him until the shock turns to something else, and he backs away. "Who's the boy? Did he do something to her? Was she drunk? Did someone drug her?"

"Drinking was involved."

"She's grounded," he fumes. "No more phone. No more sleeping out. She's done for the school year."

"She doesn't want to leave the house."

"What's wrong with her?" He turns and slams his fist against the dresser. "Why would she do this?"

"I don't know." A painful revelation ripples through me. My own mistakes bubble to the surface. He's silent. He's overthinking. The torment fills his eyes. "I'm going to kill her, and then I'm going to destroy whoever did this to her."

A deep sob escapes my chest. It's unrealistic to think I can hold it in any longer. It takes over my body.

"I want to talk to her."

I step in front of him. "Not yet. Let her sleep."

His hands comb through his hair again. The doorbell rings and cuts the tension in two. Before we can untangle our thoughts, footsteps come up the hallway.

"Where are my girls?" hollers Jonny.

"We're not finished," Bobby grumbles as we head for the kitchen. "I want to know how this happened."

Jonny's wearing the same clothes as last night. No doubt he closed up the bar and spent the night in the empty suite we set aside for employees who can't make it home. He shares the same complexion and dark hair as Bobby, though their similarities end there. He pushes the luggage cart, which is stacked with boxes, gift bags, and a tray of fresh muffins. In his hand, he's holding identical envelopes. "Where are they? Can I wake them up?"

"Too late." Lily floats past him toward the refrigerator and takes a swig from the orange juice carton.

"I've told you to use a glass," I say.

"She's fifteen," Jonny laughs. "Let her be a rebel."

"I think we've got rebel pretty covered," Lily answers dryly. She steps into Jonny's outstretched arms and lets him give her a hug before plunging into the pile.

"Watch yourself, Lily. And wait for your sister."

I adore my brother-in-law, but I would like nothing more than to politely ask him to leave.

"Where is she?" he asks.

"Where isn't she?"

"Lily," I repeat, "knock it off."

"Don't be mad at *me*," she says, twirling around and swiping a muffin from the tray.

Jonny turns to his brother. "What am I missing? Where's Zoe?"

The sinking sensation makes it hard to breathe.

"I'm right here." The hoarse voice strums through the kitchen. She enters, hair piled atop her head, each step a contemplation.

"Sweet fifteen!" Jonny hugs her, but her arms remain at her sides. "What's with the sad face?" he asks.

I want to run to her and protect her, to smooth out the swollen skin, kiss away the tears.

"I've brought your gifts. You made out pretty well. All your favorite stores and your favorite muffins from your favorite uncle."

"I'm not hungry."

Jonny's eyes narrow in on mine, and I turn away. Bobby drapes an arm over his shoulder, thanks him for the delivery, and guides him out of the kitchen. The girls and I are left with a deafening quiet. I busy myself with mindless routine like making coffee and toasting bagels. We circle each other, afraid of further hurt, afraid to say the wrong thing. The sparkly bows and shiny ribbons sit there like a tease.

Zoe rests her elbows on the table. Her silvery eyes are fixed on the food she doesn't touch. Her lips are stuck in a frown.

Lily stares at her sister. "What the heck were you thinking?"

"Please, Lilo, not from you, too. You just don't understand . . ."

"No, I don't."

"Then you shouldn't judge something you don't understand."

"You don't even know Price Hudson. Why don't you try *talking* to boys before throwing yourself at them?"

Zoe raises her voice. Her authoritative, debate voice. "I could've been drugged! You don't even care!"

This obviously affects Lily and her tirade. "Mom"—she turns to me—"is that true?"

I'm sure there are the *right* responses for these types of situations, but I never received the handbook, nor did I think this could happen to us.

"Whatever. I could've!" Zoe expects me to back her up, but I don't. "It's none of your business, Lily. Not everything's about you all the time."

Lily stands up and gets in Zoe's face. "It is about me. *I'm your sister.* And thanks to the luck of the gene pool, we happen to look a lot alike, which means your stupidity affects me." Lily doesn't stop to breathe.

Leave her alone. I'm torn. Part of me wants to help; the other wants to punish. There's no in-between. Bobby returns, stepping into a pile of crap I can't wipe clean. It doesn't last long, because his phone rings. "I've got to take this call," he says, and I'm left to stare at the back of his head as he leaves.

Zoe starts to cry. She tries to hide it from Lily, who realizes she's gone too far. Her eyes lower, and she comes around Zoe with both arms. "I'm sorry," she gasps. "We're supposed to be best friends. How could you keep this from me?" She's about to cry, too. "Why didn't you tell me?"

A lump forms in my throat. I've never had the connection they share, the ability to communicate through sheer will. It's an old twin tale, how one can sense the pain and need of the other. I long to feel their closeness. If only it could stop this nightmare.

Zoe's hair tumbles out of the rubber band when she whimpers into Lily's shoulder, "I don't know, Lilo . . . I'm sorry."

Lily's response is softer and less hostile. "You should've called me. I would've talked you out of it. I would've found you and kicked that kid in the balls. You didn't give me a chance to save you."

I dab at my eyes with a napkin. A range of emotions clamor to come out. They seethe from that place inside my soul where attacks on my children are met with dangerous impulses. Zoe's my baby. I watched her enter the world gasping for her first breath. And while she lives outside my body, her heart still beats in me. *Whoever did this to my child, you broke my heart, and I am going to break you.*

Lily grabs Zoe like she did when they were babies. It's effortless and playful. "How can I love a dumb sister so much?"

Bobby finds us huddled around the table crying. "Zoe," he says, like he's addressing an employee. "We need to talk."

CHAPTER 5

Lily disappears into her room, and the three of us face each other. Zoe stares down at her plate with the untouched bagel; she picks at her nail polish and avoids our eyes.

Bobby begins. "Why don't you start by telling us what happened."

Her hoarse voice is tired. The tears dried up. "I already told Mom."

"Is it true? Were you drinking?"

She sniffs. "Yes."

"Did you pour your own drink?"

She thinks. "I don't know. Maybe."

"It's important for you to remember, Zoe. We've talked about this."

She nods. "I did. I poured my own drink."

"Did anyone hurt you?"

I brush Bobby's arm. I get that he wants the facts, but it sounds like an interrogation, and Zoe squirms in her seat.

His eyes dig into mine. "We need to know, Emma. If someone hurt her . . . or forced her."

Zoe sits up straighter and takes a deep breath. "What do you mean?"

"You know what I mean. Did anyone hurt you? Did they force you . . ."

She stares at the wall behind him, her eyes bright red. "Nobody forced me."

"Are you sure?" he asks.

"I'm sure," she says.

His expression hardens, and he directs the next question at me. "Why exactly was she at a party with alcohol? Where were the parents?"

The blame he casts puts me on the defensive. "She told me the parents were home . . ."

"That's what they told me," Zoe says. "I didn't know they weren't going to be there."

"So you decided it'd be okay to drink? Emma, how did this happen? Who are these people?"

I don't appreciate being attacked, and I tell him, "We can't control everything, Bobby! We can lecture all we want, but they're going to face these kinds of situations. I'm just as upset as you are . . . I'm just as worried. I thought we taught them good judgment . . . and the risks."

"Like getting drunk and letting a boy take advantage of them?"

The lashing whips at me. "They're in ninth grade! They don't know the first thing about good judgment," I say.

A flush crawls up Zoe's face as she holds back a fresh set of tears. "It didn't happen like that."

"So tell me how it happened, Zoe," Bobby says.

I'm unable to move. I sit in the chair bruised and beaten like it's me being attacked. "Bobby," I say, though I'm too torn up to go on. If I speak, all my fears will land on the table, and I don't want that. Zoe being touched. Zoe liking it. Zoe on a video spreading through Miami Beach. Zoe being like me.

"It's fine, Mom." Her eyes are vacant. Her words slow and steady. "I drank. It was vodka. It tasted gross, but after a while it was okay. Kids talked to me—some older—and I liked it. I think I had another. Maybe more. Then I felt lightheaded. Everything was spinning."

I watch Bobby's expression slowly shift from disbelief to rage. It forces him to sit, and he grabs the table for support.

"I needed to get out of there. I went upstairs. Price was sitting on the stairs. He saw me stumble and asked if I was okay. I wasn't. I reached the top of the stairs and opened the first door I saw. I couldn't go back out there."

"Why didn't you call us?" I ask. "We've talked about this. No matter what it is, you pick up the phone and call us."

She takes a sip of orange juice. "It's not that easy."

Bobby shuffles in his seat, his forehead lined with worry.

"I wanted to rest for a minute. That's all. He followed me into the room and kept asking if I needed help. He drank, too. He sat next to me. We were playing around . . . taking selfies with face swap . . . he was nice. We were hanging out. Being stupid."

Bobby's not amused with the cavalier way she repeats the events. Kindness can be misleading, especially when you've let your guard down. I imagine Zoe's confusion, her pain. I grab ahold of her hand. It's weak and lifeless.

"I'd never even kissed a boy before that night," she says, her voice trembling. "He said, 'Truth or dare?' It sounded fun. He kissed me. I kissed him back."

Bobby shoots up out of his chair and starts pacing.

"You wanted to know what happened," she snaps at him.

I squeeze her fingers tighter. I know this upsets her, but I don't let up. I can help her. "We kept playing the game. I kept losing. The answers were all coming out wrong. I kept saying 'dare' when I should've been saying 'truth.'"

"Just stop," Bobby shouts. "That's enough."

But Zoe talks over him. "And the next thing I know I'm doing what I've been taught my entire life not to do: hooking up with someone I barely know."

Oh God. I can't bear to look at Bobby. His disgust will over-shadow everything else. I pull my robe tighter. "You were fourteen, Zoe. *Fourteen,*" he growls.

She has run out of answers and ducks her head instead. I feel sorry for her and for kids today. She got caught. She got videoed. The humili-ation dots my cheeks.

"Did he force you?" he asks again. "Did you at any point change your mind? Did you tell him no? Maybe he got angry."

"I lost the game, Daddy." Her eyes swell with defeat, and tears escape down her face. I hug her, hiding my sadness in her hair. "It's my fault," she says. "Me."

The heat rises in my cheeks. With all the modern technology at our fingertips, I wish we could press "Pause" or "Delete." I silently pray for this to go away. *Please, for her.*

Bobby sits back down at the table, his tone that of restraint. "Do you remember anything that happened after?"

I clear my throat to signal it's enough.

Silence dips between us, the kind that echoes what we can't take back. He taps his fingers on the table, and the noise draws Zoe out.

"You want to know about sex!" she says, latching on to his eyes. Her voice breaks. "You want to know if I took off my clothes or if someone did it for me."

I can't watch her confess her sins. With each attack, she sheds a layer of skin. A soul bound to be forever altered. But she responds to his interrogation with the fiery spirit of someone much stronger. What it must feel like for her to say these things to her own father.

"Zoe . . ." he starts.

"No," she finally says. "I didn't have sex."

"How can you be sure?" he asks.

She's adamant. "I'm sure."

"Why should I believe you?"

That's when it happens. My heart explodes. And though I asked the same questions myself, hearing them from his mouth feels worse. I get to my feet and in his face. "Trust her!" I shout. "Stop badgering her!"

He won't break the stare with Zoe and calmly moves me aside. Their eyes are locked, neither letting go.

"You can't stand it . . ." she starts, without finishing. It could mean a host of things. *I'm not perfect. I screw up.* I shudder and fall back in the chair. This is her battle to fight, but I feel responsible. Like I can somehow save her.

"Zoe," he says, his voice unsteady. "You're my child. It's a lot to take in."

"I'm sorry I embarrassed you. I'm sorry I drank." She stares downward. Her lips pressed together tight.

"I want your phone," he says, beaten. "And you're grounded."

Zoe sulks, and hands over her phone. The two of them resemble one another. It's much more than their shared sadness. Their eyes give them away, a heaviness that clouds the color; the weight makes me want to burst wide open.

"Is there anything else?" he asks. "Anything else we need to know?"

"There is," she says, a face streaked in regret. "He was nice to me. He wasn't mean."

Bobby rubs at his eyes. I am paralyzed by her disclosure.

"And I thought it would be *our* secret," she continues. "*Our* game. Nobody would ever find out. But now everybody knows, and now everybody's going to make fun of me and talk about me." She bites at her lip, and I know it can't hurt more than what she's going through.

Bobby leans against the granite. I feel the earth come out from beneath me, as though I'm suspended in air with nothing to hold on to. So I hold on to Zoe.

"It's going to be okay," I tell her, though I'm doubtful. My daughter's been bullied. The worst kind. There's no greater helplessness for a parent. "We're going to get through this." I breathe this into her hair. If I say it out loud, it has to come true.

"How, Mommy?"

"We will."

Lily saunters into the kitchen and grabs her sister's hand. "Come on, Zoe, let's go for a walk." It's difficult to let her go. She pulls away, and I cling a little tighter.

She tells me it's okay, but it's not. It's not okay at all.

Their absence lengthens the space between us, and I avoid Bobby's eyes. A flood of thoughts ravages my brain. He's lost inside himself, too. I think about what it means to get caught. How trapped Zoe must feel. But maybe she feels free—her secret no longer bottled up. I imagine him looking at me with the same disapproval in his eyes.

"How did this happen?" he asks.

His despair drags me down a spiral of darkness. Before I can answer, my cell phone buzzes. The messages from last night pile up. I read them because I can't stand to see the disappointment on Bobby's face. There are thank-yous for the party. Birthday wishes. A text from my family back in Chicago. And one last night that Bobby must have written when I was getting ready for bed: You worry too much. I love you. Great party. The ones from this morning strike a different tone. Lisa urges me to call her. Others tell me they're thinking about me. Cookie and Dara, Chelsea and Shelby's moms. They heard. They all know.

I toss the phone on the table. Bobby faces me in our white, modern kitchen, but his eyes pass right through me. He's searching for answers that aren't there. "We have no definitive proof she wasn't drugged." He raises the point again. "How would she know? It could've happened."

"She said it was consensual. I believe her."

"She doesn't remember!" he shouts. He gets up and reaches for the coffee, filling a mug from a recent bar mitzvah. The smiling face of Shelby's younger brother mocks us. "How did we not know our child was drunk at someone's house last week? How did she walk in here the next day acting like everything was fine? Are we that blind to what's right in front of us?"

I stare him in the eye. *Yes. We are.*

The doubts return. I didn't know. I should've known. The disappointment in his eyes grows, the disgust he's trying hard to muffle.

This is the side of Bobby I'd always feared most. Old-fashioned and conventional. Admirable qualities in any man, but dangerously limiting. I knew how Bobby felt about *fast* girls. Every girl Jonny fooled around with was a *slut*. And there were a lot of them those teenage years. My family often questioned our raising the twins in a flashy, untraditional setting, but we defended our choice and what the hotel provided. I scan the contemporary but lived-in space where we join together. It's a mixture of warmth and light against steel finishes and clean lines. It reflects the way we live. Sturdy and soft. But today it feels stifling, and I have to escape.

I get up, and he follows me to the balcony. The beauty that's our backyard only taunts me. Below, the girls are walking toward the ocean. Zoe's hair floats in the breeze, and her hands are stuffed in her pockets. Lily is close to her side. I shut off my phone and its symphony of notifications. It all seems so trivial. What once connected me to a bigger world is now an adversary.

Resting my hands on the railing, I watch the girls kick at the sand, arm in arm, and I study Zoe. Havoc changes a person. Beside her sister, she appears small. *Oh Zoe, what I would do to take this away from you.*

I start to cry, and Bobby tries to comfort me, but his weak arms feel more like I should comfort him. Worry shoots off my tongue. "This video . . . her reputation. What if it goes viral? What do we do about school? Her friends? That boy . . . do we call his parents?" By now I'm hysterical.

"Someone did this to her," he says. "Somebody filmed her. We have to call the boy's parents. Or get me the number of the family who threw the party. They must know something. What if it happened to other girls?"

"Do you think they're going to offer any information? They won't want to incriminate themselves. And even if there were drugs, isn't it too late to get her tested? It's been over a week. What will it prove?"

He grips the rail. "It'll prove she's not . . ."

"Don't say it!" I shout, landing a palm across his lips. "Don't you dare say it, Robert Ross. Zoe's a good kid. Whatever point you're trying to make . . . she made a mistake. Nobody did this to her."

He pulls back. "She was drunk, Emma. That boy shouldn't have touched her. He should've walked away. He should've gotten her help. Get me his number."

I'm freaking out and return to the shoreline and Zoe. The gray sky shrouds her in a thick haze, or perhaps she seems blurry to me. "She must be going through something . . . we need to help her." This forms a new swell of sadness that almost tips me over. "She's mortified. Everyone's talking about her. Anything we do will give her unnecessary attention."

"She's a teenager, Emma. She has no idea what's in her best interest. That's our job. We're supposed to keep her safe." His voice cracks, and he dabs at his eyes. A single tear breaks through.

Bobby. My arms come around him, and I force him to hug me back, but he's hardened. "I can't, Em. I'm calling the parents. I'm going after the person who did this to her." His smell mingles with the salty air, and I remember the nights we sat on this beach thinking we were invincible. "I have to do something," he says.

"I understand." And I raise my lips to his cheek, but he draws back.

His gaze bounces along the balcony. "You need to call their friends' parents and ask them to make sure the kids deleted the video." His hands choke the railing while he addresses the ocean below. "You can't trust anyone."

Trust. He holds it so heavily in his heart. Monty's face flits through my mind. His fingers running down the length of my back. I'm relieved when Bobby goes inside and I can stretch across the deck chair and stare at the clouds. I settle on a time when I was Zoe's age and how desperately I crushed on Bobby right there on the sand. "We're too young," I'd say, fighting it, fighting him, while kissing turned to touching and neither of us could stop. It wasn't our fault we had fallen in love. Being with Bobby was as natural as taking a breath. Which is why my chest is tight and the air catches in my throat.

My eyes press shut, and a chill nips at my skin. Either a cold front is moving in, or it's what happens to an insulated world when holes poke through. A vignette of memories appears, our narrative, but it is eclipsed by Bobby's reaction, how he brushed me aside. My mind wanders to my college apartment in Vermont. It's the dark place I tried to cover up and forget. Now it stares right at me, bringing forth secrets and shame. It had crossed my mind over the years, but I am able to file it away. Pretend it didn't happen. But Bobby's disappointment and the pain in Zoe's eyes make it impossible to forget.

Excuse me, do I know you?

Anything but Monty.

The worry is so potent it fills every crevice in my body.

No. You don't know me.

A banging at the door startles me, and I jump to my feet.

Ours is a private floor in the hotel, one in which access is permitted with a specific code entered by the front desk or by key card. Only a handful of people—close friends, family, and staff—can gain entry. And when they reach our glass-enclosed foyer, they still have to be buzzed in. That's where I find Chelsea, clad in her volleyball uniform.

She collapses into my arms before I can speak.

"Mrs. Ross," she cries, sweaty from practice. "How's Zoe? We're all so worried about her." The girl tries to catch her breath. Her dark ponytail falls crisply down her back. Her milky white skin is splotched in red, either from exercise or something else.

She leans against the wall, the one that has our holiday cards lined up vertically by year. Her head lines up with Zoe and Lily age eight. "We got the text at the end of the party. It started with a few of us, and then it made its way around fast. No one wanted to tell Zoe . . . or Lily. It was so mean . . . we didn't want to upset them on their birthday." She stops.

This video and its contents have scarred me. "Everyone's a suspect," I say. "You did the right thing." But I wonder if she's covering up. Or if she knows more than she's saying. "Do you have any idea who the text might have come from?"

She wipes her nose with her jersey. I should grab her a tissue, but I'm rooted in place.

"There's no way to find out," she says, sniffling. "It came from a blocked number."

"Did the message say anything? Was it only the video?"

She catches her breath. Her full lips are less pouty, and she says, "The person said happy birthday." And she stops and hands me her phone.

"You didn't delete it?"

"I should've, I know," she says, searching the floor, "but I didn't send it to anyone—my parents told me never to do that . . ." She meets my eyes. "But I thought maybe I could help Zoe . . . maybe I could show you or someone . . ."

The phone brands my hand. It's wrapped in a case of powder blue with one half of a pink heart drawn across the back. It dawns on me this is the phone I picked up only a few hours ago. I hadn't paid attention to the case, but now I wonder who has the other half of the heart.

"Here," she says, pointing at the screen and swiping through apps, though I know exactly where to go. "There." She points.

Blocked Sender: Happy Birthday! Someone's not so innocent. Which one of the birthday girls is it? SMH

The video was shocking enough that all else faded into the background, but the spite behind the words strikes me now.

46

She asks if she can see Zoe, and I explain she's on the beach with her sister. "I'm not sure she's up for company."

"Okay," she says, searching the floor. "The Zoe I know wouldn't do something like this. I can't believe this happened to her."

I replay her words. *This happened to her.* This *happened* to Zoe. Zoe didn't make it happen.

"I didn't even know she was friends with Price Hudson," she says. "None of us did."

"Can you tell me about him? I heard he just moved here."

"I don't know much." She stops, toys with her ponytail, and her eyes dart around the room. "Do you think he could've done something to Zoe? To make her do this?"

"We know about the drinking, but nothing else."

"I told her she was drinking too much. I told her to slow down," she confesses.

"You girls have to watch out for one another."

Bobby's footsteps fill the quiet between us. "Chelsea." It's cold and unwelcoming, nothing like ordinary times. He waves the Blue Book, Thatcher's student directory. Chelsea bows her head, realizing it's time for her to leave. She retraces her steps to the foyer and says a jumbled goodbye.

As soon as the elevator door closes, he comes at me. He's determined and vengeful and searches for a phone. I beg him not to. I beg him to trust Zoe, but he has a mind of his own. He believed me once. I was that convincing.

I'm cross-legged on the couch, and he paces around me. His gray jeans hug his legs, and a white pullover shows off his olive skin. I'm unprepared for this call in my Ross bathrobe. I should get dressed, but I'm lacking will.

"Mr. Hudson?" Bobby's tone is abrupt. He's holding the phone hard against his jaw. "This is Robert Ross. My daughter's Zoe Ross."

My heart pounds to the point of pain and sends a tremor through my limbs. My palms are a clammy wet. He puts the phone on speaker so I can hear. A man with a stern voice says, "I know who you are."

"This is a difficult call to make."

There's silence on the other end of the line. They know. My hand covers my eyes.

"I don't want to jump to conclusions or make accusations. My daughter drank at a party with your son."

Mr. Hudson curtly responds, "We know about the video, Mr. Ross. My wife and I are utterly shocked."

"Does your son know who might've filmed them?"

"My son's a victim, too, Mr. Ross. Did you ask your daughter?"

I drop my hand and watch Bobby walk circles around the couch. His anger darkens his features.

"With all due respect, Mr. Hudson, my daughter was drunk and underage. Your son took advantage of her. He should've stopped it. He should've never let an inebriated girl do what she did."

I encourage Bobby to sit, but he brushes me aside.

Mr. Hudson's effort at politeness turns sour, and Bobby quickens his pace. "Mr. Ross, I don't appreciate you calling my home and accusing my son of being some kind of monster." I hear a woman's voice in the background. "Hang up, Daniel." He continues. I can hear him shushing his wife through the phone. "Price is a good kid. Never any trouble. I'm hanging up, Mr. Ross. If you have something to say to me or my family, contact a lawyer."

And the line goes dead.

Perhaps none of us know each other at all.

CHAPTER 6

"I'm calling Nathan," Bobby huffs. He's our lawyer. "He knows people. There's a video of Zoe going around town, and we need to stop it."

"The kids will delete it," I assure him. "They're all friends."

"Em, half of them will forward it to a friend. The other half will be calling Zoe names for weeks. We have to shut it down. There are people who can do that."

I can't focus. There are too many darts being thrown at us at once. I descend into a quiet that allows me the freedom to obsess and ruminate about everything that's gone wrong.

"I know you're upset." He walks toward me. "I am, too. I want to know how this happened. God, I really just want to kill that kid."

Upset is the wrong word. Upset is when we couldn't fly to Florida because they were expecting a hurricane. Or when I lost the anklet he bought me for my sixteenth birthday. The time we drove to our favorite restaurant in the Keys and it was closed for renovations. This was way more than upset. He sits next to me and paints the picture for me again.

"Zoe could've been drugged. She could've been forced. Alcohol can do that to someone. Make them think it's okay to act out in ways they wouldn't have normally done."

He's going around in circles, repeating himself with the drug angle.

"Bobby." The explanations he's holding on to are pointless. "She did this. Enough with the excuses."

I don't go on. The accusation comes too close. Monty's handing me another drink, and I take it. The foolish charm. The naughty eyes. The temptation drips off his tongue. I clamp my eyes shut, but I hear the large diamond on my finger clink against the glass.

"Emma?"

"I'm here." Though I'm somewhere else.

"What happened is a crime. I don't know what kind, but if we let it go, someone gets away with hurting Zoe. And then what? It gets worse. The video goes viral. We can't let that happen!"

"Stop it!" I yell. "Stop!" My head is about to explode.

I hear the elevator chime, and wipe my eyes. Zoe strolls in behind her sister. Her gait is slow, and her eyes are dim. The question in the faded blue is directed at him. She can do that without even talking. It asks, *Do you hate me?*

He answers her by announcing he's going to his downstairs office. When he passes Zoe, I can feel the cold air between them.

Lily's breeziness helps and hurts. She's the one to maintain a sense of normalcy. She can skip over the undercurrents and ask me questions like why aren't I dressed, as if it's a normal Sunday afternoon, or if we're going to our favorite Chinese restaurant tonight. She provides a balance that reminds me to come back to earth.

"Do you have homework?" I ask.

Lily mumbles, "Yes," and Zoe says, "I'm not going to school."

I don't know if this is the best idea or the very worst.

"The kids won't be nice, Mom," says Lily. She crosses the room and picks at her face in the mirror. "It's gossip. Gossip trumps everything."

"Don't pick," I tell her. "You'll get scars."

"Why do I have to go?" Lily complains. "I'm sure there are kids who think it's me."

Zoe slumps on the couch, biting her cuticles. "I'm never going back."

I smooth her hair off her face, revealing her eyes. Today they're more gray, like mine, and I wonder what else connects us. I take her hand. "It won't always feel like this." It's what a mother says, even if she's unsure. "Maybe you should do some homework, take your mind off it. We can decide about school later."

"I texted everybody in our contacts," says Lily. "I told them to delete the video. They said they did."

Relief washes over me, brushing aside the tinge of worry that any one of them could be lying. These were good kids. They wouldn't want to hurt an innocent young girl. Trusting in our ability to contain the video, I focus on finding the coward who did this. Turning back to Zoe, I hesitate. "Honey, think. Do you have any idea who might've filmed you with Price? Did you see anyone? Could it have been him?"

I know it's a slippery slope to question her again. She pulls her hand away and stands up. "I can't talk about this anymore." She hurries out of the room, and soon a door slams.

Lily takes her place next to me, our shoulders touching. "How was she on the walk?" I ask.

"Terrible. Everyone's talking about it. I won't lie. It's the top of every newsfeed."

I want to disappear. I want to float out of the room and drift out to sea. Is it possible I passed this down to Zoe? She settles into the couch and crosses her legs. "Tell me what she said."

Lily sighs. "I asked her how things got so far so fast . . . and what it looked like."

"Lily! I hope you didn't upset her."

"Don't worry. She actually laughed. Even though she didn't remember what it looked like."

"I don't find that funny," I say. "At all."

"She's fine. She talks to me. She gives it right back. She said it was supposed to be me hooking up first. Being on the debate team hasn't really made her the Bachelorette, you know."

I think about missed opportunities, and I won't let another one go by. "I hope it's different for you, Lily. Not so public. With someone you care about."

"Mom, you of all people can't understand my generation. You've been with Dad forever. It's kinda weird."

"I love your father," I say, feeling flush.

I'm relieved she doesn't see anything peculiar in the way I defend our love. She's back on her phone, the buzzing and beeping swiping her away from me. When Lily is done, her eyes latch on to mine and she says, "She won't be drinking anytime soon. That I can promise you."

It made sense. Zoe hated throwing up. It terrified her. She'd come into our room when she wasn't feeling well and literally fight it. I can't imagine her doing it without telling me. Without needing me there. Who held her hair back? Who told her she'd be okay? Did she cry herself to sleep?

"And I'm willing to bet she wasn't drugged, Mom."

I pull myself out of the sadness and listen to Lily.

"Kids talk, and no one's saying anything about date rape drugs. No one. Price Hudson is as harmless as they come. She swears he was nothing but nice to her. They had too much to drink, and that was it."

That was it. I breathe it in and pretend it's going to be okay. Except "that was it" was recorded for everyone to see. I thank Lily for being a good sister and tell her to start her homework.

"What's the over-under on getting our permits tomorrow?" she asks, her hopes obviously diminishing.

"Be patient," I tell her. "It's not the best time."

She scoots away, shoulders stooped in disappointment, and I'm left with my worry.

I dig my phone out of my bathrobe pocket and switch it on. Seven missed calls. Twenty-two texts. And a pile of mindless notifications. Lisa is frantic. Others are genuinely concerned. The messages are well intentioned, though they're really a collective sigh of relief. *Thank God it's not my kid.*

A new message comes through. It's Lisa again. **Em, I'm so sorry. What can I do?**

Sorry. The only thing it brings to mind is death. Like a shiva house in the Jewish religion, during the grieving period for those who have been lost. It's where loved ones and friends gather to share their sympathies. They may as well have said, "Our condolences, Emma." Because, arguably, there's a loss. A piece of my daughter is gone.

My whimpers become sobs. I don't care who hears. The pain pours out of me. It's old stuff. It's new. It's everything I thought I was doing right for my girls turned into the wrong. I desperately want to help Zoe, but I don't know how. I feel like a failure. A fraud. I crumple into the cushions, grab the chenille throw, and hide my face in its fabric.

"Mommy?" It's Zoe.

She's next to me, wrapping her arms around the blanket and me.

"This is all my fault," she says.

"No!" I say, lowering the blanket.

Her eyes are puffy from crying. I wipe my cheek with the back of my hand and then reach for hers.

"I've let you down. I've let everyone down. How can I ever stand on the debate podium and be taken seriously? You said colleges might see it."

"No, honey," I say, letting her splay herself across my lap. I brush her hair with my hand and trace her forehead with my finger. "We're going to fix this." My throat is raw and my head sore from crying. "What you're seeing is love. I'm just sad for you. I'm sad to see you so upset."

As soon as the words are out of my mouth, I realize what it's done to me, to Bobby, to all of us.

"I'm so sorry for causing you so much pain," she says.

I swallow hard. "No. No. No." My vehemence surprises her, but I continue. "You're my child. I love you. With all my heart. And sometimes that love levels us. It hurts. We get disappointed. Let down. But we never give up on our kids. Ever. Do I want to make it go away? Yes. More than anything. But I'm not blaming you. And I won't lecture you anymore tonight." My voice changes. "Even though I should." The color returns to her cheeks. I rest my palm on the smooth skin. "Maybe tomorrow."

"Daddy's pissed."

A moment passes so I can process this. "He is. And he's scared, but he'll come around." I try to sound authentic, like I believe what I'm saying. I pat her on the back. "Go finish your homework. We're going to be fine."

She hugs me before she gets up, and I inhale her. Maison Louis Marie No. 4, Zoe's signature scent. The amber stays in my nose long after she's gone, and it propels me off the couch and into our room, where I throw on jeans and a camel-colored hoodie.

Our bed's unmade, the sheets a tangled mess. I pull them up and flatten the creases and fluff the pillows. The girls and their friends probably left a similar mess, but I'm depleted of energy and call for one of the housekeepers. I slide across the bed and dial Lisa. Our friendship started in Mommy and Me classes and has centered around the girls and their flurry of activities. Lisa, Drew, and Grace have been a mainstay in all our lives. The men are close through their shared positions in the real estate world, and Sabbath dinners are always entertaining, listening to the Howards' whirlwind life.

"What on earth is going on?" she asks, breathless, because she probably ran across the expanse of her Indian Creek mansion to answer the phone.

I submerge myself in the gray velvet pillows and shut my eyes. Hearing her voice makes me want to cry.

"Emma, talk to me."

Despondency is a tidal wave at the base of my throat. The rush rises, and I have no way to rein it in. All that comes out is a pitiful wail.

"Oh, Em, I'm so sorry. I'm so, so sorry. How's Zoe?"

I wipe my eyes on the pillowcase and don't even care about the black marks left by last night's makeup. "How do you think she is? She's a mess. We all are. We're upset. We're scared. I don't know if there's something wrong with my daughter. Bobby's convinced she was drugged. I think that would be easier for him to comprehend. I don't know what this will do to her, long-term." I don't even think about what I'm saying. The misery just pours out.

"You know the gossip mills go through very quick cycles. Very quick. Kids forget. They move on to the next drama." Lisa's usual high-pitched, cheery voice is subdued.

"Did you see her when they got home from the party? Did you know they were drinking?" I ask.

She pauses. "I didn't see them. We got home late, and they were sound asleep." The regret in her voice filters through. "The next morning Zoe was gone by the time I woke up."

I run my fingers through a tangle of hair. "I shouldn't have let her go to the party. I should've been there for her."

"This isn't your fault, Em. You and Bobby are terrific parents."

"Then how come I didn't know what my daughter was capable of?"

She doesn't have an answer.

"Did Grace say anything to you?" I ask.

"Em, my daughter's a teenager. She doesn't even want to be in the same room as me, sharing the same air. She sure as hell isn't about to tell me what her friends are up to."

I grip the phone to my ear. "When did it all change? When did they stop needing us?"

"They need us. Don't kid yourself," Lisa says.

"I'm not talking about chauffeuring them around town and clothes shopping," I say. "Why didn't Zoe come to me? Why'd she resort to drinking?"

"Em, most teenagers are going to experiment with alcohol. It doesn't mean Zoe has problems. I was sneaking into my parents' bar when I was thirteen."

Lisa and I are close, but I've never confided my truths. The deep, explosive ones. I've always been told that when it came to matters of relationships, you keep your private issues private. Trust no one. And I did just that. The paragon of seemingly perfect relationships. That was Bobby and me. Sweethearts for life. It was a bar held unrealistically high, and for years it fit. Until now. Until the castle began crumbling at the hand of Zoe's act. We are no longer perfect. We never were. I'm ashamed to even have this conversation.

I imagine fit Lisa with her thick, blonde, recently styled hair. She'd be pissed to know I withheld secrets over our lunches with the girls. The problem with perfection is when you can't live up to it, the exposure is that much more painful. I continue, "Did anyone else say anything to you?"

"Believe me, I tried. Cookie. Dara. We're shocked. No one expected this from Zoe."

It's always the quiet ones. Bobby says that all the time.

My mind wanders. It's thinking out loud. "I've been considering a job outside the hotel. I was going to apply at the Arsht Center or Jackie Gleason Theater. The girls have their lives . . . and it's all going to change when they start driving . . . I thought I'd put out some feelers."

"You love that hotel."

"I do. It's not work for me. It's my life. I'll always be managing it in some capacity, but I'm ready to do something else."

"That's a great idea," Lisa says, and I can see her big smile and her clear blue eyes through the phone.

"Then this happened." And I take a moment to process what I'm about to say, because up until this minute I had no inkling of what I was feeling. "Part of me is relieved Zoe needs me. It's awful to say, I know. I wouldn't wish what happened to her on anyone, but it makes me realize how much I love being her mother. I don't want that to change."

"So you're not going to get another job?"

"I don't know."

We're silent for a moment.

"What can I do?" she asks.

"Tell Grace and all the girls to delete the video. If you hear anything, let me know. Bobby's furious. He wants to go after the person who filmed them. It would help if someone knew something."

"Of course," she says. "We'll do anything for you guys. And we'll see you Wednesday, right? Dinner?"

"I'll talk to Bobby and let you know."

We hang up, and I scroll through my phone, considering the appropriate replies to the wave of inquiries. What I really want is to find the switch that makes every voyeur erase what they saw. There's a PTA meeting at Thatcher on Tuesday. A jacket was left in the Coral Room last night. The party feels like a lifetime ago. And then, from Sandra at Concierge: **Don't forget the Ocean Drive spread tomorrow. They'll be here at 9.**

I double back to my calendar and check the date. *Shit. Shit. Shit.* Tomorrow! We can't cancel again when we've already had to reschedule twice. How will Zoe manage this? And Bobby? The timing couldn't be worse. I fall back on the bed, eyes closed and fingers fisted, while despair takes over.

CHAPTER 7

Our house that's not really a house is quiet and dark. It's evening, but this darkness is different. It comes from chaos and hitches itself to the walls and ceiling. Fifteen had been ushered in with a surprising bang. The scandal stripped away order and left us all disoriented.

From the outside peering in, everything looked normal. The girls opened their birthday presents, and together we admired the kindness of their friends. Only I could see Zoe's distance. The way in which her empty eyes latched on to the gifts from her favorite stores, and when I remarked, "What a pretty top," she merely shrugged, a wooden response that meant she couldn't care less.

I scribbled the names for the corresponding gifts so the girls could send thank-you notes. Lily groaned, "Can't we send a text?"

"No. The proper thing to do is to send a note."

They told me I was old-fashioned, and I called for the bellman to pick up the chrome cart. *Damn right I'm old-fashioned.*

They sit in their usual spots at the kitchen table to do homework. Their chatter, ordinarily centered on celebrity gossip and their least favorite teachers, is steeped in quiet. Tonight, nothing is normal.

Zoe's face is tired. Dark circles frame her eyes. She pulls at her hair, frustrated over Spanish class. I get clipped answers and distracted stares.

"You don't get it," she says. "School's much more difficult than when you were growing up."

Lily's phone dings, and she reads the notification aloud. Zoe doesn't care that one of the Kardashians is all over the news for some new drama. The pressure knots the air around us.

I fend off questions about ecosystems while Zoe chews on the end of her pencil. Lily leans over and fills in the answers for her. Every so often, Lily checks her phone and we all hold our breath, waiting for a derailed train to crash.

Bobby arrives home, and I greet him at the door. He staggers, and I smell the bourbon. "Where were you?" I ask, following him to his office.

"Doing work." He avoids my eyes.

"It's Sunday. Isn't that why you put an office up here?"

He searches through a cabinet, looking for something. I feel foolish asking him what's wrong.

"How can you ask me that?" He scowls.

I come around the desk so he can't ignore me. "We have the *Ocean Drive* interview tomorrow."

He stops what he's doing and considers what this means.

"The girls won't be going to school," I tell him.

He seems reasonable. "Maybe it's for the best," he says and quickly returns to his search.

"Why are you shutting me out?"

"I'm not shutting you out, Em. I spent a great deal of time today on the phone with Nathan trying to figure out our next steps. He knows someone who specializes in situations like this. We also got the inspection results. All the marble floors need to be ripped out and repaired. Every balcony failed code. We have a major renovation to deal with."

"I thought we were up to code."

"We're not. We have ninety days to file permits and begin the work."

It's a lot to handle at once, and I try to comfort him, but he's too upset to let me in. Or drunk. His eyes are bloodshot. His steps are shaky.

The phone rings, and it's Jonny. "I told you to leave it alone, brother," Bobby says. "I have it under control."

He never talks to Jonny like this, and I chalk it up to mounting stress.

"I know what I'm doing." And he hangs up abruptly.

"Is everything okay?" I ask, but he's short.

"It's business. Don't worry about it."

I'm worried, but the conversation stalls. "Maybe we're overreacting about the video," I say. "The kids are deleting it. We can make this go away."

Yes. Let's lock it up in a box somewhere so no one ever has to see.

"I hope you're right, Em. God willing, this goes away and Zoe's learned a lesson, but I'm not convinced."

The strain between us troubles me. Instead of us figuring this out together, he's icing me out. I move in for a hug. His arms come around me, but they feel empty, like he's not even trying.

"The girls need help with biology," I say.

"I'll be there in a minute."

"You're not focusing, Zoe," he says. "The ecosystem consists of the three levels. Micro, meso, and biome. I've said it three times."

I'm preparing the marinade for a Whole Foods chicken, but I'm observing the interaction. We haven't said anything about the interview, because we're afraid of upsetting Zoe further. Bobby draws pictures and labels the energy flow along the food chain while Zoe's chin rests in her hands, and she stares off somewhere. Lily's up and down off her chair, trying on new lipsticks that came in a gift bag from Sephora. "I like that one," I say, in spite of knowing she should focus.

Bobby slams his palm on the table, and Lily's calculator crashes to the floor. "If you don't need my help, Lily, can't you go in the other room, so I can help your sister?"

"Gladly," Lily answers as she snaps a selfie of her pursed lips. She leaves with her calculator, and I hear the living room TV turn on, and Rachel and Mike from *Suits*.

He returns to Zoe, his drunkenness hiding behind a textbook. "It says here, 'Shorter food chains retain more energy than longer chains. Used-up energy is absorbed by the environment.' Zoe, are you listening?"

His impatience rattles me.

She shakes her head. I think if she opens her mouth she'll start to cry again. The struggle intensifies. He raises his voice. The *carbon cycle* and *living tissue* come out as jabs. His patience has hit its limit; he's short with her and noticeably agitated.

"I can't do this right now, Daddy," she cries, hiding her face in her hands. "I can't think straight."

He tries to slow down, to go over the diagram again, but she won't lift her head. I tell him with my eyes she's done.

"Emma, she has a huge test tomorrow."

"No, she doesn't," I correct him.

"I'm not going." She raises her head and slams the computer shut. "I can't go. I can't take this test. I can't see the kids. I don't care about the carbon cycle."

"You won't be going, Zoe," I finally say. "Tomorrow's the *Ocean Drive* interview. You and your sister will be with us."

"Great." Zoe rolls her eyes. "More people looking at me. Can't we postpone it? Can't Lily just pretend to be me?"

I approach her and rest my hand on her back. "The timing's bad, honey. I know."

She jerks away, pushing her computer aside. She gets to her feet, and the chair legs scratch the floor. Before I can stop her, she's gone. I empathize with the need to retreat, to run fast and far away from what she has to face. But what she doesn't understand is how it can come back to bite her.

Bobby plucks me from my thoughts with a question. "Have you Googled her?"

I shoot him a look, but his hand comes up. "We need to know how far this video's gone."

I stare at Zoe's abandoned seat. "I don't want to know."

Bobby slides the computer in my direction, an invitation to sit. His face is long, hard to read. "We need to know."

"I can't," I say, backing away. I watch his nimble fingers grace the keyboard. My heart picks up speed. It drums in my chest. I shiver from the chilly air. Google ignites the screen, and Bobby takes his time inputting the letters. He gets as far as *Zoe Ross*, but hesitates to hit the magnifying glass that can multiply the problem.

The unknown alarms me. What will we find? And do I really want to know? "I can't do this," I whimper, pacing the floor in my bare feet.

Our eyes meet, the screen a shield between us. His are pained and frightened. The hair on my arms stands at attention, and my whole body tightens. "I need you," he says. I dig inside my soul for lingering courage. Coming around the table, I place my fingers atop his. Together we stare at the bright screen and hit "Search." In 0.37 seconds, 12,800,000 results pop up. Our movements are jerky when we add filters. *Zoe Ross Miami Florida*. 930,000 results in 0.66 seconds. *Zoe Ross Miami Beach Florida Ross Hotel* and then *Zoe Ross Thatcher School*.

I'm pleading with the Internet gods, my heart about to jump out of its cage. With each click, each search, the threat becomes frighteningly real. Lists of results line the page, and I'm rooted to the spot, careful to read each one. Zoe Ross is the daughter of Bobby Ross, developer and owner of the iconic Ross Hotel in South Beach, Florida. She attends the Thatcher School, she has Facebook, Instagram, Twitter, Snapchat, and Pinterest accounts, and she has won numerous debate competitions across the state. I lick my lips and keep scrolling, reading the biography of Zoe's young life. No video. No indication that *Zoe Ross Does the Dirty* has spread. I thank God and exhale.

Our bodies relax with relief. "This is good," I say, trying to be convincing. "It's under control." Though there's nothing *good* about having to Google your daughter's sexual exploits on the Internet.

I look up and catch Zoe's face peering out from behind the door. Her expression softens. The color returns to her face, and the clouds in her eyes are replaced with a pale blue.

The fact that we rejoice because our daughter's sexual tryst didn't go viral indicates how far we've fallen. The respite may be temporary, Bobby reminds me, but I disagree. We can control this.

It's dark and quiet, and we're on opposite ends of the couch when he tells me he has to fly to New York later in the week. The interview tomorrow has me on edge. I'm dreading the piece on the alleged perfect family. He's propped up on a cushion, and I'm buried under a ginger blanket. This is my favorite room—creamy white with splashes of earth tones, but tonight the colors feel off.

"Now?"

He repeats it twice because the first time I pretend not to hear him. "I have a meeting in the city."

Bobby's business requires travel, though he knows how to manage his schedule for limited absences. And he never leaves on certain occasions.

"Do you really think this is the best time to leave?"

"I can't change it." He turns on the TV and flips through the channels.

"You can't or you won't?"

"Please, Emma." He's dismissive.

The noise from the TV buffers what we don't want to say. I catch his eyes and feel much farther away from him than the width of our coffee table. He may as well be holding a mirror up at me. A painful unease grips me, and I try to push it down. *The Voice* lights up the screen, and he mutes the volume.

"We need to go after the person who videoed her," he says.

"No, Bobby, we need to focus on making sure Zoe's okay."

Lily marches in and catches Blake Shelton twirling in his chair. "What's the point of watching *The Voice* without sound?" she asks. It's funny, but no one laughs. She gives me her cheek and turns to her dad. "You coming in?"

"I'll be there in a few minutes," he says as she marches out again.

I find his eyes, and the brown tugs. He's not done discussing retribution. "That's why we find the person who did this," he says. "They should be held responsible." He's pressed against the pillows, his hair dusting his forehead. His arms are toned and tan, and he looks younger than his years.

"How is punishing someone else taking care of Zoe?"

"They're not mutually exclusive."

I tug the blanket higher up my body. A question needles me. "It feels like you're disappointed it wasn't an assault."

His attention locks on the screen. "That's ridiculous."

"Is it?" I am in this moment unabashedly honest. If he looked carefully he would know. He'd see my blemishes, too. But Zoe did this. The actions were hers. Not some drug. Believing she was forced is an excuse to bury her mistake. "I know what you're doing," I say. *I've done it myself. Once. A long time ago. I made excuses. Lies.* They're so close to the surface he has to see them lurking beneath my skin.

"I'm trying to help my daughter," he says, holding up the remote and renewing his program search.

Look at me. "You want something to blame. Someone to blame."

He rubs his forehead and the platinum wedding band comes to view. "Is that so wrong?" he asks. "That I don't want it to be my daughter's fault?"

"If I see it, she can, too," I say.

"You're wrong."

"I know you, Bobby. I know how you think. You're upset . . . angry . . . but how angry? How long are you going to punish her?"

"It's been a day, Emma. Twenty-four hours."

I ask again. "How long are you going to punish her?"

He shakes his head. "Any father would feel the same. Zoe's my daughter."

"What if Zoe were a boy?" I ask.

He tosses his hands in the air. "We're not going to debate the double standard . . . I can't imagine her doing what she did . . . and so publicly. That boy used her. He didn't care about her. He didn't respect her."

It hurts to hear him say these things. It's a lashing I'd feared deep inside my bones. The swiftness with which he judges those he loves alarms me. A ball of fear plants itself inside me. It's about to implode.

"So he didn't love her," I clarify. "And she didn't love him. So it cheapens her, makes her flawed. Is that what you're saying?"

"I hate when you say it like that," he says.

"It's the truth, though? Isn't that how you feel?"

I'm staring at him so deeply I'm convinced he can read my thoughts. I want him to argue with me. To say he loves her no matter what. That whatever she did was a mistake, not a personal flaw, but his eyes tell a different story. If Zoe is feeling a fraction of what I once felt, my daughter's in a lot of pain. And dragging her through some revenge plot would make it worse.

He won't look at me. He stares at the television instead. Anderson Cooper is dapper in a polka-dotted tie, and it reminds me of the time we went to Bobby's fraternity formal and the clip from his tie got stuck. We made love with it on. In the morning it was still there. Naked Bobby wrapped in a bow of satin. He'd always been a gift. I teased him about it for years. *Even better on the inside.* Now my insides are wrought with emotions that can at any time combust.

"How are we going to manage the interview tomorrow when you can't even talk to me?" I ask. "And how can we put Zoe under another microscope?"

He crosses his legs and leans back farther into the couch. "They don't need to know what's going on with Zoe. Even off the record."

It's a personal affront, and the thunder I hear outside agrees. "You think I'd bring it up? How stupid do you think I am?"

Our eyes meet. His are unfriendly. No, they're embarrassed. "You never know what information they've dug up on us. People talk. It could come up."

My lips clamp shut, and words fight their way out. We're the perfect family in the perfect package. "I'd never betray Zoe. How can you say that?" And before I can stop them, the words shoot out of me. "Believe me, I know how to keep secrets."

"What's that supposed to mean?" he asks.

It's cruel, and I realize my mistake. "Nothing."

He eyes me a moment longer, then says, "I just don't want to talk about it. Maybe tomorrow will be good for her, a distraction."

I couldn't think of anything worse for a girl who already feels exposed than to be photographed and questioned for local media. I'd want to crawl in a hole and hide. "What about Tuesday? Do you think she'll be ready to return to school?"

"Maybe she should transfer," he says. "It might be easier for her."

I disagree. Running away isn't the answer. "Postpone New York."

"Em, it's two days."

"Can't Jonny go?"

He flips the TV off. "No, Jonny can't go. I need to be there."

I'm too exhausted to fight. I remember when his parents died and the hotel became theirs to share. Bobby's attachment was always deeper. It was understood early on he'd take the reins. There I was by his side. We chose carpets together. Paint swatches. Planned events and hired staff. His decision to leave, especially now, catches me off guard.

My phone dings. I have no interest in reading any more sympathy notes, but the name across the screen is Dr. Don Mason, the principal of Thatcher.

From: Don Mason [masond@thatcherschool.edu]
To: Emma Ross [emma.ross@rossgroup.com]; Robert Ross [robert.ross@rossgroup.com]
CC: Zelda Rubin [rubinz@thatcherschool.edu]
Subject: Zoe Ross

Mr. and Mrs. Ross,

It has come to my attention that an explicit video has been sent to many of our students that includes Zoe and another student. Thatcher has a zero-tolerance policy when it comes to sexting and the dissemination of inappropriate material. A letter to the student body and parents will go out tomorrow morning. If any student is caught forwarding or sharing said video, it will result in automatic expulsion from Thatcher. We take these matters very seriously in accordance with specific guidelines in our Student Handbook and our commitment to the well-being of our students.

I'll be in my office tomorrow morning after drop-off if you would like to discuss this matter further. Please bring Zoe. I'd like to assure her that we are here to facilitate a safe and bully-free academic environment.

I have copied Zelda Rubin, our school's counselor, on this e-mail. If there is any help or support that Ms. Rubin can provide, she is available to Zoe and your family at any time.

Warmest regards,
Dr. Don Mason
Principal, Thatcher Day School

Well, that got around fast. I'm pleased and horrified at once. "Dr. Mason wants us to come in. With Zoe. Can we go on Tuesday?"

"I can't, Em . . . and I don't think she should go. She needs time."

He never said no to anything pertaining to the girls. Ever.

I push on. "She needs to make the decision about school. We can't make it for her. If she thinks she can handle it, she should go. And you need to be there."

"Look what happened the last time she made a decision."

His words are like a bite. They leave deep marks.

There are walls between us that I never noticed before. I feel fragile, breakable, as though anything he says might crack me open for all to see. I can't be near him, and the impulse lifts me off the couch in the direction of the girls' room.

The steps to their room are long. My legs are rubbery and unsure. I don't knock, instead silently letting myself in the door. It smells like my girls, a mixture of blue jeans and cherry lip gloss, possibility and promise. Phone chargers and bags and hair ties crowd their dressers. I kiss Lily's forehead and cross the room to Zoe. I bend down to meet her cheek, ruffle her hair. I study the artifacts of a young life. I see Zoe's scattered brown hair, her tired body curled on its side in a ball. She is so at peace it's hard for me to imagine what's going on inside her mind.

I turn off their reading lamps and listen to the silence. My eyes adjust to the darkness, and I step over backpacks and shoes and computers until I land at the foot of her bed, dropping to my knees. The surge of tears starts in the pit of my stomach. They are the dreaded goodbye, the mourning of my little girl. The effort to keep the cries silent is hard. I gasp, clinging to her nearby sweatshirt. The one with the huge peace sign made of sunflowers.

The grief devours me. It's been tangled up inside, protecting me, but at the same time, inflicting more damage. Helping Zoe means helping myself. I stare up at the clock on the wall. It's a loud, clicking clock that Bobby loved as a young boy. It was his great-grandfather's, and he passed it down to the girls so its rhythmic chimes could smooth out unpredictable times. Today it makes me sad. Today it makes me hate time.

When I slide into bed, Bobby turns on his side and tells me he's tired. I'm tired, too, but I lay my hand across his back. He pretends not to notice. I clamp my eyes shut and bite down the pain.

"You didn't kiss the girls good night," I whisper into the darkness. But he doesn't answer.

CHAPTER 8

It's a morning of contradictions. Blue skies, a tranquil beach, water so clear you can see through to the bottom, and a family suppressing a bubbling secret under a painted-on smile. The girls are clad in strapless organza gowns with French lace. Zoe's emerald; Lily's sapphire. I'm amethyst. Their hair is swept back in loose buns behind their heads. Dramatic gold glitter frames their blue eyes. At a glance, they're bare-footed angels with skin dusted in soft pink.

It should have been a fun-filled day, what Lily had called her "Cinderella moment," with Bobby and Jonny in matching tuxedos, but it doesn't come close. Instead, when I look deeper, Zoe's doe-eyed expression is from lack of sleep, Lily's affair with the camera is a tamped-down excitement, and Bobby is on edge, waiting for the facade to blow.

"Beautiful," calls out Mark the photographer. "Just a few more shots outside and we'll head upstairs.

"Get closer together.

"Zoe, chin up. Smile.

"Lily, grab your sister's hand."

"I'm Zoe," she says.

"Zoe, I mean Lily, over here."

For the most part, he does an excellent job directing a family in crisis, but my face hurts from smiling, and I'm convinced our bodies don't fit together. Bobby pokes Zoe to get her to smile, and Mark applauds what he perceives as a loving gesture.

At one point, he asks, "How do you tell them apart?"

We're taking a break, and the one in sapphire chases the waves as if she's suited in Under Armour and not a designer gown. The one in emerald is hovering along the shoreline. She's contemplative when she dips a toe in the water. These people have no idea what we are living through at the moment. "Lily's always moving. Zoe's the inert one."

We return to the shoot and Mark's choreography. He snaps pictures of Bobby and Jonny and then trains his lens on us. "Bobby and Emma, move in closer."

What should come naturally feels awkward and practiced, but we know how to fake it.

"Now let me get a shot of Bobby alone with the girls."

I step aside and watch the three of them take position by the pool. Zoe's gaze is far away. She fidgets with her dress, her hair. Lily dips her toes in the water. They're told to hold hands and jump up in the air. Zoe barely gets off the ground.

"Wow," Mark says, "the dream shot," and he passes me the camera. The digital screen comes into view and I zoom in. What I saw as hesitation and Zoe's inner torment changes on the display. She's ethereal and light. Magical.

"The lens reads their faces," Mark comments. "Exquisite. The dark hair and pale complexions are very Jenner-esque."

Bobby cringes, and Zoe ducks her head under one of the pool umbrellas. Lily appraises herself. I thank him, wondering what he'd say if he knew Zoe's photo was already out there in living color.

Back in the apartment, Shari the stylist has a wardrobe change waiting. The girls and I slip into blue jeans and white tanks, and Bobby puts on jeans and a white button-down, sleeves rolled up, untucked. Jonny had his interview last night, and tension between Bobby and him has him out the door fast.

The interviewer, an attractive brunette named Lana, introduces herself and gives us a run-through on the questions while Mark snaps candids and Shari applies blush and freshens our lips. "We want to see a family working and living together. You're a Miami Beach dynasty of sorts. Let our readers into your world. Let them see the glamour and glitz juxtaposed against the day-to-day."

Our stares are blank. The apartment feels hot, and I know it's more than the lights shining down on us.

"It's okay," she says. "Be yourselves. Be the family everyone loves and adores."

Bobby's eyes meet mine, and we trade phony smiles.

The first questions center on the history of the Ross and our city. Bobby goes into detail about old Miami Beach versus new. How Art Deco and an aging demographic shifted to a cosmopolitan landscape with eclectic tastes. "I miss the old-time glamour. The beach has changed. The younger, international influence has brought forth culture and a renewed interest in the arts, but the area is transient and fickle. My parents and grandparents were raised here. I'm still influenced by their sense of tradition and history."

Hearing him talk about the city he loves always enthralls me. His voice changes, his features relax.

They discuss the competition and the newer hotels in the area and what makes the Ross stand out after all these years. "We're a family," he says. "We take care of each other. Every person who walks through these doors is one of us."

I glance at Zoe, and she's watching her father closely.

"Mrs. Ross." I hear my name. It plucks me from Zoe's soulful eyes. "Tell us how you two met."

The lights shine on me, and I feel strangely exposed. I'm not sure I want to retell our story, but Bobby's eyes meet mine, and he signals for me to begin, though it's a struggle.

"We were eight. It's hard to believe it's been that long . . . I lived in Chicago, and our grandparents had a house on Lakeview Drive. We came down to Miami to escape the cold. My stepdad and his aversion to staying in other people's homes, including his in-laws', landed us at the Ross."

It's easy to lose myself in the memory. There's no scandal. No betrayal. I almost believe I'm back there. Reliving our youth. "Bobby and Jonny would paddle around the pool throwing a ball while my sisters and I would pretend they weren't there. They'd splash us with their strokes, intentionally, unintentionally. I guess what started out as a game of pretend grew into something else."

"Make no mistake," Bobby says, "I fell for her the first time I laid eyes on her. She played hard to get."

The blush crawls up my cheek. I slip inside the story. Click goes the camera.

"Get used to this," says Lily. "They're weirdly mushy."

"This continued the first couple of trips down south. The Ross brothers were everywhere we went. There was a familiar push-pull that I suppose made us friends."

"When did it change?" Lana asks. "I'm sure it was easy to fall in love in such a magnificent setting."

Zoe meets my eyes, mildly interested.

"Bobby had a way about him. It drew me to him from the start. He was confident, but never bragged. He was funny, but never mean. My sisters told me he was trouble, but it didn't matter. He was different than the boys in Deerfield."

My mind pulls me back to those early days. My voice lowers as the memories emerge. He gets up from his seat at the bar and sits beside me. It feels good to be close. "I caught him staring. And I was always watching him. He had that ability to persuade us to follow him wherever he went."

"Did he mention the hotel in a proprietary way? Did you know back then he'd end up taking the helm?"

I shake my head and laugh. The release warms my skin. "He never wanted to run the hotel. Bobby Ross wanted to be a rock star! He'd get out his guitar and play by the ocean. We'd make bonfires when we were allowed, and half the beach would come out to listen." I turn to him when I say, "I think that's when I fell. Hard. Rolling Stones. 'Angie.'"

"How old were you?"

"Fourteen," we both say, catching each other's eyes.

"That night we stayed up all night talking. It didn't feel like enough time." I stop to let the redness recede from my face. The girls' watching makes the story that much more sincere. "I couldn't pretend anymore. As soon as our car pulled into the Ross driveway, Bobby and I were inseparable. He'd rearrange his entire week for my visits and show up wherever I went. He'd send my favorite flowers to our room. Peonies. And he made sure our beach towels with the monogrammed quotes had extra meaningful messages sewn into the fabric for me: *Sweet as Tupelo Honey, My Gray-Eyed Girl, Heart of Gold*. They always had to do with music."

I'm falling with every word of our story. Lana is, too. Her brown eyes are stuck in a wistful longing, and I feel myself embracing my role in the joyful scene. "The Ross opened its doors on the day John Lennon was born. And Bobby was born the same day, years later. To him it's no coincidence. He worships Lennon. 'Music royalty,' he calls him. Fitting for the crown jewel of Miami Beach. I loved that he loved her so much, how he talked endlessly of her. And how he could just as deeply love me the same way. By the time we were fifteen I'd say we were . . . in love. We've been together ever since."

The number echoes through the living room, and Zoe rises. "May I be excused?"

Lily chases after her.

"You have nice girls," Lana remarks. "Polite. Friendly. Are there challenges to raising teenagers in a luxury hotel on South Beach?"

The glow that had captured our story scatters like sand.

Bobby is quick to respond. "Raising teenagers anywhere poses challenges. Teenagers are scary people!" His eyes find mine, and we hold the stare longer than we should. "It's not easy. Like every parent, we do the best we can."

The girls return and calmly take their seats beside us. My heart slowly picks up speed, and I have to embellish. "I didn't grow up like this. We agreed early on that we wouldn't let material things influence the girls. We talk about values a lot. Being good people. We have our own definition of what success means."

Bobby's compelled to sell our perfect little family to this room of strangers. "We encourage the girls to give back to the community. Zoe volunteers at the Humane Society. Lily, well, she's getting there." He chuckles. "The girls clean their room and make their beds. Emma cooks dinner. People have this misperception that we have chef-prepared meals every night. I'll never forget, when the girls were ten, I'm not sure which one it was . . ."

"It was Lily," Zoe replies.

"Lily, right. Lily complained about her dinner from the restaurant, making a scene as if we were starving her to death. The next day, I took them fishing. Dragged them out of bed at five. I showed them how some people have to get their food. You know what? They never complained about a meal again. Most people don't get it, but we're a normal family living probably—to some—in an abnormal home, but it's no different than anyone else's."

Lana taps her pen against her pad. "It must be hard at times to watch them grow up."

Zoe's fingers sweat in mine. I eye Bobby, and he repositions himself on the couch, crossing and uncrossing his legs. I wonder if Lana and her crew see the flame rise in me. They can't possibly know what happened, but Zoe's ordeal is sneaking into the conversation. Her eyes dart around the room, and she nibbles on what's left of her nail polish.

Lana must see she's tapped into something, and she smiles. "You're all so tense! Don't worry, Mr. Ross. I'm asking these questions to paint a picture. There's a misconception about family in today's socioeconomic climate. Part of this piece is to illustrate how not all families conform to such stereotypes. The Ross is an upstanding name in the community." And she looks at the girls when she adds, "You're clearly raising delightful teenagers. I'd think all of our South Florida readers will find your story refreshing."

I'm frozen in my seat. This is a mistake. We are a fraud.

"No problem at all, Lana," Bobby answers. "There's a lot of temptation out there. Emma and I try to provide the girls with the skills to manage tough situations. Like any parent."

"Well, you're doing a great job," she says. "Now back to the Ross. So you two fell in love . . ."

"We fell in love," he says, relieved to be steering us away from the hidden truths. "We did the long-distance thing for a while. Quite a while, actually. High school. College. Emma was an actress back then. A real performer."

I nod, still tightly wound. *I was. The best.* I pretend-smile again. *Come on, Bobby, look closely. Can't you see?* "He never came to see me perform." I jab him with my elbow. "He had a jealous streak this long." I hold my hands far apart.

"She was good," he says, while I hold on to the memory and pretend it means nothing. "Except when she was kissing other men."

"Gross, Dad," Lily says.

I put on my best act, laugh, and playfully swat him. "He never got used to the roles I'd play or the job requirements."

"Gross, Mom," Lily repeats.

Lana smiles. "The jealous type, Mr. Ross. I think we found your one flaw." She has no idea what her comment suggests, and after a brief silence, she moves to the next question. "Emma"—she turns to me—"you moved to Miami after college, and the two of you got married?"

"Yes." A whisper.

"That's a long time to be together."

Bobby pulls me closer. "Yes," he says. "We're very lucky. It's always been the two of us. *Solo tú,* we say." Snap. Click.

"The wedding was here at the hotel?"

"It was," I say. "It was beautiful." We were barefoot on the beach, smiling so hard our faces hurt. I feel as if I'm about to cry.

"And then tragedy struck," he says.

"Yes." I squeeze his hand. "Bobby lost both parents within weeks of our wedding." I pause. "Laura went first, peacefully, in her sleep, while Tropical Storm Mayda battered the beach in a late June storm. Zane passed four days later."

Bobby lowers his head. Mark stops taking pictures, and the room silences.

Lana motions with her hand. "Let's take a break, everyone."

The crew takes five, and no one speaks. Zoe's fingers play with her bottom lip, Lily brushes the strands of the knit throw, and Bobby holds my hand, though I know if I let go, nothing will hold us together.

"I'm getting hungry," Lily says.

Zoe is quiet.

"You doing all right?" I ask her.

"I wonder what they'd think if they knew the truth," she whispers to me.

It's a question I'd been asking of myself. "It's none of their business." But I can't silence the voices telling me otherwise.

It's getting late, and I can tell the girls have had enough. When the crew returns, I ask them how much longer.

"Just a few more questions," Lana says. She begins by asking the girls to recount a typical day at the Ross, and the monotony proves that living in a hotel is not much different than a day in the life of their peers.

"My mom still yells at us to wake up for school," Lily says. "And would you believe we have to do homework every day? And clean up around the house?" She giggles and moves on to lacrosse. Zoe shares a few snapshots about her work with animals and debate.

"What's your favorite thing about living here?" Lana asks.

Lily is first. "I can never pick just one. The beach is my backyard. I have a huge family. And it makes me proud to see what my parents have created. Oh, and room service is a nice benefit."

Zoe's next. She's not in the mood to talk. "Certainty." We wait for her to say more, and when she sees she's confused us she goes on. "The sun rises every morning outside my window. It sets each night. I like being there to see it happen. It's reassuring, and I trust it."

Lana's impressed, and she doesn't hide it. "That was beautiful, girls. You were great. Now you're free to go."

Lily and Zoe get up, thank Lana and Mark, and hug Shari, who tells them they're superstars. When they're out of sight, Lana begins again.

The next hour is spent talking about the early years and how the brothers zigzagged through a real estate boom and a recession while remaining faithful to their parents' intentions for the hotel: family values and commitment to the guest. It was a time of great change, and Bobby steered the hotel through some rough patches. The twins arrived, and the question of raising them in a "transient and untraditional" setting came up, but it was no longer a choice. The Ross was our home, and we'd raise the girls here. Bobby says, "I think growing up on the beach roots us to the earth. Keeps us grounded."

I add, "Bobby's a great father. He used to take the girls every morning in their double stroller on his walk-through of the hotel and grounds. As they got older, it became board meetings and staff parties. The sounds of little girls infused life into the walls. And the hotel anchored them to their past, and to the grandparents they never met."

Bobby discusses his other properties sprinkled around Miami: the Mirage, the Water Tower, and the newly renovated Seaport in Sunny Isles. Lana calls us the "First Family" of Miami Beach. It should make me feel proud, but a rush of unease slides down my legs.

When she asks about the future of the Ross, Bobby lets me finish. I'm thinking about the massive remodel ahead of us, but I don't divulge many details. "Like all hotels, you have to adapt to the changing times and the shifting demographics, but change is good. Every part of this building contributes to the success of its whole, and we'll improve where needed." I pause. "The heart of the Ross remains unspoiled. *That* will never change."

"She's the boss." Bobby smiles, and Lana says we're done.

It is only then that I push back on the cushions and release a long exhale into the air.

CHAPTER 9

We're sitting around the dinner table picking at our food when Bobby says, "I'm proud of you girls. Today wasn't easy. You rallied, and it meant a lot to us."

I glance at Zoe, who's stuck inside her head. Her eyes are fixed on her plate, but she's not eating. She hasn't said much since the interview.

Bobby twirls pasta on his fork. By the way he scrunches his brow, I can tell he's in deep thought. He directs his eyes on the girls. "All this talk about the hotel, I'm wondering if you girls have ever thought about living somewhere else? Like an actual house?"

I stop chewing and meet his eyes.

Zoe remains unaffected while Lily's intrigued. "What do you mean? We love it here."

He forks the food into his mouth, absently chews, and swallows. "At times I wonder if you girls would be better off away from all this."

I watch him closely.

Zoe's voice is a mixture of denial and defensiveness. "The Ross is all we know. We don't have anything to compare it to." She pauses. "And Daddy, it didn't happen because we live in a hotel."

The cold, hard stare I give him clashes with his beliefs. *You're looking for an excuse.* He brings the glass of water to his mouth and backs down. "I'm curious. It's a conversation we've never had."

"Because we've always been happy here," I bark. "Why would you ask such a thing?"

Lily gets up and drops her plate in the sink. "I'm going to read the most boring book in America: *Jane Eyre*. When are they going to assign us Sarah Dessen?"

"Oh God, school. Do I have to go?" Zoe asks. "Everyone's seen me! Everyone's watched that video. How can I go? You think I can sit through a test?"

Bobby mutters a snide remark, but we hear him loud and clear. "No. Because you barely understand the material," and Zoe turns her back on him.

I remind her she won't be alone, that we'd be with her, walking her in, and there by her side when she meets with Dr. Mason.

"As if this can't get any worse. Dr. Mason knows about the video." Her face has gone slack, and her shoulders sag. When she stands up and makes her way past me, I reach for her arm, but she slinks away. "I'm fine, Mom."

The rejection stings, but it's no worse than being left at the table with Bobby and feeling alone. All the nostalgia threaded through our stroll down memory lane has vanished.

"It was only a question," he says. "You didn't have to attack me."

I stand up and clear the table, too exhausted to argue.

"I raised the question. I think it's a good one, considering the situation we find ourselves in."

I'm rinsing plates when he joins me in loading the dishwasher. "How can you ask that question after today?" And when he thinks about this, I say, "You can't blame what she did on the hotel. It's not that simple." We're standing shoulder to shoulder, but it feels farther. "Actually"—I stop and face him—"sometimes it is very simple, but it's not the hotel's fault. It's no one's *fault*."

He tugs at his shirt collar. "Why are you so quick to defend her? What if she starts doing this all the time? What if she's . . . what if . . ."

"What, Bobby? You're worried your daughter may have a reputation? Is that it? You're worried she may actually like fooling around with boys?"

"It's different."

"How convenient. The old double standard again."

"Whatever. Maybe it's best I'm leaving. I'm too irritated to be around her."

His disregard frightens me. My secret unravels, spreading through my body. "You're ashamed of Zoe. Is it so bad you have to leave?"

"It's business, Em."

"You've always been able to shift things around for us."

"I can't this time," he says.

"Does this have something to do with Jonny's phone call?"

"No."

It's a flimsy response, and I let it go.

The dishes are done, and an awkward quiet settles between us. We stand on either side of the island facing each other.

"It went well today," he says. "It should be a nice piece."

My fingers grab the countertop, and I lean into them for support. *The piece.* As long as the piece is okay. As long as it paints the perfect picture. June, Ward, Wally, and Beaver, shiny and spotless like our great hotel. Agreeing with him is continuing the charade.

His eyes narrow in question. "What's wrong with you?"

I push off the counter, grab a dishcloth, and wipe imaginary grime from the table.

An eruption builds. It burns the nerves up and down my body. There's no stopping what comes out of my mouth. "Everything's wrong."

He comes toward me, and I fling him away. I'm wiping the table down, long, hurried strokes that make no difference in the porcelain white. Zoe's face tacked to the bulletin board stares down at me. It's her school photo, taken a few weeks ago. Her smile is pure, her eyes cheerful. Summer had come to an end, and her skin was more olive than pale.

This is about her. Not you. I wipe and wipe as though my hands can erase the last forty-eight hours. But Zoe still would've done what she did; we just wouldn't have known about it.

By now I'm crying, cold drops that stream down my face and land on the table I'm trying to clean.

"Everything's wrong," I repeat. "And you, you're worried about a magazine article that is so chock full of cracks that anyone looking close can see?"

He stands over me, and I can tell he wants to touch me, but it's too painful, and he turns away. Eventually, I drop the rag and collapse in a chair. "What do you want me to do?" he asks.

"Stop fighting her. Listen to her. Don't push her away. I feel it every time you look at her. She feels it, too."

"Why aren't I entitled to have an opinion about this? Why can't I be angry? Should I be like, 'Hey, Zoe, great job. Let's go shoot some pool downstairs'?"

"I'm not saying that."

"Then what are you saying?"

I drop my head. I hate arguing with him. "I don't know."

But I do know. I'm scared he's going to look at me the way he looks at Zoe.

CHAPTER 10

Bobby sleeps soundlessly by my side. I toss and turn, staring at the clock, watching the hours tick past. I roll over again and face the stars that dot the black sky. They used to bring me back to earth. As my nerves begin to settle, I replay the day. Faking happiness is grueling work. We've erected facades and walls, and what's beneath it all tugs on old memories. The Ross holds that history—the girls touching the Atlantic for the first time, Bobby and I vowing to love each other forever, the miles that separated us, the lonely hours apart. Yet she's as imperfect as the rest of us. How easily we can deceive ourselves and each other.

I was told that first love was as fleeting as its powerful pull. That wasn't how it was for Bobby and me. Each passing year, our minds became a little more enrapt, our bodies intrinsically bound. There was so much more than what I'd shared with Lana and the magazine.

During our high school years, when I was in Chicago and he was in Miami, I daydreamed about returning to the Ross. While performing in *A Midsummer Night's Dream* and *Romeo and Juliet*, I used my acting skills as a coping mechanism. No matter who played my Romeo or Lysander or Demetrius, when I closed my eyes, I saw only one man: Bobby Ross.

Friends tried to set me up, but the prospects never evoked in me what Bobby could. My sisters loved him. And with each visit down south, a stretch of summer, winter break, a long weekend in May, our growing relationship became the ideal for all future relationships.

When our family ventured to the palm-tree-lined streets of Miami, I immersed myself in Bobby's world. As quickly as I could shed my winter coat and boots, I was following him around the city that he loved. For Valentine's Day, he took me to Joe's Stone Crabs and introduced me to their famous claws and buttery sauce. We spent afternoons biking along Lincoln Road and walking the beach, hand in hand, sharing the minutiae of our respective lives. He knew all about my girlfriends back home, and I knew all about his world within the hotel walls. He taught me Spanish. *Flaca*, he called me, when I appeared too thin after exams. *Bonita*, because he said I was pretty. *Te extraño y te amo*, because he said he loved me and missed me more than the English language could convey. To which I learned to reply, *No puedo vivir sin ti*. His response, *I can't live without you either. Solo tú.* Only you.

Nothing about Bobby was cursory. And as we aged, we were no longer young kids with a crush. When he'd play with my hair, he was fingering the blueprint of my internal history; when he ran his fingers up and down my arms, he was tapping into my tender spots, the ones that said I love him and only him.

Lana's presumption was correct: Bobby had a jealous streak that ran the length of the Atlantic. As kids skipping along the beach playing a game of two-hand touch, he staked his claim. I was his. It was me and my sisters, Jonny, and Stuart and Jeff, two brothers who visited often from Long Island. It was winter break, and I was clad in a purple bikini that I had bought with Bobby in mind. The style was small and stringy, and he had already taken it off me once before. The weather in Chicago had been unusually cold that December. I was anxious to be back at the Ross beside Bobby, though I was a senior, and I knew college was nearing.

So when Stuart chased me into the end zone and grabbed the thin string, part of my top became exposed. My left breast, to be exact. His eyes popped open, and he lunged closer.

"Hey, asshole!" Bobby yelled, loud enough for them to hear in Islamorada. His nostrils flared, and he shoved Stuart aside and covered me with his arms. His ownership of my body excited me. It excited him, too. He kissed me long and hard on the lips while his hands expertly retied the strings. Stuart never bothered me again.

Zoe doesn't get it, and most kids don't. We were teenagers once. Beneath the bickering and brattiness, feelings were unearthed and comingled. Instead of rushing into the sexual pull, we relished being close. Bobby never pressured me. When we kissed, I took those lips home to Chicago, closing my eyes and imagining them somewhere else, somewhere I'd never let a boy go before. The years that followed were bottled up in the scent of sunscreen and salt. Back home, I would smell Bobby in the faint breeze of the Coppertone I'd leave by my bed. The sensations would sustain me when we were apart.

At seventeen, we stayed out all night on the beach with an oversize blanket Bobby had swiped from the laundry room. We told each other we were going to watch the sun rise, and around midnight, we covered the sand with the blanket and our bodies.

As if sensing where my mind has gone, Bobby moves beside me. He's turned on his side away from me, and I think about curling around him and drawing him close, but I don't.

It's still dark when Zoe crawls in bed alongside me. The alarm isn't set to go off for another hour.

"Why are you up?" I ask, rounding my body to make room for her. She is warm from sleep.

"I don't know what to do." She presses into me. "I don't want to go."

I brush the tangled hair off her face. "Whatever you decide, honey, we'll support you. There's no wrong answer."

"What would you do?" she asks, her voice prodding me for answers.

"I can't answer that, Zoe." I want to, but there's a distinct difference between what's right and what's easy.

"Please, Mom. I want to know."

I sigh and consider the circumstances. "I guess I'd go. I'd think of it as a performance. Like acting." Bobby shuffles next to me, and I lower my voice. Our bodies soften each other. "Imagine you're at a debate. It's a type of performance. Don't let them get to you. If they see you upset, it'll give them something to talk about. Don't give them anything more to talk about." A memory flashes. It's quick. Snap. I'm walking into class, and the girls stop talking. One laughs. Another mouths a dirty word. I channel Rosalind Russell in *Gypsy* and lift my chin. "Pretend."

I spoon-feed Zoe the same lines over her untouched breakfast. The girls are dressed in their school uniforms, polos and khaki shorts. Thatcher is generous with variety, and they wear different colors to prevent confusion, though their temperament sets them apart. Lily nibbles on a croissant, animated and talking fast about Thursday's lacrosse match. She wears her hair pulled back in a messy swirl of brown and appears well rested. Zoe is silent and motionless. Her hair spreads down her shoulders and hides some of her face. Her expression is blank, leaving us guessing whether she's actually going to make it out the front door.

"I'm scared," she says, her voice a heavy whisper.

I grip her eyes in mine. "I know."

Bobby pours himself coffee and takes a seat at the table. He's dressed in a dark suit and the red tie we bought last year when we visited my sisters up north. He's stuck in his head and far from his animated self. I wonder if he remembers turning away from me last night.

"How long do you think this meeting with Dr. Mason will go?" he asks, as though he's doing me a favor by joining us. He cuts into a bagel and slathers it with cream cheese, avoiding eye contact. Zoe's mouth opens to say something, but she changes her mind.

I don't press her about going to school. I focus on things we can try to control. "Dr. Mason's confident the video's contained. No one wants to make this worse. We're behind you, Zoe. Whatever you need."

Her head rests in her hands, and we wait for some indication of her decision. I don't want to push her. She needs to be comfortable with her choice. She surprises us by standing up and grabbing her backpack from the floor. "Let's get this over with. Maybe he'll excuse me from taking the biology test."

Lily surprises me, too. Always the one armed with a quick comeback about the unfairness of things, instead she's mum.

We pass through the hotel lobby, and the stares and laughs of guests who are merely being friendly feel like something else. No one in our sphere seems to know, and it's nothing like what Zoe will soon face. Her wound is raw, and the phony smiles and callous whispers of her peers are sure to hurt. There's no way I can shield her from what's to come.

Lily listens to music through her headphones, and Zoe sulks. Bobby's by my side, though we don't touch. He's focused on his building, and I imagine he's studying the white marble floors that need to be replaced and how the demolition will affect the gold mosaic columns that stretch toward the high ceilings. Their tiles reflect the surrounding candlelight. Most days, when I enter the vast space, the possibilities envelop me. Today, the giant white pots overflowing with plants greet me, the pale leather couches and soft lights graze my skin, but that is all. There's an emptiness in my belly I don't know how to fill.

The staff at the ivory modular desk smile at us like they do each morning. Lily waves, and Zoe stares ahead. Heather, one of the welcome staff, comes out from behind the desk and approaches Bobby. Her expression means it's important.

"Go ahead," he says. "I'll meet you out front."

Guests mill around, some feeling the joy of checking in, others feeling melancholy over checking out. The Beckers' little boy approaches and thanks me for a *super* time. His parents smile and wave. We won't see them for another year, and the nostalgia twists inside.

Alberto greets us like he does each morning, though today is different. He's holding the door for us to pass through. "Today's the day! Driving permits, yes?"

Lily appears beaten. "Not quite, Poppy Berto."

Zoe's lips are pressed together. I manage a smile for the two of them, and we touch briefly on the cooler weather moving through South Florida as we descend the stairs.

We wait for the car to be brought around the circular drive, and Alberto remarks on how grown-up the girls are. "Do you see the resemblance? They look very much like their *abuela*. Same eyes," he says, and he focuses on Zoe when he adds, "and very serious."

When the car arrives, I turn from Alberto, and greet the valet as he holds the door. The forced smile hurts, quickly sliding off my face.

"Señora Ross," Alberto says, joining me by the passenger's side, "I've upset you . . ."

"No, Alberto." He squeezes my fingers. My eyes well up again. How I miss Laura and Zane Ross. With everything falling apart around us, Bobby could use his father's common sense and his mother's intense adoration. I have to believe they're near. That's when I see Bobby approaching.

"Thank you, Alberto. We'll be fine." But when I steal a glance at my girls in the back seat, I'm really not so sure.

The Thatcher campus is lush and green—unheard of in Miami. Perched on a generous piece of land, the property houses state-of-the-art classrooms, a three-hundred-seat theater, a television studio, a sports complex, a farm-to-table food hall, an aquatics center, and numerous other amenities that make it one of the most desirable private schools in Dade County.

Bobby drops us off at the front of the two-story high school before heading to the covered parking garage. "I'll meet you in Dr. Mason's office," I say to him over my shoulder. Lily runs ahead while Zoe takes her time. My arm wants to pull her close, but I know she won't allow it. Every step of the way, I worry. Is someone looking at her? Are they pointing? Are they saying unkind things?

School offices are always unnerving. Zoe glumly sits with her hands in her lap while Dr. Mason politely asks how she's doing. She shrugs; embarrassment creeps up her face. Bobby takes an empty seat and we begin.

"Let me start by saying we've prepared a letter to parents and students outlining the risks of filming, uploading, viewing, and distributing inappropriate videos and photos." He hands us a copy, and we read it together. "Zoe and Price are unnamed. Anyone found partaking in the listed offenses will be reported to the authorities and receive an immediate expulsion from Thatcher," he warns.

Bobby nods. "Has the school heard anything else? We'd like to find out who's behind the filming."

"I have not," he says, dropping his hands to the desk. "But I can assure you if we hear anything you'll be the first to know."

I study the middle-aged man with wavy brown hair and an angular face. "Do you think maybe Zoe can talk to Dr. Rubin today?" I turn to Zoe. "Do you want to talk to the school's counselor? Maybe it would help."

"Zoe," Dr. Mason says, clasping his hands. "We're taking every step to ease this transition for you. We're here to help. Whatever you need. Talking to Dr. Rubin might be a good first step. I'll schedule something that won't interfere with your classes."

"Can you make it during biology? I have it third period. There's a test I have to make up . . ." She struggles to finish.

"That shouldn't be a problem," he says, swiveling his chair to the computer. "I'll send a message to Mr. Musso about a different makeup day, and Dr. Rubin will see you third period."

When he finishes, he turns around and faces us. "Zoe, I'm impressed to see you here today, though not surprised. The kids look up to you. Your teachers have nothing but glowing reports. In my experience, the best thing you can do is walk out there and do what you've always done. We'll take care of the rest."

Loud voices suddenly infiltrate the office—a boy's voice, something I can't make out, a slapping sound, and then "Shut your mouth!" *Lily.*

My heart thuds, and I dart a look at Bobby, who is doing a wonderful job, by his blank expression, of being blissfully unaware. I'm on my feet before any of them acknowledge the commotion, and dash out the doorway. Zoe is not far behind.

There, in the hallway, surrounded by a group of teenagers, Lily's waging her own war. "Bobby!" I call out.

"You're in big trouble," she says to a scrawny boy with frightened eyes. She has him cornered by a row of lockers. He backs up, the tight navy-blue Thatcher polo squeezing his skinny arms. The brown of his eyes matches his Justin Bieber haircut.

"You're not being fair!" he cries out, a shot of injustice pouring from a mouth full of braces. "You agreed to do it."

I am frozen, face-to-face with Price Hudson. My heart pounds in my ears. Bobby's about to move in closer. I stop him with my arm. "Don't."

"You're such an idiot." Lily pounces, her hands on her hips. "You don't even know I'm not Zoe."

"Lily!" I shout. I want to punish this kid, but it gets lost in my wish for my daughter to be a lady.

Dr. Mason is directing students and demands they get to class. "Lily, Price, that means you, too." Price's face is stricken with fresh panic. Everyone knows Zoe is compliant and sweet. Her sister is the firecracker.

"She didn't want it!" Lily shouts. "And she definitely didn't want it filmed!"

"I'm going to kill this kid," whispers Bobby. He takes a single step, and fear spreads through my veins. One hand grabs hold of his shoulder while another comes around his waist. His body tightens beneath my grasp; I'm restraining him with all my might.

Dr. Mason shouts, "Lily and Price, now!" while Grace Howard, with a flip of her hair, tries to intervene. "Lily! What are you doing? We have to get to class."

Price yells back, "I would've never forced her. It was a game. She lost. She said it was fun!"

The words are hardly out of his mouth, lingering in the air, when his head yanks to one side, and he grunts. It takes me a moment to realize what happened—Lily has just punched Price.

"Lily!"

The boy is holding his jaw and whimpering, dazed by the force of her fist. I am angry and ashamed, but I restrain myself from rushing to Lily with praise or punishment.

"That's my girl," Bobby says under his breath.

The crowd splits, and the boy hides his face. Grace seems torn between defending Lily and comforting Price. Her cheeks are blushed, and confusion clouds her eyes. I come around Lily and lead her away. She calls over her shoulder, "Never say those things about my sister again!"

Dr. Mason fumes when he addresses Lily. "In my office."

Which is how both Lily and Zoe end up seated in the principal's office at the strike of the bell for first period.

I remain standing, and glower at Lily. "Are you kidding me?"

"Price Hudson is a complete jerk," she rants. "He shouldn't be allowed in school. What a putz."

"Lily!" I hiss, while Bobby's unmistakable grin crosses his face.

Zoe slides down the chair and melts into its plastic.

"Lily," begins Dr. Mason, rolling a pen between two fingers, "we appreciate your concern for your sister, but one act of misconduct won't negate another. Thatcher has rules. We abide by them."

Price passes the doorway, followed by the school nurse. He has an ice pack against his face. Lily turns to Zoe. "You can't let people treat you like that and get away with it. If I can't defend you, who will?" She nurses her hand while continuing her assault. "I'm not sorry. He deserved it. He took advantage of my sister. I should've done it a few more times."

Zoe's face is a spectacle of color. It starts out a pale, filmy white and ends with a fiery red. Bobby's beside her, pleased. His smug look is hard to miss.

"That doesn't give you the right to touch him!" I raise my voice. "What's happening to you girls?" I drop into the chair while the chaos swirls around us. "Bobby, say something!"

"You don't want to hear what I have to say," he replies.

I cover my face with my hands, humiliated that Dr. Mason sees us like this. Then it hits me. And when it hits, it hits hard. Dr. Mason was a small fraction of the humiliation. Zoe's on a video in the digital universe, and we've been judged by hundreds if not thousands. It doesn't matter that we do our best. It doesn't matter that we thought we did everything right. It doesn't matter that Zoe loves dogs and gets straight A's. She will forever be marked with her own scarlet letters: *B* and *J*.

My mind plays this spectacle over and over again, and concentrating on Dr. Mason and the broken pieces of my family is difficult. He tells Lily to compose herself. I hear the phrase "forced to suspend you."

Dr. Mason's eyes fill with sympathy. The cringe-worthy kind. "The Hudsons are my next appointment. Perhaps they'll be willing to overlook this matter."

Fantastic, I think. They're going to walk in here any minute. I'm furious with Bobby. His silence is a personal affront. "You're condoning your daughter hitting someone," I whisper.

"Typical," Lily adds. "My sister gets a reputation, and Price is a hero."

The reminder of this unwanted label transforms Zoe from her catatonic state to impulsive. She jumps up and makes a beeline for the door, her red shirt and face a shock against the pale yellow walls. I stand up, annoyed with Lily, and knock over a pile of papers on Dr. Mason's desk. Bending over to pick them up, I fume at her, "You're treading on thin ice."

"Lily," Dr. Mason admonishes, clearing his throat, "I'm not going to say it again. Watch yourself."

Bobby remains seated while I chase after Zoe. As I leave, my eyes are on Lily, but hers lower. She mouths, "I'm not sorry."

"You're going to be when I get through with you," I say.

I step out the doorway and collide with the Hudsons. They look like any normal Thatcher parents, but I can tell by the sorrow that lines their faces and the way they're hunched into each other that, like us, they're a family under siege. Sympathy turns to dislike and grips my body, making it difficult to take the next steps. Mr. Hudson holds the door open because he has no idea who I am. Our gray eyes meet, and my heart beats so loudly I'm sure he can hear it. Mrs. Hudson looks away but soon returns her eyes to me. My mouth opens, but it's more out of shock than having something to say. The loathing floods my senses. What I saw moments ago as *normal* is now a woman who's too thin and blonde and a man who's big and overbearing.

We slip through the small space, and my breath fills my starving lungs. I turn around and study his arm draped around her shoulder. How he's holding her up. My eyes are shouting, *Your son is the devil.*

94

I quicken my pace to catch up to Zoe. The kids disperse into their classrooms, and the hallway is deserted and quiet. Zoe exits a door leading outside, and soon she's gone from my sight. I find her seated on a lone bench that borders a pond separating the high school from the middle and elementary schools. A nearby tree drips with vibrant green leaves, and the contrast blinds me.

"I shouldn't have come," she says. "I made a huge mistake. It's all too much."

"We can leave," I tell her, taking a seat. She's still, hunched over, and I assure her it'll be okay. But I'm not sure it will. "Let's get in the car. We can try again tomorrow."

She thinks about this. I tuck a lock of hair behind her ear. "It's all right. You've been through a lot."

"No," she says, changing her mind, "I should stay. The first day of anything always stinks. I want to get it over with."

"I know how you feel," I begin. A leaf lands in her hair, and I want to believe it symbolizes something. How things fall down and get back up.

Zoe's empty stare disagrees. "You could never know how I feel."

This is what it's like to be on the edge of a cliff staring down at the jagged rocks and water below. *Oh, Zoe, I do. I was made fun of once. I walked into a room with a label stuck to my back. And it multiplied into something far worse, a horrible mistake that I'll never be able to erase. Ever.* But I could never tell her. No matter how much she pulls, it would kill me to tell her. "I do, Zoe."

The wind swipes at Zoe's face. If she replies, the breeze picks it up and carries it away.

There's space between us on the bench—not a lot, but enough for me to be concerned. "We all screw up," I tell her. "It's part of growing up. There's nothing you can do that will change my love for you. Nothing."

"I don't believe you," she blurts out. "You'd never do something like this."

She has no idea what her words mean to me, no idea of the visceral power of their suggestion. It's been harder and harder to silence the sounds of my fight with Bobby all those years ago. *"Monty's there? He's in your apartment? Are you fucking him?"* How one lie became a lifetime of lies. How his accusations became the truth. And the sin lay dormant through milestones and memories, until now. This moment. When it landed in my daughter's soul. I'd been plugging the holes in the dam, confusing my story with hers, and trying to understand her through my colored lens. It's unbearable for me to watch her suffer so intimately and publicly. I give her the only thing I can. "I've made questionable decisions like you."

"Please. What did you do? Sneak onto an airplane before they called your group number?"

How they love to tease me about being a rule follower. I haven't always been. There's a knot the size of a grapefruit forming in my belly. The secret part of myself unravels, the one I hadn't wanted anyone to see.

Her eyes fix on the grass. Small, purple flowers make the weeds look alive and healthy. "No one has any idea how it feels. Everyone talking about you . . ."

"I can't imagine," I whisper, leaning in closer, lessening the gap. Modern technology had stripped Zoe of her privacy. There were no devices recording my transgression and what came after. Either way, the shame didn't have to be seen to be felt.

She shakes when she speaks. "What I've done, the reach is too far and too fast."

I hug her tighter and feel her heart against my chest. Tears sprout from my eyes. I can't make them stop.

"There's a monster out there," she says. "It can be anyone pushing a button and ruining my life. I can't see them, but they're out there, and I'm terrified."

I feel the monster, too. So close.

"We're fighting back, Zoe. You're not alone. The school's e-mailed everyone . . . they've deleted it . . . your friends will back you up . . . and we will, too. Everyone knows who you are."

She pulls back and faces me with her freckles and damp eyes. "It's unrealistic for you to think you can fight the Internet, Mom. And Dad is mad. He wants to blame this on someone."

"You're his little girl," I say, stopping to catch my breath. "He wants you to make smart decisions. So do I."

The sun peeks from behind a puff of white and casts a glow on Zoe's face. It's the kind of shine that highlights everything she wishes to hide. There's remorse, there's humiliation, and something else bouncing off her skin. "Why is this happening to me?"

Her eyes glaze over. I'm sad to see her so distraught, so distrusting of the world. I swallow my inner torment and tell her what she needs to hear. "Bad things happen to good people, Zoe. It doesn't mean you're bad. It means the universe found a warrior in you. It chose carefully. It's up to you how to move forward. You can choose to be the victim, or you can choose to be the warrior."

"I don't know how," she sniffles.

"Hold that beautiful head of yours up high. Show everyone that you're better than their stares and daggers. You're bigger and stronger than what's on that recording. It captured your body, but it could never capture your spirit."

Her posture relaxes. She unfolds her fingers and takes my hand.

"We're going to have a helluva fight," I tell her. "But we won't give up. Even when it hurts." She wipes her eyes, and I can hear the soft inhale. "That's what you do for people you love, Zoe. That's what you do."

CHAPTER 11

Zoe squeezes me hard when we walk back inside and say goodbye.

"You can do this," I assure her, cupping her face in my hands so she's forced to look at me. "Talk to Dr. Rubin. She can help sort out some of your feelings."

Bobby waits in the car out front. He's angry and short. He curses the Hudsons and their irresponsibility and blames Price for pretty much everything including global warming.

"Is Lily in trouble?" I ask.

"Let them come down on my daughter for defending her sister."

My head throbs, and I buckle my seat belt. "I don't know how to handle much more of this."

He doesn't answer. He tries to console me by caressing my arm. His fingers feel cold. Wrong. Like the first time I saw him after our big fight about Monty. Zoe's suffering feels like déjà vu, and I slowly pull my hand away.

"I'm impressed with Dr. Mason," he says. "He seems to have the situation under control."

I'm thinking about far more important things. "How will she get through her classes?"

"Kids are resilient."

"Do you think she should see a real psychologist? Maybe there's something else going on."

"She was drunk and fell prey to a boy, Emma. There's your diagnosis." He scratches at a surface that soon gives way. "I blame that boy," he says. "He did this to her."

I cross my arms against my chest and stare out the window. Miami is a bright, beautiful city, though today it hurts my eyes.

We take the steps up to the lobby side by side, but there's an ocean between us. He leaves me for the executive offices, and it's a relief to be alone. Nearby guests are oblivious to the heaviness of my heart. Every time my phone rings or beeps, I prepare for "Come pick me up." I approach the front desk with a list of tasks I can't complete. It's useless to think about burying myself in hotel responsibilities. I'm on heightened alert, my children filling every viable space in my body. The delivery of Chiavari chairs and LED screens for this weekend's wedding will have to be monitored by someone else. Concierge can handle placing the order for our new guest room amenities. Alberto can reschedule the meeting with the new landscapers. And I beg Heather to ask our IT consultant to come as soon as possible to figure out why the Wi-Fi keeps dropping on the seventh floor.

"Are you all right, Mrs. Ross?" she asks.

I tell her I am, though I'm not. Then I text Lily. **You OK? Everything OK with Mason?**

She sends me the thumbs-up emoji, and I try to relax.

The apartment is quiet, and the sun streams through the windows and brightens the walls and furnishings. I disappear down the hall into the office I share with Bobby and see the laptop open on the desk. During ordinary times, I'd scroll through Facebook or search for inspiration on Pinterest. Now those time-sucking activities elude me. Besides, I am afraid to see the notifications piled up—all that I'd missed—other people's happiness. I stare at the blank screen and wonder how an honest status update would bode: "What's on your mind? My teenage daughter has publicly embarrassed herself and most of your kids have seen it." Like me now?

I'm surprised to see Bobby come up for lunch. He folds his jacket on the back of a chair and rolls up his sleeves. He's brought two kale salads and my favorite guacamole from the beachside restaurant and suggests we eat on the balcony. It's a peace offering, and I take it, but I should have been paying closer attention to his motivation. My instincts are off, and my obsessing over what's going on at school makes it worse. I want to talk about Zoe. But his olive branch precludes me from bringing her up.

He's preoccupied, and we discuss the restoration. "It's going to be expensive and disruptive."

"What's our alternative?" I ask, deferring to him and his knowledge of these types of things. "Don't we have to do it?"

A gentle wind ruffles his hair, and a strand falls in front of his eye. "We do. And we have the money to cover it . . . it's just . . ." I lean in to brush the hair away, but he gets there first. I sit back and think about the grand decisions we've made together on the hotel's behalf. Decisions about her care and growth, how to maintain her beautiful charm. I wait for him to continue, but he stops. "I don't know."

"What is it, Bobby?" It's a stupid question, considering, but he's acting strange. There's a different kind of distance pulling us apart. He has to feel it, too. He drops a chip into the guacamole, and our fingertips touch.

"I think we should sell."

The wind picks up, and I'm sure it's mangled his words. It sounded like he said we should sell.

"The market's ripe. It's a good time to consider options."

I wasn't imagining it. The wind hadn't deceived me. He's talking about selling. It's why he questioned the girls. I laugh. "You can't be serious."

"We should have a house."

I don't know who this man is, because the person I know never expressed any interest in a house. This is our home. The prospect weakens me. The food that moments ago looked appetizing has me squeamish. I manage another bite of salad, but it's like dust scratching my throat. "I don't want to move."

He grabs an ice cube out of his glass and pops it in his mouth. After hearing about what happened to Zoe, I didn't think there was any room left in my body for fear, but something tells me I need to be afraid. Very afraid. He's entertaining this idea for reasons he's too proud to share. We're far apart, like that night all those years ago. And this is what we do when we don't want to hurt each other—we lie.

No, Em, I tell myself, *you're being paranoid. He's thinking out loud. You stopped trusting yourself, so you don't trust him.*

"Are you being serious?" I ask him. "You're planning to sell the hotel?" My heart has been hit with so many things I'm sure it's gone numb.

"I'm thinking about it."

Lily walks in first. I'm staring at the ocean with Bobby's announcement weighing on my mind when I hear her spring through the door. *We're not selling.* It's what I told him, and I would tell him again. But he left for work, and the conversation ended abruptly. She throws her backpack on the floor and meets me in the kitchen.

"Where's Zoe?" I ask.

"She's coming. Someone in the lobby has a mini doodle, and she's playing dog whisperer."

I wish I hadn't handed off my projects. Then I could pretend I didn't waste an entire day worrying about their every move and cursing Bobby under my breath. I should wait a few minutes to pounce, but I can't. "How was it?"

Lily stands at the table drinking Gatorade that turns her lips blue. Her eyes dim when she says, "It was pretty bad." My heart sinks, and I don't reprimand her for drinking out of the bottle. She details the texts and Instagram posts and Snapchat stories that highlighted Zoe's public shaming. Zoe and Price were the stars. I am shocked that kids can be so mean. "Someone needs to tell the school. They shouldn't be allowed to do these things!"

"By tomorrow it'll be someone else," she says, taking another swig. "You know how these things go."

My head falls into my hands. Revulsion spreads to my fingers and toes. The weapons they throw at Zoe will cause more damage than her actions. Labels that won't go away. *That Emma Grant isn't so perfect after all. Who knew she had it in her?* The voices taunt. The years have made them louder than before. She takes a seat beside me and rifles through her backpack until she finds her phone. "Please don't tell her what they're saying about her," I say. "She'll be devastated."

She uh-huhs me and scrolls through her phone, an endless reel documenting every move through poses and selfies. I sit back and watch as she immerses herself in the feed. We've had multiple conversations about this hallmark of pop culture, and I'd love to rip the phone away. This generation believes the number of likes is proportional to self-worth. I don't understand the phenomenon. I don't understand my daughter flashing herself on a screen while someone swipes across her face, wiping out her meaningful parts.

"When I was in high school, a boy who stared at us in the hallway was our big excitement. I suppose that's what you girls feel when someone likes your post."

Lily taps on the screen without looking up and laughs. "Are you comparing a boy staring at your ass with a thousand likes?"

"I guess I am." Even if it's an entirely disproportionate level of attention—and need. "Self-esteem tied up in likes and swipes is misleading."

"Mom, you are seriously antiquated."

If I hear one more time how their world is so different from ours I might scream. Technology can never replace real-life interaction. And insults hurt, no matter the vehicle delivering them.

"It's sweet," she says, and it feels more like an effort to get me to be quiet.

What good was preaching to her about the way their father and I grew up? Not only had the Internet opened up new corners of the law, but dating had changed, too. Just a few weeks ago, Bobby and I were in a cabana by the pool, and I was giving him the highlights from a recent article about Tinder.

"Casual sex is pandemic. Romance is gone. Emotional intimacy nonexistent." He was trying to work, but I could tell he was interested. And I didn't think at the time the conversation would come back to haunt me. Haunt us. "Do you have any idea what this will do to the institution of marriage?"

He had told me to stop freaking out. "I wish I was growing up in this era," he joked, but I didn't laugh.

"It makes me sad," I said. "This generation may never experience the thrill of a first date."

He rolled over, dropped his papers aside, and planted a kiss on my forehead. "Always my worrier," he said.

"It's my job," I replied, wondering if our girls would ever have what we had.

Then he traced a finger down my shoulder and kissed the soft skin. "They have you inside them. Plenty of romantic gushiness."

Now the conversation seemed like a lifetime ago. I ask myself, what's the point of lecturing and teaching and comparing one generation to the next when my daughter becomes the poster child for teenage promiscuity? What is the point of preparing her for boys and self-respect when a boy can wrest it all away in a heartbeat? Her choices are my choices. And if I will ever understand what she did, I must first understand what I did—and that comes with culpability.

I hear the elevator and greet Zoe at the door. She collapses into my arms, almost knocking me over. Yesterday we had to restrain ourselves from sharing; today the cork's come out of the bottle. Her sobs are regretful and deep, as though she's given up. I wrap my arm around her and steer her toward the kitchen. Her pain sits inside and makes it hard for me to breathe.

I whisper into her tangled hair, "I'm sorry you had a bad day."

"It sucked. It was like being a dead frog. Everyone was dissecting me." She sets her backpack on the table beside her sister. "You wouldn't believe the things they were saying. They think our family is in the mafia. And we have drug deals in our bathrooms. And of course there's no supervision."

The insults are crushing. "I'm sorry, honey. But you made it through the worst part."

Her expression disagrees. It brandishes all the signs of weakening. A deep-seated humiliation sculpts her cheeks. I want to wash it away.

"How was Dr. Rubin?"

She pulls a chair out and plops herself in it. "We played chess."

"Nice," says Lily. "You get to play chess, and I have to take an exam."

Zoe rolls her eyes. "I'll trade places with you, Lily. Gladly."

I press her for more information.

"She was nice. After a while I didn't feel like playing, and she could tell. She said I shouldn't be afraid to speak up for myself."

Lily laughs. "Oh, that's real subtle."

I glare at her. "Enough commentary. Let her finish."

"I told her I didn't have to speak up for myself with Price, that he didn't force me to do anything. She told me we didn't have to talk about Price and what happened on that video."

She wanted this to happen. My heart quickens.

Lily asks, "So what did you discuss for an hour?"

Zoe turns away and stares out at the balcony. "Stuff."

Lily groans when I tell her to give us a few minutes. When we're alone, it doesn't take Zoe long to start talking.

"I'm sorry," she says again. "I'm sorry I've disappointed you." She's zipping and unzipping her Thatcher sweatshirt as though she's undecided about which one of us she's talking to.

I don't know what to say to her. I really don't. I turn away and focus on the appliances, the light fixture in the ceiling, anything to hide my discomfort.

"Why'd you do it, Zoe?"

"Mom." She looks me squarely in the eye. "Don't. Don't judge me."

Monty's memory swirls around me, and if someone had asked why, I doubt I'd have the answer. It was impulsive and maybe out of character, but it satisfied a need. A want. A freedom I'd never experienced. Literally never. I cower.

"I'm sorry. I'm trying. I am." But I'm not. I'm trying to figure out what connects us. Neediness? Curiosity? Alcohol? I'm wondering how I didn't get caught and she did. I'm wondering why I'm drawing these comparisons so clearly, as if there's a red pen in my palm and the strokes of our dalliances are written across the sky.

"Today was hard enough," she begins again. "The kids were jerks." She hugs her legs to her chest and rests her chin on her knees. "Everybody stared. Even the teachers heard what happened."

"Did anything else happen with Price?"

"No," she says, picking at something on her shorts. "He avoided me. And I avoided him. Lily's lucky she didn't get suspended."

The silence that follows is full of questions. I tread lightly when I ask, "Is there any chance Price could've had something to do with you being filmed?"

Zoe is adamant when she disagrees. "It wasn't him. I told you. He was as shocked as I was. I don't care who filmed it. I just want everyone to erase it from their phones."

"How can you be so sure?"

"Because I am," she insists. "He wouldn't do that to me."

Three days ago I'd never even heard this boy's name, and now Zoe is the barometer of his behavior. I study the denial spreading across her face, because it so closely resembles mine. Her actions, the exposure, the willingness to push it away. Suppressing humiliation only doubles its power.

"How will we know if kids are deleting the video?" she asks, swiping at her eyes and the torment buried there. I notice her fingernails are bitten down to the quick. I'm convinced it signifies something deeper.

"They are. You have to trust it."

"I don't trust anyone!" She crumples, and her hair hides her face. "This is who I am now."

An angry steam collects in my throat. "No, you're wrong. That one action doesn't define you. It was a mistake."

Zoe shrugs. The last few days have aged her into someone older than fifteen. "It's bad enough that everyone's talking about me, but no one knows the real story. It wasn't as scandalous as everyone thinks." She pauses and finds my eyes. "Dr. Rubin is the only one who's not trying to pull some reason out of me." Her features thaw one by one as she returns her gaze to the table and to me. "I feel like you want to make this into something much more than it is."

It already is. It has seeped into my bones and spread like a disease. "If you did this to feel good about yourself, I want to know."

"Why?" It comes out as a whimper. "Will it make you feel better? Or will it make you feel worse?"

She's touched a nerve, and I back away.

When she speaks again, she talks to the floor, kicking at it with her sneakered foot. "Plenty of girls like fooling around, Mom."

She just punched me. My daughter just punched me. Smack in the gut.

Thick emotions clog my throat. "Sure, Zoe, when they're older, mature enough to handle it . . . sex is powerful . . ." I can't finish my thought. Her words chip at my resistance. I see Bobby in the flecks of her eyes, and I'm trying to convince him that it was a mistake.

I suck in my breath and let the elephant in the room simmer. Am I judging her too harshly? Is this just a different culture? Kids hook up without feelings? "You're so young, Zoe. Hardly mature enough to understand the repercussions or even the dangers. I'm sure he didn't wear a condom. It can't just happen. You have to think about it."

"A lot of girls don't think about it."

"Those girls are confused," I say. "It feels nice at first, but sometime after, I bet they want more. They regret it."

"How would you know?" she snaps back. "Daddy's the only person you've ever been with!"

I avert my eyes and focus on getting my point across. "You girls are young. You think you know everything, but you're so far from it. Even if they're *all doing it*, claiming it's fun, I doubt they believe it. Deep inside. When they're alone with themselves and wishing the boy cared."

I want to say, *Where's the eye contact? The intimacy? Does being on your knees like that feel good, doing all the work for someone you don't know?* But I stop myself from the harsh, cruel judgments that stem from personal scrutiny.

"I remember being your age and thinking I was so grown-up and knew what was right for me and my body, but I didn't." My voice quavers. "You're a minute into fifteen with command of a phone and a new wave of technology. That doesn't make you an expert on everything. There are far more important things. Like self-respect. Intimacy. Trust.

Do you know how easy it is to get naked or undress for someone? But getting to know someone, *really know someone*, is being naked. When you drink and lose your inhibitions, you can hurt yourself—deep, deep inside—and those kinds of scars are way worse than physical bruises."

I preach as though she's one of those girls who gives herself to a boy to fill a need. I preach to her as a mother who wants to be sure she's setting the right example and hitting the right notes. I preach to her the age-appropriate lessons because she's young, and the conversation may shift in ten years. It's all meaningful and righteous, but with every word that leaves my lips, the sutures pull apart and the wound slowly opens. I got drunk. I may have been lonely. I was definitely mad. I did something out of character. I lost my inhibitions. It felt good. Then I woke up in a puddle of regret facing terrifying repercussions.

Zoe gets up and opens the refrigerator. I wait for her to turn around before I stand up and give her what I so desperately needed all those years ago.

"I love you, Zoe. More than you'll ever understand. I want you to live a full life. I want you to make good choices and be proud of those choices." I continue on autopilot. Pure, untarnished Emma being Super Mom. "There's a part of me that doesn't understand how it happened. I'm old-fashioned that way. I want you to love and be loved. But more than anything, I want you to love yourself."

Her eyes blink back tears.

"Daddy and I love you and support you. We'll do whatever we can to protect you . . . but I want you to understand your actions, too, as a young woman."

"I hear you," she says. "That's why this was my private business no one needed to know about."

The words I preach to Zoe are whirring in my head. They're hypocritical, but they're the best I can do, the best I can give her. This isn't how I want her to experience intimacy. She needs to know the thrill of meeting someone new and experiencing that exciting jolt. And what it's like to talk to each other all night and uncover the secret places that make you one. And how it feels to touch the person you love for the first time. The anticipation of that first kiss. They're all the sensations that mean you'll never be the same. How you'll lose part of your heart, but you'll gain someone else's.

Zoe's eyes flood. I search for the glimmer of what once was. If only my nearness could erase some of her pain. "I'm so sorry you have to go through this, Zoe. I'm sorry it had to be like this."

"It's so easy for you. So easy for Lily." Her voice cracks and she surrenders. "I'm not like you. I'll never be like you."

"What does that even mean?"

She sucks in her breath about to answer, but changes her mind. I feel her pull away. "I really don't want to talk about it. I really just want to forget it."

"Zoe." My eyes narrow on hers. "Where'd you just go?"

"Please, Mom, I'm not a baby anymore." Her hands jam inside her jacket pockets, and she bends her head down low. Before she backs away, she adds, "And I'm quitting debate."

She stands in front of me, but she's escaping me. I'm searching the memory bank for clues, indications as to why our elder twin by a mere fifteen minutes is suddenly someone else. It's far more than passing through the gates of teenagedom, or the onset of hormones, or being old enough to acquire a learner's permit. It's something that when added to adolescent milestones makes them slippery and dangerous. It's complicated and simple all at the same time. It's boys.

CHAPTER 12

While Bobby showers and gets ready for bed, I slip under the covers and away from the things he said earlier. He's upset and being rash. Selling the hotel is not the answer. The wind slaps the windows, and the howling sounds like suffering. I scroll through messages—Lisa Howard confirms our dinner plans for tomorrow, my sisters complain about the Chicago weather, and there's an e-mail from the guidance counselor, Dr. Rubin.

> Zoe and I had a good talk today. There's nothing striking to me that indicates a more serious behavioral issue. Zoe appears comfortable and accepting of her actions. Her reaction to the exposure is quantitatively normal, and her feelings fall within the range of age-appropriate. Mrs. Ross, you raised a special girl. It's going to be an uncomfortable few weeks, but she'll be back on track in no time. I will continue to work with her.

I slip the phone on the nightstand and feel for the first time we're going to survive this. Bobby comes out of the bathroom wrapped in a towel while he dries his hair with another. His body is beautiful to look at. After all these years, he's still in shape—big and broad-shouldered—and I watch him get dressed.

I show him the e-mail from the school, and without responding, he climbs into bed and starts playing with his phone. He doesn't try to smooth things over. He doesn't tell me we're not selling the hotel. And he doesn't tell me he had a meaningful talk with Zoe after school, because he didn't.

The space between us threatens me. I get up from the bed and stare out at the darkness. He comes up behind me, and we watch the black waves shimmy onto the shore, their crests reflecting the moon.

"I love you," he says. It's a fragile voice that nips my ear. It's an apology, or an attempt, and I'm willing to listen. But then he says this: "And I want you to understand what I'm about to tell you."

I turn to face him. "You're scaring me."

His finger brushes my lips. "The meeting in New York is with a potential buyer." His eyes fasten on mine. "For the Ross."

I back away.

His hopeful expression fades. "I tried to tell you . . . this wasn't an easy decision."

Words won't form. I stop and start, but nothing makes sense. I shake my head, thinking I heard him wrong. "This is your meeting? This is why Jonny can't go?"

"It's a meeting, Em. It can't hurt to hear what they have to say."

I suck in my breath and whip him with my words. "How could you? What about everything you told Lana? You said you loved this place . . . did you mean any of it?"

He clasps his hands behind his head and searches the ceiling. "It's one meeting, Emma."

"You can't do this!" I shout, fighting the tears that burn my eyes. "This is our home. You heard the girls. This is all they know. They love it here. I love it here."

"We have an offer. It's a big one. We haven't had one like this in a long time. They know about the improvements. They want her as is."

"So we're done? You just sell out?" I turn away from him and pace the floor. When I speak, I'm bordering on hysterical. "I don't believe you. You'd never consider selling the hotel. She's your baby . . . our entire history is wrapped in her walls. Is there something you're not telling me? Are we in financial trouble?" And I stop because I'm out of breath.

"We're fine," he says, following me, reaching for my arm, but I'm quick to back away. "Our mortgage is paid off. The Ross has never been more stable."

"We're far from fine!" My words are weapons scratching at my throat. "*Fine* was talking through major decisions together. *Fine* wasn't selling our home."

His eyes fall in defeat. "This may not be the best place to raise teenage girls. It's only going to get harder as they get older."

"They're good girls!" I yell. "We uproot them for one single mistake? Have you no empathy for what Zoe's going through?" I stammer, unable to comprehend. He's really doing this. It wasn't just thinking out loud. "This will kill her!"

He tries to calm me down. He comes close, but I step back. "Miami has beautiful homes on the water. We can have a backyard. Privacy. There won't be so much scrutiny."

"But you love this hotel . . ." I am crying into my hands. "How can you even consider leaving?"

He is stubborn. And determined. "I love her. I'll always love her, but the Ross is a business, Em. Selling now is a viable option. Our other properties keep me busy, and the renovation's going to be pricey. Why drop millions of dollars into her when the girls have a few more years and then they'll be in college? I'd love to have a home with you. We can get a boat, be alone, instead of sharing our backyard with hundreds of guests."

"These people are our family." It comes out as a sob, and I shake my head. "I won't do it. I'm not moving."

He searches the floor, and his reply is icy. "You may not have a choice."

Our history unravels. The seam of our story rips open. "How can you do this? What about Jonny? Why are you arguing? Is it because of this?"

He won't meet my eyes. "I'm waiting to hear the offer . . ."

"He'll never agree to this," I argue. "Never."

He looks pained. Removed. Far, far away. The big-hearted boy I'd fallen in love with was slowly disappearing. "Jonny trusts the way I manage the hotel's business."

"This is about Zoe, isn't it?" I persist.

"No," he says, finally meeting my eyes. "Let's listen to the offer."

"I'm never going to agree on selling. We made a life here. This is our home. The staff . . . this will devastate them."

He's stone-faced. He never likes to see me cry.

"Please don't do this," I beg. "The Ross is the one thing I've come to count on. The one thing. Please don't take her away from us."

He grabs me and cradles me in his arms. I try to resist, but he pulls me tighter, tugging while he whispers to my hair, "It's going to be all right, Em . . . I promise you."

"Zoe will think it's her fault," I cry.

"Shhhh," he says and kisses my forehead. "She'll be happier. We all will."

He leads me to the bed, where we fumble beneath the covers. My sobs subside. My heart, though damaged, returns to its usual pace. He thinks curling around me can defuse what he's thrown at me. It can't. I let him do it because it feels better to have his arms around me than to be apart. I fall into a fitful sleep only to be jerked awake by troublesome dreams. I stare at Bobby's face while his peacefulness mocks me. It hurts to look at his tanned, rugged complexion, his lips that have loved me in ways I'll never explain. I don't know this man, but perhaps we don't know each other.

All I want is to slip back inside our memories, to be on the beach again with Bobby holding me, free from secrets and scandals. He's tugging at my bathing suit while we slip beneath the ocean's waves. He's reaching for my hand as we shuffle through a crowded nightclub. He's pressing himself against me as we lounge in the hammocks behind the hotel. He's staring at me, his eyes telling me I should be having his babies.

Because what came after changed everything.

CHAPTER 13

Upon graduation from high school, Bobby enrolled at the University of Miami, and I entered a small liberal arts college in Vermont. He would tease me about my dreams of becoming an actress, and in between the laughter, he'd whisper in my ear how I'd move to Florida and run the hotel by his side.

"Is that a proposal?" I'd laughed. When I gave myself to him on that beach, I had promised all of me, to him, *solo tú*, wholly, for the rest of our lives. I had become his Achilles heel, the area of rare weakness. And this need to have me, while making me forbidden to anyone else, made him foolish at times. He could be jealous, stormy mad when I called him late at night to tell him about the scene with the fancy New Yorker, or the cowboy from Kentucky. He knew it was only acting, but he struggled. "How do you touch these guys every night?" It was why he rarely came to my performances. Our bond was tight, and though his jealousy was childish and unwarranted at times, he did his best to block out the intimacy I shared with others. Those were the nights we'd fall asleep with our ears pressed to the phone receiver, me holed up in my room beneath a light snow, he with the traffic crackling on US 1.

"I wish you were next to me."

"Feel that?" he said. "My hand is on your leg."

I laughed. "Bobby."

"Spread a little wider. Let me in."

I always did what he asked.

"Do you feel me, Em?"

"Uh huh."

"I'm going to put my lips on you. Is that all right?"

I giggled. "Yes."

His voice dropped. His own breaths were deep and winded. "You're so pretty, Em. I'm looking into your eyes. Can you see me?"

"I see you."

"What do you see?"

"You want me."

"Do you want me?"

"Yes."

"Touch me."

"I am."

"How does it feel?"

"Go deeper."

"I don't think I can be any deeper inside you."

"I love you, Bobby Ross."

"I love you, Emma Grant."

The memory thrusts forward and lodges deep inside. Bobby turns away from me in his sleep, and it reminds me how separate we are. In those moments, on those phone calls, all we had wished for was a way to see each other through the wires. We could have never predicted the future—that one day our own child would have that capability and it would cause her so much pain.

The girls in my freshman dorm couldn't understand staying faithful to someone who lived so far away. "I can't help the way I feel," I'd say.

"But you're so young," they'd continue. "You should be out having fun."

Physical separation was inconsequential. We were never really apart. He was planted in my soul, and I in his.

"Don't you want to know what it feels like to be with another guy?" one of them asked.

I had watched Bobby's parents for years. When your cheating father abandons your mother, you're drawn to loving couples. Abel, our stepdad, came into my and my sisters' life as though he'd always been there. And our parents were content, but there was something about the elder Rosses that had me observing them like a favorite play. The answer to my friends' question rested in Mrs. Ross's speech at an anniversary dinner in the grand ballroom. She toasted to her groom, their love, and never needing more than what they had. "That's what it means to be happy." And I tucked that notion inside my heart. I was happy with Bobby; it was uncomplicated. I never needed anything or anyone else. Until first semester senior year. Until Monty Greer.

His name sheaths my cheeks in shame. Until recently, I hadn't thought about him in years. I could do that. Make it so it didn't happen. Pretend I'm the immaculate bride. When it crept up, I knew how to bury it back in its tomb. People who lie actually believe their lies. I believed my lie. Because that's how badly I wanted it to be true.

Monty was the fellow actor whose perfectly arranged features and natural talent were trumped by his brash behavior. He was the kind girls were warned against. Charming and dangerous, he had a seductive side that always enraptured those in his pursuit. Because of his sharp acting skills, it was impossible to know when the honesty stopped and the game began.

Monty was used to getting what he wanted. And he wanted me. He mistook my soulful eyes and flushed cheeks to mean something when we were playing Antony and Cleopatra. And he'd hold me a little tighter, kiss me a little longer, and I chalked it up to being in character.

Unlike the girls at our small college, I knew how to distance myself. My roommates thought I was crazy. "He's hot. He's going to Broadway." Unless we were in production, I felt nothing for Monty. And the more I felt nothing for him, the more he tried to change my mind.

Bobby and I were engaged the week before we returned to school. It was a romantic beach proposal, and I was completely caught off guard when my parents and sisters showed up at our celebratory dinner. Bobby was careful and kind when planning the weekend. He toasted to the two of us. *Solo tú. You and me forever.*

Plans were under way for a June wedding in Miami. It was the happiest time of my life—and the scariest. I'd been feeling overwhelmed those last few weeks, agitated and on edge. Whoever said the engagement was a blissful period hadn't stepped inside my story. Early feelings of loss and abandonment surfaced. I loved Bobby wholly, but I was terrified to be a wife—to love one person for the rest of my life. My father couldn't do it, and I wondered how much of him lived within me. My sisters and I were busy choosing dresses and flowers, on the phone for all hours of the night. What they didn't know was when they'd squeal, "You're the luckiest girl in the world," I would hang up the phone and throw up in the bathroom. I couldn't accept the goodness coming my way. I was afraid things were moving too fast. I was afraid to have regrets. I was worried about graduation and starting a career. And mostly, I was petrified of marriage. Petrified of making mistakes. Learning I wasn't lovable enough. The anxiety darkened my sleep and affected my schoolwork and performances.

An article in the school's paper gave me a less-than-glowing review of a performance I'd put my all into. "Stiff and forgettable" felt harsh and unjustified. Bobby was pressuring me to transfer to Miami to be with him, and his demands, coupled with planning a wedding, classes, and the troupe, were beginning to take their toll on me. Bobby arrived for a visit; he said he had a "surprise" for me. I don't like surprises, and he knew it. We argued. Our one disappointing attempt at sex was just that. He chalked it up to nerves. I chalked it up to poor planning. He left, and something within us was broken. He never did end up giving me the surprise.

Later that same week, Monty and I were rehearsing in my apartment. I don't even remember the reasons why we ended up there, but at that point it was entirely innocent. One minute we were pulling apart a scene and the next, the stage was set for disaster. I left the room for a bathroom break and returned to Monty waiting at the door. "Bobby's on the phone."

The panic swept up my body. "You answered my phone?"

I pushed past him, and he went outside to smoke a cigarette. "Bobby?"

"Monty's there? He's in your apartment?" Bobby despised Monty. He'd been accusing me for months of flirting with him. Mostly in a playful, teasing way—how we'd kiss on stage—but now he was furious. I saw him through the phone. Nostrils flared. Pacing the floor. "Are you fucking him? Is he the reason you didn't want me to come last week?"

I stared at the round diamond. "Don't," I said, his jealousy unleashed on me like a weapon. "We're getting married in a few months. I've never given you reason to doubt me." My voice was broken, shaky, but deep down I was pissed. I was tired of the jokes about Monty. Tired of the unjustified accusations. Tired of having to defend myself without cause. Tired of dress swatches and tablecloths. Bobby yelled. Cast blame. Made threats. Questions I didn't want to justify. The miles that separated us had come to a head. We always knew it wouldn't be easy.

Monty returned, and I told Bobby I had to go. "I'll call you when we're done rehearsing."

"What the fuck, Emma? I want to talk to you."

"All you're doing is screaming at me and accusing me of things I'd never do! I'm sick of it." It was our biggest fight ever. The accusations couldn't be taken back. My head was dizzy from yelling.

The last thing he said to me before hanging up was "Maybe he can make you happy." He had never hung up on me before. Ever. Seconds passed, and he called me right back. I didn't pick up the phone. It was my turn to be furious. When the incessant ringing continued, I threw the phone off the hook.

Practicing scenes after that was impossible. I was dead inside, but I couldn't give Monty the satisfaction of knowing he was at the center of our argument. I knew the divide between Bobby and me was taking its toll, but his attack was unjustified, and it triggered a flare in me I couldn't tamp down.

It was late in the afternoon when we called it a day. The fight was resting on my conscience, but I agreed to join Monty and our theater group downtown for drinks and a revival of *The Philadelphia Story*. I thought a night out would be good for me. Instead, I was Tracy Lord, the Hepburn character who had gotten herself drunk (for the second time in her life) and took an innocent dip in a pool with someone the night before her wedding to another man. Lord's fiancé, George, saw her in the pool, assumed the worst, and when he confronted her, she turned it around and broke off the engagement, citing his lack of trust. By then, the rest of the story didn't make a difference. I was living it.

I normally wouldn't drink so much, but I was exhausted by decisions that had to be made for the wedding and riddled with growing confusion. Bobby. His anger. The unwarranted attack. Soon it became automatic. My cup was empty, and someone would fill it. It didn't matter if I liked it or not. It numbed the worry and muffled Bobby's voice.

The rolling hills of Vermont had produced a chilly mist, and one by one, the group began to fade, until it was Monty and me nursing our beers. His antenna reached inside me, sensing a weakened resistance. At once he settled into himself.

"You look pretty when you're vulnerable," he said. It was subtle enough to feel authentic.

"It hurts," I told him, the wound still fresh from the recent review, the alcohol making me flimsy.

"It's the artist's way," he said. "We hang from the sky on a delicate string while random strangers criticize. Besides," he continued, "it's supposed to hurt. That's how you get better." His green eyes latched on to mine, and I could understand Bobby's jealousy. "You're good, Emma. One of the best."

Monty and I had shared many hours together rehearsing and role-playing, touching and being close, though there was nothing intimate about us. That he became my confidant was a quirk of fate I should've paid attention to. We talked about everything but the theater. Music. Politics. What our futures looked like.

"Did you grow up a Bears fan? Do you think you'll go back there after college?" he asked.

For the first time, I didn't know the answer.

He didn't mention Bobby once. Neither did I. The ring between us, though garish in size, was invisible to Monty. And to me. I was so angry at Bobby. Each sip lessened the ability to care. I was in a daze. The alcohol was a cozy shawl I had no problem sinking into.

Without costume and theatrical makeup hiding his face, Monty could be sincere and kind. Alone, without an audience, he was a hand-some blond with expressive green eyes. Someone whose lips were sensual and exciting. I welled up when he talked of his brother's passing and rested my hand on his palm.

We left the bar. It had been a wicked, biting cold, the kind of chill that sliced through your skin. It reminded me of Chicago. So when we arrived at the door of my building, and he asked me if he could come up before making the long walk home, I didn't think twice about letting him in.

As the night wore on, he became better looking. Wittier. This is what getting drunk did to people. Or maybe my feelings for Bobby prevented me from *seeing* anyone else. My roommate was out, and we were sitting on the couch watching *Melrose Place*. His hands were freezing. He snuck his fingers against the back of my neck, and I fell into him, laughing.

"You're incredibly sexy, Emma."

I smiled, feeling the crimson cover my face. Giddy Emma. I tried to hide it with my hands, but he grabbed them instead. In retrospect, I couldn't believe how easily I let him in. And then things got kind of blurry and he said, "Do you have anything here to drink?"

"I can't," I said, noticing how woozy I'd become. Was it only a few hours ago that we watched *The Philadelphia Story*? The innocent dip in the pool. A friendly walk home. Then the splintering of things. The fight with Bobby that launched that night hit me with a freezing punch. He handed me a glass, and the cold liquid slid through my body. And then another.

His lips came down on mine with an unexpected force. He moved in closer and grabbed my face and my hair. I closed my eyes and smelled that pinch of Bobby in the air, but it wasn't enough to make me move away. This was something else. Scorching hot, a term my mom would use when she described the Florida summer. But this wasn't the Florida I knew. This was dangerous, a collision of temperatures that had me all mixed up.

I kissed him back, opening my mouth wider. We'd kissed before in front of hundreds of people, but this was nothing like a scene from a play. His lips were icy cold, steamy hot, King Lear, and Romeo suffused with something treacherous. A gear switched in me, and I had no way of pulling it back. I was playing another role, one that satisfied a host of dangerous needs.

Bobby was a million miles away. My mind was cluttered with lights and movement. Everything around me was whirling and swaying, and it centered on the feeling deep inside that I couldn't stall. It felt good. It felt so good to be kissed and touched and wanted. To be with someone else.

He lifted me off the couch and carried me through the door of my room. My bed was unmade, and he dropped me on the sheets and lay on top of me. I closed my eyes, and flecks of light floated in the air around us. It could have been the snow outside my window. I slipped inside the dream I was having, the one where I was awake and alive, the one where I was beautiful and free. I didn't stop him. I didn't push him away. I didn't say no. I slid the ring off my finger and plopped it in a drawer.

I was completely lost in Monty Greer. It was like no role I'd played before. Soon he was peeling off my pants. My shirt came off over my head, and he was kissing my neck, my eyes, my hair. I could touch every inch of him and still feel it wasn't enough. I wanted him inside me. What took Bobby and me years to reach, Monty and I mastered in less than a few hours. I was too drunk to have regrets. Too excited to stop.

There was only one boy I'd ever touched, and I surprised myself with how I could handle someone else. I liked the way he felt different, the newness of his skin, the length of his body. The way he'd cup my face in his hands and stare deep into my eyes, as though he were lost in me. Needing only this.

We didn't sleep much. When I dozed, he rolled on top of me and started again. He was gentle and caring. I was warmed by his touch.

I woke up first, opening my eyes, half expecting to see Bobby there. But it was Monty, and the sobering realization of what I had done shot through my body like a piercing alarm. I jumped up, searching for my clothes, my ring, something to cover my body. And my guilt.

I thought of Bobby. Monty's lean body was curled inside my blankets. He looked so peaceful.

"You have to go." I shoved him awake.

He opened his eyes with a smile that mistakenly thought I wanted more.

My voice, buried deep within my throat, trembled. "You have to leave."

Disappointment clouded his face, and he got up and found his clothes. I sat on the bed, shaking. Before walking out the door, he came to my side of the bed and lifted my chin with his fingers. His eyes tried to catch mine, but I resisted.

"Last night was amazing."

CHAPTER 14

Midtown Miami is packed this time of year. The newly developed neighborhood north of downtown hosts an eclectic range of trendy shops and restaurants, and tonight we're seated at a table by the window in MC Kitchen.

"Miami's beginning to feel a lot like Soho," Bobby observes. The Howards are running late, and the extra minutes alone are filled with small talk, like the changing Miami landscape.

"You're avoiding the issue," I say.

He closes the menu. "What do you want to talk about, Em?"

He doesn't mean to patronize, but it's there, in his voice. We've spoken very little since last night, and it's added to an already uncomfortable strain. I fell asleep to Monty wedged between us and woke up to Bobby gone. He didn't see the girls in the morning; meetings kept him tied up most of the afternoon. "You dropped a bomb on me . . . we should talk about it."

"Em, I understand you're upset, but there's not much else to discuss. It's only a meeting."

I signal the waitress and sit stiffly while tension gnaws at us. "Zoe's threatening to quit debate. And Lily got a C minus on her math test."

"Moving will be good for us," he says without looking up.

The attractive brunette arrives and pours water into the glasses on the table while Bobby asks for something stronger. She leans over him with the drink menu, and her perky breasts bounce between us.

"You should've been there this morning," I say. "Zoe put her contact lenses in a cup of water, and Lily drank them. The screaming went on for hours. Zoe's pissed she has to wear her glasses. It's hard enough being made fun of. Now the glasses."

"Doesn't she have another pair?"

"It was her last."

He picks up his phone and responds to a text.

"We should've canceled," I tell him, peering over my shoulder at the crowded restaurant. "I should be home with Zoe."

"Drew knows the group vying for the Ross. I want to talk to him about it."

I grab my napkin, and the silverware clatters against the table. "I'm never going to agree to this."

"You might," he says, finding my eyes and holding. "When you and the girls are lounging in your private pool in your new backyard."

Sexy Waitress returns with Bobby's drink. Her eyes rest on his longer than I like. Placing the glass on the table is an art form for her. I expect her to land in his lap.

"We've never cared about that stuff," I say, watching him down the shot in one gulp. My eyes fill with sadness, and I wonder if he can see. A whisper escapes. "Please don't go."

He motions for another shot. "I have to go. Besides, Em, you're better at this. I don't know what to say to Zoe."

"You're being stubborn. Take her for new contacts. Do something. Anything!" I plead.

And this is who I married. The man who can turn away from the people he loves after they've shown their true colors. "You think I don't have feelings about what happened to Zoe?" My words are broken, and I would scream them out loud, but they are stuck in my throat. "I have huge feelings, but I don't get to voice them. I don't get to ignore her or fly to New York because it's too hard to look at. I have feelings, Bobby. Deeper than you'll ever know."

The stirrings of a forgotten time. My secret is so close. I'm sure he can feel it tickling his neck, skipping down his spine. I need to escape. From him and from his judgments.

"It's different. She's different." His eyes lower when he says this. "I failed her somehow. I should've been able to stop her from hurting herself."

What would it do to him if I said she hadn't hurt herself? That she said it wasn't a big deal?

"Come on, Em." He appraises the set of breasts that are refilling my glass of water. "Can't we be normal people for one night?"

My fingers play with the buttons on my blouse. "Normal people?" I scoff. "Tell me what we should talk about. You want to talk about the neighborhood again? How about we talk about our waitress's bra size? Or I know. Let's talk about the magazine article again. We can tiptoe through the tulips in our little denial parade."

He swallows the drink in a single swig, and silence descends like a curtain. The noisy restaurant accentuates the rift growing between us.

"We can talk about Elle and Kinsley," he says, leaning back in his chair and wiping lint from his blazer.

I lean back in my chair, too. "Now? We're going to revert to talking about our employees and their impending marriage?"

"You've said yourself they're more than our employees."

He's not wrong. I'm just too tense to comply.

"They've set a date," he continues. "I'm going to officiate." His deep brown eyes burrow into mine. "Thanksgiving Day. A celebration on the beach, like we had."

Headlights shine through the window, lighting up the glasses on the table. The Howards' Mercedes pulls in to the valet, and I take a sip of water. "That's terrible timing. It's too soon."

"His mother's not well. They want her there."

The news snaps me back to reality. Kinsley's mom, Fern MacNeill, has always been dear to us. Fern ran our beach for more than twenty years before turning the reins over to her son. Kinsley was Lily's first crush, even though he is years older. He crafted matching step stools when the girls were three. He carved their names into the wood. Red and pink for Lily. Yellow and orange for Zoe. Lily thought her colors signified love. Now Fern was sick. We'd put them in touch with our doctors and promised her the best care. But it was a bad cancer. And we knew it was only a matter of time.

"The girls will have something to look forward to," he says.

I pluck myself from the melancholy doom of a wedding framed in death. "Zoe doesn't want to go to a wedding, Bobby. She wants to hide in her room and pretend she's invisible."

His response is lukewarm. "It's a little too late for that, don't you think?" He averts his eyes, and not even my stare can pin them down.

He is quiet, which is almost worse than blaming and disapproval. I've known him long enough to know where his mind ventures when it involves the women he loves. Possessive and a tad insecure. He can't fix everything, but he tries. It's maddening for him to imagine any of his girls being touched, exploited, harmed. That's why I had to safeguard him all those years ago.

Outside, Lisa is staring at her long legs in the window's reflection, and I am bracing myself for what's to come. My gaze rests on the changing sky. Whether shifting from day to night or night to day, the canvas is always on the cusp of something new and magical. I want to trust the beauty of the purple and gold.

"Let's make this quick," I say.

The Howards approach the table. Bobby rises and shakes Drew's hand, while I force myself to greet Lisa. She hugs me hard. People do that because they think they can take away your pain. These are the times when I wished for a drink. I could drown myself at the bottom of a glass, flail in the abyss where others numb their problems. But after Monty, I vowed never to drink again. It was easy to explain to Bobby that alcohol didn't agree with me, how it made me literally sick. Instead, I take turns digging my fingernails into the palms of my hands and drinking enough water to have me fleeing multiple times to the bathroom.

It's not Lisa's fault I'm bad company. Each time she sinks her pitying blue eyes into mine, I want to get up from the table and run. Under a mane of blonde, freshly blown hair she says, "I can't imagine what you're going through, Em. Zoe's such a good girl. Who would do this to her?" She rubs my shoulder when she says, "It's terrible."

I thank her. Multiple times. But I have little more to say. *I shouldn't have come.* I try to catch Bobby's eyes, but he's deep in business. I can always tell by the hypnotic stare, how they latch on to topics like foreclosures and market fluctuations, Miami's ever-present diversity.

Lisa talks, her red lips sip some colorful drink, and I feel bad that no matter what she says, it's not going to help. When we get off the subject of Zoe, she informs me of all the latest celebrity gossip. It's what she does best. And she has a way of sharing it like she's doing us all a favor.

"I can't even make you laugh tonight," she says, giving up. "Not even with the story about Amy Schumer? Oh, honey. Let's do a girls' day. You, me, Dara, Cookie. We can go to Palm Beach. Get out of town."

"I can't leave Zoe, Lisa."

"We'll take the girls!"

"I can't," I tell her, tying my napkin in knots. "We need to be home."

"Grace is really upset. She feels horrible for Zoe. All the girls do. We love her. Whatever we can do."

I appreciate her kindness, but I can't help reading into what she's saying and not saying: she's happy it's not Grace.

The food arrives, and I have never been less interested in pan-seared snapper and garlic spinach in my life. I move it around the plate with my fork, because I can't get it to my mouth.

"You have such discipline," Lisa says. "I starve myself all day for a good dinner."

This is not about staying thin, and I scoot closer to Bobby. That's how I hear him tell Drew about his meeting in New York and vie for information about the buyers.

It happens quickly. One minute, I think I can survive on denial and celebrity hook-ups, but then Bobby's foolish notion of selling the hotel grabs me by the neck, and I'm fighting for air. Lisa gabs about a shop that opened in Bal Harbour, how they're invited to the VIP opening, and I should come with her. "It'll be good for you to get out."

I'm grinding my fingers into Bobby's thigh. "It's an awful idea, Drew, don't you agree?"

Bobby shoots me a look.

"The Ross is a legendary hotel," Drew replies with his rounded cheeks while the ravine between Bobby and me widens. "She's one of the original landmarks. I'm sure you have courters contacting you all the time."

"We do," I say, reminding the men how we've never entertained them before.

"The market's shifting again, Emma," Drew explains. "There's a rise in newer, pricier, commercial competition." The exact term is *trendy* and how South Beach is one of the hottest luxury destinations. "It doesn't hurt to listen to an offer. I know these guys at STK. They're impressive."

He prompts Bobby to define what makes the Ross stand out, and Bobby thinks about it. His eyes fill up with the love she brings forth in him. "So much of it is the people. Other hotels and their modern designs can't emulate it."

"So why do you want to let her go?" Drew asks, his light eyes glimmering with interest. "Maybe I'll take her off your hands."

The table is quiet, awaiting Bobby's response. There's no way he's going to tell them the truth. He'll turn it into an opportunity, but I know differently and so does he. I force a smile at Lisa, who is always bored by business conversations. If I succumb to my irritation, I'll hurl plates.

Lisa shrugs it off, though with her recent Botox it's hard to decipher the emotion. "Boys and their toys." She waves her polished fingers in the air.

I disagree. The Ross is way more than a plaything.

"Let them be," she says. Then she shimmies closer to me like she has breaking news. "You missed a classic PTA meeting. Stacey Fisher lured parents with the promise to wear her high school prom dress. It was standing room only! She looked like a jar of pink frosting. It was fantastic."

This is why we've remained friends as long as we have. She could always make me laugh. Though tonight my lips are pressed together. "I know you're trying, Lisa. I'm just not in the mood."

Dessert arrives, and Lisa polishes off an entire chocolate *budino* by herself. The men sip coffee, and I sit in numbed silence, the next crisis filling my veins.

When we get to the car, the door hasn't even shut before I rip into Bobby. "You're making a big mistake."

"Emma, I'm sorry. I know you're upset."

"You have no idea how I feel. None. You're not sorry, so why do you keep saying it?" Our knees practically touch in the compact car, but there is nothing connecting us. The engine roars to life, and we make our way down a deserted Miami street. His eyes on the road are cold and unreachable. "I'm such an idiot. I really thought you'd drop it. I thought you'd change your mind."

He doesn't answer. His jaw is tight. I place my palm on his leg, and he covers mine with his. "You're angry," I say. "You're not seeing things clearly . . ."

"Emma, don't."

His fingers wriggle away, and I latch on tighter. "Bobby, this is crazy. You said it yourself, the Ross has what no other hotel on the beach has. We've redone floors and balconies before. Isn't this drastic?"

"It's a meeting," he repeats.

We're stopped at a light, and my silence turns his head. He'd have to notice my eyes, how they're inconsolable, how my lips are sealed shut. When I speak, my words are a desperate plea. "Why are you doing this?"

His tone is unconvincing. "I like these buyers. It feels right."

"You're confused! You're angry! It's not a reason to sell our home!" I feel a headache coming on. "I'm as invested as anyone. I've been there through the ups and downs. I've watched you turn her around. Against the odds, against the competition, you've survived. Why now?"

"We can make a nice profit on a sale."

"Bullshit. You've never cared about the money."

His head is turning from side to side, and he refuses to listen. Frustration fills me, the kind that wants to grab hold of him and shake.

"Answer me," I plead.

Sadness washes out of his eyes. His lips part, but nothing comes out.

He doesn't know, but I do. If he rids himself of the Ross, maybe it will erase what Zoe did. We start over—start fresh. It wipes out the pain and embarrassment. We've always referred to the Ross as our third daughter. Her maturation comes at a time when he's fragile and wounded. How easy to sell her rather than to deal with the changes. It crosses my mind I was right to lie all those years ago. He would've gotten rid of me, too.

Bobby drives faster than usual along the Julia Tuttle Causeway. By now, I've released his fingers, though I wish I didn't have to. I almost tell him to slow down, but keep my mouth shut as I look out the window. The bay is speckled in flashing lights, and the city sparkles in the distance. Before long, we are pulling up to the hotel. The valet greets us and asks about our night, but neither of us replies. We step inside; the noise and activity collect around us. The elevator ride is silent. We face each other with an aged pageant queen between us. When she departs on her floor, her pungent scent remains. He moves in front of me and peers into my eyes. We are locked in a battle until I turn away.

After checking on the girls, we take careful steps toward our bedroom. "Look around," I demand, turning to our family portraits on the wall, Lily's backpack thrown on the floor, our wedding picture framed along the bar. "This is our life . . . our kids . . . our home." It's not easy trusting what I have to say, but I reach deep inside. "You don't get to give up on us."

He's stubborn and unconvinced when he says, "I'm doing what's best for us and the hotel."

"You think moving is going to change what happened? You think we're going to start over playing house somewhere else? It's not going to fix what happened."

"Emma, please, it makes sense. You can't see it now, but it does."

"No, you're wrong," I say. "You have three girls here. All of them are growing. So what do you do? You sell one and abandon the other. And what will happen to the third?" I will only ask him one more time. "Please don't do this, Bobby."

"I have to."

And it really doesn't matter that he's leaving, because he's already gone.

CHAPTER 15

"Mom, what's wrong?" Zoe's the child who is attuned to the changes in my temperament. It's after school, and we're driving to Lily's lacrosse scrimmage in Plantation. Lily sits shotgun, and Zoe is in the back.

I catch Zoe's eyes in the rearview mirror, and she seems better today, other than her outdated glasses. "I'm fine, honey."

Bobby left on an early morning flight and has been in meetings ever since. Lily's beside me complaining that *she* should be driving the car, reminding me for the umpteenth time about getting their permits. I clutch the wheel. I can't think of anything worse than being in a car driven by one of my kids. Well, maybe I can.

Lacrosse doesn't begin until January, though Lily plays on the club team in the off-season to practice her stick skills. Zoe calls them the *Cavemen* due to the rough and tough nature of the sport. Today the skies are clear blue without a cloud in sight. The perfect weather for a match.

"How was school?" I ask.

Zoe stares out the window, and Lily replies on her behalf.

"She's fine, Mom. We've got her covered."

But I need details. "Did anyone bother you?" I ask Zoe. "Did you take the biology test?"

She looks up, but a nearby horn blasts through the car and takes her response with it. It's the signal that the conversation is over. Lily puts in her earbuds, and I try again.

"Did you talk to Mr. Harmon? You're too talented to quit debate."

She loosens her seat belt, hangs over my seat, and pats my shoulder. "I'm fine, Mom, really."

Her insistence warms me. "Are you really?"

She settles back. "I promise."

Other than the spectacles that hide her face, Zoe looks like herself. It's me who is the mess. Me who is judging—gauging how she's supposed to feel, what she's supposed to look like—because I remember what I went through, how I fell apart. Lily sings along to a song on her phone. She has a beautiful voice. Zoe's eyes are shut, and she rests her forehead on the window. She's tired but seemingly content. Her hair falls down her face, and a wistfulness surrounds her. Lily's on to the next song, one I've heard a thousand times before. I never noticed the phrase "Everything comes back to you."

We enter Central Park and follow the veering road toward the parking lot. Lily meets a group of girls who smile and high-five her. Some are in their team jerseys; the others are dressed in tight-fitting shorts and T-shirts cinched at the waist. I'm unloading the chairs and cooler, and Zoe offers to help, but I tell her to go on ahead. She trails behind with her backpack slung on her shoulders. She doesn't even try to keep up.

The fields are filled with boys and girls in padded uniforms that look more like combat armor. The lacrosse culture is like any other team sport where parents and players rely on an assortment of very good and very bad behaviors. No amount of healthy competition or team building can defuse the heightened energy of parents watching their prodigies excel on a field. Lily gets her athletic ability from my sisters. They both lettered in high school lacrosse and were offered scholarships out of state.

We set up our chairs along the sideline with the other parents. Some I know well; others are from the opposing team. Evan Griggs is the team mom. She's front and center under a collapsible canopy with our team name, Dolphins, emblazoned across the top. She moves over and makes room for us under the tent. Her daughter is the goalie, so her nerves should be the most rattled, but she's always tough as nails. And sharp as a tack. She's surrounded by Kami Frankel and Donna Benson. Their designer bags cost more than the coach's monthly salary. They stop talking when we approach. Donna whispers something out of the corner of her mouth to Kami and another mom, Elena. I'm fuming, but I won't let Zoe see. The last thing I need is their pity, so I give them my brightest smile and wave.

The game is under way, and Lily's finesse is in full swing. She plays attack, and by the end of the first period she leads the team in goals, 5–0. She's that good. Probably better than my sisters.

The team fathers stand. They don't know how to sit. They cluster together like a pack of wolves pacing the sidelines. Only one of them has the willingness to congratulate me on Lily's effort.

"She's really good," he says.

And I smile while the eyes of the other mothers burn holes in the back of my head.

Screams come from another game. They're louder than the usual "C'mon, son!" All eyes turn to the adjacent field, where coaches and players charge the grass.

"I told you this sport is barbaric," Zoe says.

A mess of pads and sticks crash into each other. The metal sounds of helmet on helmet silence the other games. A whistle blows, and referees from all over the park race to break up a fight. The entire team is in the middle of the field except for one lone boy sitting on the bench. My eyes find him because Zoe's watching, too. He stands up and walks off the field toward the bathrooms. Then he turns around again. Zoe gets up and heads in his direction.

"Where are you going?" I ask.

"I have to save somebody."

"Who?" I ask.

"Price Hudson."

My heart skips, and I follow her gaze. The boy is suspended between joining the ruckus and disappearing. One final turn, and he's walking with purpose toward the action. There is nothing mean about his face, but he suddenly looks angry. Zoe stands in front of him, blocking his path, and I can tell by the way his hands come up, he's telling her to get out of his way.

Worry curdles my stomach.

His arms come back down, and a grin spreads across Zoe's face. An impasse. Is she laughing? In her glasses? They look like characters in a John Green movie, not the stars of an awful after-school special. Then I notice the moms around me watching, too, and I'm faced with the deep-seated need to defend my child from their stares.

Breathe. Let her do this. Whatever this is.

The chaos from the opposite field subsides, and soon, games resume and teams are in motion. I plant myself in my seat and wait for the sign that says *Save me*. So when someone taps my shoulder, I jump.

"I'm sorry," she says, "I didn't mean to scare you." The woman is at once recognizable and unfamiliar, but I draw a blank. "I'm Price's mom," she says. "Monica Hudson."

I'd been so consumed at the time, wrestling with devastation and damage control, that I hardly remembered the face of the woman entering the principal's office.

Studying her carefully, I notice her height and the windblown blonde hair. She's still skinny, bony like her son, but far prettier than the woman I passed in the doorway. Her face is free of makeup, and she doesn't appear to mind the faint lines that cross her forehead. Her smile is hesitant, her lips uncertain. Her pale-blue eyes squint in the sunlight, first at me, and then at the kids standing behind us.

"You're Zoe's mom, yes?" There's a hint of an accent in her tone.

I steal a glance at the kids and nod. "Yes, I'm Zoe's mom. Emma Ross."

"I'm sorry," she says.

I watch her lips move and feel sick inside. I hate this woman. I hate everything she stands for. I hate that she didn't teach her son to respect girls. I hate that we're connected in this drama. I hate that our kids have been exploited. And I hate that I hate, because at the center of it all is blame.

"I've been meaning to call you," she says, while a small, cherubic girl approaches and asks her mom for some pop. The girl can't be more than seven. Price has a sister.

With a water bottle in her hands instead, the little girl, Ruby, takes off running, her yellow dress whistling in the breeze.

"How did this happen?" I blurt.

Monica studies the grass before she finds my eyes again. "I'm not sure. We're new here. Nothing like this has ever happened at home." Then she asks if we can talk. "In private." And she points to the adjacent park with plenty of trees.

I'm rooted to the seat. The other moms have stopped cheering. I'm not imagining them leaning closer.

"Please?"

I hesitate, watching Zoe face her enemy. But the whispers guide me to my feet. Monica reminds Ruby to stay close to her brother. We walk in silence side by side along the field. I glance back at Zoe. "I'm not comfortable leaving my daughter over there."

She has a casual breeziness about her when she says, "I think we need to learn to trust them again. Give them some time to work through this themselves."

I release a long, held-in breath. "They've had enough alone time. He's a boy. He took advantage of her."

She settles onto the park bench and stares down at her fingers. I stand off to the side, leaning on a wooden beam that's part of a fitness trail. "I deserve that," she says. "If it were my daughter, I'd probably feel the same way."

Sounds of whistles and screaming coaches pass through the wind, and the cheers of parents and teammates carry the tune. "You hate me," she says.

I shuffle along the apparatus. "I do."

"It's okay," she says. "I've made a voodoo doll of your daughter."

"My daughter doesn't do stuff like this."

"Mrs. Ross, your daughter *did* do this. They both *did* this. You think girls never go after boys? Do you know what it's like for a teenage boy to say no to a willing teenage girl?" The breeziness is turning into a weapon. "What if I told you that Price is an honors student and has never gotten into any trouble in or out of school?"

"I'd say the same about Zoe."

A vibration stops me from listing the litany of superlatives that describe Zoe, and I take my cell phone from my back pocket and hit "Ignore."

"I see you're upset, Mrs. Ross," she says.

"Upset? Upset isn't close to what I'm feeling. I have no idea how this will affect Zoe. I don't know how many kids are watching that video, sharing it with their friends, and"—I pause—"laughing at her."

Her fair skin turns bright pink. "I understand," she says. "When we made mistakes, nobody saw. I'm scared for Price. And it's not only the kids. The parents are just as mean."

Bobby's face flashes in my mind. Monica's voice takes on a softer tone. "We can't make it go away. Whether I blame you or you blame me, the community has formed their opinions about us. We're negligent, irresponsible. We've been judged. Our kids have been judged." She looks off into the clear blue sky then circles back to me. "This is such a small percentage of who my son is. If it's a numbers game, five percent.

That's what it comes down to. In Price's short life, he's been decent for ninety-five percent of the time. But no one sees that. They'll hold on to this. And that percentage will stick to him like glue.

"We don't promote this type of behavior," she continues, ignoring my quiet. "We've tried to be good role models." The wind picks up, kicking the trees and rustling leaves. "Despite our good intentions, we never expected this." Her eyes fill up with weakness. "I never fully realized what being a mom meant. I knew you felt what your child felt, deeply, but I never ever thought it would hurt this much . . . to be unable to protect them . . . to take away their pain."

A flicker of sympathy spreads through my body. I want to hold on to it; I want to fall into those words and let their meaning soften me.

Shouts and cheers dissolve my worry, and I turn to see Lily charging the field with the ball in her net. Zoe yells her name—actually, her nickname, *Wheels*, because she can drive past anyone who gets in her path. When she raises her stick, we all know it will go right in, and it does. Her teammates pat her on the back, the coach claps, and I set aside my distress to make room for pride.

"She's a natural, eh?" Monica says.

Her compliment dissolves some of my anger. "She always has been."

"The girls are twins, yes?"

I nod, but I won't look into her eyes. Instead, I stare at the field. "Fifteen minutes apart." I pause, my thoughts willing me to go on. "I never thought it would be Zoe. Lily was always physically faster."

Her eyes flash a hint of understanding. "I never thought it could be Price. I still don't." Funny how that happens. How wrong we can be. "What our kids did was one thing, but whoever held that record button down, they're the offenders. They violated their privacy and didn't think anything of humiliating them publicly. They're the ones who should be punished." She says this, and there's nothing smug about her now.

Unwinding the story has come to this: I was so intent on Zoe's actions I'd forgotten to read the remaining pages of the script. A fury that had welled up inside me scrambles to come out. We could leave it alone and trust that the kids learned a mighty lesson, deleted the video from their phones, and moved on to the next sordid story. Or we could go after the culprit and teach these kids a bigger lesson.

"What do you plan to do?" I ask.

"We're conflicted. The kids have deleted it. We want it to go away. Seeking justice may have the opposite effect. It's a tough call."

My phone vibrates again, the buzzing too persistent to ignore. It's a text from Bobby. **STK wants the hotel. Howard's group, too. We're in the best position to negotiate. B**

The words shout at me from the screen.

But before I can fully process them, Zoe and Price bolt our way. Zoe's face is an explosion of sadness. Price is on the verge of crying, his skinny knees banging into each other as he approaches his mother's side. Zoe is out of breath, and panic returns. Price hands his mother his phone.

"What is it?" she shrieks.

I watch Monica's eyes and the way her fingers handle the keypad. Zoe's gaze tells me not to look. She's hunched over, the prospect forcing her to look away and hide her face. It's a YouTube video. Their names are plastered beneath. I reach out to touch her, but she collapses to the ground. I join her there, wrapping her in my arms. My eyes close, and I let her sob into my chest.

"Mommy . . . Mommy . . ." she says, unable to finish.

I hug her hard while her body shakes, a violent tremble I can't slow down. I thought I could protect her, and I failed. No matter how hard you try, no matter the level of wishful thinking, there are some things that are beyond our control.

"I'm here, baby. I'm here."

CHAPTER 16

Zoe fights me. She pushes me away and runs toward the car.

"Leave me alone," she cries, the tears streaming down her face. I get up and chase after her, all while I dial Bobby.

"You need to come home," I cry into the cell phone. "You need to come home now."

There's panic in his voice. "What's wrong?"

It's painful to say aloud. "Zoe's on the Internet."

Silence echoes through the phone.

"Bobby . . . Bobby, are you there?"

"Jesus, Emma. How the hell did this happen?"

I can't even begin to answer all the ways that question can be interpreted. When I reach the car, I find Zoe planted on the ground by the passenger door. "I'll call you right back . . ."

She howls, curled up in a ball. I try to lift her, but she flings me away. "Stop! Leave me alone. My life is over."

"Zoe," I say, choking on the emotion, "get up and get in the car."

She refuses, hyperventilating, kicking at me when I get too close. Kids walk by and stare. I try to block their view, but her noises can't be camouflaged. My fingers shake when I text Lily to get a ride home with one of her teammates.

"Zoe, please get up," I beg. "I'll take you home. We need to do something. We can't do that with you sitting on the ground."

My phone rings, and it's Bobby. "Talk to me."

Zoe's on her feet, and I'm holding the car door for her. She crawls inside, sinking into her seat. Her body slumps, and she throws her glasses on the floor before her head collapses against the window.

My voice shakes when I answer. "We're getting in the car. What do we do?"

"We're calling Jo Jo Sturner. She's the lawyer Nathan told me about." He pauses. "The expert on cybercrimes. I was hoping it wouldn't come to this."

Cybercrimes crashes into me, and I weaken from the force. I maneuver the car out of the parking lot, but I'm physically sick, dissolving into the leather cushion. The phone transfers to Bluetooth, and Bobby comes back with a woman on the line.

His voice trembles. He is caught between embarrassment and rage. "Our daughter, she's fifteen . . . she was at a party . . . now there's a video of her . . . on YouTube."

I'm not sure I can breathe.

"Nathan said I might hear from you." She sounds young but firm. "I'm sorry you have to bear witness to how unkind the modern world can be."

Zoe stares out the window. God only knows what she's thinking.

The deception has ravaged my ability to reason. My earlier hostility is now turned on someone else, someone less worthy of forgiveness.

"How can this happen?" Bobby asks. "Anyone can upload a child to any site? There are no restrictions? No content provisions? Nothing?"

"Slow down, Mr. Ross. We'll get to the parameters and regulations. There's a lot to cover. First and foremost, the video needs to be flagged as inappropriate. Go to the site and report it. Usually it takes twenty-four to forty-eight hours for them to comply."

"What if it spreads?" I yell. "That's too long!"

"I want to know who did this." His tone is flat, but the threat is loud. Zoe covers her face with her hands. "I want this asshole to go to jail," he says. "Whoever did this needs to be punished."

He's right. We have to make the person pay, the one who committed this horrible crime against our daughter.

"I understand," she says. "This is very painful for families. We take sexual cyberharassment and cyberbullying very seriously." The weight of her words shuts the world down around us. "My people can start a full investigation . . . your daughter's friends, anyone at the party who might've seen or heard anything . . . YouTube . . . we have ways to find out who did this."

"No, Mommy," Zoe pleads. "I don't want to do that."

My fingers squeeze hers so tight it makes her cry worse, and she pulls away. I grip the wheel instead. My knuckles turn a painful white, but it does nothing for the nausea slamming against my stomach. Bobby is silent, but I know he's pacing back and forth somewhere in New York, ready to go through the roof.

"Whatever we need to do," he says. "Just do it."

Jo Jo continues talking about laws and managing fallout, but I only hear the plan to meet at her office tomorrow. It's a rope that pulls me to safety. She hangs up, and Bobby says he's changing his flight. Tears pound at my eyes to come out. I push them back, trying to be strong for Zoe. I am heartbroken, afraid to look at her and see the anguish on her face. My fingers dig into the wheel.

She whimpers, "One stupid mistake and my life is ruined!"

The world tilts, and I can't steady the road—disturbing thoughts swirl deep inside. *How much more can she take?* My foot wants to stomp on the accelerator. It's impossible to sit still when all I want to do is scream. The elements around us sense our agony. Heavy gray clouds darken the sky, and soon the rain is slapping the windows.

"I'm sorry," she cries.

"Zoe, don't. You didn't ask for this. We're not going to let this person hurt you any more."

The Ross appears, and the line of cars waiting for valet backs up onto the street. I pull off to the side and park in a loading zone. The wind and rain batter us, and I signal to the guys that the keys are in the car. Lightning flashes at our feet, and we run for the doors. In my rush, I remember the cooler and chairs left under the tent. *Damn.*

Zoe disappears ahead. The floors are slick with cautionary yellow signs. Sandra approaches with concern in her eyes. My clothes are soaked, and I shiver from the cold.

"Mrs. Ross, are you okay? Can I get you a towel?"

"I'm fine," I tell her. "I'll change upstairs."

"I won't keep you," she says. "Jenny's sent the new arrangement. They called a few times to see if you're pleased. And the Golans left a note after their recent stay." She passes me the sealed envelope, which I take before slipping away. "Are you sure you're okay, Mrs. Ross?" she asks, though I'm too far ahead to answer.

I step through the bustling lobby without acknowledging my staff. I don't smile at the girls behind the front desk or engage them in our usual discussions. They are the conductors who bring the hotel to life, the people who anchor it deep inside my heart. Today, those pieces escape me. I don't know how to reel them back.

The elevator ride is a momentary pause. A chilly plume of air snakes around me, and I drop to the floor. Zoe's one single mishap is broadcast very publicly. I try not to judge. I try to be her mother, understanding and calm about a daughter who's experimenting in her sexuality, but my judgment is skewed. I imagine pressing the emergency button to stop the nightmare from spreading. I could hide in this metal box where digital access is useless.

Get up, Emma.

My body wants to. The damp clothes make it hard to move. And I'm tired and I'm overwhelmed. Someone's attacked my child. I get up. I stand. I remember: fight back.

The elevator doors open, and I manage the few steps through the doorway. Jonny's there—Bobby must have called him—and I collapse into his arms.

"It'll be okay," he says.

"I don't see how." I'm crying. "We need to get that video down. People are watching it!"

"I'm here," he says to the top of my damp head. "We'll get to the bottom of this. I won't let anyone get away with exploiting my niece—who, by the way, has locked herself in her room."

I pull back and wipe my nose with the back of my hand. He hands me a napkin, but all I do is crumple it in my fist. He follows me to the office and to the computer. "This is crazy," I say. "Do you know how to flag a video?" I feel lunch making its way up. "Zoe!" I call down the hall. "She'll know what to do."

"Em, relax."

I fling his hand away from me. "Don't tell me to relax, Jonny. I can't make this go away for her. I can't promise her she'll be fine. How will she find her self-confidence? How will she ever trust again?" I blink back tears and push away the shocking stories in the news. Victims of cyberbullying who lose all hope. Innocent, helpless kids who resort to harmful behaviors. What if Zoe hurts herself? What if she's trapped? A whisper escapes. "Kids kill themselves over this sort of stuff."

He takes hold of my shoulders and forces me to look at him. "Zoe will persevere. She's strong and has plenty of people who love her."

"Did we do this?" I break down.

"This isn't your fault," he says, pulling me close.

"I swear I didn't see this coming. At all." I look him square in the eyes when I say, "I never thought it could be my kid at the center of some scandal."

Zoe slinks into the room. Her hair is dripping from the rain, and there are splotches on her cheeks. She takes a seat at the desk. She hesitates, her fingers seemingly afraid the computer might bite.

"Honey," I begin, but I don't have the strength to finish. We face each other. Our puffy eyes and long faces reflect our shame. It's useless to ask if she's okay. She may never be okay, and we all know it.

Jonny rubs her shoulder while she clicks on the mouse. "If I had known turning fifteen would suck this much," she says, "I would've enjoyed being fourteen a lot more."

I stare at the computer as it lights up. I wonder how something so cold and artificial can heat me up like flames. I finger the phone in my back pocket, thinking I should call the police, let them deal with this madness. Why should Zoe have to find herself in a search engine? But Jonny's nudged her aside, and he's tapping the keyboard.

"Who would do this to me?" Zoe asks. The absolute horror in her voice stings. The tears rush, and I have to hold her shoulders up. I pluck words from the sacred space I save for those I love most. It comes out as a whisper, but with vigor.

"Zoe, we're going to get through this."

She burrows deeper into me and nods. "Uncle Jonny, did you find it?"

He doesn't answer. We break apart and see his eyes locked on the screen. Zoe brushes him aside. "Let me do it."

She sighs like only broken children know how and faces the computer. Her gaze is fixed, and the tears leave a trail of sadness on her skin. I glance at the monitor and there's Zoe and Price. It sucks the air out of me. Tiny print tells me the video went live last night. *Last night.* While we were at dinner. While Zoe began to return to normalcy and neglected to Google her name for the hundredth time. Comments have accrued. I don't read them, pretending the video is of somebody else. Jonny rubs Zoe's shoulders, but he doesn't look at the screen. My hand rests on the curve of her back. Determination fills her chest and travels through to her fingers.

Zoe maneuvers around the mouse pad, and I watch the arrow stop on "More." In the drop-down menu, she clicks "Report." Now she's asked to choose a reason for flagging. She selects "Sexual Content." "Please provide additional details," it prompts. *Someone posted this of me. I'm fifteen. PLEASE take it down.* And with a pressing thud, Zoe takes a step toward healing herself and her reputation.

"Submit." She says it aloud.

"Submit," I repeat.

She turns from the computer and collapses in my arms. I thank Jonny for being there with us, and he reminds us that he's always there, for whatever we need. Our eyes lock, and I want to ask what's going on between Bobby and him, but it'll have to wait. "Can we talk later?" I ask as Zoe turns back to the computer.

"If it's about my mule of a brother, Em . . ."

"You know?"

"Yes, I know."

I steal a glance at Zoe, who's deep in thought in front of the screen. I don't respond.

"Whatever happens," he says, "you have to trust that he does everything for you and the girls. All four of you. Even if his decisions don't always make sense."

I'm not sure what he means, but now's not the time to dig further.

"Love you, Zoe," he says as he walks out the door, but her eyes are glazed over in a digital coma.

"Zoe," I say, refocusing my attention on her, "we should call the school. They need to know."

Dr. Mason had given me his private number for emergencies; this constitutes an emergency. Dr. Rubin follows. She wonders if Zoe might benefit from seeing someone outside of school. She offers three recommendations for private therapists, but Zoe says no.

"She prefers to talk to you," I tell Dr. Rubin.

Her calm voice reassures me. "Your daughter's in good hands."

Soon Lily races into the apartment, out of breath. She holds her lacrosse stick in one hand and her phone in the other. A line of dirt coats her shorts; her face is flushed. The phone beeps and dings.

"Everyone knows," she says, her eyes sympathizing with Zoe. "We can't stop this."

"We're dealing with it," I tell her. "Daddy's coming home. We're taking care of it."

Zoe drops her head on the table.

"Are you okay?" Lily asks.

"No," Zoe mumbles into her arms. "Would you be okay?"

I try to comfort her, but she pushes me away. "We're getting it taken down."

I don't know that I believe that. I thought we had contained the video, that her "friends" were deleting it. Nothing makes sense, and then there's Bobby. And Jonny. And something in his voice troubles me.

Lily showers and begins working on a project. She has to make a video of herself giving a weather report in Spanish. She enlists Zoe's help, to distract her from her misery, but it fails. Zoe locks herself in her room again, and I'm left to film Lily desecrating the Spanish language.

Bobby calls from the plane as it's taxiing before takeoff. "How is she?"

I want to climb inside the phone so he's next to me. "Horrible."

"I'll be there soon," he says.

The quiet that follows chokes me. He tries to bring up the meeting because he doesn't want to talk about Zoe on the Internet, and I cut him off.

"I don't care about the meeting."

"Where is she?"

"Locked in her room." The phone feels icy cold. Like his words. "Can you talk to her?"

"What time is the meeting with the attorney tomorrow?" he asks.

"Did you hear me?" I raise my voice. "You need to talk to her. You need to let her know it's okay . . . she needs her father . . ."

"Is she going to school?"

He's not hearing me. He's slipping away. A physical ache spreads through me. "I don't know what to do, Bobby. I need your help. I need you to say something. She's your child, for God's sake. Talk to her!"

My hysteria matches his stoicism and how removed he is. He speaks cruelly, a flat tone that slaps my ears. "The daughter I know would have never done something like this. The daughter I know had common sense."

I hear the captain tell the flight attendants to prepare for departure. "We're taking off," he says. And the phone disconnects.

Stunned, I cradle the phone against my ear and sob. And I know that while Monty revealed our first crack, here is the evidence of another. And I'm terrified. Not only for Zoe. For all of us.

CHAPTER 17

The day is hours too long. I peel off my clothes and drop them in the hamper before taking a warm bath and stepping into my pajamas. The cold apartment chills my skin. The rain outside smacks the windows, and the pounding thunder shakes the walls. A black robe hangs on a hook, and I wrap myself in its thick fabric. It's Bobby's. His smell reaches my nose. I've been tracking his flight, and he should be home soon, unless the weather has other plans for him.

Besides matters of family, I have never been much of an emotional type. Raised strong and strong-willed, I rarely yielded to the worries that plagued kids my age. But pain had never felt like this. Even when my father eventually left, instead of being angry for his absence, I felt oddly relieved. When Mom married Abel, I learned from him what it took to love a child. Even someone else's. Being Zoe's mom means my heart lives outside my body, and though I try, I can't always keep it safe. I thought all the love I had for her would turn this horrid interruption in our lives around, but now I'm not so sure my love is enough.

A dull ache in my forehead forces me to lie down, and when I do, I see Zoe on a well-known website. I see her body, her lips, and it fills me with such anger I punch the pillows. I punch and punch, out of breath, and I realize I'm punching him. Monty. And I hear his voice: *Last night was amazing.*

And then there's Bobby and me twirling on a merry-go-round. I'm so dizzy. I had just told him about my cheating father. He had said, "I'll never hurt you like him. That will never happen to us."

I punch. The hatred rises in me like a volcano. And even though I kicked Monty out, the shock at what I'd done was pervasive. It wasn't him I hated—it was myself. I'd been wound up in principles that slowly broke apart. I had become my father, and I was disgusted.

Spent, I collapse on the same pillow I've used as a punching bag. The realization magnifies Zoe's mistakes and the pain she must be experiencing. What will become of her if the video doesn't come down? What about Bobby? At the time, lying was my only option. He loved me all these years even with this part of me tucked away. The thought of telling him the truth sends a burst of fear through me. It's freeing and frightening all at once. My phone dings, and it's him. He's landed.

"Good night, Mom," whispers Lily, as I bend over to kiss both her cheeks. I cross the room to Zoe, who lets me kiss her on the forehead and only that much. She hides under her comforter, the sheet and blanket a shield.

I don't immediately leave the room upon turning out their light. When they were babies, I'd listen for their steady breaths to signal they were safely tucked away in sleep. Lily's always came first, her tiny body submitting. Then Zoe. Fitful at first. Erratic. And then a stable rhythm. The front door plucks me away from the measured peace. I tiptoe out of the room, closing the door behind me, as Bobby approaches.

"Are they asleep?" He looks as tired as his girls, his face unsettled.

My arms are crossed, and I don't greet him warmly. "You should go in."

"I don't want to wake them," he says, though that had never mattered before. One of our few arguments was about settling the girls down for bed. He had a way of riling them up when I needed them to wind down.

He is halfway down the hall when I catch him, forcing him to stop. "Don't do this to her." He doesn't move, his body painfully stiff. "And don't do this to me."

His head dips downward, and while he's much bigger than I am, it feels as though I'm holding him up. "Why'd she have to be so careless?" he asks. "How are we supposed to fix this for her?"

"Bobby." I touch his face. "We may not be able to fix this."

His tie is undone, splayed unevenly around his neck. His eyes are dark. "I don't know how to love her through this."

His uncertainty pulls at me. I'd never seen him so stripped and afraid. "You do," I say. "You love her better than anyone."

He opens his mouth to say something else, but nothing comes out.

I back up against the wall, and he eyes my silk pajamas. "I've really missed you," he says.

Helplessness collides with loneliness, and I ache to be close again.

He unties the bathrobe and brings a hand around my waist. His eyes follow the line of my top down to the satin ribbon of my bottoms. He tugs at the delicate string while finding my eyes. I want to punish him, push him away, but I let his fingers undo the bow that sets us apart.

His hands travel up my body and rest on my shoulders. From there they stroke my face. I arch to meet him, my toes balancing me so I can fall deeper into his grasp. When his lips come down on mine, they're terribly sad. The stubble scratches at my cheeks. His mouth is urgent, but mostly needy. We stop, and he hugs me instead. It's all either of us can manage. A week ago, he would have taken me right there in the hallway. He would have lifted my top over my head and held my arms up while he tasted my neck and breasts. He would have ripped the tie from my pants, letting them fall to the floor at my feet, and he'd start slowly, his fingers tracing my thighs, his lips following.

"Daddy?"

Zoe's voice pulls us apart. He lets go and yanks on the tie around his neck. I retreat, the spaces inside me hungry, but hushed. Zoe looks so small walking toward us in her boxer shorts and T-shirt. Her glasses sit awkwardly on her face.

He doesn't want to, but he turns around. She picks up speed and races to his chest, throwing herself into him. I can tell his arms want to fit around her, but they don't. He kisses the top of her head where he had once kissed her cheeks. It drains my body of the tenderness I felt moments ago, and I shake my head at him.

"How was New York?" she asks.

"It was okay, Squirt," he says, using the name he hasn't called her since she was four.

"I'm sorry, Daddy." Her raspy voice is tired with sleep. She sounds as though she's given up. "I had no idea this would happen. Please help me."

"I'm doing everything I can, honey," he says, patting her on the head and nothing else. "Get some sleep. You have school tomorrow. We'll talk when you get home."

"Aren't you driving us?" She pulls away and stares up at his face. "It's Friday."

Years ago, when I had tried to talk him out of their Friday morning drive with its hour-and-fifteen-minute round-trip, his response had been "I won't get those minutes in the car back."

"Mom and I have an early meeting. I'll see you when you get home."

Zoe's disappointment crawls through me. "You can drop the girls off, and I'll meet you," I say.

"I can't, Emma." He's hiding behind his contempt, and I wonder if Zoe can see through it, too.

"I'll make it up to you, kiddo," he adds.

But she turns from him, the rejection crowding her face. She throws herself in my arms. "Go to bed," I say, hugging her.

She slips down the hall, shoulders slouched. I take off in the opposite direction. Bobby tries to say something, and when I'm almost at our bedroom door, he grabs my arm and forces me to face him.

"What's wrong with you?" he says.

"Do you see what you're doing to her?" I fling his hand away and step inside our room.

He follows and takes a seat at the foot of our bed. "Don't make it more than it is. I'm not good at this stuff. My fourteen-year-old daughter with a boy doesn't make sense."

"You don't get to pick and choose. She needs you."

"Fathers aren't supposed to know their daughter's exploits," he argues back. "I'll deal with the investigation."

He tiptoes around the truth, and all it does is open my eyes. I see the whole of him, and it alarms me. "How can you judge her like this?"

"How can I not?" he snaps back.

"You don't get to do that to someone you love!"

"She doesn't love herself! If she did, she wouldn't give herself to a boy like that. Someone she doesn't even care about."

His lips are moving, but I'm somewhere else. Every nerve in my body is inflamed, about to catch fire. He just ripped into my chest and swiped at my soul.

His phone rings, and he answers it while I take a seat in the corner of the room and rock back and forth. Maybe the soothing motion will wipe out what he's just said.

As soon as the door closed behind Monty, I ran to the bathroom and threw up. Sitting against the cold tile, I cried until there were no more tears. I washed my face, dumped the bottles of tequila in the garbage, and climbed into bed. That's when I saw the phone off the hook. Hours he must've spent worked up and suspicious. I set the receiver back on the cradle. It was seconds before it began ringing. I knew it was him, and this was long before caller ID. There was silence on the other end. Not at all like the comfortable kind we'd fallen asleep to.

"Bobby." It was a whisper.

He only needed to say one word, "Em," and I was plagued with regret. "I've been calling you all night."

I was crying too hard to answer, but I covered the phone so he couldn't hear. I reached inside the drawer for the ring, placing it back on my finger, knowing it was forever marked.

"You were with him." His voice was broken. "Emma, just tell me. Is he there?"

"Bobby, please don't do this . . . I really don't feel well." I had no recourse. Pretending to be sick was the only excuse. Everything he'd accused me of, I'd done. His self-fulfilling prophecy had come true. I was a cheat.

"Please tell me you weren't with him," he begged.

I was gasping. "I wasn't with him."

"Thank God," he said, the relief a loud breath he'd been holding in. "You have no idea where my mind went. All I could think about was the two of you . . . I didn't sleep all night." He was going on and on, and I was only half listening, biting back the lies. "I'm so sorry, Em. I love you so much. Being away from you makes me crazy sometimes. I get jealous. He's with you. I wish it were me. Only me. Only you."

It wasn't even a complete sentence. But it was everything. Bile rose from my stomach. I was horrified by my actions; shame was a physical threat.

"My schedule's been crazy." I forced the words. "I missed a rehearsal. We had to do it here."

"I was wrong. It'll never happen again. I'm sorry, Em. I'm sorry I said what I said. Please forgive me."

And I listened and quietly whimpered while he apologized. Hearing his love didn't feel good. The truth was like a nail lodged inside my heart; rusty and cold, it twisted my soul. All the love I felt for him coated my words with a disgusting shame.

Fear makes you do terrible things. Mine let him take the blame. The lies just kept growing, though some of them were true. I was sick that night and the morning after. And a little crazy, too. Over the subsequent weeks, no matter how hard I tried to conceal and to forget what I'd done, the betrayal found its way back. Then a jolt of truth made it impossible to forget.

My period was late. Very late.

His voice snaps me back to the present. "Emma." And I wonder if he can see that the story I constructed is coming apart, and the messiness is pouring out.

"Zoe needs love," I say. My voice is heavy with the weight of memory, the depth of what we both need most. "She needs forgiveness."

"I'm doing that!" he yells, and I flinch. He slumps on the bed and talks to the ceiling. "I'm getting us out of here. We'll find a nice house in a nice community where no one will know what happened. I'm giving her her life back!"

My face is hot. Monty's touching me, and I push him away. My chest hurts. I'm no better than my daughter. In fact, I'm worse. My voice shakes. "You think that'll make it go away? We sweep it under the rug, and it magically disappears? Are you that ashamed? You'd rather sell our home and hide?"

He sits up again. "Give me a chance to process it! It just happened. I need time to absorb it, to understand it." He avoids my eyes as he says, "No father wants to think of his daughter like that."

A desperate ache settles in my heart.

"I need time," he says, finally looking at me. "I need to think about what she's done. Can't you give me that?"

I'm in Vermont, waiting the two minutes for the pregnancy test to signal my results.

A miserable quiet fills the air.

"They've lived in this fairy tale for too long," he says. "Balance will be good for them."

I'm no match for his logic, though I try. "Wasn't being here good enough for you and Jonny?" And the name is a subtle reminder. "You'd tell me if there were problems with the hotel, wouldn't you?"

"We're fine, Emma. The world is different."

"Why can't you look at me when you say that?"

"Enough!" It feels like a slap across my cheek.

"You can't shield them from what's out there," I say. "What keeps them out of trouble is in here." My palm lands on my chest. "You can't rip them from the only home they've ever had. This is where they grew up. This is where your parents would want us to be."

His hair nips his forehead. He brushes it back and sighs. "They raised us to be better people than this. We raised those girls to be better than this. I'm giving them another chance."

"And we just pull them out of school? What about their friends? They have a full life here! Why would you punish them like this?"

"You're too easy on them," he says, turning away from me. "Someone has to be tough. I know how boys think. Boys will see her one way. They'll take advantage of her . . . they'll think she's . . ."

"Don't say it," I begin, stumbling on the words. "You can't really think . . ."

"It doesn't matter what I think. This is the right move," he says.

"It's *our* decision, Bobby. The family. You don't get to decide! You said it yourself. They need balance. Stability. The whole world is watching her, and she's exposed and scared. You need to figure out a way to love her. This little experimentation of hers could lead to something worse if you turn her away. She's not that one single mistake. There's so much more to her than a single mistake."

This is how I convince myself that lying wasn't wrong. I was saving us, saving myself. I could bury it so it didn't happen. Then I wouldn't be bad, used, and duplicitous. But maybe he needs to see I'm no different than Zoe. That our weaknesses tie us together, but we are lovable and worthy. It comes to me so fast I wonder how I didn't see it before. It's not scary. It's a gentle tap on my heart, waking it up, reminding me of its worth. *Tell him.*

I shake the words away. Banish them the way I'd done all those years ago, but they are no longer containable. To pretend it didn't happen is impossible, especially as I watch my daughter suffer so publicly. The past had entered the present with a mighty clap, and turning away from it wasn't working. Clamping my eyes shut, I will the answer to appear. But nothing is clear. Except a new sound: *it's time.*

He heads for the bathroom, unbuttoning his shirt along the way. I watch him from behind, the way the fabric slides off his arms and accentuates his muscles. He'll be beside me in a few minutes, and I don't know if I should try to love some sense back into him, or merely turn away. I think about letting him inside me and having his eyes hold on to mine when I break the news. Divulging the true story of what occurred so long ago could only happen when we were as close as two people could be, when our love was unquestionable and enduring. Then he would understand that love was pure and fluid, and imperfections could fade into the background.

I lift the blanket and slide underneath. I hear his steps on the floor as he shuts off the light. The blinds are up, and a luminous moon floats outside the window. The silver sky guides him to his side of the bed. When he's under the covers, he rolls over with his back to me.

There's something I want to tell you, I begin, in my mind. *It's going to hurt.* He'd sit upright, and his eyes would grab hold of mine. *People are imperfect, some tainted, some scarred. It's possible to love someone who's made a mistake.*

He'd say, *What are you talking about?*

And I'd reply, *I screwed up, Bobby. Like Zoe, I'm not perfect.*

He'd grab me under the covers, remind me I'm beautiful and a great wife and mother. And I'd pull away. *You love me. I know. I feel it in every part of my body. But you don't know everything about me.* Then the deep breath would follow to make room for my confession. He loved me unconditionally and unknowingly, but now he is snoring while the conversation I've imagined evaporates into the air. On most nights, I would tap him on the shoulder, but tonight I give him a firm shove against the back until he readjusts himself, and the grunts become softer and lower. I pray that he will understand that true love can exist even when you hide parts of yourself you don't want anyone to see.

I curl into a ball.

The truth was hard to look at. It slid inside my dreams for weeks thereafter, sinful and interminable. I felt guilty and irresponsible. A string of what-ifs filtered through my mind: *What if I hadn't taken the phone off the hook? What if Monty hadn't answered the phone? What if it had been a different movie that night? What if I hadn't drunk?* Despite how hard he pushed me that day, I did this. Our perfect love was no longer perfect. And it was all my fault.

Now my child is bound in the same prison of shame. Where the only criticism that is worse than the one coming from those around you is the one that comes from within. Nothing is louder than that voice. It wrecks perceptions and clouds judgment. When it says you are bad, you believe it.

My secret might have lived a long and silent life, but watching Zoe struggle has unleashed its fury. I was wrong all those years ago for not trusting him enough to tell him the truth. Maybe it's my body next to his, or that he has rolled over and his arm has draped across my chest. We are momentarily united again. But it feels wrong and artificial, and I know what I must do to make it right.

CHAPTER 18

Zoe slumps at the breakfast table, Googling herself. She doesn't touch her bagel, preferring to check the Internet every thirty seconds to see if the video is down. She bangs the keys each time she sees herself on the screen.

"Mom said it could take up to a day, Zoe." Lily's fingers tug Zoe's hand away from the monitor. "Stop torturing yourself." Zoe stares longingly at the balcony and the faraway sky, and I do my best to hush the noise buzzing in my head. *Is my daughter okay?* Her face bears the signs of a restless sleep.

Bobby slips into the room, and I can tell by his edginess he's not going to join us. *I'll never hurt you.* He does a good job at isolating himself, and Lily asks him what's wrong.

"Tired. Long travel day." He kisses the top of her head and walks over to Zoe's side of the table. She turns away from him; he doesn't even try to fix it.

To me he says, "I'll meet you in the lobby. Call me when you're close." I don't get up to straighten his tie or make him coffee, and he seems not to care.

"Everyone in this house is acting crazy." Lily sighs.

"Are you sure you want to go?" I ask Zoe. "It's okay if you stay home."

I can hardly make out her answer. Instead she grabs her backpack and stuffs it with her computer and the Tylenols I'd given her for a headache.

When we arrive at Thatcher after a drive that consists of me giving a pep talk to Zoe's one-word replies, I instruct Lily, "Please look out for your sister."

She pops a breath mint in her mouth. "I always do."

I watch them enter the building, joined by Shelby and Grace, who turn around to wave as I ride off.

I'm lost in thought and forget to call Bobby. As I near the corner of 26th and Collins, he calls. "I'm waiting in the lobby."

I turn into the circular drive; I see him before he sees me.

With the spate of cooler temperatures, he's dressed in a camel cashmere sweater with a gray collared shirt poking out. His black slacks frame his lean legs. He's chatting with the valet and bellman. They adore him; it shows on their faces. When he notices me waiting, he shakes their hands, gives them his warmest smile, and takes my place behind the wheel.

On the way to downtown, we touch on everything but Zoe. It's the kind of fall day that makes up for the fiery hot of summer. Bicyclists crowd the streets; dogs are out walking their caregivers. The air is clean and fresh. Inside the car we are suffocating.

"Have you met with the team about the wedding?" Bobby asks.

Shit. I forgot. "I'll talk to them this afternoon."

"We need a walkway for the wheelchair. And I want Mirielle to make those turkey sandwiches in the hot, buttery ciabatta rolls. Nothing fancy. But festive."

I yes him, because I'm kind of shocked that he can think about buttery sandwiches as we're heading to meet with lawyers about our daughter's video.

"Did you see in the paper today the Arsht Center is looking for someone?" he asks.

I turn to him with a fury in my eyes. "Seriously, Bobby? Like I can think about that now? The girls need me. Now more than ever."

He acts as though I've kicked him, and we refrain from talking. Whatever. I cross my arms at my chest and brush a hair off the top of my silk blouse. It's black. So are my pants. I've decided I'm in mourning.

The building in downtown is one of Miami's tallest. The circular drive through the parking garage makes me more nauseous than I already am. I hold on to the dashboard for support. We pass through the glass double doors and board one of the blocks of elevators. Bobby hits thirty-nine, and we stare at the walls in silence.

"Mrs. Ross. Mr. Ross." The petite blonde greets us in the lobby of the impressive modern office high in the sky. The views from any window capture the Miami skyline and east to the beaches. "Jo Jo Sturner." She smiles and gives us her hand. "And this is my investigator." She gestures at the wiry man by her side. "Javier Harden."

I appraise her. The young woman's gaze is firm, apologetic, and she reminds me of Reese Witherspoon with her turned-up nose and smiling blue eyes.

Bobby thanks her for seeing us on short notice, and we follow her through a maze of corridors to her office. She motions for us to sit across from her in matching chairs, while Javier stands nearby. We take her card from her outstretched hand.

"Nathan's a close friend. He's familiar with my work with the Cyber Civil Rights Legal Project, the pro bono work I do for online sexual abuse and harassment. Javier used to be with the State Attorney's office. He retired after 9/11; he specializes in cyber sex crimes. Most families don't know how to proceed. I'll lay down the groundwork, explain Zoe's rights, and provide facts about what we're dealing with."

Their combined sensitivity and grit are well matched. They assure us they are there to help. "Our number-one priority is your daughter's psychological health. Beyond that, there are victim's rights, and because she's a minor, strict laws are in place to protect her. I'll help you navigate the inner workings of the Internet, sexual cybercrimes,

162

and emerging laws, and Javier here can explain the scope of computer crimes. It'll be up to you to handle the toughest part—Zoe's emotional well-being."

A collection of grief prohibits me from saying much. "It's tough."

Jo Jo looks directly at me. "This doesn't define her. No one action ever does."

I want to believe that. The tears gather, ready to fall. A box of tissues sits on her desk.

Jo Jo sits up straighter. "Mrs. Ross, let's start at the beginning."

Hearing myself retell the story makes me uneasy. I'm sure the sharp pain between my eyes is defeat as I tell Jo Jo and the wordless Javier about the bathroom and the video Zoe got herself trapped in. "We thought the kids were deleting it."

Javier finds a notepad tucked inside his pocket. He doesn't look old enough to be retired, but 9/11 changed people. His fingers curl around a pen, and he asks, in perfect English but for the tiniest accent, "Do you have any idea if Zoe was coerced into the act, Mrs. Ross? Is there any indication she may have been harmed?"

"We have no reason to believe she was assaulted," Bobby says. "I'm not sure if she remembers or if she's being completely up front. This is very out of character for her."

"Can Zoe substantiate that the acts were consensual?" Javier asks.

I'm stone-faced. Fingernails cut into my palms.

"These are uncomfortable questions, Mrs. Ross," Javier continues. "We need the facts."

I dab at my eyes and continue. "They were drinking. Maybe someone slipped something into her drink. We'll never know, but she said it was consensual." The flush crawls up my back.

"I've been doing this a long time, Mr. and Mrs. Ross," says Jo Jo. "It's unpleasant. It might be a long, arduous process." She leans in closer. She has flawless skin. "But she has parents who love and support her."

Something in her drawl reels me in. What she says makes sense, but it's tough to accept when it's your child, the person you were supposed to save from everything, including herself.

"Teenagers don't have a clue as to the broader scope of their actions," Jo Jo says. "They think they live in an inviolable bubble that cushions them from threats. Javier can attest. If there's one thing we'd like to get through to the families, it's this: The Internet is like Pandora's box. Once you let something out and online, it's virtually impossible to put it back in. I tell folks, be watchful of recording devices, and be borderline paranoid of your surroundings."

Jo Jo turns this into everyday fodder, as though we're discussing teaching children to safely cross the street.

"Isn't it a little late for this conversation?" Bobby asks, the color draining from his skin.

I finger the collar of my blouse. Nervousness has me licking my lips until the lipstick is gone.

"We'd been firm with the girls," I say. "We talked about that stuff all the time."

"How serious is this?" Bobby asks.

Jo Jo leans forward when she replies. "Your daughter's a minor. If she was coerced in any way, or if someone drugged her, those are significant offenses, punishable by law. Further, whoever videoed her and shared it can be charged. However, it's exponentially worse once it hits the Internet. We're in the age of digital voyeurism, Technological Tom, as in Peeping. Child erotica, porn, sexting, they're all dangerous. Whoever filmed her is in trouble. And whoever watched it, and anyone who sent it to their friends can be charged with possession and distribution of child pornography. That means every kid at Zoe's school could face some form of penalty even if they did nothing but receive the video on their phone." She pauses while we absorb the severity. "Let me be clear. If an adult watches or shares the video, myself included, they can be charged, too. If convicted, they'll have to register as a sex offender."

I never fully appreciated the term *Coming out of my skin* until this very moment. The discomfort, the agony—it creeps up and down my arms and legs. This is criminal. I look at Bobby. His empty eyes stare at the floor.

"Look," Jo Jo begins, "it might be wise for all of you to talk to someone, professionally. Zoe needs a confidant she can trust, someone she feels she's not letting down. It's hard sometimes for a young girl to expose herself to her parents. There are counselors at the Cyber Civil Rights Initiative who work with victims, unfortunately, all the time."

"She's seeing the guidance counselor at school," I say.

"What about you two? How are you holding up?"

Neither of us responds.

Jo Jo shuffles papers on her desk. "You flagged the video as I instructed?"

"We did," I say.

She turns to her computer and types. "It's still there."

The news is a blow, and I wish there were a way to pull the Internet plug.

"Did Zoe have any indication she might have been videoed? Could she have videoed it herself?"

Bobby's indignant. "Zoe was videoed unknowingly."

Javier eyes us sympathetically. "Every parent wants to believe they know everything about their child. It's not always the case."

Excuse me, do I know you? No. No. No. I know my daughter. But the question gnaws at me.

Jo Jo interrupts my denials. "We've established that while Zoe's underage, she agreed to the acts performed in the video. Blood work at this time is pointless, and there's no evidence of physical assault. But there is a cybercrime. You said her face is identifiable?"

"Yes," I answer. "And it says her name. And the boy's."

Bobby clears his throat, and I stare at my clasped fingers. Jo Jo lets that sink in before moving forward. "The laws are getting tougher and stricter pertaining to sexting when a minor's involved. There's sexual cyberharassment and the distribution of child porn." The words spring from her mouth as though she's repeated them one too many times. "Sexual cyberharassment covers materials uploaded to the Internet, ones where the victim is clearly recognizable or identified. It does not cover those spread via texting. It's a lot of information I'm throwing at you, but you need to understand."

My head lowers farther toward my lap, and I'm studying my fingers and nails. I need clarity. With each second that passes there is a new fact to remember, a new concept to absorb. I should probably grab a pen and paper, but I'm afraid of what I'd do with a sharp object. I clench the chair handles instead. Bobby is pale and defenseless. We are sequestered in our seats, apart. And Jo Jo, she keeps talking.

Trying to decide which issue to deal with has me woozy. The room feels unsteady, as if it might collapse under the weight of our worry. Javier joins in, but I've shut my eyes and begun massaging my temples. The pain is worsening. I want Zoe. I need to be near her, comforting her, loving this away from her.

It's only then that I notice Jo Jo's clothes. Rather than focusing on what she's saying that has Javier writing furiously on his pad, I'm making note of the floral top and the navy slacks. The black flats with the silver buckle. Her fingers are bare of jewelry. What kind of person chose a field like this? The helplessness has to be agonizing.

"Why would someone do this to her?" I finally ask.

"Hurt people hurt people," Javier answers. "Their goal is to shame the victim with a virtual attack. The real slimy bastards download their cache to underground sites. They're virtually impossible to shut down." He opens and closes his eyes in deference. "We have no control at that point."

I'm washed down by debilitating fright. "What are you saying?" I stutter, unable to form a thought, shackled by a raging venom. "We may never get rid of this video? How can this be?"

Bobby's eyes change. Their warm brown shifts to black. The disappointment spreads across his face. "It's about choices," he says. "Why would anyone put themselves in this position?"

"Bobby." I'm unable to meet his gaze. "She had no idea this would happen."

"How do we know that?" he asks. "She may not even remember."

"I trust her!"

Javier stares down at his pad of paper.

"It's understandable to be upset," says Jo Jo.

"Maybe Emma will divorce me in twenty years and forget she has a video of us stashed in her hard drive."

Divorce. The word startles me, and I hardly hear the rest.

"Then she gets a virus," he continues, "and wham, we're an overnight sensation. It's not the people I trust who I worry about—it's the predators who hack into your private lives. I operate with a heightened sense of mistrust. Don't take chances. Be smart. That's the solution."

I know all about mistrust. Our eyes finally meet, and I don't recognize who's inside him.

"Mr. Ross," Jo Jo asserts, "you're correct in your vigilance, but kids today don't think in the abstract like we do. Right now, Zoe needs love and compassion. Support. We may never know the reasons why this happened, and you'll have to accept that, and her. Zoe's well-being relies on it."

It feels like a tiny victory, and Bobby backs down. I cross and uncross my legs before questioning Jo Jo. "Yesterday, my husband asked about YouTube's parameters for content. Can anyone post this stuff?"

Jo Jo feels around her bag and retrieves an inhaler. She takes two puffs before putting it back. The minor threat to her health almost goes unnoticed; she's composed and focused. "There's no way for YouTube or any of these sites to censor the amount of material uploaded daily. Monitors can flag explicit content, but there are simply too many uploads to review every single one. Once a video gets taken down, the same one often crops up on another site under a different account with a different name. It's the Internet version of Whac-A-Mole."

My voice shakes, and panic rises up my throat. "How do we stop it? How do we stop it from going to that underground place? Or to another site?"

"I know this is difficult to hear," she says, "but there's a possibility we may not. This is the reality we're facing. Internet crimes are radically different from a catfight in the cafeteria and, unfortunately, longer lasting." Her blue eyes narrow in regret. "I'm sorry. Technology is a predator with way too much power. I've seen more than my share of young girls in this situation. It's always somebody's daughter."

I let this threat coil around me and drag me underwater. It's always somebody's daughter. Now it's ours.

"We'll do everything we can to bring these criminals to justice," Jo Jo says. "Limiting distribution is key. Once we have that under control, we can focus on liability and recourse."

"Meaning?" asks Bobby.

"To upload to YouTube, you have to have a Google account. We have methods of following the tracks, and my people in law enforcement can expedite this through their subpoena power. We'll know pretty quickly if we're dealing with a juvenile or a more sophisticated cybercriminal. The latter has ways of hiding their identity." She pauses, checking the calendar on her desk. "Is Zoe able to meet with us today after school?"

Bobby searches my face for the answer.

"Sure." I nod.

"Great," Jo Jo says. "We'll come around four. Javier will get started on the preliminaries. We'll contact the boy's family as well. A full investigation."

At the mention of his name, Javier crosses the room to shake our hands. "I have young daughters, Mr. and Mrs. Ross. I'll treat your case as if Zoe were one of my own."

Jo Jo stands up and leads us out of her office. "I'm sorry we had to meet under these circumstances, Mr. and Mrs. Ross. Call me anytime. Day or night. Whatever you need. See you this afternoon."

CHAPTER 19

Our conversation on the ride home is bitter and short. Bobby drives with one hand on the wheel while the other massages his temple. "What was she thinking?"

I want to say, *She's a young, impressionable girl doing what a lot of girls do. Only she got caught.* I swallow it instead. My voice is shaky, but loud. "You have no idea how Zoe feels. You have no idea how she's suffering or why she did this. You do this. You judge. It hurts people. I know you can't believe what happened in that room, but your accusations . . . sitting on that pillar of moral virtue . . . Zoe made a mistake. She has to live with it. You're only making it worse."

He feels my gaze and turns.

"It's sad we can't be on the same side," I add.

He doesn't care. He ignores me, closing me out. When we get to the hotel, he disappears to his office, and I actually follow through on the wedding matters. Oozy butter sandwiches and all.

The girls walk in after school, and I pull Zoe aside to ask about her day. She sulks. "I survived." I inform her of Jo Jo's visit. Her eyes glaze over, and her shoulders sag from her backpack. "I can't."

"Zoe, we have to. What this person did . . . we can't let them get away with it. Or do it to someone else."

"I don't want to talk about it anymore."

I won't give up on her. I won't let her give up on herself. "You have to."

"I want it to end. I want to make it go away."

I wish for that, too, but not by burying it. My daughter must stand up for herself and fight. She must do what I was too afraid to do.

They unload their computers at the kitchen table, and Zoe types in her name. "It's still not down."

Bobby comes through the door, and his nearness puts me on the defensive. He doesn't joke with the girls about recent Instagram posts from Random Turtle and UberFacts or join in the conversation when the girls bring up a summer trip. Today he's closed off and focused on revenge.

"I got an A on the Spanish project," Lily says.

He half smiles. "Good job, Lil."

"Mr. Harmon is pressuring me about debate," offers Zoe. "I'm excused from practice and the next tournament, but I don't want to do it anymore. Period. I can't imagine being the center of anything right now. Why doesn't anyone listen?"

"Debate looks good for college," he says without looking at her. He opens the refrigerator, asking for blueberries. He loves blueberries.

"I'll call downstairs and have them send some up," I say.

He's annoyed. I'm a terrible wife. Luckily for me his phone rings, and he takes the call in the other room. Zoe follows him, but it's to go to the bathroom and put in the new contacts I bought.

"Daddy's acting really weird," Lily says.

"He's got a lot going on with work. And he's very worried about your sister."

The front desk texts me, letting me know that Jo Jo and Javier are on their way up.

I meet the pair at the door and usher them toward the kitchen. Jo Jo is poised, admiring our views along the way. Lily looks up from her phone and smiles.

"Zoe?" Jo Jo asks.

"Lily," she corrects her. "Nice to meet you."

Zoe returns with fresh eyes.

Jo Jo's expression is part sympathetic and part fearless. She introduces herself and extends her hand. "I'm an attorney. And this is Javier Harden. He's a private investigator."

Zoe and Jo Jo study each other while Javier nods his greeting and vanishes to the periphery. Zoe caves into herself, shrinking before my very eyes.

Lily watches her sister, waits, then asks, "Do you want me to go in the other room?"

"No," I say. "You stay here. We'll go into the living room."

"Unless Zoe wants me to stay," she adds, searching her sister's eyes.

Zoe tells her it's fine. "Finish your homework. At least one of us will pass ninth grade." A signal passes between them that's hard to miss.

"Listen to them, Zoe," Lily whispers. "They're here to help."

Jo Jo takes a seat on our couch and offers Zoe the space beside her. I sit on the other side so she feels me close. Her body hunches over as if she's fighting the temptation to flee. Bobby walks in and shakes their hands before sitting across from us. He doesn't look at me. He's cracking his knuckles and tense. Javier, with his slight frame and trimmed goatee, prefers to stand.

"Am I in trouble?" Zoe asks, her blue eyes wide.

It's hard for me to watch her. Blotches cover her skin and her features are tight, pressed on her face. My eyes rest on the gray fabric hiding the part child, part woman underneath, a contradiction of age and body and mind. Her posture closes her off, but she is bursting to grow up.

"I didn't know you girls were twins," Jo Jo says. "It must be fun."

Zoe stares ahead blankly. "It's all right." She folds deeper into the couch and sneaks a glimpse at Javier. "Am I in trouble?" she asks again. "I know I'm in trouble with my parents, but with the police?"

"Zoe," Jo Jo begins, her blue eyes full of sympathy, "I was telling your mom and dad how I work for people who have had Internet crimes committed against them."

Zoe blinks.

"You're a child in the eyes of the justice system," Jo Jo continues, "and no matter how this video came to be, we have laws against filming them, laws against posting them on the Internet, or even sending them to a friend through a text."

I can tell by the way Zoe is fidgeting with the string on her hoodie that she is spooked.

"You're not in trouble," Jo Jo reassures her. "We're here to help."

"What about the video?" Zoe asks. "When will it come down?"

Jo Jo's high-pitched voice hammers away at the quiet. "As of about fifteen minutes ago, the video's officially down. It didn't have many views . . . a couple hundred."

Bobby stretches back in his chair. "Thank God."

I'm partially listening. I'm thinking of Zoe and how a couple hundred people have now formed their opinions of my daughter. How they're judging her. Laughing. And God only knows what else. Jo Jo's trying to make it better by saying we're lucky, how it wasn't thousands or hundreds of thousands. That it's very contained.

I want to tell her there's no such thing when it's your daughter engaged in sexual activity on a video on the Internet. Will she ever be able to apply for a job without it coming up? Will it affect her entrance to college? I stare at Zoe's face while the thoughts attack.

"If it's okay with you, Zoe," Jo Jo says, "we'd like to ask a few questions and figure out what happened that night."

"Why?" I think Zoe is about to cry again. "What's it going to change?"

"Zoe, just listen to Ms. Sturner," Bobby says.

I don't tell her what to do. I move in closer and let her feel me near.

"You have rights," says Jo Jo, "and you have to defend those rights. We're not going to ask only you questions. We're going to ask Price Hudson the same ones, and anyone who received the video."

Zoe pulls the sleeves of her hoodie down past her wrists so her hands are hidden. "You may as well bring in the whole school." She groans. "Stuff like this gets around quicker than a Snapchat."

"Only it doesn't disappear in twenty-four hours."

Jo Jo's knowledge of the girls' favorite social stream seems to pique Zoe's interest. She turns in my direction, because she's beginning to understand the gravity of what she's up against.

"I know this doesn't feel good," I say. "I know it hurts. I'm here."

Jo Jo sets down her legal pad, and her eyes tell Zoe she's here to fight for her, too. "We're going to do everything we can to fix this."

The momentary rally of support softens Zoe's face. "Okay."

"Miss Ross," Javier begins, fixing his attention on Zoe. He has a nice voice, deep and full. "Do you have any idea who might've recorded you?"

She shakes her head.

"Did anyone threaten you?"

Another shake of her head.

"Was there anything out of the ordinary that night? Anything that stands out?"

"Other than a bunch of teenagers drinking and being stupid?"

Javier cracks a reassuring smile, and Zoe lightens.

"Is there anyone who would benefit from posting about you?"

She carries the weight of all of us on her shoulders. Her eyes stare down at the floor. "There were only the two of us in the room. No one else was around. I don't know who would do this."

"Think about your surroundings."

She shakes her head again. "I would know if someone else was there. There wasn't."

"What about the boy? His friends? Could they have set you up?"

"No."

"Zoe, you didn't film this, did you? Sometimes kids do it for fun. They think no one will see it."

"Okay, enough!" shouts Bobby, standing in Javier's face. "I've told you, someone filmed her. My daughter's not responsible for this!"

I should be angry, but his reaction only makes me feel sorry for him.

"I would never do that," Zoe cries. "And Price wouldn't either."

Jo Jo waves her hand in the air. "Zoe, some of our questions might make you uncomfortable. It's understandable. We're building a case, and we need to cover every angle."

Bobby's hunched over, eyes locked on the floor.

I tell myself to let them do their job, but I'm really thinking, *These strangers are in our home, watching our every move, deciding if we're evil or just plain stupid.*

Bobby's inner agony is impossible to rein in. "You're all sitting here talking about this video like it's not my child. Like it's some random person . . ." He stops himself, because the pain is too hard to share. "My daughter . . . someone exploited her." He sits and puts his head in his hands, saying, finally, "I don't understand how this happened."

"I didn't know, Daddy!" Zoe wails. "I didn't know someone would be filming me!"

I catch his eyes, and he scowls at me. It feels like I've been stabbed.

"Zoe," I whisper, tucking her hair back off her face, "we know you didn't have anything to do with the video. We know."

"You can't excuse her like that, Emma."

When I speak, my voice to Bobby is vehement. "You need to stop. You need to stop right now."

174

Lily comes in and bends over the couch to defend Zoe. "Leave her alone!" she shouts. The girls have never raised their voices to him before. "You're making it worse!"

"He hates me!" Zoe shouts, her face red.

"I don't hate you, Zoe," he says, but he doesn't look at her either. It's a failed attempt, weak and unconvincing. "I hate what you did."

"Take it back!" I shout. "Take it back now!"

"Mr. Ross," interrupts Jo Jo, perturbed, "Zoe needs your support. If you're unwilling or unable to provide it, I suggest you leave the room."

Indecision spreads across his face. He turns to Jo Jo when he says, "It's not that simple . . . do you have a daughter?"

"I don't," she says, "and perhaps that puts me in a better position to be objective."

My eyes blink in disbelief when Bobby stands.

"Dad?" Zoe says, her teary eyes wide.

Slowly, he walks out of the room. Every fiber of my being tells me to get up and follow him. The sensations scream *Just do it. Introduce him to Emma Grant. She's flawed. Imperfect. Like his daughter.* But Zoe needs me more. Lily goes after him in my place.

"You okay there, Zoe?" Javier asks.

Her bottom lip quivers. She sniffles. Nods.

"We can stop for today, if you'd like."

I like the kindness in Javier's voice. How his eyes train on Zoe with concern. She feels it, too.

"Let's finish," she says.

"Do you have possession of the video? Did you send it to anyone?"

The look she gives him means she'd have to be crazy to forward the video.

"I'm not trying to scare you. The laws haven't caught up with the technology, and the way in which we proceed depends on your answers. They'll trigger different laws."

Zoe rubs her eyes. It's exhausting and a lot for her mind to process.

"We'll need a list of everyone at the party that night," says Jo Jo. "Your close friends, anyone you know who got a copy. I'd also like your cell phone and your computer."

"My dad has my phone," she says.

As Jo Jo speaks of lists and laws, Bobby returns to our fold, followed by Lily. He sits, but he's still agitated. His leg bounces; I want to reach across the room and slap it. We avoid each other. Our eyes. Our bodies. Nothing connects us, and it makes everything going on in the room feel worse.

Jo Jo turns to me. "The person who videoed your daughter might not be the same person who uploaded it to the Internet."

"Then we go after both of them," Bobby says.

"Javier's made some calls. Our friends are happy to pull favors, especially when kids are involved. But before we go down this road, be clear of your intentions. Some families think the exposure and vulnerability isn't worth it—not to them, not to their child, even to the accused. Then we have families who see no way to heal other than retribution. Make no mistake, there are devastating repercussions associated with sexting and cybercrimes. Being underage doesn't protect you anymore. And once we find the person, it's up to you to decide to press charges. All we have to do is alert the authorities to make this an official case."

As if sensing our disconnect, she lowers her tone and says, "Talk to each other. Make an informed decision."

Bobby speaks up. "I won't feel bad for going after someone who's deliberately hurting my daughter."

"I'm simply telling you the impact it's going to have, Mr. Ross. The consequences are far-reaching, and it can drag on for some time." She holds his stare until he's the one to look away.

I'm relieved she doesn't tell Zoe how once a video is uploaded to the Internet, it makes it almost impossible to take down. How the underground trolls can snatch it, burying it in their polluted holes.

"This isn't my first rodeo," she says. "I've helped hundreds of victims across the country. I'll do whatever it takes for the sake of justice."

Jo Jo motions for Javier, and the pair stand up. "It's been a long day," she says. "We'll leave you all to mull this over. I'll be in touch."

Zoe hugs my chest, and I rock her back and forth like I did when she was a baby. Jo Jo gives Javier instructions, and I'm through listening. Bobby walks them to the elevator.

When he returns, he runs his fingers through his hair. "What a mess."

Zoe jumps off the couch and approaches him with her hands on her hips. "You think it's hard for you? What about me?" If she has any tears left, they're tucked away.

He won't face her.

"I know how you feel about me, Daddy."

"No, you don't, Zoe. You'll never know how I feel about you . . ." He stuffs down the despair, but it leaks through. "You'll never know how much I wish I could make this go away. To protect you. To save you. You'll never understand until you have your own child . . ."

It hurts to watch him weak and powerless, but it hurts worse to question his sincerity. I'm not sure how much of it is motivated by love or by the desire to erase what's happened.

"I just wish you used better judgment. That's all."

"You see?" she says. "You ruin everything!" And she storms off to her room.

I turn to him. "When's the persecution going to end?"

He shakes his head, unable to answer.

We settle in for dinner, and Zoe picks at her food.

Bobby sits across from her and struggles to speak. "I'm sorry, Zoe." It's unfeeling and mildly sincere.

Zoe hisses, "You can't take it back."

The only sounds are the scrapes of our utensils against the plate. I try to swallow. Each spoonful is a struggle.

Lily tries to change the subject. She brings up Chelsea's birthday dinner tomorrow night. "It's at the Edition," she says.

The Edition is one of the newer hotels and has an ice-skating rink and bowling alley. There's also a club, the Basement.

"You should let Zoe come," she says.

"She's grounded," Bobby growls.

"I wouldn't want to go anyway," Zoe says, chewing on a piece of steak. "Walking into that party would be like walking in naked."

Bobby spills his cup of water, and I don't move to clean it up.

"It's a dinner," Lily argues. "Her parents will be there. She's our best friend!"

I give him *the look*, but he doesn't budge.

"I'm not making this mistake again, Emma. They need supervision, not running around South Beach hotels."

"You have to trust them again," I say. *You'll have to trust me again.*

"Am I allowed to have the girls over to the pool tomorrow?" Lily asks.

I look to Zoe.

"It's fine," she says.

"Are you sure, Zoe? Lily can go to one of their houses . . ."

"They're my best friends, Mom. It's fine."

The rest of the conversation is stilted and bare. Bobby asks if we've heard anything from *Ocean Drive*, and we discuss Kinsley's wedding. Safe subjects that don't evoke reaction.

Lily brings up the party again, but Bobby shuts her down. Zoe excuses herself from the table and heads toward the china cabinet. With the Shabbat candlesticks in hand, she opens the drawer where we keep our candles and matches.

That's when I realize what day it is. We're not religious, but the candle lighting is something we look forward to each Friday at sundown. Particularly Zoe. She came home from Sunday school years ago quoting her teacher, Mrs. Landman. "Mommy, we have to prepare the home for peace and harmony. We have to light the candles on Friday nights." Since then, we haven't missed the practice.

Same prayer. Same white candles. The girls stand, welcoming the Sabbath with their hands. They cover their faces. When they finish, the flames brighten their cheeks, and I think we might be okay. We have this ritual connecting us, always reminding us of our love for one another. That despite everything, there is always a glimmer of hope.

But all the sameness has changed. My arms are around the girls. Bobby is off to the side. I want to yank him close, the holiness of the Sabbath guiding me, but my emotions make it impossible. The candles warm my cheeks, and I stare into their bright glow.

I pray for peace and harmony this Shabbat.

I also pray for forgiveness.

CHAPTER 20

I'm stuck inside a dream. Teenage Bobby whispers his worry in my ear: "All night, Emma. I thought you were with him." I was facing my bedroom mirror at the time: you're a liar, Emma Grant. And I heard my mother's voice: "You share your body with someone you love." The voices were coming at me, and I dropped my head into my hands and screamed.

"Emma!" Bobby shakes me awake.

I'm covered in sweat, shouting words that make no sense.

"You're having a bad dream," he says.

Only it's not a dream. The pounding of my heart begins to settle, and I tell him I'm fine, though my voice is unsure. Rather than comfort me, he rolls back over.

It's dawn, and there's no sense trying to sleep. I get out of bed and watch the sun rise from our balcony. There's something calming about the rising flame rippling on the water. New beginnings await. Zoe was right. The sun is the one glorious thing we can count on each day.

The memory eclipses what comes so beautifully and naturally. There's Bobby, after our fight, professing his love to me, apologizing for the things he said. I'm clutching the phone, mouthing the words back. After what I'd done, did *I love you* hold any weight? *Do I know you?* he asks. He should've known me. He should've seen right through me, but distance destroyed the ability to read each other's eyes. Of course Bobby's mad with Zoe. He would've been furious with me. I would've lost him forever.

He was so relieved that morning when I said, "No, I wasn't with him." What pained me brought him joy. Days later he was still focusing on those hours we were out of touch. "I can't imagine either one of us being with anyone else. You're the only girl I've ever wanted." Like that, all the joy faded, like swirling water down a drain. It took with it my pride, and guilt became the sinister badge that followed me around. That's how quickly my "fun" turned into shame. Monty and I resumed our roles. Acting. The game of pretend. I was angry I'd given him a piece of me. Resentful. He was the blip on the radar I could never take back. He didn't deserve what I gave him. The hostility. The rejection. *How did I let it get so far?* It was me I hated. The embarrassment too great.

Word got around, as it usually does. *Emma Grant cheated on her fiancé!* The snickers and sneers when I walked into the theater were hurtful. Or worse, how they stopped talking when I approached.

But none of the sabotage, either external or self-inflicted, prepared me for the blue line that revealed I was pregnant. To add insult to injury, I had no idea who might be the father. It was a time of inner torment, a great struggle to hide a life-altering betrayal. The stress spread throughout my body, and I fell ill, though the nausea-laced symptoms could have been maternal. How would I tell Bobby? How could I keep this secret that would seep into our forever—a lifetime of lies? With no one to turn to, I retreated within myself. It was a lonely time marked by a quiet suffering. I went to sleep each night with parts of me broken, impossible to repair. I loved Bobby. I was sure of that, but what was love without the truth?

Hours later, I escape the haunted past in a lounge chair by the pool. Bobby is playing golf with Jonny at Doral, and I'm left to read the newspaper and dissect current events in my head. Both print and real life. I attempted to lure him to the cabana with me, a pastime we both enjoyed. He brushed me aside. "Another time," he had said. When we went our separate ways in the lobby, my eyes pressed against his backside, willing him to turn around. He refused.

The girls and their friends are lined up in nearby lounges. Zoe seems more relaxed among those she trusts, and I'm happy to see her interacting like she once used to do. I'm under an umbrella fully clothed, reading the *New York Times* because I'm too old for half my bathing suits and terrified of skin cancer.

The article I'm attempting to read has me questioning if my diet is gut friendly when I hear Shelby say, "Why are you going after the person who recorded the video? I mean, why put yourself through it? Just be done with it. That's what I'd do."

The girls are in a row. Lily's in the middle, Zoe's on the outside next to Grace. Chelsea is the first to respond to Shelby's comment. "I'd want to know," she says, her dark hair pulled on top of her head. "And I'd want them to pay for what they did."

"Maybe," Shelby says, lathering herself up with a fresh layer of sunscreen. "I guess I'd want it to go away. Fast."

Grace is playing with her phone and not joining in. At least one of them has common sense.

Zoe rolls over onto her stomach. The frown lines sour her face. "You'll never understand what it feels like," she says, dragging her words. "Not unless it happens to you. And I wouldn't wish it upon my worst enemy."

Shelby holds her phone up while she talks, snapping pictures of the sky, the trees, herself. "You can count on us. You know that."

The support touches Zoe. It's not the sun turning her face and neck red.

Shelby continues. "I heard they're coming to all our houses. They may have to search our computers."

"I don't think they'll come to our house," Grace says, releasing her honey-blonde hair from an elastic band. "My father will just tell his friends at the station that I'm your friend."

"They came to my house this morning," admits Chelsea. "They wanted to know if I knew where the video was filmed. If I recognized the background. Then they asked if anyone had a problem with Zoe. If they ever threatened her—"

Lily interrupts. "Hey, guys! We're talking about my sister like she's not here. Can we talk about something else?"

That's when Zoe calmly asks, "Do any of you know anything about who filmed the video?" She pauses, brushing her hair with her fingers. "You can tell me, you know."

"I asked Ava," says Shelby. "She says nobody's talking. Nobody's ratting out their friends."

"How do you know it's a friend?" asks Grace. "It could be anyone."

I listen and fight to keep my mouth shut. The conversation deflates me. I want to guard Zoe from their ignorance, but I know I can't intervene. All signs point to a "friend," but I will never believe it. No one can be that cruel.

The rest of the afternoon is spent listening for clues. Hints. Anything to help me understand the dynamic of these kids. The girls, like Zoe, have no idea of the severity of the case. In some ways, their naiveté is refreshing. Zoe's lucky to have a close, supportive group. After some time, I get bored hearing about boys, Netflix, and Chelsea's upcoming birthday. And when they order lunch, I'm relieved to see Zoe smile again.

The ongoing argument about Chelsea's party ends in a stalemate. Lily goes. Zoe accompanies Jonny to Cirque de Soleil. We had invited her to be with us, at least I did, but she was actually looking forward to the time with her uncle. He had a way of comforting her that none of us could.

In happier times, Bobby and I might have made an evening of the drop-off. We'd stop in at Market or the bar at the Matador Room with our friends. Tonight Bobby says he needs to get back to the hotel and work. I am prickly mad.

"Why'd you even bother coming?" I ask, which is met with more of his empty stare. His exchange with Lily as we reached the valet had been impersonal and brief—he may as well have been her Uber driver—but it was better than the empty wave he'd given Zoe across our living room.

We're heading south on Collins and only a few blocks from the Ross. The traffic lights, a blur of green, yellow, and red, reflect on the windshield, mixing with an earlier drizzle. Charlie Puth plays on the radio, and I turn the dial to make it louder. It's a song Bobby knows I love, the one Puth sings with Selena that we'd duet together. Tonight he shoves my hand away and mutes their silky voices. "I have a headache," he says, and his abruptness cuts deep inside.

The light shifts from yellow to red, and a rush of emotion overwhelms me. I reach for the door handle and look at Bobby one more time before unclicking my seat belt and pushing the door open. I can't be in here one second longer.

"Emma!" he shouts, but it's too late. I'm gone, taking off on the crowded sidewalk, hiding my sadness among a sea of strangers. The streets are narrow and difficult to maneuver in heels, but more so on a Saturday night in season. It'll be impossible for him to get to me, but Bobby might find a way. I don't know where I'm going. The jeans I'm wearing hug my hips and thighs, slowing me down. I hear him honking, which incites the other drivers, and they honk back, cursing at him to get out of their way.

I slip inside the throngs of people strolling up and down the street. Young couples in flip-flops and shorts. Scantily clad women. They steer themselves on platformed feet, and nearby men gawk. All walks of life. All heading toward something or someone. And then there's me, walking away. The Ross is a mere block ahead. I can't go back. What once welcomed me and sustained the balanced rhythm of my heart is now a sentence in isolation. I need to be somewhere else, somewhere that doesn't remind me that I am somebody's mom. And how much it can hurt.

The Sagamore comes into view, and I take the steps to the rounded driveway. We'd always had an affable relationship with the hotel and recommended each other's properties or amenities when in need. I long to tuck myself into something familiar yet foreign. The Sagamore lobby with its trendy, bustling crowd is just the place.

I take an empty seat at the bar and signal for the bartender. He greets me with a smile.

"Mrs. Ross, nice to see you again." I'm polite and friendly, but offer very little. He hands me a Perrier with lime, and I thank him for remembering. I twist around to study the crowds filling the nearby tables.

Bobby descends on me before I have a chance to take a sip. He is large and looming, regret in his eyes. "Emma."

The bartender greets him, though Bobby rebuffs his pleasantries.

"Leave me alone, Bobby," I say, wresting my arm from his grip.

"What are you doing?" he demands.

I can't take the pounding of his stare. Sliding off the stool, I grab the Perrier and make off into the crowd. He's behind me, dropping cash on the bar, and follows me down the bright hallway covered in expensive art. When I exit the doors to the pool and beach, I'm greeted by the sound of loud music on the patio below. A party is in full swing, and hundreds of guests spread across the lawn, dancing and celebrating. I make it to the bottom of the stairs, and a Caribbean tune overtakes me, buoying me in its rhythm.

I'm floating through the crowd, my white, off-the-shoulder top rustling in the breeze. I let myself relax to the music. It's not long before

Bobby takes hold of my fingers and leads me away. I don't resist. The rhythm steers me. I shut my eyes and let him guide me the way he did long ago.

The area is enclosed by security and tall shrubs. Beach access is restricted, and there is nowhere for us to go. He presses my hand tighter in his, leading me to the edge of the property. The music isn't as loud, but the vibration cushions us as we stand face-to-face. Nearby, a tiki torch burns.

"You promised you'd never hurt me," I say, placing my empty glass on the rim of the wooden fence. He stares past me at the ocean. I say it again. "You're hurting me." The words break through the noise around us and crash into him.

He whispers, "I'm doing the best I can."

"It's not enough."

His palm sweeps across my face, and he stares into my eyes like when we were kids and I'd give in. This time, I turn away. His fingers slip down my neck and along my shoulder.

I have to move. I step back, and his hand drops. "That won't work." Torment fills his eyes. "You need to talk to me, not touch me."

He comes closer. His breath is all that's between us. "I love you," he says.

"No." I shake my head. "We need to talk about Zoe."

He turns away. "You think I hurt you?" he asks, his voice rising over the drumming sounds around us. "What about what she did? *That hurts.*"

The beach is so beautiful. The breeze caressing the waves. The smell of salt. But his words chase it all away. There's nothing beautiful about being here with him.

"I don't know how to love her," he says, looking back down at the ground.

And then I have to say it. "You loved me when I wasn't perfect. I've made mistakes."

"What do you want from me?" he asks, his eyes trained on my face, unaware that I'm inching toward the truth. "How did this happen, Em? How did this happen to our girl? One minute she was five, climbing on my back, and the next she's . . ." He can't finish. The only time I'd seen him this grief-stricken was at his parents' funeral. The music blares, loud and pervasive.

"I try," he says. "I tell myself, *Today I'm going to talk to her . . . I'm going to take her to that juice bar she likes, and she'll sit and talk to me, and she'll be Zoe again, drinking her favorite smoothie.*"

"She'll always be Zoe."

"Do you remember the first day of preschool? She grabbed our legs and wouldn't let go."

I nod, blinking back the tears.

"And the time she asked us where babies came from, and we told her from in here?" He points at his chest.

I finish the sentence for him. My voice is hoarse and dry. "We told her that Mommy and Daddy's hugs created her and her sister."

"And she believed us."

"It was true," I say.

"Then why wasn't it enough?" he asks. I search his eyes for some fleeting recognition of family, some memory of what once was—how it could still be—but he's lost inside himself, and I can't break through. "Why the hell wasn't it enough?"

I'm going to tell him the truth. Right now. He needs to know. He needs to know who I am so he understands love and acceptance and how nothing is ever as it seems.

"There are girls who are okay with their sexuality, Bobby. They accept themselves. They make peace with it."

"Impossible," he says. "No young girl can feel good about that kind of behavior."

"Is that what you think?"

"That boy used her!"

187

I try not to sound defensive. I try to sound calm. "What if she used him?"

"Are you crazy?" His eyes narrow, and a scowl covers his face. "What did she get out of it? Girls like that do shit like that because they feel bad about themselves. They think getting with a boy will make them likable. It gives them some bullshit confidence boost."

I stare into his eyes. *Is that what it was for me? Is that what you think?* All this time, Zoe's been trying to tell me something. She doesn't feel the way I felt. She never felt the way I felt. I'm the one who needs to be like her. And the first step is telling him the truth.

"Bobby." It begins as a whisper. "There's something I want to tell you."

But his phone rings. Of course it rings. He walks away from me, the noise, and the music. I follow while my heart pounds so loudly it drowns out the sounds. *She's not you,* I remind myself. *She's living with her truth. Accepting it.* The idea begins to free me from the well of despair I'd been drowning in. *It's going to be okay.* He'll be angry, but he'll understand.

He covers his ear with one hand and holds the phone with the other. "Speak up, I can't hear you."

I'm ready. As soon as he hangs up.

"Wait, can you repeat that?"

I practice saying it again. "Bobby, I have something to tell you."

The beating of my heart continues, louder and sharper. Bobby moves the phone between us and puts Jo Jo on speaker. "The person who uploaded the video didn't cover their tracks. The IP address is irrefutable."

She must be using her inhaler, because I hear the faint whistle through the speaker. When the sound fades, she says, "We'll have the name very soon."

I'd reached the top of the mountain but was told there was another one to climb. The dread of what's to come moves closer and closer, like the waves along the beach. My courage drifts back out to sea. The secret folds itself back up, but it no longer fits inside. I have no choice but to wait.

"This is good, right?" He's yelling over the music and wind. "We can catch the person?"

Jo Jo is silent. When she addresses us, her voice is cautious. "There's more. As predicted, all evidence confirms it's a peer. Someone who goes to school with the girls, most likely a friend or acquaintance."

I am shaking my head. Nameless and faceless was much easier to accept.

"This makes it tricky," she says.

I let it simmer and find Bobby's eyes. He's cursing at the sea.

"I'll call you tomorrow," she says. "Hang in there. We're close."

He leans against the fence, and the ocean's wails sound a lot like his cries. I stand beside him and feel the wind against my face. I was moments from shattering his reality. Now we're faced with a different wound. He makes no effort to console me. The remoteness of it all hurts, reminding me how far apart we are. The bargaining returns. It started with praying it wouldn't be some sexual deviant filming Zoe through a window. Now it's praying it's not someone we know.

"They're no friend to Zoe if they can do something like this," he says, more to the black sky than to me. "This was deliberate. I have no problem going after them and their entire family."

"I can't believe this," I say.

"Believe it," he sneers. "I told you this was bad. I told you she messed up."

Oh, Zoe. We all mess up. "This is going to destroy her," I say.

He backs away from the railing and heads toward the crowd. I follow him. The music blares. People laugh and shout. Suddenly, the noise feels like it's suffocating me. I hold my hands to my ears and try to keep up with Bobby. He walks fast, as though it'll make everything around him disappear. Soon we're on the street and the short path connecting the two hotels. I am behind him. There's more than a foot between us.

We cross through the doors of the Ross with our heads bowed low. He says, "This is unconscionable."

The lights are dimmed, and the soft candlelight exudes warmth. The glow makes the floors appear flawless, but it's easy to be fooled. It's unconscionable, and he doesn't know the half of it.

When we arrive upstairs, we don't talk about what we've learned. He's plotting revenge, and I'm still bargaining. He pours himself a drink and closes himself off in his office. I switch on the TV and wait for the girls. After an hour, he joins me, and I play Words With Friends on my phone while he flips through the news and *Saturday Night Live*. He's on one side of the couch, and I'm on the other. During commercials, he mutes the TV, and the only sound is the clinking of the ice in his glass. When I look at him, all I see is disgust on his face.

When he finally came to visit me in Vermont six weeks later, the traces of that night lingered on my body. The touch of his fingers made me freeze up; it wasn't easy letting him in. I was in a state of constant fear that he'd find out, that we'd be somewhere and someone would slip. And when his hands rubbed against my belly, I froze. His fingers splayed across my secret made me jump from the bed and into the bathroom, where I proceeded to vomit. He eyed me curiously, counting back to his last visit. "Are you feeling okay?" He even chuckled when he said, "Maybe you're pregnant."

And in bed, when he whispered in my ear, "I want a daughter one day who looks just like you," my face gave it away.

"Emma?" he asked, suddenly sitting up. "Are you pregnant?"

We were a couple about to be married. It wasn't planned, but even the best-laid plans went awry.

"Oh my God," he said, a smile covering his face. "You're pregnant!"

He was so happy, I didn't have the heart to let him down. He mistook my tears for joy, and the blank expression on my face for something else. "We're getting married, Em! We're going to be a family! With our little baby." He placed his hand on my stomach, kissed me gently on the lips, then pulled back, smiling ear to ear.

I stared hard into his eyes while thoughts burned my pupils: *How can you not see through me? Love means you'd know I'm a liar.* And that's when I understood what it means to know someone, *really* know someone.

He wrapped me in his arms, already convinced it was a girl, and took the news home with him to Miami. We'd agreed to keep it our secret, *my dirty little secret*, and the shame made me physically sick. The stress shook me to the very core, and the resolution came a week later in the form of stabbing cramps and a fiery red liquid.

I had miscarried.

Feelings of relief and sadness mingled, though Bobby was devastated. He mourned the baby girl who would've looked like me, while I bit back a well of tears. I accepted my fate as a sign of some greater power. I'd never know if it was my greatest loss or my greatest shot at a second chance.

I swathed myself in the cocoon of wedding plans and buried the terrible slip. We would be husband and wife; we would have plenty of time to think about children. I also quit acting that final semester, something I loved more than anything.

Time went on, and the wound healed. There were moments I felt guilty and exposed. When we'd hear of a couple's indiscretion, when we'd talk about trust with the girls—being honest with us whatever the cost. And when we recited to one another *"Solo tú,"* I'd freeze but quickly bounce back. Cover it with the love I felt. Deep love. I was an actress. I slipped inside the new role, the memories began to fade, and we were again Emma and Bobby. And I marched forward with a good life, a healthy marriage, and two girls he was sure looked just like me. The past was where it belonged, behind us. There was no sense looking back.

His laugh startles me, and I blink. He has no idea where my mind has traveled, but I'm going to tell him.

The girls come in simultaneously, because it always happens that way with twins. Lily talks a mile a minute about the Edition and how the manager, Scott, let them go bowling after dinner. "Everyone asked for you, Zoe. You were missed."

Zoe smiles, but she also looks tired and uninterested. She doesn't sit for very long. She's careful to take a seat next to me on the couch, far from her father.

"How was the show?" he asks.

"Good."

"You hungry?"

"No."

I brush her hair with my fingers. He doesn't look at her when he asks. He focuses on Michael Che on the *SNL* news, and she follows Lily to their room. I am sick for what she's about to learn and the cruelty of it all. Then I wonder if the person who did this was at the girls' birthday party. And I can't think of anything worse than a friend's betrayal.

"I'm going to bed," I announce.

When I'm almost out of the room he asks, "What is it you wanted to tell me?"

I stand there contemplating turning around and emptying my soul. Every nerve and muscle in my body wants to get rid of it, but something stops me. Maybe it's Zoe. Maybe it's fear. Whatever it is, I back away. "Nothing."

CHAPTER 21

Morning arrives with a surge of threats. In my latest dream, Bobby screams. He knows the truth, and I'm chasing him down a dark, deserted street. He won't stop. He won't turn around. I'm running and the road zigzags and I can't see him. All is black. I wake up trembling. I lift myself out of the bed and go into the bathroom, where I study myself in the mirror.

The wide glass can't hide what's in front of me: brown hair tickling the bridge of my shoulders, delicate features, gray eyes framed by thin eyebrows. My complexion was always my best feature, making me look years younger than the other moms, but today the shadows and lines are more pronounced. I tug on my forehead to see what I'd look like with a face-lift, an injection, anything. I'd definitely look more awake and alert. When I let go, the skin puckers in its usual spots. Concealer has become a very good friend.

I see him in the mirror as he comes up behind me. His face is worn. The youthfulness all but vanished. He avoids getting too close and hovers in the doorway. I step out of my pajama bottoms and drop them in the hamper.

"How long are we going to do this?" I ask, as he slides closer and sits on its metal top.

"As long as I have to. As long as someone is held responsible."

I'm wearing nothing, only my silky pajama top, grazing my thighs. It makes what's coming out of my mouth more difficult to say. "Isn't there a way to fight your cause without treating her like some cheap whore?"

Neither of us hear Zoe approach, but she enters the bathroom and drops her beach bag on the floor. "Is that what you think of me?" she cries. "Jesus, Mom, put on some clothes."

I wrap a towel around my waist and move toward her, but she pulls away.

"Zoe, that's not what I meant . . . you misunderstood!"

"I understood perfectly!" she screams.

I gaze at Bobby, pleading for his help. He's tight-lipped, which makes it worse. "Zoe, you're taking it out of context."

"You called me a whore!" Her flip-flops smack the floor as she storms away from us and into our bedroom.

Each time I hear the word I cringe a little inside. I try to get closer. "That's not what I meant . . ."

"But that's what you think. That's what everybody thinks."

Bobby lets me fight her. Alone. I'm pissed, but I have to convince her. I can't let her think I'd ever call her that horrible name.

"No, honey," I argue, in her face, latching on to her eyes. "That's not true."

"How can you say that?" she pleads, tugging on her terry-cloth cover-up. "You know it's true. You said it yourself."

Lily enters the bedroom with a gold sarong around her hips. "I can hear you guys from down the hall," she says. Everything about her is crisp and alert. Her eyes match the bright blue of her bikini, her hair frames her face, and her legs are toned and tanned from lacrosse.

Seeing her twin sister makes Zoe erupt in a fresh bout of hysterics. "Look at her," she cries. "Look at how perfect she is. Everyone loves her. They're only friends with me because I'm her sister, or they're mixing us up," she shouts, pushing past us. "I hate all of you!"

I grab a pair of sweatpants from my drawer, but it's too late. By the time I reach her, the elevator chimes, and she's gone.

Lily turns to me and asks, "What did I do?"

Bobby slips between us, dressed for the office.

"Thanks a lot," I say.

"I told you I had a meeting with STK. Drew's interest has them on their toes."

I am a pot about to boil over. "They're here? In Miami?" I stomp my foot on the floor like Zoe did moments ago. "What the hell, Bobby? It's Sunday. When were you going to tell me?"

Lily's eyes are confused. She shifts from one leg to the next in a pattern of worry.

I block Bobby from walking out of the room. "Please go to her. Tell her. Tell her that's not what we think of her."

His voice rises. "I have a meeting, Emma."

"There's always a meeting!"

He turns to Lily with a scowl on his face. "Where are you going, and where are the rest of your clothes?"

She shifts her eyes and pulls her sarong up over her chest. "To Grace's pool. I thought Zoe was coming with. And why are you being so mean to her?"

He grabs his briefcase and leaves us. I circle back to Lily, who's as perplexed as me. "Why are you guys so mad at each other?" she asks. "You're starting to scare me." It's then I notice an overwhelming smell that assaults my nose and makes me nauseous.

"You don't need so much perfume!" I say.

"Mom, are you and Daddy okay?"

Heat colors my cheeks. "We're fine," I say. "It's been a tough week."

It's convincing, and she returns her attention to her phone.

"Lily," I begin, knowing it's a crap shoot whether or not I can get my daughter to have a conversation before ten in the morning. "Is it true? Is it true what Zoe said about her friends?"

Today's my lucky day. I get the attentive, put-my-phone-in-my-beach-bag Lily. It's like winning the teenage lottery. She plays with the knot on her wrap when she faces me. "She's upset. We're all friends. She and I are a package."

"That's the problem, I think."

Lily stammers at first, "Mom, really, people like Zoe. She's being sensitive." She pauses and then continues with a little more vigor. "We get compared. All siblings do. Especially twins. When you look so much like someone else, kids need to find that one thing that makes you different. It doesn't mean you're better or worse. It gives them a point of reference. Kids need that kind of stuff. I don't know."

"And what makes Zoe different from you?"

Lily picks at her face when she's uncomfortable. She's vigorously picking again. I swat her fingers away until she faces me. "She's quiet. Nothing earth-shattering. Just different from when she debates. I think the kids expect her to be that way in person."

How well I knew about hiding behind the guise of scripts and lines. Acting provided a platform to say and feel without having to think about what came next. There was a manual, a set of guidelines that told me what to wear, how to be, who to love. Only this mastery didn't trickle into real life.

Lily's phone vibrates, signaling the girls are downstairs. I use the extra minutes waiting for the elevator to let her know I appreciate the way she supports her sister. "Tell Zoe we'll be at Grace's if she wants to come," she says, stepping inside the elevator. "And Mom, they better find the person who did this. I don't like seeing what this has done to her. I miss my sister."

"I miss her, too."

Like me, Zoe finds solace on the sand behind our hotel. I see her from our balcony, pacing the shoreline, and I get myself dressed to meet her.

As I pass through the rear lobby doors, I spot Bobby and a group of men walking the grounds. I pick up speed and hide my face in the hopes they won't notice me pass. I'm not fast enough.

"Gentlemen," he announces to the trio of expensive suits and extends his hand in my direction, "meet my better half, Emma." I slink to his side, and the STK group appraises me. I'm seething, forcing a smile on my face as he introduces me. Reluctantly, I offer my hand.

"You have a stunning hotel here," says one of the men, short and overweight, a nasty cigar dripping from his lips. "Tell me about the purple flowers," he says, leering at me a little too long, smacking his mouth around the vile smoke.

When I'm asked about the bougainvillea, I'm usually happy to engage.

"Tell them, Emma," Bobby urges.

Sucking in my breath and blistering rage, I steady my gaze on the pudgy cheeks of the man who goes by the name of Frederick. "The elder Mrs. Ross cherished her vines. They're not actually flowers, Mister . . ."

I stop myself until he says, "Summer. Like the season."

"Mr. Summer," I repeat, displeased with the insult to such a glorious time of the year. I walk toward the spidery vines, and the group of men follow. The last thing I want to do is give the men who are about to take my hotel a lecture on botany, but there are some duties I can't avoid.

I grasp one of the vines, and the group gathers around for a closer look. Bobby enjoys watching. For a second, I see a familiar kindness in his eyes, but it's not enough to erase the recent divide.

"See here," I begin again, holding up the vine. "Most people are confused about the flower." I point at the vibrant color spilling off the stems. "The pink is actually the leaf." I carefully peel the colorful petals away to reveal my find. "The bougainvillea flower is the small, white circle." I hold it out for them to see. I'm being polite so they don't notice how I am patronizing their ignorance. "These vines have been here for generations." And I stare at Bobby hard when I say, "They meant everything to Mrs. Ross."

"I'll be damned," Summer says. Then he turns to his lackey, a string bean of a man who's swiping an iPad and recording whatever Frederick Summer says. "The vines are collateral damage, folks. We'll be sending in a team of landscapers to spruce this place up."

I don't know what's worse. His breath on my face, or his blatant disregard for our home.

Bobby abruptly turns his cheek, afraid to meet my gaze. He's leading the group back inside, but he's not quick enough. I'm in his face, and guests are strolling past us. The words are jammed between my teeth, masked by a gritty smile. "While you attend to your business of ruining our hotel, I'll be out back with Zoe . . . our daughter."

He stops me with his eyes. "Not now." But I'm stormy mad and don't care who hears. And as I'm about to lay into him some more, Zoe's thin, narrow frame heads in our direction.

"We'll discuss this later," I say between clenched teeth.

"Who are they?" Zoe asks as we walk back through the pool area and down the steps to the beach. I'm irritated and short when I tell her, "Nobody." My brain is shouting, *Assholes*.

The sun is strong, and the fresh air feels good. I roll up my sweat-pants and let my legs breathe. Jen Ross, the well-known mommy blog-ger and no relation to the hotel Rosses, objects to sweatpants for any woman, but I'm convinced she'd make an exception for me.

We approach one of our private beachside cabanas with Ross towels thrown across the quilted cushions. Zoe's side is covered in magazines and the book she's reading, *Joshua: A Brooklyn Tale*. The quote on her towel reads, *Feels like Home*. Mine says, *Sink Your Feet into the Sand*. At once, Kinsley approaches and asks if we need anything. His blond hair is pulled off his face in a man bun. I'd like to tell him we need lots of things, none of which he can give, and instead ask for a pitcher of water and some fruit.

When enough time passes between Zoe flipping the pages and closing me out, I know to push harder. "I'm sorry you had to hear Daddy and me arguing. What I said, you took it out of context." Zoe keeps reading, or pretending to read. "Talk to me," I plead.

She sets down the faces of Orlando Bloom and whomever he's dating at the moment. The beach begins to fill up with chairs and umbrellas. Locals walk along the shore, and a handful of guests test the cool water. The winds pick up, and our thoughts are carried through the breeze. Something about the water slapping the sand and the crackling of the crispy white foam relaxes me.

Kinsley returns with the fruit and a basket of chocolate croissants. He knows the girls' favorite snacks and always tries to please them. He sets the tray down and tells me how excited his mother is for the upcoming wedding. I politely listen, asking about her health, while Zoe makes her way to the beach.

"I'm sorry." He searches the sand. "What you and Mr. Ross must be going through."

I catch his eyes as they travel from the ground to Zoe's back. The sun glistens on his hair, the strands a bright golden hue. It's been a week since we learned of Zoe's tryst. It was bound to make it around the hotel. He recognizes my quiet and his mistake. "I'm sorry. It's wrong for me to go on about the wedding."

He walks away from me, embarrassed. "Wait," I call out.

He stops and turns around.

"Don't be sorry, Kinsley. I know how much you love the girls. This is tough for all of us."

"There must be some way to straighten it all out," he says.

"I wish there was." I pause. "Knowing you care means a lot. Especially to Zoe."

"She's like my baby sister. I watched her grow up."

"Thank you for caring, Kinsley."

He holds on to my eyes before turning again and marching away.

I return to watching Zoe. When she reaches the slushy sand, she buries her toes in the shallow water. It fans out around her, and the waves crackle with laughter. I don't immediately follow her. I let her think this through, find her center, as I try to sort through mine.

Soon I'm off the chair. Love and devotion carry me in Zoe's direction. She looks up as I approach. "Let's walk." Shoulder to shoulder we shuffle along the sand. "Want to talk about it?"

"Everyone likes her more than they like me. She's perfect. And she's prettier."

The girls are identical twins, genetically wired to be clones of one another. And because of that, I'm genuinely concerned with my daughter's perception of perfect, a superficial assessment based on external miscues.

"You're down on yourself. None of what you're saying is true."

"We're always compared," she says. "It's nothing new. One of us is friendlier, so the other is a bitch. One has better grades, and the other one is dumb. Even if the difference is so slight. People make it more than it is. Now everyone has *that thing* to tell us apart."

"You both have wonderful qualities. You're different and the same in many ways. Watch each other. Take the best qualities and learn from the not-so-good ones. Do you have any idea of the relationship the two of you are creating? How it will take you long and far into your futures? There's no friend in the world who can provide you with as much love and understanding as your sister. Even I can never come close to sharing what the two of you have."

"She's always been more popular. Boys have always wanted to be her friend."

"I don't believe that," I say. "You never know what people are thinking. Everyone has their stuff. Boys will always be there. I promise you. When the time is right. Don't rush it."

Zoe's body follows even when her mind resists. I don't even have to look at her to know she's torn. I feel it in her limp fingers. When she opens her mouth, it's an unrecognizable voice. "Why did this happen to me?" she asks.

I stop and rest my hands on her shoulders. We are face-to-face. It's unbearable to read the sadness in her cheeks. "I don't know, Zoe. But I know we don't give up. It sucks, and it hurts, but we keep fighting back."

I force her to keep moving. If we keep moving, we'll reach the end of this mess. The air will buoy us; the water will soften the blow. Zoe half walks, half drags herself through the brash waves. Her limbs carry her, though I'm the propeller that guides her forward.

"Something like this would never happen to you."

I stop and force her to look in my eyes. "Is that what you think?"

She searches the sand below. Her toes draw lines and shapes, things that don't make sense.

"You're wrong," I continue. "It can happen to anybody. And it does."

This gets Zoe's attention. She looks up, and her eyes fill with questions. A wave bursts into us and soaks our legs. We don't move; we stand there. Drops of ocean speckle our feet.

"Have you ever wanted to be someone else?" she cries. Her shoulders slump forward, and in one fluid movement we collide into one. "I was somebody else that night."

I hold her harder than I've ever held on before. I hold her to break the pain away, to hurl it out to sea piece by piece. If I hold her hard enough and long enough, the bad stuff will disappear into the cloudless sky while the wind takes it far, far away.

"I understand, Zoe," I whisper in her ear.

"I liked being somebody else," she cries. "I liked kissing him . . . I liked . . ."

"Until it stopped feeling good," I finish for her. I let that pierce her skin before she continues. She backs away and leads us south along the beach. She makes sure I'm by her side and not trailing behind.

"You felt free," I say. "Maybe you were a little curious."

She doesn't refute anything I'm saying. Tears slowly drip from her eyes, the kind that are governed by relief, not pain. They make her look defenseless and small.

"And you did something out of character," I continue. "Something you would've answered, had you ever been asked, *I'd never do something like that.*"

She tries to hide her face.

We stop just before our chairs, and I raise her chin to me. "Listen to me, Zoe." The desperate need to repair this hinges on my next sentence. "I understand."

"You can't," she replies, her eyes narrowing in disbelief, yanking herself away from me. "No one gets it unless they've lived it."

I am bursting inside. My own brokenness about to break through.

We fall against the cabana's cushions; the canopy hides us from view. Zoe shifts awkwardly on the lounge. "It happens, Zoe . . . all the time . . . to people just like me and you."

"Not to you, Mom," she responds, in that lofty voice that teenagers have perfected. "You would never be so stupid."

My mind races through scenarios, closing in on the one that I could best convey to her. The truth has been tucked inside me for too long, but Zoe needs to understand she wasn't the only one who got caught up. She needs to know that we are all capable. Holding it in for this long has had one result: it has fueled my shame, stunted my growth. I'll tell shame who's boss. Lift the lid. Set it free.

"Zoe." This time louder and with more might. She turns from the honeydew she's about to toss in her mouth because she hears it, too, and the confession trickles out of me. "I was someone else."

Her silence hushes the entire beach. The breeze seems to disappear; the waves file out to sea. Even the children's laughter ceases to skip through the air. She releases her fork, falls back into the chair, and drapes the towel around her shoulders. "I wasn't quite your age," I begin. "I was older, in college."

I snap my fingers. "That's how quickly everything changed. One minute I was drinking, a lot, and the next I was doing something I'd never thought I'd do, with someone I didn't even care about." The admission knocks the breath out of me. She stares at me strangely. I can't tell if she's disgusted or if our souls have just found each other.

"Granted, I was older, but the feelings . . . my God, I stuffed them away. They're the same. And they grew too big for me to handle. You were called names. So was I. But no one criticized me more than I did. The self-loathing affected my whole life. I quit acting, something I loved. And I blamed my behavior on outside influences. I made mistakes. Trust me. Big ones."

She's quiet. Too quiet. She gazes up from the towel she's studying. "I'm not ashamed of what I did with Price, Mom. I'm ashamed of the video. Not what I did."

A breeze sweeps into us, and I wipe sand from her lip. A simple gesture before the big reveal. "I know."

She looks at me funny, not understanding.

"I couldn't see it at first. Maybe I didn't want to. I should've. I made it about me. And my experience. You see, Zoe, you're stronger than I ever was. I lived with a lot of self-loathing for many, many years. I still wish you had waited until you were a little older to experiment, but I'm glad you don't feel what I felt."

"I don't. I promise." Her face is lighter, like a load has been lifted. Her voice is less strained.

She pulls the towel tighter around her. The folds cover the quote, and all that's staring out is *Feels*. "This is kinda weird," she says, turning toward the water and away from my face. Our parallels collide. Sure it's weird. But I feel us joining together in a way I hadn't felt in weeks.

"You need to trust that you're not alone. Things happen to each of us that not everyone understands. You think you won't make it through, but you will."

"Easy for you to say. You're not on the Internet."

"No, I'm not on the Internet," I say, thankful my indiscretions had never been broadcast to the world, "but Zoe, I respect you for getting up every day and going to school and for taking ownership of what you've done."

This gives her satisfaction.

I continue. "I should've been more like you. When I made my mistake, I should've been honest with myself and the people I loved."

"Was he as hard on you as he's been on me? I always thought it was weird you were only with Daddy. Your whole life. It must've driven him crazy for you to be with someone else."

The picture she paints is blurred. I don't know how to answer. She seems genuinely concerned and asks again, "Was he?"

A phone rings, and the sound startles me. I look up. He's standing in his dress shirt and slacks and presses a button that sends the call to voice mail. Bobby. I don't know how long he's been listening. My heart stops. There's a hollowness to his eyes, and when they burrow into mine, fear shoots through me.

Zoe shrinks into her seat and half smiles at her father. The wind ruffles his hair and his shirt. He leans over to kiss my cheek, but it's a whisper instead: "Tell me, Emma, was I hard on you?" My cell phone blares, and I pick it up. My fingers shake. His eyes crawl up and down my skin. It makes it hard to hear the voice on the other end of the line. *Excuse me, do I know you?*

I cover my other ear with the palm of my hand. "Jo Jo?"

Silence crashes into us as though it knows what's about to come. My eyes slam shut. "Your husband didn't pick up." She's out of breath. "We have the name of the person who did this."

I see him out of the corner of my eye. Zoe is oblivious, facing the ocean, facing better things.

"Can you hear me, Mrs. Ross?" She says again, "We have a name. I'd like to tell you in person."

There's a name. A face. A human being. *Was Daddy hard on you?* "I hear you," I whisper.

He turns toward the hotel. His legs pounce on the sand. I need to go after him. I let go of the phone and rub Zoe's leg, letting my touch comfort us both. "Zoe, Jo Jo's on her way." I wait a beat. "They have a name."

She rolls over on her stomach and hides her face in her hands. "I don't want to know," she says.

I'm watching him leave, but I feel Zoe's reaction. He's almost out of sight, and I need to get up and catch him, but I don't want to alarm her.

My hand lingers on her back. "I understand."

I'm frantic inside, but she can't tell. I stand up and slip on my shoes.

"She'll be here in an hour, Zoe. You'll meet us upstairs?"

She brushes me off without lifting her head, forgetting how moments before, we were one.

I want to stay with her. I should stay with her, but I need to go to him. "Don't be late, please."

If I hurry I can catch him.

CHAPTER 22

He's crossing the pool deck when I reach him. "Bobby, wait."

He waves me away and continues at a fast pace. I can hardly keep up. He stares ahead and pretends I'm not there.

"Please wait."

He doesn't answer but slows down. My heart is fragile, like it's about to slip out of its cage onto the floor. We pass the pool and the patio gardens and pretend smile at the guests.

Kinsley approaches. "Mr. Ross, do you have a minute?"

"Not now, Kinsley," Bobby says, waving him off.

The double doors open, and a plume of cool air hits my face. I know where we're headed when he leads me down a deserted hallway to the empty ballroom. This is where we go to be alone. The airy space is vacant, and the soundproofing we had installed years ago cushions the room in an eerie calm. He has to hear the beating sound banging in my chest. I try to quiet it with the palm of my hand.

The large tables are put away, and the chairs are stacked one on top of the other against the cedar walls. White sheer curtains slip from the ceiling, and we stand face-to-face, the Steinway nearby.

"Was I hard on you?" he shouts, rage spilling into the air. "When you were with someone else? How'd I react? Refresh my memory, because I don't recall having that conversation."

My eyes hurt to look at him. "Bobby . . ."

"You were with him that night." He's in my face, his eyes wildly mad. "That night. Our fight. I knew it. We were engaged, Emma! What the hell?"

My entire body is squeezed in fear. Words are hard to compose. "Let me explain." He's about to explode. "I wanted to tell you," I cry. "I tried."

"You wanted to tell me?" A vein pops out of his neck. "You had *years* to tell me." I push him away, and he grips me tighter, making it impossible for me to move. He's whispering in my ear, "Tell me, Emma. Tell me the truth. Now. All of it."

It takes remarkable courage to share what I've hidden for so long. The words are haunted and loud, plucked from a sacred space. "You're right," I cry. "I lied." My face reddens. "I lied. I was with him. I was with Monty."

His response is barely audible, and his cheeks dull. "How could you? How could you lie to me all these years?"

A tear rolls down my face. My voice shakes. "Because of this."

"You said nothing happened. You said . . ."

I can't meet his eyes. I search the floor.

"Monty fucking Greer?" He sneers and backs away, the hurt so deep it colors his skin and hardens his eyes. I take a few steps toward him. But when I touch him, he makes that tiny, unavoidable step back.

He brushes past me toward the piano and sits. I go after him until I'm close to his side. The back of his dark linen shirt is wrinkled, and tufts of his hair meet the collar around his neck.

"You didn't trust me," I cry. "You pushed, and you pushed . . ."

"So it's my fault?" he yells.

My voice shakes. "Please listen to me."

His hand slams the keyboard, and I wince. "I always hated that bastard."

I sit beside him on the bench and wait for the flare-up.

His voice splinters when he speaks. "I knew it. He was always after you."

"That's not what happened. You and I fought. You stopped trusting me . . . the wedding . . . it was too much at once . . . graduation . . ."

Silence.

"We went out with the troupe that night. I was upset. I drank. A lot. Why do you think I can't stand the sight of alcohol? How the smell makes me gag? It's not an excuse, but it blurred the lines. One thing led to another and . . ."

"You were with him. Did you have sex with him?"

I take a breath. He won't look at me. "I did."

The hurt buries itself deep in his eyes.

I'm crying. "God, Bobby, it was an awful mistake. It should've never happened. I was scared and stupid, and I lost myself."

"Please stop," he says. "I can't. We were engaged, Emma. *Engaged.*"

"That's why I couldn't tell you. I'd betrayed your trust. I thought I'd lose you." A sob escapes me when I add, "I couldn't bear the thought of losing you."

He's quiet, which is almost worse than his screams.

"I punished myself for years. Deep down inside I thought I was a bad person, *a slut.* Wouldn't you have judged me, too? You would've given me that look. That same look you've been giving Zoe. And it would've killed me inside for your eyes not to love me. I was terrified, Bobby. Terrified to see the disappointment." I twist my wedding band on my finger.

"How could you?" His words are like ice. "Him? Of all people? Why, Em? You knew how I felt about him."

"What if I had told you?" I say. "Would you have accepted me?" I follow the lines on his face, the olive skin against the dark eyes. "Do you have any idea how embarrassed I was? You were always saying how much you loved that you were my only one. I didn't want to take that from you. I know how Zoe feels . . ."

"I never lied to you," he says. "We've never lied to each other."

"Bobby." My eyes fall, and the gravity of what I'm about to admit rises. "Bobby . . . when I found out I was pregnant . . . there was no way of knowing . . ."

He shakes his head to stop the story from unraveling. Then his hands hide his face.

I continue, my voice shaking. "I think I caused it . . . the miscarriage. All the guilt and shame I felt . . . I did this. I'm sorry. I'm so sorry."

He raises his head and stares at me as if he doesn't know me, the truth about our baby tearing him in two.

"I mourned that baby, Emma. I thought she was ours. You let me believe she was ours!"

"I wanted her to be!"

"You can't do that. You can't play with people's lives like that . . ."

Tears spout from my eyes. "Believe me, if I could've taken it back, I would have. There were times I convinced myself it didn't happen, that my story was the truth. That our story was the truth. Our baby."

Rage coats his eyes. "Were you ever going to tell me?" he asks. "Were you going to have the baby and let me believe it was mine?"

"I don't know what I was going to do," I cry. "I didn't have a plan . . . I . . ."

He stops me. "I thought this grief was ours, but it wasn't . . ." The lines on his face are etched with a pain I can't erase. "How could you keep all this from me?"

I can't face him. "Because of this." The silence is terrifying. I imagine him walking out and never coming back. "You brought up his name . . . and Zoe got herself into trouble . . . and I couldn't hold it in anymore."

"I don't understand. I don't understand any of this."

"It never went away, Bobby, that fear you'd find out I wasn't who you thought I was, that you'd compare me to my father," I say, looking at him, but he avoids my gaze. "Watching Zoe and seeing your reactions to her, it brought it all back. Maybe it's too soon for you to understand, but we *both* stepped out. We both faced repercussions. I wanted to make her feel less alone. And you know what? She doesn't regret what she did. She's taken responsibility for her sexual curiosity . . . her sexperimentation. I'm the only one who's hating herself."

He's listening, but he still won't look at me. I'm sure he cringes inside when I say those words. "I know this is a lot for you to take in, but you have to believe I'm still the same person who has loved you all these years. That's the whole point. I'm Emma. I'm the girl you love. And Zoe's the same, too."

"Tell me what I'm supposed to do with this!" he shouts. "Tell me."

"Be angry at me!" I yell. "I deserve it. Lying was wrong. But we were young, and that's the time in our lives to make mistakes. My actions don't change who I am or what we created together. We're all flawed. Me, Zoe, the hotel, you, every one of us."

He strokes the keys lightly. "It makes me sick. It makes me sick to think of Zoe doing that. To think she thought so little of herself."

"Don't you mean me?" My eyes fill with tears.

He turns to me. "She's not a woman, Emma. She's a teenager."

He's torn. I can see inside, the lethal mix of emotions. At one end of his thoughts is Zoe. At the other is me. The hotel teeters between us. Nothing is stable anymore.

"I don't know who you are." His palm comes down hard on the keys.

I'm angry and sad all at once. "Yes, you do."

He fiddles with the keys. His pain becomes music, and he starts to play a song I haven't heard in years: "This Woman's Work." The melody haunts me, and I wonder if he chose this song on purpose. If his intent is for Kate Bush to call me out on all the things I should've said, but didn't. His fingers slow down, and to drive his point home, he makes one final slap on the keys. The sound tells me he's in mourning again.

"How can you sit here," I ask, "in this room, and say you don't know me?"

He doesn't answer. His eyes well up.

"I never meant to hurt you," I say.

"But you did."

"I know." I lower my eyes. "And it was a mistake."

"Lying isn't a mistake, Emma. It's a decision."

Our phones beep, reeling us back to the present.

"It's Jo Jo and Javier," I tell him. "They're here. And they have a name."

CHAPTER 23

I close my eyes and inhale deeply. The time is now. I text Zoe to head upstairs, and she says she's already there. Bobby gets up from his seat and smooths out his slacks. A layer of deceit is pinned to his face.

"We're not done," he says.

I follow him out of the ballroom and through to the lobby and elevator. Jo Jo is waiting in our foyer with an oversize briefcase and appears less perky than usual. In all these years, I've hardly ever craved a drink, but at the moment, I am ready to break my own rules.

"Zoe?" I call out, walking toward the living room.

"I'm in here," she says in a shaky voice.

"Have a seat," Jo Jo instructs, motioning for us to sit. "Let me begin by saying I'm relieved it's not someone with technical expertise. We'd have had a difficult time tracking a person who didn't want to be tracked." She's talking slowly, taking her time, and it's unsettling.

My legs are pressed together, and the suspense chips away at my nerves.

"Let me be clear. We had every indication it was heading in this direction." She sucks in her breath. "The IP address matches a family on the beach. Their child attends Thatcher. She's in Zoe's grade."

I am unable to move. Bobby sits across from me, and he refuses to make eye contact. His fingers are clasped. Zoe. Well, Zoe, is slumped against the chair.

Jo Jo pulls out a legal pad and searches the page. "Does the name Grace Howard mean anything to you?"

Every nerve in my body stands on heightened alert. "Yes. She's Zoe's friend. One of her best friends."

Jo Jo sets the pad on the coffee table while my heart thumps in my ears. "The video came from the Howards' address. We believe Grace posted it on the Internet."

Bobby gets up. "Impossible! Grace is one of her closest friends."

I can't feel the floor beneath my feet.

"What?" It's not my voice; it's Zoe's. She's pacing. "No! No! Not Grace. That's a mistake. She wouldn't do this to me! How could she do this to me?"

She is hysterical and shouting. Her cries spill across the room. I jump to my feet and throw my arms around her. Grace Howard. The name slices through me. It stops my breath. Not the girl who played here for years after school and on the weekends. How can this be? These are our friends. My hand covers my mouth, and shock ripples through me.

Bobby stands and grabs the back of his chair. He's fuming, and it looks like he might toss it across the room. "God dammit."

Zoe wriggles away from me and stands in front of him. "Just leave!" she screams up at him. "Why are you even here?"

My arms come around her. I try to restrain her. Comfort her. Make her feel loved enough for the two of us.

He doesn't back down. He peers deep into Zoe's eyes. "Don't you dare disrespect me like that. I'm your father!"

Jo Jo stands up and moves toward Bobby. "Mr. Ross, please calm down."

"Please stop, Bobby!" I plead.

Zoe straightens herself and gets in his face. "You haven't been my father," she wails. "The second this happened, I didn't exist." Her eyes hold his firmly, and each word is a testament to her courage. "It's bad enough living with what I've done. The whole town thinks I'm a slut, Daddy, but you know what? Nothing feels worse than having you look at me like that."

I am both proud and sick for Zoe. The public wrath is one thing, but her dad's denunciation is another. I fit around her and hold on tight. *Her friend did this to her. It's not possible.* "Your father's upset, honey. He loves you. So much." Now I'm crying.

Jo Jo's eyes lock on mine, and she gives me a nod. *Talk to each other.* Our lowest point is on display, though none of us wince. This can't be new to her: families torn apart, couples divided, and the host of problems that follow unfortunate crimes.

I return to Bobby. The word *slut* sits between us like an open sore. Bobby can't look at it, and he refuses to touch it.

"I'm sorry." He shrugs. "I'm sorry I can't separate you from your actions. It's just, God, Zoe, you're just a kid."

"Bobby, stop." I'm in his face. I refuse to let him condemn her like that.

"This wasn't supposed to happen." They're not words; they're sobs. He marches across the room and forces Zoe to look at him. "Didn't we love you enough? Didn't I love you enough?"

Zoe's lips start to tremble, but she doesn't cry. "I'm still Zoe. I'm still the same girl. The one you taught to play corn hole. To thumb wrestle. The one you gave a song to. Do you remember? You said it was for me." Her voice cracks, and this final blow breaks him in half. Usually an entire head taller than she is, he is pulled to the ground by his grief, and he appears weak and small. "Stop hating me." Her eyes leave his face, find mine, and return. "Please."

She has far more insight than I had at her age. What Bobby was saying to her, he should've been saying to me. And I should've given him the chance. We could've fought for each other.

Minutes pass before anyone moves. Zoe slinks down on the couch, and I lean over to Bobby and whisper, "I'm the one you're angry at. I'm the one you want to go after. Not Zoe. Not Grace."

He raises his hand. "Stop it, Emma. Not now."

I witness a change in Zoe, a revival. If she can stand up to her father, she can stand up to anyone. She moves from the couch to take a seat on the coffee table right in front of Jo Jo and asks pointedly, "What do we do next?"

Bobby's hunched over in his chair. I'm too shocked to sit, so I pace. *Grace Howard.* "How can you be sure it's her?" I say. "Could there be a mistake?"

"I'm sorry, Mr. and Mrs. Ross," says Jo Jo. "I know this is difficult. My guys were able to match the IP address. Apparently the video was sent to YouTube the same night the text went out. We're not sure why it didn't go live sooner. We've seen it take upward of forty-eight hours, but rarely more than that. Grace didn't cover her tracks. And there's no disputing a digital footprint."

"This can't be." But I won't argue with Jo Jo's evidence. I stop myself from texting Lisa. From calling her and screaming. "I speak to Grace's mother every day!" I say.

"I'd put a moratorium on that. In legal terms, I advise against it. Let our investigators deal directly with the family."

"What about Zoe? And Lily? They can't avoid one of their best friends in school."

Jo Jo speaks over my torment, and the words sound like a warning. "We're waiting for a warrant," she says.

Javier finishes Jo Jo's thought. "As soon as it's issued, detectives will go to the home. They'll search her phone, her computer. When the video turns up, which we suspect it will, you have to decide whether or not you want to press charges."

Charges against a stranger is one thing. Grace Howard is another. I'm suddenly riddled with doubt.

"We want to press charges," Bobby insists. "No matter who it is."

"If that's the case, we'll go to the SA's office," Jo Jo says. "We'll provide the evidence, and they'll take over. They'll consult with Zoe, who will merely be a witness. The case becomes the State versus the accused. Going after this person sends a very strong message. The laws don't take these crimes lightly. If convicted, the suspect has a permanent record."

The details make my head spin. Now that it's Grace, everything's changed. It'll be her house they'll invade. Her bedroom. Her computer. The same house where we spent Saturdays barbecuing by the pool. An idea takes root and slowly moves through me. I can barely string the sentence together. "Does this mean Grace filmed Zoe?"

"We won't know until we get the warrant for her phone. Right now we have the forensic link from her IP address to the upload."

I'm crushed.

"Computers and phones are tricky. The State will have to prove no one other than Grace used either one. Sometimes it's a matter of password protection. If Grace is the only one who knows the password, it would be hard to prove someone else got in."

My hands squeeze into fists. That had to be it. Someone used Grace's computer. Someone used her phone. There's no other explanation.

Zoe shifts in her seat. "Will Grace be arrested?"

"If we do our job correctly," answers Jo Jo, "then yes."

I fall back in the chair and stare at the ceiling, shocked that this is happening.

"What will she be charged with?" Zoe asks, her shoulders deflating.

"That depends on the State Attorney. The gamut runs from cyberstalking to sexual cyberharassment to possession and distribution of child pornography. The number of counts is based on the number of uploads."

The room silences. We are fastened to our seats; the horror of this moment unspools around us. I watch Bobby. His lips press together. His forehead is lined with worry. His eyes are in shadow. And then he explodes.

"What the fuck was Grace thinking? What the hell is wrong with her? I swear I'm going after her. I'm going after the whole family. They'll have nothing when I'm done with them. Nothing. How dare she do this to Zoe!"

I gasp. I think about Lisa and me pushing the girls in their strollers along Ocean Drive. At Fisher Park. A string of memories whittled down until they're meaningless.

"Grace will pay for what she did," Bobby scoffs. "And I won't feel sorry about it. She's not the victim. Zoe is. I'll be happy to see that family go through half of what they've put us through."

I twist around when I hear this. *Victim.* It's a tiny fissure that lets humanity through. It shines on Zoe's face. I see her searching her father's eyes for approval, to trust that maybe he's on her side.

"Me too," she whispers, getting up and standing beside him. "Whatever I have to do."

I should interrupt. I should stop this madness from spiraling. But I know it's too late. The wheels are in motion. We needed to know, and now we do. But how could we have suspected it would be Grace?

Bobby is nodding. "I don't really care how justice happens, only that it does, and fast."

"I spoke with Price Hudson's parents," Jo Jo continues. "They're intent on the State formally pressing charges. In fact, they specifically stated they concur with whatever the Ross family decides."

I'm adrift, my eyes glazed, taking it all in. My mind is somewhere else altogether. I want to fight for Zoe, but Lisa's face stops me. It's the line between crime and punishment, revenge and forgiveness. I am straddling a fence I can't bring myself to cross. Go forward. Go back. Someone gets hurt. Someone suffers. Nobody wins.

"The decision is in your hands," says Jo Jo, packing up her briefcase and standing up. "If you're after justice, we have to file a case. I suggest thinking about it. We'll be in touch."

Jo Jo's departure leaves us in eerie silence. Zoe remains seated between Bobby and me, twisting her fingers. Bobby stares out the window, plotting revenge.

I squeeze Zoe's hand. "Are you okay?"

"I don't know," she says.

"How could Grace do this?" Bobby asks. "*Why* would Grace do this?"

The questions crowd around us, and there are many. Answers are hidden in boxes we can't open. Lisa loved Zoe. Her concern was genuine. What would this do to her? What would this do to our friendship? *Hurt people hurt people.* What was inside Grace, hurting her to the point of lashing out?

Bobby jumps up. "I'm calling Drew."

"You can't!" I say.

"Grace broke the rules. I'll do whatever I want."

"Daddy, don't," Zoe begs.

"Bobby," I begin, "we should talk about this. Do you really want to go after our friends? A family we've known for years? Maybe we can settle this alone . . . in a civilized manner?"

He rears his head at me. "Grace bullied Zoe. The worst form of bullying. They all need to be held accountable. Yes, we're going after them."

I'm thinking about the players involved. Everyone's a victim. Everyone suffers. And my heart has split open wide. How Grace intentionally did this and sat in our home watching Zoe suffer kills me.

The door opens, and in walks Lily.

"Welcome to the shit show," Zoe says to a clueless Lily, who comes over to kiss me hello. She smells like coconut, and her cheeks are pink from the sun.

"What's wrong?" she asks.

"It was Grace!" Zoe yells. "Grace uploaded the video to YouTube."

"No way," she says, her mouth open in a perfect circle. "No way." She says it again, because she can't believe it. "No freaking way."

"Yup. Grace did this to me."

Lily drops her bag on the floor and sits next to her sister. "Why would she do that? I don't understand . . ."

I'd been asking myself that same question and drawing a blank.

"C'mon, Zoe. Maybe someone took her computer or her phone. She's one of our best friends!" She searches my face for an explanation, but I can only shake my head.

"She's no friend of mine," Zoe says. "The girl's basically ruined my high school existence. I'm marked for life."

Lily takes her sister's hand. "Have you spoken to her? Have Mom and Dad called the Howards?"

"We're not allowed to talk to them during the investigation," I interject. "The police are handling it.

"Oh my God, this is crazy!" Lily manages. "I can't believe it. I don't get it."

"It's easy," Zoe says. "Grace is a bitch." Then she starts to cry again. "I've never had a friend betray me in such a mean way. It has to be a mix-up. It can't be Grace." She stops to wipe her eyes. "I hate her. She didn't give me a chance. She picked something that was nonnegotiable, something she could never take back. What do I do?"

"We hold her accountable, Zoe," Bobby says. "You defend yourself. You don't let her get away with hurting you."

I'm not sure this is the answer, but I'm not sure of anything at the moment. He wants to seek justice, but his intentions are blurry.

"I'm not going back to school. It makes me want to throw up, thinking about my friend doing this to me. It's unforgivable. I can't look at her."

I realize I'm digging my nails into my palm. There's blood, and I don't bother to wipe it off. I get up to console her, to give her the little strength I have left, but she gets up first and heads for her room. Lily is close behind.

Bobby sits beside me with his head bent into his hands. I want to comfort him. I want him to comfort me, but we are too divided. I remember how we used to find each other in the dark. How he could sense my moods and make me laugh, capture me in his arms. Now we are strangers pitted against each other. I don't know if we can find our way back, and a cold chill nips at my skin.

"Please talk to me," I whisper. "Please."

"For fuck's sake, Emma . . . what the hell do you want from me?"

"I want to be a family again. I want to help our daughter together. I want you to understand why I did what I did. That I loved you that much. Forgive me. Forgive Zoe . . ." And when I think I'm finished, I add, "Love us. Unconditionally."

Nothing's getting through to him. He swipes at his arm as though my words touched him and he's flicking them away. "People are never what they seem," he sighs. "How a friend of Zoe's could do this. Someone this close to us." He shakes his head and stares down at the floor. "I don't know you either. Do I?"

His disappointment climbs deep inside me, clawing at my defenses. "You know me, Bobby."

He clasps his hands, and I notice his bare finger. "Where's your ring?"

"Where's my ring?" he repeats, his beautiful eyes gone cold and dark. "Where was your ring when you slept with someone else?"

The harshness strips me of a response.

He says, "I'm going to stay in the suite tonight."

The employee suite. The pressure against my chest—I can't catch my breath. Everything I've feared has risen to the surface, and he's actually leaving. I hold on to the cushions. Dizzy. "Bobby . . . you can't do that."

"I can," he says, turning away from me. "There are too many lies . . ."

A lone tear runs down my cheek. I'm helpless to undo the pain I've caused.

I try to apologize, but the words are muffled in sobs. "I should've told you. But losing the baby . . . it was over. I could forget about what I did . . ."

Tears drown the black of his eyes, and his lips tremble.

"I feel so betrayed," he says. "That baby I mourned . . . what am I supposed to do with those feelings?"

My body is without life, my eyes soulless and dead. I told myself all those years ago that it was Monty's baby. It had to be. My voice breaks, and another round of tears escapes. "When I was pregnant with the girls . . . it was different. I felt different." I try to get him to look at me.

His mind is somewhere else, so I retrace how we got here. "Monty didn't mean anything to me. He wasn't you. He could never be you."

"Stop." His hands cover his face. "I don't want to think about that night. Every time you mention his name, I imagine what you were wearing . . . him touching you . . . how you looked in his eyes." The anguish drowns his words. "I can't."

If only I could take away the pain. Instead I cower in raw, immeasurable shame. He gets up and leaves me there alone, and all I can do is collapse and wonder, *What have I done?*

CHAPTER 24

The space Bobby has vacated is cold. I don't go after him. I don't beg. Lying was wrong, and his resentment is real and deserved. A wide range of emotions wash through me, and the anger mounts for thinking I was protecting either of us by hiding the truth. Anger at him—fairly or unfairly—for the unwillingness to accept the many parts of the people he loves.

I check on the girls, and they're showering. Lily's phone is on her nightstand, and several missed calls from Grace have piled up. I want to delete her from Lily's contacts. Delete her from our lives. But I know some things can never be completely erased.

My phone rings, and Lisa's picture flashes across the screen. I hit "Reject," and she texts me immediately. Where are you? Everything ok? Haven't heard from you.

Zoe walks in swathed in her Ross robe and her hair wrapped in a towel. I sit on her bed, and she plops herself on the blanket beside me.

"You okay?" I ask. My arm comes around her.

The towel slips to the floor, and neither of us picks it up. Her damp, dark hair shades her face.

"What do you think?" I ask. "Do you want to make a case of this?"

She shrugs her shoulders. "I think so."

"You need to be sure."

"I don't know," she says. Lily is drying her hair in the bathroom. The whirring of the blower floats through the doorway.

"I know." I hug her close. "None of it makes sense."

"Do I have to go to school? I can't look at her. I can't."

I wipe the hair away from her eyes. "No. I'll e-mail Dr. Mason. One day at a time. But maybe we should call Dr. Rubin. Maybe she can offer some advice over the phone."

She nods. "Is Daddy mad at you?"

I'd hate for her to know how he's refused to sleep beside me. "I think Daddy's disappointed in a lot of things right now."

"The kids at school talk," she says. "They say I have to feel really bad about myself to do what I did."

"But that's not you. We talked about that."

"I know. But everyone wants some deeper reason. Even Chelsea asked me the other day. I drank and got carried away. It wasn't anything more than that."

"Your outburst the other day led me to believe otherwise . . . are you sure there's nothing more you think we need to talk about?"

"I feel that way sometimes, I do. I have insecurities and doubts, but that's not why I did what I did."

"And that's your story. Trust it." My hands squeeze hers hard so she knows how much I mean it. "Sometimes reasons are others' excuses— for themselves. Things happen. Circumstances. Inhibitions. Some reasons are out of our awareness completely.

"I never want you to feel betrayed by your body or your actions. You're going to grow up and experience a lot. Society isn't always kind to women. Make sure you're aware of your intentions. Respect yourself. And please, please, be careful. There's a lot of scary stuff out there."

"Tell that to the girls who call sex a recreational sport."

"I still think they're too young. But this is good. It's important for us to have this talk."

"It's weird."

"Yeah, I suppose the stork dropping you off is easier to take in."

She laughs, and my heart fits back into place.

"Zoe, you can experience sex in a beautiful way." I'm thinking about her father, and the memories are long. "If you're doing it to make a boy like you, I think you'll be disappointed. You don't have to touch someone to feel close. The closeness comes from knowing each other and trusting each other. And that's when sex will surprise you in ways you never imagined."

Her eyes lighten. The pain dissolves. There is more blue than silver.

"And yes, there are women who merely enjoy sex. When they're older, responsible adults."

"Oh geez," she says, covering her eyes. "It wasn't like that. I promise."

"I know, Zoe. I've accepted what you did and who you are."

She nods. "I would love to have a boyfriend and be a girlfriend. Like Molly and Sam," she says. They're the celebrity couple at Thatcher. "To like someone like you and Daddy. I love hearing your stories about the beach and the hotel. Price and me . . . we were different . . . but I accept what happened. I'm a good person, Mom. I know I am."

I hug her hard. "I know you are. And I love you."

"But I won't accept what Grace did. It was wrong, and we have to do something about it." She gets up and saunters over to her closet. Lily joins us, and the girls take their time getting dressed.

My phone dings. An e-mail from *Ocean Drive*. The proofs are ready. The Royal Family. It feels like a lifetime ago.

Lily handles her phone while she reminds me she needs new sneakers for lacrosse. Her eyes change when she sees the missed calls from Grace on the screen. She holds up the phone and asks, "What do I do?"

"You do nothing," I say. "You let the authorities handle it."

"What is it?" Zoe asks.

"Grace is blowing up my phone." I imagine calling her and giving her an earful. I imagine saying things I can never take back.

"I'll never forgive her," says Lily.

Hours later, we're at the dinner table, and Bobby is badgering Zoe about Grace in between bites of kung pao chicken and Mongolian beef. His bag is packed and hidden in our room. I had watched him fill the leather case, feeling my heart turn over with each item he packed. He had said he'll slip out after dinner.

"Why hide it from the girls?" I had asked, prickly mad.

"This is something different," he'd said. "This is between me and you." But I knew he was lying. We were all a part of his departure. It hurt worse, because it was directed at me.

We used to enjoy Sunday night dinners at Tropical Chinese. Tonight we're huddled around the table with takeout from Sum Yum Gai. Bobby is eating out of the carton with chopsticks, while I pretend not to notice. We have far bigger problems to deal with than germs.

"Did you and Grace have a fight?" he asks.

She hesitates. "We all argue and fight. *Nothing* warranted this."

"You can't think of a single reason why she would do this?"

I reach for my glass, and my hand brushes against Bobby's. He jerks his away, and the glass slips from my hand and spills across the table.

"I didn't do anything," Zoe shoots back.

I snatch a paper towel from the counter and wipe it up while they're locked in a stare.

Lily decides to weigh in. "Sometimes Grace does things for attention. She doesn't mean anything by it most of the time." She spoons a wonton into her mouth.

"This crossed a line, Lily," he says. "This is a serious offense." Bobby ignores me as I lean over him. The energy between us is all wrong. "Zoe," he says, "we need to let Jo Jo know our decision."

Zoe wrinkles her brow. Her whisper silences the table. "Let's do it."

"Maybe we should give it a day or two? Some time to talk this over . . . think this through," I say.

Bobby is ripping the duck-sauce packet with his teeth when he says, "What more is there to say? The girl screwed up. She needs to pay."

Like me? His harshness fills the air, and it makes it difficult for me to swallow.

Lily must sense the rift between us; she breaks the awkward quiet. "Can we go downstairs for movie night?" It's a monthly ritual on the beach with a large screen, popcorn, and blankets, plus the hotel's best desserts. "They're showing *3 Days to Kill*. Kevin Costner. Mom, you love him."

"Bobby?" I ask in a tone that's forced. "It's a beautiful night. Why don't we join the girls?"

"You know I can't," he says. His eyes are apologetic. "I have a call in a half hour." He looks at his watch to drive his point home. "And I'll be working downstairs late tonight. Number crunching last month's financials. You know how due diligence works."

"Girls," I say, "why don't you go down? Uncle Jonny will be there. It'll be fun."

A dark black canvas of sky surrounds me. I usually love November in Miami, and the way the cool air reminds us of the coming season. Now I'm numb to its touch. I'm standing on the terrace staring down at the crowd gathered by the movie screen. Kevin Costner's plastered across the screen, and his voice travels up the building. Coincidences happen to me often. Fate. I log in to Facebook, and the top post will be something of real relevance to me. A friend's loss. An anniversary. I've always felt there is meaning in the timing. So when I see this particular scene on-screen, I'm not surprised it's one of Kevin Costner and his estranged teenage daughter discussing an upcoming dance with a boy. She's explaining she doesn't know how to dance, and he leads her off the couch. It's obvious the young girl doesn't want to dance with her old man. She backs away; he pulls her close. And soon she's standing on his feet dancing with him to her mother's favorite song.

It sends goose bumps up and down my legs. Not only because I love watching a teenage girl dance with her father, but the song . . . the song is one of ours. Mine and Bobby's.

Bobby comes up next to me, and he hears it, too. He drops his bag on the floor. We're watching this young girl, so much like Zoe.

We don't talk. Side by side we watch the drama unfold on the screen, mirroring our own. They're at the kitchen table laughing and drinking wine when the mom encourages Kevin Costner to tell their daughter he loves her. He stares into her eyes with more love than I can stand when he says that his daughter already knows. Because he loves her as much as he loves her mother.

Our hands curl around the railing, but not close enough to meet.

"Say something," I say.

"What can I say?" he asks.

"Say you love me. Say you love her. Say you're not leaving."

He stares out at the night sky. His voice is wistful and sad. "This isn't a movie, Em."

"I know. It's much more than that."

"I wish it were that simple."

"I screwed up. I should've been honest. He meant nothing to me. It's always been you. It's always been us. *Solo tú.*"

He kicks at the wall. "I spoke to Jo Jo. We're pressing charges. You can help by supporting me." He's talking to the sea, and I study the lines across his cheek. I envision Zoe's face at the table and how she agreed to this.

"How do we know it won't make things worse?"

He faces me. But his eyes shift from side to side. "You made a decision once."

It stings. "I'm sorry." I hope my eyes will tell him how much. "I shouldn't have lied. I should've never lied. Not to you, of all people."

He says, "You're right," and the guilt floods me. It has been a life-time of quiet humiliation. Fear of full disclosure did that to me. He punished me, unknowingly. I wouldn't let him do that to our child. When I think of her, I find my voice.

"Zoe's confused. She thinks if she agrees with you it means you forgive her. Are you ready to do that?"

"What do you want to do, Emma? You want to go to the Howards' for coffee, slap Grace on the wrist, and fly to Cabo together for spring break? It doesn't work like that. This is a game changer."

"It's a better solution than you putting Grace in jail and selling our home!"

"You don't understand," he hisses. "Everything I'm doing is to save us. Everything. How come you don't see that?"

I have nothing more to lose. I stand in front of him and reach for his arms. He draws back, and I reach for him again. Our eyes meet. His are empty, a dark, dark brown. "Because it hurts. Because it's lonely without you. Because I miss you."

He tries to pull away. One of his hands swipes at his eyes.

"Because I made a mistake once. Because I love her. Because I love you, Bobby. More than anything in the world."

We face each other, and I see us as young kids frolicking along the beach. I see him chasing me until the sun slips from the sky and the moon becomes our compass. I see him laughing when he pulls my bathing-suit string, and the delicate way he ties it back together again. His hands graze my back and nip my shoulders. The goose bumps dot my skin. He's smil-ing that smile that could make me do anything. And in his hand is the diamond that he pulled from a nearby shell. I jump into his waiting arms, circle my legs around his waist, and we fall back in the sand. The rush of time is like waves bashing the shore. It soaks me, and the salt teases my lips.

But he turns away. He leaves me on the balcony and slams the door. I drop into the chair beside me and hug my knees to my chest. This loss is like nothing I've ever felt.

His side of the bed is a loud reminder of my loneliness. I stare at our ketubah and remember the day we hung it up. He had to go to the emergency room after smashing his finger with the hammer. *This is how it's going to end.* How will I ever replace the frame with something else? A wall of bricks tumble down. Our daughters. Us. Our home. It's too painful to think about. I grab my iPad and scroll through the pictures from the magazine shoot instead.

The magic of the Ross is lit up against a fiery sky. Our girls float across the sand with the deep blue sea dancing behind them. The four of us hold hands, traipsing along the gardens, and the smiling guests stare in our direction. I swipe forward to the individual shots of the hotel interior. They capture her mystical beauty, her simple sophistication. It's hard not to fall in love with her again. She's breathtaking. And the minor flaws and imperfections make her the hero of our story.

The spread takes my breath away. Bittersweet, but elegant and understated. I want to touch the screen and capture the loveliness in my hand. Lily looks angelic. Zoe a blushing beauty. There's no sign of scandal on our faces. No signs of a fault line pulling us apart. Bobby looks handsome and refined, like one of those men in the perfume ads. Dark and magnetic. Sexy as all hell. We look composed and happy, the all-American family. How misleading. I almost wish the camera caught our vulnerability. It would make us more human.

I pick up my cell phone and text Bobby. I love you. I'm sorry. You know me. You know me better than anyone.

CHAPTER 25

Bobby slips in with the sun. I've woken Lily, and I'm stepping out of the girls' room when I catch him sneaking in. The bags under his eyes tell me he slept less than I did, and he brushes past me with a cursory nod.

Lily's unusually slow. Zoe normally motivates her in the morning, but with her decision to stay home and avoid facing Grace, Lily's taking her time. They've already called three times from downstairs to tell us her ride is waiting. Bobby's yelling, and it only slows Lily down more. I wipe the sleep from her eyes and send her on her way.

He's sitting at the table drinking a cup of coffee. The field between us is wide. "What's Zoe doing all day?" he asks. Not *How are you. Let's talk. Let's fix this.*

"She can follow you around like she used to do."

"Not today." He takes a sip without lifting his eyes from the *Miami Herald.*

We never started our days like this. He always looked at me, touched me in some form. Or he'd leave a love note under my coffee cup, surprise me with breakfast in bed. Uncomfortable silence didn't work for us.

"What are we supposed to do?" I ask. "Sit and wait for them to arrest Grace?"

He nods and blinks as though he's listening, but he's somewhere else.

"Do you want to meet us for a quick lunch?" I ask. I'm nervous. He makes me nervous.

"I can't."

"I'm trying, Bobby."

He is silent. The only sound is the paper rustling between his fingers as he turns the page.

"Be angry at me," I say. "But not Zoe. Please."

He gets up, and I watch him walk away, taking my fight with him.

My phone buzzes, and it's a text from Lisa Howard. I'm starting to worry. You haven't answered any of my calls. The police are here asking for Grace's computer. What's going on?

Her name across the screen tugs at my stomach. My friend. What will this do to us? My finger rests on the tiny picture near her name, and I slowly move the tip across it. Part of me wants to call her. We would dissect the situation like we'd always done when it came to the kids. But I delete her message and shut my eyes instead. Until the phone buzzes again. It's Lily. I don't know how I can avoid Grace. If you think punching Price was wrong, just wait.

I write back. Stay cool, honey. For your sister.

She gives me the thumbs-up. And then proceeds to complain about how slow Chelsea's mom drives.

I have three missed calls from Monica Hudson, Price's mom. The messages are all the same. "Emma, I'm sorry to bother you . . . I'd like to talk about the case. Who is this Grace Howard? Do you know her? This is awkward, I know. I'd still like to talk. Can you call me back?" No one's been this eager to talk to me in weeks.

I dial the number on the screen for no other reason than I need someone to talk to, someone who understands.

She answers on the second ring. Her voice echoes my own. The muffled tone means she's in mourning, too. "I'm so glad you called. This Grace Howard . . . she sounds like a bad kid."

I fight the urge to defend Grace.

"Do you know much about her? Why she would do this?" She either has a cold or she's been crying. I explain the relationship and how we've been close friends for years.

She gasps. "Why on earth . . ."

I don't have an answer.

"I'm sorry. The kids don't deserve this." She blows her nose. "And I'm sorry this happened so publicly. But even with the news about this Grace person, my husband and I have had to accept that Price made a bad judgment call. He's capable of mistakes." She pauses. "It's difficult to realize we don't know him as well as we thought."

Bobby's face appears in my mind. Blame it on Price. Blame it on a drug. Even blaming it on Miami, comparing it to the wholesome upbringing I had in Deerfield. It doesn't matter. Chicago. Miami. Girls. Boys. Good parents. Bad parents. None of us are immune.

She asks how Zoe's doing, and I decide to tell her the truth. "She's home today. She didn't want to face Grace. She's been going to school up until now and managing, but this set her off. What about Price?"

"He's okay. He's trying to focus on his schoolwork and lacrosse."

I'm hugging the phone to my cheek. I close my eyes and imagine she's lying under a blanket on her couch like I am.

"My eyes have been opened," she says. "The labels, the misperceptions. Girls are sluts, boys are the devil. Whichever side you're on, the name-calling is wrong."

It would've been so easy to be angry at Monica the way I am at the Howards. But it's the opposite. I like her, and I find comfort in our strange alliance. "Thank you."

"For what?" She sounds confused.

"Nobody understands. It's nice to talk to someone who does."

"I wasn't joking when I said I made a voodoo doll of Zoe. I'm as guilty as the next guy. I'm not proud of that. But I see things very differently from where I sit. Now."

When parents say to each other, "We're all in this together," it's utter bullshit. When your child screws up and you're the subject of idle gossip, watch who stays and watch who goes.

Zoe slides into the room and sits beside me on the couch. "Monica, Zoe's awake. Can we talk later?"

"How about coffee sometime? I'm not very popular at Thatcher."

"Of course," I say. "That would be nice."

"Was that Price's mom?" Zoe asks after I hang up.

I say yes, and she's quiet. "Are you okay with that?" I ask.

"It's fine."

"How about you get dressed and come with me downstairs? Hotel business. You used to love joining me." She pulls a blanket over her and presses the remote. She prefers to flip through mindless TV instead.

My phone rings, and it's Lana from *Ocean Drive*. I get off the couch and head to my room. She gushes about the proofs. "We'll send a copy of the interview well before we go to print. Did you love the pictures? We can provide you with copies. Let us know which you like best."

Sandra from Concierge interrupts with a list of questions she's probably been accruing for days. I'm rifling through the mail that hasn't been opened. Invitations and events we've missed. RSVPs we've forgotten to respond to. "I'm sorry I haven't been around. We're having some issues with the girls."

"I know, Mrs. Ross." Of course she did.

She offers to help, but there's nothing she can do. "Have Kinsley and Elle turned in their list?" I ask. "Do we have a count?"

"Yes. Seventy-eight. They're in Mr. Ross's office going over tables."

"We need to lay down a ramp for Fern MacNeill's wheelchair."

"Got it."

"What about our numbers for this upcoming week? Are we within range from last year?" The busyness keeps me distracted. For a few brief moments I forget.

"We're up ten percent," she says. "And I took the liberty of signing off on the Smiths' F&B. You always take care of them when they come to town."

I thank her and finish getting ready.

"Meet me for lunch," I call out to Zoe.

She prefers I bring food back, but I think it's a mistake. "You need to get out."

"I'm fine," she says. "Uncle Jonny has some dogs for me to walk later."

The elevator doors open to a bustling lobby. Guests and staff are in a hurry as I step through. Some are gathered at the front desk; others are lined up at Concierge. Businessmen are en route to meetings. Vacationers are preparing for an afternoon at the beach or poolside. A couple is sitting nearby sipping mojitos. A young man is typing away on his laptop. The sweeping ceilings make every footstep a resounding noise, every laugh a menacing jab. The music piped through the walls is too loud, and the glowing candles reflect all I wish to hide. We are all linked under one roof, but traveling in different directions. The energy once made me feel vibrant and alive. Now the instability alarms me.

I walk deeper into my hotel's belly and notice Alberto teasing a little girl with pigtails. Soon he'll pull a quarter out of her hair and make her laugh. Sandra tends to a guest with her affable smile. A waiter carries a tray of mimosas to the front desk, libations for our guests checking in. Our staff is cheerful and friendly, thorough and attentive. A warm rush reminds me of all I had forgotten. No, I could never give this up. Never.

A text comes from Bobby. Can you come up?

I don't immediately respond. I have rounds to run, meaning a walk-through on a certain floor and paperwork to clear in registration. When I finish, I text him I'm on my way.

They're gathered in Bobby's office—Kinsley and Elle—and they're going over the floor plan for the wedding. They greet me with shared smiles; Bobby doesn't look up. His words are gruff. "There's some staff we're having trouble seating."

"I hope you don't mind, Mrs. Ross," says Elle.

I smile, reminding her it's my pleasure to help. Latching on to their hopefulness allows me to forget my unhappiness. They thank me and leave us alone to strategize.

The spreadsheet with the guests is laid across his desk, and the floor plan is pinned to the wall. I notice documents with STK across the top and an offer letter from the Howard Group. I pick it up and shove it in his face. "You can't possibly be entertaining his offer."

He walks over to the shredder in the corner of the room and sends it through the feeder. The whirring sound is the only thing we've agreed upon.

I study the contents of his office. Years of marriage unwind around us. The pictures of the girls as babies. An enlarged black-and-white of Laura and Zane Ross in front of the hotel, with Bobby and Jonny in strollers. A guest had sent a miniature model of the Ross with a pink satin banner draped across the front. It was a replica from the day the girls were born, and Bobby dressed the front of the hotel in hot pink. Instead of a sign that read "It's a Girl," he had a customized banner with "Two Girls" fitted across the veneer.

Tabitha slips through the door carrying a manila envelope with Bobby's name. "It's the documents you requested from the vault, Mr. Ross."

The deed to the hotel. A vise slides though my chest and squeezes. I search Bobby's face, but he won't look up. Tabitha catches my eyes instead. It's her job to know he's sleeping somewhere else, and her sympathetic eyes hide nothing. She tiptoes out of the room, closing the door behind her.

If I had told him all those years ago that he'd one day consider selling, he would have cast me off as ridiculous. He has put so much love into the hotel's care and evolution, adjusting to her changes—the growth spurts—and remaining competitive among the other hotels in the area. Giving it up is not a solution.

I return to the table chart with my eyes misty. I know exactly where to put all the players. He watches me.

"What happened to us?" he asks.

I don't have the energy to fight.

"Emma?"

I glare at him. "I'm right here. I'm the same person I was a week ago. I've apologized. I've begged for your forgiveness. What happened to us?" I ask. "What happened to *you*?"

"I want to go back to the way it was before."

"We can't do that," I whisper. "But we can be something better, stronger."

A few minutes pass before he speaks. He's staring at a gorgeous framed photo of the Ross against the wall. I study it, too. The sweeping walls and windows, the surrounding trees and grass, the people. They form the soul of our home. And whether it's a body or a building, how can anything develop without giving it the love to grow?

"Remember how much we used to love being here?" he begins, his words an echo of regret.

"I still love it here," I reply. "I'll always love it here."

"It's time," he whispers.

"Don't do this," I beg.

"Things will be better. You'll see."

"No, you're wrong. You love this place. Your kids love this place. It was never about the walls or the carpet. It was the people." I recall the memories that are etched in my heart. Laughing until we cried, until our bellies ached, our long, breezy goodbyes, sitting at the bar and ordering Shirley Temples and then shots of tequila, telling him *I do.* "We always said that words could never describe her. It's always been a feeling . . . inside."

He shakes his head. "Emotions screw up sound business decisions."

I take a step forward, unsure if I should touch him.

"You're not going to be able to fix everything, Bobby. I know you want to. I know it's in your blood to protect those you love, but it's not always possible. Moving won't bring your little girl back. Or make what she did go away." Then I add, "Or change what I did."

"That's not what it's about."

My voice is uneven but determined. "I know you're pissed. It's warranted. But walking away, selling the hotel, having Grace arrested, and rejecting Zoe—it's wrong. You can move us out of here, you can ignore Zoe, ruin Grace's life, but all it's doing is destroying us."

"You already did that," he says with callous eyes, "when you lied to me."

This is exactly how I'd imagined it. Maybe even worse.

"How can you let Grace get away with hurting our family?"

"Our family?" I stab back. "This isn't a family. When was the last time we were a family, and I don't mean in a glammed-up, phony interview? Family doesn't abandon each other at tough times. Families don't pick and choose the parts to love. Families fight for each other no matter what tries to break them apart."

"I don't know my family anymore . . ." His voice cracks.

My face flushes with heat. Words like *I'm leaving* or *separation* had never touched us, but neither did words like *sexual cyberharassment*. Monty Greer is the nail in our coffin. "What are you saying, Bobby? You want a divorce? You're done? Tell me!"

His eyes fill with tears. "I love you." He says it like it's the first time, and he's not sure I'll believe it. It's a flimsy string holding us together.

"Those are hollow, empty words—worthless if you leave."

"I don't know how to do this, Em. I don't know how to give her what she needs. I don't know how to forgive you. To stop seeing you with him. To stop hating what you've done—what you've kept from me. It's playing over and over in my mind. How can I make it stop?"

My eyes shut, and I inhale deeply. When I open them, I take the few steps between us, and grab hold of his eyes. "Let me tell you what love means. It means we're all profoundly human. That we make mistakes, and we accept each other's faults. It means we value each other more than our pride." My voice changes. "I love you, Bobby. I loved you all those years ago on the beach, even when I didn't know it myself. And I wish I could go back and change what I did, but I can't. And when I tell you I love you, I'm giving you all of me—including my commitment to make us whole again."

His eyes fill with confusion. He doesn't move.

"I'll face your anger. I deserve it. I'll love you better than before . . . you can count on that. But please support Zoe. It's bad enough she has to live with her inner critic. Having her father denounce her is almost worse." Then I change my mind. "No, actually, it is worse. For her, it's much worse."

I wait for his arms to wrap around me.

"Everything's changed," he says, not making a move. He had never backed away from me before. He was always the one to touch me first, to love me last.

"You think I've changed? You think I'm different?"

"The person I knew before didn't keep things from me," he replies.

"And the person I knew didn't turn his back on his daughter and sell her home."

"Don't," he says. "I'm going after those assholes. I don't give a damn how much money the Howards have or how much influence they have in town. They're going to pay for what they did to Zoe."

"Go ahead," I say. "I can't change your mind. You think it's going to make it easier for you to hug Zoe again? To love her? To love me?"

But he's not listening. He's got it in his head that this is the battle he's going to fight. If he can exact revenge on the Howards, maybe he'll feel that he's in control. Over Monty Greer, over Zoe, over Price Hudson, over me, over the hotel industry, over everything.

"You're not going to be able to fix this, Bobby," I say. "Not like this. The wrongs won't go away. They'll still be part of us."

He studies me, searching my eyes. "Watch me," he says.

Back in the apartment, Zoe's draped across the couch, and I hand her a sandwich from the pool bar. My nerves are rattled, and I can't bring myself to eat. She's deep in a *Damages* binge, and I tell her how much I enjoy Rose Byrne.

"Mr. Harmon called," she says between bites. "I think he was expecting you to answer."

"What'd he say?"

"He told me it's time to come back to debate. He won't let me quit."

"And?"

"Ugh. He gave me this whole story about how he was a teenager once."

Mr. Harmon resembles the cantor from our temple. He's tall. Lots of gray hair. A big, bushy beard that tumbles down his face. The kids in debate love him, but imagining him as a teenager has to be an interesting visual.

"He said I'm too talented to give it up."

"You are," I say, tickling the foot that sticks out of elephant-dotted pajama pants.

"Dr. Rubin says I need time to heal. I told Mr. Harmon that. And being watched and pointed at is not the best way for me to heal. Then he challenged me to debate him." She smiles. "I like that he cares," she says. "I'll think about it."

I close my eyes and hug her hard. She's been forced to face what she did. I, on the other hand, lived a hidden humiliation that no one knew about. My own private little Idaho.

"Do you regret what you did, Mom?"

I hesitate at first. "I did. For a long time." I brush her hair away from her face and behind her ear. "Every experience is a piece of our own personal puzzle. It's part of our history. I wish I had figured that out sooner. It makes me wonder what might've been different. Giving up theater was a mistake."

"You can go back."

I laugh and stretch my legs across the cushions. "Nobody wants a middle-aged Rose Byrne. But I've been thinking about doing some volunteer work for one of the local theaters. For now, you girls are my priority." Then I ask, "What about you?"

She tucks her feet beneath her. "This is a memory I'd like to scatter, like we used to do when we'd blow on dandelions. You know what I'm talking about? Some of the pieces stick to the flower, and the others disappear into the air. I'm not sure I'd want to keep them all."

Her hair smells like strawberries. How astute she is. How insightful. I watch her in amazement. "Those are parts of you, Zoe. The good and the bad. They're there to teach you something." I smile. "Don't ever wish them away."

CHAPTER 26

Over the next few nights, Bobby keeps up his charade. He's home for what he calls "after work" and then disappears when the girls go to bed, slipping back during the early morning. It's a routine that reminds me daily of what I've done, but he seems to find it satisfying.

"Am I that repulsive you can't lie next to me?"

"I need space, Em. I need to think."

I vacillate between understanding and affliction and spend hours walking the beach with my thoughts. The temperatures have dipped to a breezy seventy, but instead of relishing the clear skies and crisp air, I sink into the sand and stare at the waves. Their repetition is something I can trust.

Lisa's been calling and texting. She's persistent when she wants something, and she's not used to my silence. It's been days since Jo Jo's team of investigators arrived at her house and took Grace's computer. Avoiding her has been a challenge.

Zoe returns to school after two more days at home. I could get back in bed and hide under the covers, but I won't. My daughter got herself ready and went out the door, and I will, too. She'll fake-smile to the kids in the hall, and I'll do the same with our staff and our guests.

Before I head downstairs, I enter the study and take a seat at Bobby's desk, where the Mac stares up at me. It's been a while since I had any interest in visiting the Internet, even though it was once a morning ritual, logging in and studying the latest news. After opening the laptop and powering up, I scroll through CNN and the *Huffington Post* before landing on my Facebook page. Emma Grant Ross. I scan the feed and all the posts I'd missed. Dogs are still being abused around the world, friends are sparring over politics, and my high school classmate David Collins is still cracking the best jokes.

Bright red notifications line the top of the screen. Monica Hudson sent me a friend request, and I immediately accept. Friends have left words of encouragement, cryptic in nature, but real, on my wall. A few have posted a string of emoticons to illustrate how they feel. I visit the girls' pages. Zoe's account has been frozen until the investigation concludes, so I punch in Lily's name and admire her profile picture—she and Zoe sitting on a raft floating in the ocean. She has hundreds of birthday wishes and collages with her friends. Grace's birthday wish is there. *Love my besties forever.* It's a picture of the three of them when they were five.

Everyone looks happy and content in Facebook bliss, and I'm reminded how different real life is compared to the one suspended on social media. Fakebook. I face the computer in a dull fog. And I am terribly sorry for my girls experiencing a harsh reality. They live in a land where expectation is unrealistically high. The crux of the digital world. Everything is documented with precise perfection. No one's posting about their dirty laundry or the cat puke they had to clean up. But if someone gets ahold of your secrets and the flaws you wish to hide, the age of connectivity and accessibility makes it impossible to contain.

I reflect on my teenage years, nothing like the years that cement Zoe's mistakes into technological memory. My girls don't get to screw up. There will always be someone to document their fall, the fatal error that turned them left instead of right. Memory was once personal, a fluid, perception-based luxury. We could pull back on it as much as we liked. Or we could add to it as we wished. Now it was permanently engraved into history. No editing, no filters. It was no wonder the girls always needed to look their best, show their "prettiest side, be skinny enough."

I have to see her page before I log off. Lisa. Her face lights up the screen, and I try not to miss her deep laugh. Her last post was a few nights ago. A dinner at the Palm. She and Drew were smiling at the camera without a care in the world. I hover over the "Unfriend" button. But before I officially cut our Facebook cord, giving mortality to years of friendship, I study her feed, the pictures and posts that make Lisa dimensional and real. After scrolling through their recent trip to Anguilla, the numerous bags and shoes with designer labels, an inordinate number of selfies with ironed-out hair and fake eyelashes, and their dog dressed in a tiara, I feel too sorry for Lisa Howard to press "Delete." Her life, which had all the frills to make it full and complete, seems at times cold and artificial.

And then I see the pictures of the four of us. And I remember the woman who drove my kids home from school every time I couldn't be there. And how she could make me laugh until I almost wet my pants with her witty sense of humor. She was the one to show up at our tennis matches with a jug of sangria and always hire a driver to take us home. She could be generous and easygoing. She had texted me every day since the scandal. Who was the one judging now? I know I'm not supposed to contact her, but the years of friendship have to mean something. I saw how keeping quiet had hurt someone I loved. Lisa deserved to hear it from me. She was owed that much.

I pick up the phone and dial her number. My hands are shaking, and my heart pounds through the phone. The call goes directly to voice mail, and I'm shamefully relieved. "Lisa. I should've called sooner . . . I'm sorry . . . I'm sure you know by now . . . this thing with the girls . . . Grace . . . we had no choice. Bobby's so angry. He didn't see any other way." I stop to take a breath. "Please call me. We need to talk."

I'm downstairs in the lobby when Elle's wedding dress arrives. Bobby exits the elevator simultaneously, and we bump into each other like strangers. The delivery man smiles at us, mistaking my blush to mean something else. "I have a special delivery for the bride." It's an enormous garment bag filled with wishes and dreams. I signal Sandra to call for Elle, but Bobby insists we take it to his office for safekeeping.

Our fingers brush as we carry the bundle through the lobby. I consider the dress—its white satin bodice and fine lace—and I imagine being at the start of a great romance. Having a chance to do it all over again. I remember my own gown, now in a box preserved for safekeeping. Maybe one of the girls will wear it. Maybe they'll want something with fewer memories.

I don't know what I'm thinking. I'm holding the dress like a bridesmaid might, careful not to let the train—even though it's covered in plastic—drag along the floor. When we near the end of the hallway, he'll let go of the dress and lift me across the threshold. He had done that numerous times before when we were teenagers. We'd sneak into guest rooms, pretend we were husband and wife. Sometimes we didn't make it to the bed.

But he doesn't notice when we walk across the threshold. He hangs the dress in a nearby closet and instructs Tabitha to let Elle know it's there. And it's safe. She hands him his schedule for the day, and he takes a phone call. I feel let down. Misplaced. I'm somewhere I'm not supposed to be. So I leave.

I'm driving down Collins Avenue to the 41st Street Walgreen's when I get a text from Lily. The car speaks her message to me. "Grace is a no-show today."

My stomach flip-flops. I get through the dry cleaners, Epicure, and a stop at the dermatologist's office for some eye cream. I'm approaching the car when the call comes through from Jo Jo. "Grace Howard was taken into custody."

Jo Jo says it again, but I can't bring myself to respond. There's a band around my chest, pulling and contracting. It's difficult for me to speak. *Lisa didn't answer the phone. It's too late. They were taking Grace away.*

"Mrs. Ross? You there?"

I step into the car, trembling. "Yes, I'm here," I say, though I'm far away. I'm outside looking in on the soiled fragments of our former friendship. I imagine Grace shackled like a criminal. Her blue eyes rounded in fright. Drew Howard curses, threatening to take us down with the wave of his hand. And poor Lisa, my friend, is cowering in a corner wishing her status could make it all go away.

"Mrs. Ross, it's going to be okay," Jo Jo says, though it doesn't feel that way at all.

I am still, fleshing out my thoughts, blinking away the images of Grace being carried away.

"I'll call you when I have more information," she says.

We hang up, and a text comes through from Monica. **Are we making a mistake?**

Yes, I want to shout. It's all one huge, colossal mistake that we're making worse and worse, but I don't know how to stop it.

The phone rings, and I know who it is before I see Lisa's name sprawled across the glass. *Don't answer it. It's too fresh. She's too angry.*

I let it go to voice mail. It's a safe place for her to unleash her rage.

Sitting in the parking lot, I wait for the incoming message alert, but it doesn't come. The car waiting to take my spot honks.

The phone rings again.

I feel the desperation in the shrill sound. Lisa's name juts pinpricks into my skin. It's a mistake, but then it's all a mistake. I can't ignore the actions of a desperate mother. We had been friends for years.

"Lisa."

Her voice is stripped, hoarse, and breathy, and when she describes in detail what has become of her daughter, she's a mother begging for mercy. "They showed up at our house today, Emma. *Our home.* They're treating Grace like a criminal . . . I don't know what she'll do if she has to stay overnight. Grace never sleeps out. I don't know how she'll survive."

Lisa's voice is flat, though I can hear the melancholy thrum, the whisper of defeat, the brittle words that are battling tears. Talking about sleepovers is a necessary way to cope.

"How could you do this?" She breaks. "How could you let this happen? Couldn't you have come to us before letting Grace be taken away like some animal?"

I'm wavering. I ball my free hand while the other grips the phone. "I tried. It was too late." But then I see Zoe's fragile face and the pain Grace caused. "We didn't do this to Grace, Lisa."

"Grace didn't do this to Zoe. It's a mistake. Grace would never, never do something like this. Someone must've taken her computer or her phone. She loves Zoe. She doesn't even know how to upload a video to the Internet." The dam has burst wide open, and with it, her rationale.

I remember having the same reaction when it was Zoe. None of us want to believe it's our kids. I raise my voice. "Every one of them has it in them to do questionable things. They're all capable. Put any one of them in the wrong situation at the wrong time, and it happens. You think I thought Zoe would do what she did?"

"Grace would never do this, Emma. She'd never do this to Zoe!" All I hear is her gasping.

"Lisa, there's evidence linking Grace to the crime. Besides being against the law, it was mean. Why would she do this?" I feel myself welling up and make every effort to hold it in.

Lisa lets out a whisper. I can hardly hear the words, tightly knit in denial. "I'll say it again. Grace would never do this. You've made a grave mistake in coming after our family. You'll regret this, Emma." And the call ends.

Her threats chill me to the very core. I can't hide my disbelief or my sadness. *Mistake.* Sure, it would be nice to hear that Zoe had been tricked. That someone had drugged her so she wasn't liable for her actions. Then there would be someone to blame instead of her. Looking inward meant stripping away layers. And was it ever that easy? There were too many pieces to string together.

The car behind me has given up while I stare out at the crowded parking lot. Lisa's voice echoes in my ears. I flip between compassion and retaliation. I pick up my phone and dial Bobby's number, change my mind, and hang up. I need time to wade through my thoughts and Lisa's threats. But as soon as I place it on the console, it rings.

Jo Jo is in my ear updating me, but I tell her to stop. My brain is overloaded. My words bang into each other. A flurry of chaos. "I know how today went, and I'm not sure how much more we can take . . . Zoe's best friend betrays her, her mother is livid, my husband plans to sell our hotel. The timing couldn't be worse. He's not thinking clearly. None of us are. Are you sure this is the right thing to do?"

"I don't know anything about hotels."

"This case," I correct her, bordering on hysterical, "this arrest. It's spiraling out of control."

"Mrs. Ross, I thought I was clear. Once the case gets picked up by the authorities, it's not yours anymore. The State prosecutes with or without your consent or Zoe's testimony."

"How do we undo it?" There's panic in my voice.

"I'm not sure you can. The prosecution's tough. Cases like this are growing at an alarming rate. The State wants to prove a point." I hear her inhaling again. "Talk to your husband. See if he's willing to recuse the kids from testifying. The Hudsons, too. But know that Grace could still be prosecuted."

"It's not enough," I argue. "I know you told us what would happen once the ball started rolling, but we need to stop the ball. Immediately."

"You can't possibly want that, Mrs. Ross. Grace Howard committed a serious offense against your child."

The quiet between us is unsettling.

"I told you and Mr. Ross to think this through. When it's someone you're close to, objectivity is compromised. I can't advise you either way, and certainly not how to feel." She pauses. "I'm surprised Mrs. Howard contacted you. Her attorney—I'm sure she has a team of them—had to have advised against it." I leave out the part where I called her first.

My thoughts get mixed with Jo Jo's voice discussing bail. "Since she's a minor, she's protected. Her name won't be disclosed. The records are sealed."

The hypocrisy travels down my body and back up again. I can't accept the unfairness—how our daughter can be publicly shamed while Grace gets to hide behind the same laws that couldn't protect Zoe.

Call waiting blares in my ear, and it's Bobby. I used to love when the picture from the Keys, his hair messy and the sexy beard, would flash across my screen. He's without a shirt, and the twinge inside reminds me that I'm not dead. I switch calls fast.

"Em?"

I listen as the call transfers to the surrounding speakers that make him sound like he's whispering in my ear. "Em, you there?" I want to bury myself in the deep, gravelly tone. We had fallen more and more in love over the phone when the connection laced us together, eyes closed, words kissing our necks and cheeks. "I'm here," I say.

I finally make my way out of the parking lot. The car weaves in and out of traffic. It's a dreary day, one that echoes the winters up north, though many degrees warmer. The sky is gray, the air still and thick.

One puff of wind and something might drip from the sky—rain, or some other form of sadness.

"They took the Howard girl in."

"Grace," I say louder than I should.

"I don't know that girl. And you shouldn't feel sorry for her."

"*That girl* spent years in our home, Bobby. The Howards were our friends."

"We should've used better judgment. She destroyed Zoe. The law agrees."

I should pull over. We had always told the girls that if they were upset or tired they should never get behind the wheel of a car.

"Bobby, this is Grace. This isn't some nameless, faceless stranger." I wait a beat. "We need to stop it. I want to stop it. We can't go through with this."

"It's too late, Emma. If it's a mistake, then I guess we're all guilty."

I push "End," sending him to the dropped-call graveyard.

Hours later I'm following the windy roads that lead to Thatcher. Apprehension has me on edge, a bomb in me about to go off. I'm early, so I'm the lone car in the circular drive. Lily is first to exit the building. She's half walking, half jogging, her backpack slung over one shoulder, causing her to tilt to one side. She opens the car door and flings herself on the seat beside me.

I lean over to greet her. She smells like school lunch and stale air-conditioning. Zoe's next. She is cautious and slow. Her bag hunches her forward as she glides toward the car, her face wearing the crookedness of her mood. She climbs into the back and lies across the row of seats.

I'm steering the car out of the cul-de-sac with both hands on the wheel, the building receding behind us. I need to tell them. "How was your day?"

"School starts too early," Lily complains. "High schoolers should get an extra hour in the morning."

"Look," I begin, not knowing how to say this, so I just say it. "I don't want you hearing this from somebody else. The reason Grace was absent today was because she was taken into custody. She's been charged."

Lily processes the information first. "Wow." She must feel Zoe's stare. "She deserves it, but the entire school is going to hate us. We're going to be the laughingstock of the grade."

The color fades from Zoe's face, and the twins are no longer in sync.

Lily is undecided. "Grace is wrong, whatever, but having her arrested? Meddling parents are the worst."

"Lily," I begin, "what Grace did to your sister was way more than wrong."

"I agree, but wasn't there some other way?" she asks. The blue in her eyes matches her disposition. Yes, there was. Only we didn't think it was enough.

"Mom." Zoe's voice is wobbly. "Is Grace in jail?"

The term sounds dirty. "I don't know. The laws are different for minors. I'm not sure where she is, or if they're going to charge her as an adult."

"She's just a kid!" The shock stumbles from her mouth.

My head pounds. I stretch my neck against the headrest. Zoe's taking it all in. She's in deep thought. I know this, because I watch her in the mirror. Lines furrow her forehead, and her lips move without speaking. The stress of the last few weeks has taken its toll on her. Thoughts glide off her tongue and into the universe.

"Do you think they'll let her bring her Prada bag with her?" she deadpans. "She doesn't like to go anywhere without it." She laughs. At first it's guarded, but then it's a hearty chuckle and releases some of the tension. "I'm sure they don't have Pratesi sheets in jail," she continues. "She's not gonna be happy."

"Orange is the new black," Lily joins in.

"She won't spend the night," Zoe adds. "Mr. Howard has probably jetted in from a business trip to bail her out. Like the affluenza kid."

"Girls," I chide. I imagine Grace and her pleading blue eyes crying out for her parents to save her. Sympathy for the young girl overwhelms me. Or young adult. Depending on where the spokes of the wheel turn.

"She's never getting that BMW she's been bragging about since she was ten," Lily continues.

"Of course she will," adds Zoe, rolling her eyes.

I should stop them. They're talking about our friends, a family we had trusted. But God, it's good to hear them laugh again. If this is how they make sense of things, let them. They're angry. They're exposed. When Lily can't find anything else to poke fun at, she turns to me and asks for a second time, "Was an arrest really necessary?"

"You're upset," I say, her doubt echoing my own. "But Grace broke the law."

A quiet envelops us. We are stuck in our individual minds playing multiple scenarios. One is more awful than the next.

Lily's phone begins to buzz and beep. A series of notifications that can only mean one thing: Grace Howard's arrest is trending at the top of every news feed. "It's out," she says.

I don't want to go home. "How about we stop at the seamstress and see if your dresses for the wedding are ready?"

Lily can't break away from the phone, but she says, "Sure," while Zoe leans back in her seat and grunts, "Six months ago. That's where I want to go. Today was a hundred days long."

I make the turn to the shop on Lincoln Road. The girls are quiet, Lily engrossed in her phone, Zoe staring out at the trafficked streets of Miami. I flip through the stations until I find a song we can all agree on. It's never an easy task. Train. Macklemore. We settle on Adele.

❧

"Perfection," says Flora the seamstress, as the girls twirl in front of us. They're the same color palette, coral and lilac, but the styles are totally different. I catch them smiling at themselves in the mirror. I could cry, they look so grown-up.

"If you have the time," the older woman says, "I can finish these seams, and you won't have to come back."

I smile. "We'll wait."

The girls run next door to the bakery, returning with cookies and iced coffees. They plop down on the velvety blue cushions, one on each side of me. When they're done, Lily rolls over and rests her head in my lap. I wipe the lingering crumbs and finger the pale freckles lining her jaw.

We don't bring up Grace or YouTube. We huddle together, talking about normal things that girls their age talk about: shoes, Justin Bieber performing at Fontainebleau, and driving permits. But Zoe withdraws again. Without the dress, she slips back into sadness. Lily tries to fill the quiet.

"Lyndsey's having a *quinceañera*," she says.

"She's Jewish," says Zoe. "She had a bat mitzvah."

Lily giggles when she repeats Lyndsey's reasoning, "She thinks because we live in a city where English is practically the second language, it gives her dual citizenship."

Zoe fights her smile, but I see it cross her face.

"I switched advisory today," Lily says.

"You can't do that," replies Zoe. "They don't allow it."

"Oh yes, I can. I went to my counselor and told her I'm graduating with my twin sister."

I'm confused. "What does advisory have to do with graduation?"

"Advisory is your homeroom for the four years of high school. You sit with them at the graduation ceremony."

"You really switched?" Zoe asks. "For me?"

"I did," Lily says. "Why are you surprised?"

"I don't know. I didn't think it mattered that much to you."

"Zoe," Lily says again, turning to face her sister. "You matter to me. You've always mattered to me. We're different, but come on, do you know how many times I've wished I could speak like you? Your debate wins are all over the school. Have you watched the videos? The recaps on the morning announcements?"

"No one cares about that stuff," Zoe says, brushing her off. "Your lacrosse games are much more exciting and cool. *You're* much more exciting and cool."

"Geez," Lily says. "I should've told you . . . I should've said it more often . . ."

"What?" Zoe asks.

"You have it all wrong. I'm the one who's always wanted to be more like you."

Zoe's face changes, her surprise evident. Then a small smile forms. "You might want to rethink that statement," she finally says.

"I'm sorry this happened to you," Lily says, twirling her hair in her hand.

Zoe stops chewing. I can tell she's embarrassed at the pain she's caused. "You're not mad?"

"It's fine," Lily says. "Grace deserves it."

My arms come around both girls, and I hug them tight. The nearby doors leading outside are opening and closing, the steel barriers that separate letting someone in and sending them out. Zoe says, "I love you, Lilo."

"I know," Lily says. "Because I love you, too."

CHAPTER 27

The girls are asleep, and I slide into the empty bed. Bobby texted me earlier. I won't be home for dinner. Kiss the girls.

He hasn't called, and I assume he's not going to pop in before returning to his suite. My mind is numb with worry, and I switch between *Downton Abbey* and old episodes of *The Killing*, before diving into the book that has been sitting by the bed taunting me.

A bookmark pops out, and I'm surprised to find it's the envelope Sandra handed me days ago from the Golans. I'd become careless. I rip the paper open and see the scrawly handwriting of Dalia Golan.

> *Emma & Bobby,*
>
> *Thank you for the special touches during our most recent visit. Reaching our twenty-fifth was monumental in itself, but the attention and kindness from your staff truly made our stay memorable. Did you know that someone pulled a picture of us from Facebook, had it blown up, framed, and waiting for us when we entered our room? And I know we didn't reserve the suite overlooking the ocean, but you remembered. It was where we spent our first anniversary. It was a difficult time, and Laura Ross found a way to bring us back to life. Thank you for*

*that wonderful gift. Thank you for honoring a tradition
with human kindness. If we weren't spoiled enough, the
champagne and chocolate-covered strawberries arrived.
How can we ever thank you for these generous gifts? For
making us feel a part of your family year after year? For
making us feel like home.*

In gratitude and in friendship,
Dalia & Morris Golan

Dalia was diagnosed with breast cancer the day before their first
anniversary. It was a bittersweet time. Laura Ross saw to it that the
young couple would forget, for a weekend, the battle they had ahead.
And when Dalia went into remission, the Golans decided that as long
as she was alive, they'd celebrate anniversaries at the Ross.

I fold the note in my hands and hold it close to my heart. I check
and recheck the phone. I get up and stare out the window, as if he'll
appear in the blackness. Nothing.

I slide back under the comforter and turn my back to the empty
space. If he could have seen the girls today. They were so pretty and
grown-up in their dresses, he would have never turned away. They were
flawed and testing limits, but they were delicious kids. They had good
intentions; they would balk at Pratesi sheets.

I must have dozed off, because I am startled awake by his sounds.
They're vague and unpronounced, but they're familiar and mean he's
close. I smell his cologne, the faint whiff of citrus woods commingling
with the scent of the lobby candles. Before, I would've turned over and
lifted the blanket for him to meet me, but tonight I'm confused. He's
quiet and doesn't turn on the light. I listen to his choppy breaths as he
undresses and heads to the bathroom to wash up. The door is open, and
I feel him in the reflection of the mirrors that frame the walls. I stare. I
can't help myself. He weakens me.

I wonder if he's come to his senses. I want so much for him to curl around me and whisper he loves me. *I'm here for you. I'll never let you go.* He may find me under the covers, or he may simply turn away. If the Howards are weighing on him, or Monty and Zoe, or if the interested investors are giving him a hard time with the sale, it will push him farther away. We are at a crossroads, and it's anyone's guess whether we'll survive.

His presence nears, chilling the air around me. I hear his breaths, his feet against the floor. I am so still and quiet I'm sure the faint beating of his heart inside his chest is the sound I hear bouncing off the walls. He is staring at me, watching me while I sleep. He had always loved seeing me when nobody else could. He would slip his hand alongside my neck. Then my lips. I'm not sure why I'm playing this little charade. I wonder if he can see the flicker behind my eyes, the way I tighten my fists to keep still. I have missed him, and I want him back.

After a few minutes, he heads out the door. The rejection drains out of me in a release of breath. I'm sure the sound reaches him, but he pays no mind. The balcony doors open, and curious, I shoot up from the bed and follow his path. I find him outside, seated on the wicker sofa. In his hand is last year's Shutterfly album. I had tried to keep up with the years through annual albums. We'd always enjoyed the recap—how we all had grown and changed.

The truths about Zoe and me have tested his faith. It's why he's sitting alone on our balcony staring at what once used to be.

As I open the door, the breeze wraps around my ankles and thighs. The chill nips at my shoulders. He looks up, and though it's dark, I can see his sadness in the moonlight. All the arguing and silences have led to this.

"Look at her," he says, turning the album in my direction. It's Zoe at a debate tournament where she upset her opponent on why dress codes should be abolished in high schools. The win didn't carry over to Thatcher's policy, but it may as well have, knowing she had the power to be that convincing. "She's poised, articulate," he continues. "She's got everything going for her."

I remain still, unsure where this is heading. He decides, scooting over for me to sit. I am hesitant, but I take a seat, allowing the nearness of his body to mean something.

"She looks happy," he says.

"She is."

He closes the book. "When you're happy . . . you don't . . . you don't do those things."

I turn to face him. "That's not true."

"My daughter drinks. She acts out. Does that mean there's something inherently wrong with her? Other kids drink. They don't end up giving a stranger a blow job."

His body is fire against mine. Finally, I say, "Zoe did what could happen to any kid in a similar circumstance. There's nothing wrong with her."

Our faces stare back at us from the album's cover. We're in the Canadian Rockies on a spectacular tour of the Athabasca Glacier. You can barely make out our smiles from beneath the hats and scarves, but they're there. It was a gorgeous summer day in a breathtaking part of the world. He rubs the page with his palm. I'm not sure if he is trying to erase us or love us.

"Today was tough," he says, leaning back and crossing his arms. My hands are tucked beneath me. "I had to fight myself not to show up at Drew Howard's office, and Kinsley, poor guy, his mom's real bad. We made final arrangements." I think about touching him. "It was really hard to watch."

"When do you plan on telling the girls that you're thinking about selling?" I ask. "They're going to hear soon. And the staff."

"Let's tell them tomorrow. We'll take them to dinner."

I turn slightly to meet his eyes. He's so close I can feel his chest moving up and down with each breath. "What will you say?"

"The truth," he says, but not to me. He's talking to the sky above. "A real home is good for us. We have an offer we can't refuse. I want to focus on our newer properties. The Ross needs a renovation."

We're touching, though I wonder why he let me sit next to him when his words say he wants to be far away.

"I thought I'd be able to get through to you. There once was a time I could have," I say.

I feel clumsy beside him. My skin is sensitive to his touch, the signals between us all crossed. Anger collides with resentment, a flood of feelings that make me sad. I have never doubted our love, but now the pieces won't fit back together.

I move to a nearby chair and study the sky. Earlier in the evening, I couldn't make out the stars. They were covered by dense clouds. But now I see them scattered, tiny bright lights dotting the black. They give me a subtle glimpse of hope I hadn't felt in weeks. "Are you staying here tonight?" I ask.

"I don't know."

Silence.

"They won't keep Grace in custody for long," he says, changing the subject. "They don't do that with minors. She's probably been released."

I have a hard time imagining Lisa and Drew in their pricey mansion sleeping while their young daughter lay imprisoned somewhere.

He doesn't want to talk about what Grace's betrayal is doing to Zoe. He doesn't want to talk about how we lost our close friends. He wants to talk about payback. "The chief of cybercrimes—who knew there was such a person?—explained what happened."

"I know," I say. "I got an earful from Lisa. It sounded uncivilized."

"That's not how it went down." He pauses, holding the book to his chest. "The police let Lisa and Drew take her in themselves. It was very civilized. She wasn't handcuffed."

"She made it sound barbaric."

"She was upset," he says. "I'm sure it felt as bad as she described."

"She's so young. She couldn't have known . . ."

"She should've known," he says. "They all should've known."

The more focused he becomes on vengeance, the more I am forced to play both sides. I grip the chair handles and squeeze. "We're making an example of Grace Howard."

"It's too late for righteousness, Em. Doing nothing sends the wrong message."

"What kind of lesson is it to rip someone's life apart? We didn't like it done to our child, so why do it to someone else's?" I say. "It feels wrong."

"What's wrong is you're not seeing the difference. What's wrong is . . ." He stops himself.

He tosses the book on my lap, and it opens to another page. There we are. He can disappear all he wants, but our life is right in front of us: Zoe and Lily taking selfies in Jasper along the blue-green glacial water; dinner at Barton G with the famed oversize cotton-candy dessert overtaking the picture; a community service trip to Costa Rica with a group of families, including the Howards; and the one when Zoe captured Bobby hugging me from behind. The hotel appears in the distance, and from this angle, it's magnificent. I analyze our casual togetherness, something we hadn't had to fight for. His arm was around me; my petite frame was buried in his chest.

My fingers touch the page, pointing at his face, and his eyes follow their path. A breeze flutters around us, and the howls creep along the side of the building.

"What more can I do?" I ask. "Tell me what to do."

He lets out a sigh. "Why don't you go back to bed?" He doesn't reach for me. He doesn't give me any more. Disheartened, I get up and leave him alone. The book falls to the side, the pages of our life open, the proof of our happiness, flapping in the breeze.

He never makes it to bed, and I fall into a deep sleep. My dreams are fitful and disturbing. By dawn I am afraid to close my eyes, so I lie back and let the light wash over me in whispers of golden orange. The ocean is flat, the sun's reflection fanning out for miles. The girls will be awake soon. I'll have to make excuses for him. I'll have to tell them he went for a run, or had a breakfast meeting. They won't believe me.

It's not long before I'm dressed and seated at the table, and I hand over those lies. Zoe says, "Stop covering for him, Mom."

Lily stops chewing on her granola bar while her eyes go from her sister to me. She says, "We know he's mad."

Zoe stirs her bowl of cereal. "It's because of me."

"Daddy's busy," I hear myself say. "Daddy and I are fine."

I can't even look at them when I say this.

Later that afternoon, Bobby and I are seated beside Jo Jo and the Hudsons in the Graham Building off the Dolphin Expressway. Renovated and modernized, the office divides itself between Children's, Criminal, and Family crimes. The State Attorney's office is a cold, functional space on the fifth floor. We are surrounded by officials trained in this new form of domestic violence, "sexual cyberharassment." We're meeting with the State Attorney herself, Carla Rodriguez, and the worst has yet to escape from her mouth.

"Grace Howard was taken to a local hospital last night for a psychological evaluation."

"What does that mean?" I ask, frantically trying to understand.

Bobby is next to me, but we are careful not to touch. Our division is more than physical. He spent the twenty-minute drive on a conference call with Jonny, and I could feel the tension between them. When it got to be too much, I stuck my headphones in my ears and tuned him out.

Jo Jo moves in closer and whispers, "We're told she's having an anxiety reaction of some kind. They'll evaluate for the next twenty-four hours, and then she'll go home."

I return to the night Zoe found out she was videoed. It wasn't jail, but it may as well have been. I think I might get sick. I turn around in my chair. "We can't go through with this." I'm searching Bobby's eyes, but he's too stubborn. "Why are we doing this? I told you this wouldn't change anything. It's hurting everybody."

All eyes pass from me to Bobby. The differences in our opinions are present in our faces and body language.

Rodriguez, with thick, brown hair and an unsmiling face, is unsympathetic and outlines the reasons we've all been called together in the first place. "Grace Howard was formally charged yesterday. She was booked, fingerprinted, and she's pleading not guilty. Her father, as most of you know, has a lot of influence in this town, and he's already threatened my staff with lawsuits and things I won't repeat.

"I'd like to take a few minutes to update you on procedure. We're building a case against the accused. Thus far the evidence is indisputable. The video is on the defendant's computer with a pathway linking it to the YouTube upload. I'll be sharing copies of our findings when they're complete."

"What about the person who videoed the kids?" Mr. Hudson asks, the brawny blond counterpart to his attractive wife.

"They're one and the same," Rodriguez says.

I lower my gaze to the floor while my insides curdle. Adrenaline hisses through me, and I want to hurt Grace with my bare hands. "How can you be sure?" I ask.

"Kids talk. Sometimes they cover their tracks and try to protect their friends, but like anything else, you can get to the bottom of who was there, who wasn't, who may have perjured themselves unknowingly. Despite her efforts to delete any trace of the video from her phone and computer, we have corroborated evidence that Grace Howard did this. She allegedly told a witness she was in the en suite bathroom when Zoe and Price entered the bedroom. She filmed them from a crack in the door."

The shock and disbelief spread through me. "How can one person be so mean?"

Rodriguez doesn't answer me, reserving her judgment for the courtroom.

"How can I tell my daughter this?" I ask.

I feel a hand on my shoulder. It's Jo Jo. She whispers in my ear, "We can safeguard Zoe from all the testimony."

Rodriguez continues, though I'm miles away. "We've advised the accused of the no social media and no Internet orders, with the exception of school purposes, and she had to surrender all other digital devices—phones, tablets, laptops, et cetera. We're charging her with aggravated cyberstalking as a minor and sexual cyberharassment."

"What is expected of Zoe and Price?" Bobby asks. He'd never acknowledged them as a pair until now, never used their names in the same sentence.

"As they are the victims, their testimony is essential to the case. An entire courtroom will be privy to the video."

We let this idea wrap around our heads, and I consider the emotional ramifications for Zoe, for Price, for all those involved.

"What will happen with Grace?" I ask.

"Grace Howard's psychological well-being can't be ignored," Rodriguez says. "She's a minor, and we must comply with all applicable laws. The last thing we want is her father slapping us with a lawsuit." She shuffles the papers on her desk and proceeds. "The family's hired a psychiatrist and a team of doctors to report on her mental state. There have been threats that she might harm herself."

We may as well have placed a gun in Grace's hand. What she did was despicable, but I'm struggling with the punishment. "How long can we expect this to go on?" I ask.

"That depends on Grace and our other cases. There's always a backlog. The arresting officers gave the Howards a courtesy by allowing them to bring Grace to the station on their own. We tried to work out a plea. We offered her the minimum to resolve this quickly. They declined. That stretches it out and sets us up for trial."

Punishment. It comes in many forms. Within. Without. It's unclear which one is worse. They both hurt. We all suffer.

We take the steps out of the courthouse into the streets of downtown. Bobby and Mr. Hudson awkwardly shake hands. Monica gives me a hug—the human touch momentarily consoles me.

"Mr. Ross," she says, training her light eyes on Bobby, "it's unfortunate to have to meet on these terms. Under different circumstances, I'd like to think we might be friends." She squeezes my hand while Bobby nods. We watch her long blonde hair flow behind her in the breeze.

The not-so-new-anymore baseball stadium stands in the distance, and I consider how things have changed: landscapes, buildings, lives. We're walking silently toward Bobby's car, which is parked a few blocks away. It's hard to believe that it's almost December when the temperatures are back up to the eighties. The sun pounds the pavement around us, and I shed the blazer I threw around my shoulders that morning. It's hot. And it's more than the temperature. I'm worked up and agitated, the details from the State Attorney's mouth hammering away at my temples. I'm watching the planes fly overhead en route to Miami International Airport and wishing I could hitch myself to their wings.

We step into the car and strap ourselves in. He has one hand on the wheel and the other on his cell phone. He's doing everything in his power not to look at it, but he glances at his e-mails from time to time. Usually it drives me crazy. Today I don't even care.

"Bobby, we can't let Zoe testify. Please."

"Were you in the same meeting I was in? Did you hear what Grace did?"

"Did *you* hear?" I shout back. "Grace is falling apart. This won't be good for anyone!" He doesn't see what I see. How revenge and punishment destroy lives. How sometimes our own private hell is enough of a sentence. Regret can be a remarkable lesson.

"What about Zoe?" he asks, his words short, his eyes vacant. "She needs to defend herself. She needs to learn that now."

"No, Bobby. She needs to learn compassion and acceptance. She needs to know forgiveness. It's way more important than exacting revenge."

There's something spreading deep in his eyes. I've had enough of the silence. I've had enough of the punitive way he's cast me aside like he had no hand in what went down with Monty that night.

"I was with Monty. I was drunk. Stupid. Lonely. And sick of being accused of something I hadn't done." There. I've said it. "I should've talked to you about it instead of turning to him. What came after . . . it was unforgivable to keep that part from you. But for God's sake, we were barely out of our teens and thousands of miles apart. I refuse to feel as though I'm some dirty slut because you say it's so. I did it to myself for too long. Needing to be perfect—for you. I refuse to continue like this. If Zoe can own her actions, so will I. And you . . . you're going to have to own them, too."

He accelerates, and we shoot past every car on the road. He stares straight ahead. I'm out of breath, terrified and relieved all at once. I grab on to the door handle. He jerks the car faster.

My words come out hushed in regret. "What I did never changed my love for you. Never. We've built a beautiful life since then. I have never loved anyone more than I have loved you. I have never needed anyone other than you. I'm sorry. I'll say it as many times as you'll listen. But you need to find a way to accept me, without judging. Years. We've had years. This one blip on our radar can't wipe out all we created."

I stare out the window as we pass midtown and the Arena. The shiny buildings and colorful architecture hurt my eyes. The traffic is backed up on the MacArthur, so he makes a U-turn and heads toward 95, then north to 195 and the Julia Tuttle. When we were younger and he first got his driver's license, we would drive across the set of bridges with the top down on his old Mustang. The city spread out around us, the crystal water colliding with the stately, waterfront homes. It was paradise and why I loved being at the Ross, overlooking the ocean and the endless sunrise.

"I'm trying, Em."

"You're not trying," I cry. "You're miles away. And I need you to come back to me."

He's about to say something. I watch his lips part, then quickly close. Our hands touch, his skin warm like our childhood memories.

And for a brief moment, he doesn't pull away.

CHAPTER 28

An afternoon downpour drops the unseasonable temperature to a mild sixty-eight. Dinner is on Mandolin's outdoor patio with its shady trees and long wooden tables. Lily's still in her lacrosse uniform and complaining about needing a shower. Zoe's grumpy because we wouldn't let her light the candles before leaving the house.

"Your mom and I want to talk to you girls."

Zoe wriggles in her chair and finds her sister's eyes. "I have no idea what they want to talk to us about. I swear. It's not about me."

Lily is dead serious when she asks, "Are you getting a divorce?"

Bobby loosens his tie and sips a glass of wine. "I want to discuss the hotel."

"Whatever it is," says Lily, "I didn't do it." Her long ponytail falls past her shoulders and down her back.

"It's not you," he continues. "But it affects you."

I sit beside him while he takes another swig. Last night, we drove the rest of the way home in silence, and he closed the door on me when we got upstairs. His struggles were a knot of indecision. I could tell he wanted to reach out, to talk, to touch, but he buried himself in work and left me to sleep alone.

"There's no easy way to tell you this. I'm just going to say it. We're selling the hotel."

Zoe is first to speak. Her eyes are accusation and anger, the wrinkle on her brow pronounced. "What?" she shouts, standing up from the table as she's been trained to do in her debates. She is fire and flame, kicking at her chair, while Lily laughs.

"Come on, Dad. You love that place. You're joking, right?" Lily says.

"It's not a joke. Sit down, Zoe. I've had some time to think about it. Change is good. The hotel is ready for new ownership. I think we've run our course."

This is his battle. I'm silent.

"The Ross is our home," Zoe stutters, caught between sorrow and fury. "You can't. That's not fair."

I want to hug her. I want to make it so it isn't so.

Lily is uncharacteristically quiet. She lets her sister speak for the two of them.

"Zoe, it's not that simple," Bobby says. "We have an offer we may never get again." He pauses, and I can see this is hard for him, but he fights through it. "It'll be good for you girls to have your own home— maybe something on the water with a pool and a big backyard."

"We have a backyard," Zoe argues. "We have the entire ocean. It's where we grew up. Why would you make us leave?"

"It's a building, Zoe. Don't get carried away," he says.

"How can you say that?" Zoe's eyes are aflame while her arms cross at her chest. "I'm not moving," she declares.

The waiter interrupts to take our order. He's Latino with bushy eyebrows, and he looks like someone we know. At another time, we would have played a game, taking turns guessing, but tonight we're not in the mood for fun.

When he leaves, disappointed no one wanted their famous Greek sampler, Zoe persists. "I'm not moving. You've spent your whole life talking about how great it is. How could you make us fall in love with it if you were going to take it away?"

"What about Alberto and Luz?" Lily asks. "And Kinsley and Elle? Where will they go?"

"Mom," Zoe says, "you don't agree with this, do you?"

I can't face them when I say, "I don't." I look at Bobby instead, holding on to his eyes until he's forced to look away.

"Girls, it's a good time for us to sell. The Ross may be where we live, but it's also a business. We forget that sometimes. The hotel needs some major improvements. Now's a good time to get out."

"This is what you do," Zoe says, cocking her face to the side. "You give up. When something breaks, you just walk away."

"I love that place." His fist slams the table, and the water glasses spill, startling the waiter, who's serving warm pita and complimentary hummus.

"Then how can you let her go?" Zoe asks.

Lily grabs hold of her sister's hand. "It sounds like Daddy's trying to do the right thing for the hotel. I'm sure he's thought this through. He thinks there's no other way. Right, Daddy?"

He doesn't answer.

Zoe continues her assault. "You always told us that the one thing that makes a hotel special is the people inside. Anything wrong with the Ross can be repaired."

Before he can respond, the shadow of two people approaches our table. They stand over us and stare. The restaurant is noisy, packed with customers, but suddenly it's quiet. "It must be nice to be able to go out and enjoy your family," says Drew Howard, with Lisa by his side.

"Come on," Lisa says, tugging on Drew's arm. "Let's not make a scene." But he pretends not to hear her, intent on making that scene.

I avoid eye contact with Lisa, though her presence shrinks me in my seat. Bobby stands up, throwing his napkin on the table. He towers over the shorter, rounder Drew.

"Don't do this here," he says, wiping his hands on his jeans. "You're making a mistake."

"You made the mistake, going after my daughter."

"The State went after your daughter," Bobby corrects. "I'm asking you, respectfully, to step aside and let my family eat in peace."

I catch Zoe's eyes to reassure her it's okay, but she's gone white.

"We could've talked!" Drew shouts, raising a fist, while nearby customers pause from their meals to stare. "We could've resolved this between us . . . figured out a way to work through it. Charging her is reprehensible! The girls have been friends their whole lives."

"What kind of friend does this?" Bobby lashes back.

Lisa is withdrawn and silent. Her blonde hair is pulled off her face, and deep swells of worry hide her eyes. She grabs Drew's arm and again attempts to steer him away from the table. I can't face her. I stare at my plate instead.

"Both girls made mistakes," Drew says, snatching his hand away from Lisa's. "Hell, we all made mistakes at their age. You could've come to us. You *should've* come to us. Grace is sorry. She made a mistake. I don't know if she'll survive this."

I look at Lisa. I'm telling her with my stare, *I don't know if my daughter will survive this, either.* She breaks away first, and I feel regret seep through my veins.

Bobby's face is explosive. His palm comes up in Drew's face. "There was an investigation, Drew! We had no reason to think it'd be a friend of Zoe's! Why would we? We were shocked to find out it was Grace!"

Lisa thrusts herself forward, knocking into her husband and the table. Her voice, once familiar, sounds like a stranger's. "The court will prove Grace's innocence," she says. "You'll see. You'll have dragged her through this for nothing. For what? You want to send my child to jail?" She begins to break down. "You were our friends!" Then she turns to me. "Emma, please . . . please don't do this."

I can't look up. I'm studying the table and the grooves in the wood, the cobalt-blue lanterns and jar of fresh olive oil. My mind whispers, *Please go away. Please.*

Drew shifts his eyes from me to Bobby. "Is this what you really want? To punish Grace?"

"Do you have any idea what she's done?" Bobby asks. "The impact? How long that video will haunt Zoe? Grace needs to know the consequences of her behavior. She needs to pay for what she did!"

"Think if it was your kid, Bobby . . ."

"It *is* my kid!" he yells, pointing a finger in Drew's face. "It happened to her! That video may never go away."

Drew's voice is a pleading whisper. "I'm not threatening you . . . I could create lawsuits that will have you tangled up for years, but I won't. I'm begging you, father to father, please don't do this . . . please don't do this to Grace."

I tug on Bobby's jacket so he'll back off.

"What about Zoe?" he says, pulling away and motioning toward the silent figure, who is now hiding her face in her hands. "Do you have any idea what that video did to her? She has to live with it. And she'll do it, because she has no choice. Grace . . . she had a choice."

"Bobby," I say. "It's enough. Sit."

Drew talks over me. "They're kids, Bobby. They screwed up. I don't know what happened with the two of them. I'll make it my business to understand." He turns to walk away but changes his mind and growls, "There were ways we could've dealt with this. You're going to be sorry."

Defeated, the Howards and our long-standing friendship vanish. Patrons go back to their meals, and the breath I'd been holding releases into the air.

"This is a mistake," I say. "A terrible mistake." It's too painful to think about the repercussions.

I lean into Zoe, smoothing out her hair. "Are you okay?" She doesn't answer, falling farther into me instead. I hold her tight and feel her body wrack. "I'm sorry." My heart hurts for the Howards. It hurts for Zoe, and it even hurts for Bobby. Lily pulls out her phone and snaps a picture of the Howards' backsides. I demand she delete it or she's going to lose her phone like her sister did. "Haven't you learned anything from this experience?"

"How is this our fault?" she asks.

Bobby takes a swig of his drink before flagging down the waiter and asking for another. "It's not," he says. "They're upset. Everyone's upset."

All eyes rest on Zoe, who hides her face in her hands. "I did this." When her main course arrives, she pushes the plate away.

"You didn't do this," I argue. "You made a choice in that room. It was personal and private." Bobby's eyes shoot missiles in my direction, but I don't stop. "It was your choice. Your body. Nobody got hurt in the process. What Grace did with it was wrong. She was the one who took advantage of you. Her actions were deliberate."

Bobby listens to me comfort our daughter and stabs at his food with a renewed vigor. "Zoe, I didn't appreciate your outburst."

"Bobby," I plead.

"It's the truth," Zoe bites back in response to her father. "It's what you do. You don't like something. You leave."

"I can't expect you to understand," he says.

She's tough when she releases herself from my grip. "I understand. The hotel is a little broken. You can't stand to see it that way. Are you embarrassed?"

I bring the glass of water to my lips, hoping the cool liquid will quench the heat.

"Watch your tone, young lady. After what you've pulled, you're lucky you're allowed out of the house. Keep disrespecting me and I'll come down on you even harder. You won't like it."

"Bobby," I interrupt. "That's enough."

Zoe shrugs and whispers to her sister, but loud enough for us to hear, "Whatever." Lily finds her sister's hand again and curls it into her own.

"Zoe," he begins again, this time his expression weakening, "do you have any idea how badly I want to fix this for you? To make it right? It's my job to make it go away, to protect you."

"That's just it, Daddy. It's not going away. It's always going to be there. Someone's always going to remember me as that girl. They'll have the video on their phone even if they never show it to anyone. They'll have that part of me that not even you can fix."

"You're wrong," he says, digging his knife into a piece of lamb.

"I'm not," she says, summing it all up in two words. "I'm doing better than you are with this. I've had to get up for school every day and pretend it didn't happen, that people aren't looking at me, talking about me. And you know what? I've done it. It's been tough, and it sucks, but I do it. Every day. And I'll do it again tomorrow. And you . . . you need to stop figuring out ways to fix this, because you can't. You're going to have to accept it. And me."

My hand lands on Zoe's leg, and I gently pat her thigh. My daughter has done what I should've done all those years ago. She freed herself. Had I done the same, it might have fused Bobby and me together, instead of tearing us apart.

During the car ride home, it's silent except for the breeze floating through the open windows. No one dares bring up the sale of the hotel. The encounter with the Howards leaves us lost in a flurry of thoughts that slam into each other. I watch the girls in the back seat. Lily is passed out, which happens after a grueling practice. Zoe is staring blindly out the window, the world different and imposing. I am struck by how she teaches us things we don't understand ourselves.

Hours later, the girls are asleep, the Shabbat lights burn, and Bobby informs me he's going to meet Mr. Summer and his team of investors at the bar. Reality sets in and silences me. I want to ask if he's coming home, but I fear the rejection.

I get into bed, feeling horrible. My phone buzzes, and it's Jo Jo calling. She asks me if I've seen the news about a certain school in Dade

County that suspended students for *receiving* a sext from another class-mate. Parents were outraged that some of the kids in question hadn't even opened the text.

"These phones are affecting the world around us. Too much access to too much stuff," she says. "I'm not sure what it's going to take for kids to realize the consequences of their actions."

But that isn't why Jo Jo is calling. She's calling because we received a tentative date for Grace Howard's trial in juvenile court. "Assuming she passes the psychological screenings, pencil in December 4. We're lucky we got in before the holidays. You'll need to come down Monday for an informal meeting. That includes Zoe."

The finality of it all comes at me like crashing waves. Lisa is pleading for us to stop. Grace is begging for forgiveness, for absolution, and the phone call means there's none. Though it's the beginning, it's really the end. The chain of events has spread like a virus across our porte cochere. We are powerless to stop it. I text Bobby with the date for his calendar. Before I hit "Send," I add **See what you've done.**

I'm not sure how long I'm asleep. A voice from the hallway trickles through our door and jostles me awake. I tiptoe to the living room. It's Zoe. She's seated in the living room with her back to me. I know it's Zoe by her throaty voice. She's comforting someone.

"Grace," she whispers into the phone, presumably Lily's, "you shouldn't be calling."

I am thankful for the dozens of times I told the girls not to hold their phones against their heads. Because of that, Zoe is holding the phone in her hand, and I hear Grace's whimpering voice through the speaker. "I'm in the hospital for the night," she says. "I'm sorry. It was stupid. I don't know what I was thinking. You have to believe me."

"Why would you do this to me?" Zoe cries out. "We were friends!"

Grace is sniffling into the phone. "I don't know . . . I was mad at you. I was so mad at you!"

"What did I do?"

"You know what you did. With Price."

"I don't understand."

"Come on, Zoe, you know. I told you!"

"Told me what?"

"I told you I liked him! I told you that night!"

"What are you talking about? You never told me!"

Grace quiets, and I hear her blow her nose. I think about her in the hospital. A dark room alone. Zoe sounds clearly shocked. *Price Hudson? All this because of a boy?*

"We were walking into the party . . . I told you I wanted to hang with him."

"You never said his name, Grace. I would've never . . ."

"I was in the bathroom. The room was spinning. I was so sick. I heard voices in the bedroom . . . I didn't flush. I was drunk and furious."

"Wait. You filmed us?"

I burst into the living room, needing to shield her from this bombshell. She's stunned, motionless, and my arms come around her. She's shaking. Her finger's on "End" when Grace begins to cry again. I'm about to explain, but Zoe shushes me.

"Zoe, please," Grace cries, "you have to forgive me. I can't live with this. I can't live without you!"

"You think videoing me and posting it on the Internet is the way to get back at me? Did you think that would get Price to like you? Are you crazy?"

"I am," she whispers. "I did it. I wasn't thinking. I was upset." She stops herself. "I made a horrible mistake. I wish I could take it back. I'm so sorry."

"If you were watching us, you had to know we were drunk and being stupid. You could've stopped it! You could've helped! You didn't.

You watched me. And you recorded it. And you put it on YouTube! Why would you do that?"

The agony in Grace's voice is difficult to hear. The mistakes these girls made—in the blink of an eye—and the fallout too deep to comprehend.

"Zoe, I swear, I don't know." She is hysterical. Her words are a jumble of sobs and regret. "He was being so sweet with you. He was looking at you . . . the way I wished he'd look at me. You have to believe me. I couldn't stand it! Remember how drunk we were? I didn't know what I was doing. I didn't remember even posting it. It didn't go live for days. They said there could've been a glitch. I don't know. I completely forgot about it! And then it went live, and it was too late."

"You sent a text to everyone. On my birthday! You blocked your number."

The line goes quiet.

"I don't have an excuse for that. I wish I could take it back. Google is full of information. It's not hard to find ways to block your number to send a text."

"You knew it was wrong. You ruined my life, Grace. It was mean. You hurt me. There's no taking it back." I tighten my grasp around her.

"Why can you be forgiven, but I can't?" she begs. "I swear I don't remember posting it."

"I told you already. There's a big difference between stupidity and being plain old mean."

Grace's words are buried in her sobs. "Do you know what it's like to do something stupid that you're going to regret for the rest of your life? You did it at the time because you weren't thinking. Everyone keeps asking me why, and my reason is stupid! I have no excuse. None. Zoe, I was so jealous. And mad."

"Why didn't you take it down? You saw what it did to me! To my family. You sat in my house and lied to me. To everyone."

"I deleted everything from my computer and phone. I didn't know it could be traced to me, and I didn't want to go near YouTube again. I thought it would go away. I didn't think the police would get involved and they'd be searching my room! I'm sorry, Zoe. If I could take it back, I would, I really, really would. Your family has always been so nice to me. I loved being at the hotel with you. You always made me feel like a part of your family."

Zoe is torn, mangled by indecision.

Grace says it again. "Please forgive me, Zoe."

"I can't. I just can't."

Her finger presses "End," and she collapses in my arms.

"I'm so sorry, honey."

"I feel bad for her, and I shouldn't," she cries.

"You're human, honey. You have a wonderful empathy for others. Don't punish yourself. It's what makes you special."

The outline of her face is dressed in faint rays of light. I'm rubbing her hair, and tears drip down her cheeks.

"I really had no idea she liked Price."

My mind ventures to Bobby and what forgiveness means. "You're a brave girl, Zoe. Forgiveness is a gift. Not everyone can give it."

"I feel sorry for her," she says. "I'm not sure I'll ever forgive her. I want to hate her. I want to make her life a living hell. When she says she's sorry like that, I can't hold on to it. I try, but I can't."

I smooth the tendrils of hair that escape the cloth band. "I want to hate her, too," I say.

"She has everything she wants," she adds. "Everything. She has no idea how many people are jealous of her."

"They're only things, honey."

"I don't know. I like the Howards. They're nice, and it's always a fun time when they're around. Grace never likes to be with them. Even with all that stuff, she came here. We were an instant family to her."

"Remember we talked about when people feel lost or empty on the inside, they do things to fill themselves up?"

"I guess that makes sense," she says, adding, "I'm an idiot."

"You're not an idiot. Not even close."

"I'll be a bigger idiot if I ruin Grace's life like this. It'll make me feel worse."

"I understand, but you didn't do this to Grace. She did this to herself. She had plenty of time to think about what she was doing."

"Grace is stupid sometimes," she says. "She likes to be funny. She gets a lot of attention that way. I think she's lonely. And I think she's sad."

"Needing and seeking attention is dangerous. It can end up hurting you and the people you love. I'm sorry she hurt you, honey. Grace isn't the only one who wishes she could take it away."

Footsteps fall along the hall. I don't know if it's relief or something else that washes over me.

"Who's that?" Zoe asks.

"Your father."

"Where was he?"

"Work."

"He's doing a lot of that lately."

This revelation makes me sad, because we're all feeling his absence.

"I don't want Grace to be punished any more than she is," she says. "I really don't. Isn't it my choice to continue?"

I repeat Jo Jo's words from the other day. "The State has a case, and your testimony helps, but it's not necessary to prove it."

She nods. "I don't want to deal with lawyers and courtrooms and Grace's face staring down at me when I go to sleep at night."

"The courts say a crime was committed, honey."

"It was *my* crime! The crime was committed against me! Don't I have a say in it?"

"No, not anymore," I sadly whisper.

"You said what I did isn't who I am. This can't be who Grace is. Every kid at school passed that video around. Are we going to go after everyone?"

"Zoe, I love how you see the good in people, but some people aren't innately good. I don't know if this is the case with Grace. Maybe this will change her, but we need to let the courts do their job. They're standing up for you, defending you. You're making a difference."

This is not how I feel, but at this point, I don't believe we have another option.

"I don't want them to!" She's yelling, her voice fierce. "And I don't want to leave the Ross. It's one or the other, but not both. I'm not leaving the only home I've ever had *and* helping with this case against Grace. You can tell Daddy that."

Before I have a chance to answer, he steps in the room and says, "You just did."

CHAPTER 29

Bobby turns on the light and sits next to us on the couch. His jacket is thrown over his shoulder, and his eyes are red.

Before I can ask him what's wrong, Zoe says, "Do I have to testify? I don't want to . . . Daddy, please." She gets up and parks herself on the floor in front of him. "Daddy, just listen to me. Please. I know you're angry and upset. But look at me. I made a mistake. Grace made a mistake. We all make mistakes. You taught me to be strong, but you also showed me how to care about people. You. And Mom. We can make this right. We can. It doesn't have to be like this."

His eyes have lost their fight. His shoulders are slumped. He stares at Zoe and blinks back tears. I can't decide if her message has sunk in or if he's drunk.

"Zoe, can I talk to your mom alone? I heard you, but can we talk tomorrow?"

She leans toward him. "You're not going to talk to me. You never want to hear what I have to say."

He grabs her hand and pulls her up toward him. She sits on his lap like she used to when she was a kid. He nuzzles close to her and whispers in her ear, "Everything I do is because I love you. It doesn't always feel that way, but it's the truth. Do you hear me, Zoe? I love you."

I watch them, and it breaks my heart and puts it back together all at once.

"I love you, too, Daddy." She slouches and lets him kiss the top of her head. Satisfied, she rises and walks toward her room.

When she's out of earshot, he drops his head in his hands. "I fucked up, Em." His words are tinged with grief.

I slide closer to him. My hand on his shoulder feels the despair. His arms come around me, and he collapses. "I love her," he whispers into me. "You know that, don't you?"

"I do."

"I love you, too," he says.

The words plant themselves deep in my soul.

"It's hard watching her grow up. It happens so fast." He pulls away but only to wipe his eyes. "I want her to stay my little girl a little longer."

"So do I."

When he speaks again, he says, "Kinsley's mom passed."

Sadness washes through me. It's a painful loss that presses us together. "I'm so sorry, Bobby. I know how much this hurts."

"Mr. Summer and I were at the bar with his men," he begins, swallowing the pain. "Alberto came by to let me know. I had to tell him the rumors about the sale were true. My men, my family, they'd have to find new jobs. I know I've let him down . . . he asked me about Zoe. 'Señorita Zoe,' he calls her. I told him I wished my old man were here. Guidance. I need some guidance." His eyes well up. "He said he's here. Always here." Then he turns to me. "I don't feel him, Em. I haven't felt him in a long time."

"He's in there," I say, pointing at his chest. "He's in Zoe. Lily. All of us."

"I've been horrible to her." All that moves is the lone tear that slides down his face. "And then I heard her voice. I heard her talking to Grace . . . and to you . . . and I listened, Emma, I really listened. She's an amazing kid. She's able to do things I never could."

"I know."

"I thought I lost her. Someone took my place. I was angry, but dammit, I was sad. And when you told me about Monty . . . I lost you both at once." He stops and finds my eyes. "Life is too precious and too short. I don't ever want to know what it feels like to lose either one of you."

I cup his face and force him to look in my eyes. "You're not losing me. And you haven't lost Zoe. We've been here all along."

He puts his arm around me and pulls me to his side. I curl into him and close my eyes. He's a thick tree, and I'm wrapped in his roots. I feel the steady rhythm of his heart, and I want to climb inside.

"Em, there's something I have to tell you."

I nuzzle into him. "This is hard on all of us," I assure him. "It's okay."

"You need to listen to me," he whispers into my hair.

It sounds serious; I pull back to face him.

He shakes his head and stares at the floor. My body tenses, and there's regret in his eyes that I hadn't seen before.

"The Ross is in trouble. I made a bad business decision."

I get up from the couch, and he reaches for me. I snatch my arm back, and he jumps up and comes around me. When I try to break away, he grips me tighter, making it impossible for me to move. He's whispering in my ear, and I'm wondering how many lies string us together.

His voice breaks. "I've been judging Zoe . . . and you . . . I'm no better."

My body begins to weaken, and I listen.

"I took out a mortgage on the hotel last year to invest in what I thought would be a profitable deal. Turns out it was bad. We owe a lot of money to the bank."

I sit with this. The lie. The betrayal. How we shield ourselves from those we love. I have no right to ask, but I do. "Why, Bobby? Why didn't you tell me?"

He doesn't answer. He only holds on tighter while our mistakes make us one.

Minutes pass before he says, "I've been so angry at you. At Zoe. At the Howards. Price. But the person I'm most mad at is myself. Jonny was against it. I didn't listen to him." He grasps my eyes in his. "I thought I could make it go away. I thought I could protect you girls . . . and now it's out of my hands."

A twisted relief presses me against him. The tears are streaming down my cheeks. I am sobbing. Our collective pain locks us in its grip. I imagine him holding on to his lie—the cover-up—and like me, his insides are hollow and worn.

"You were right," he insists. "We're all capable of screwing up. I'm going to fix this. And I'm going to do right by Zoe. I've been terribly selfish and stubborn. I didn't want to see it. I didn't want to accept it. Zoe's braver than anyone I know. Much more than I'll ever be."

I close my eyes while a thread of memories ties us together. All the reasons we fell in love weave through us, all the ways in which we promised to take care of each other. He's hurting, and it feels good to be needed, but it breaks my heart a little, too.

"How do we fix it?" I ask. "Is selling the only option?"

He doesn't answer, and I don't know what that means.

I grab his hand and lead him across the room. His eyes question me, but he follows. We head to the balcony outside. "Look at this place," I say, staring out at the blackened ocean, the rising swells reminding us of what's out there.

"We're all here. Nobody's gone anywhere. It feels different, but we're just changing and growing and finding out who we are. We'll always have each other. Always."

His lips come down on my mouth. They're ravenous, desperate. My entire body comes alive. The feel of him against the ocean breeze fills my every sense. If we lose the Ross, who am I to judge? We could have lost each other, and that would've been far worse.

"I've missed you," he says.

"I've missed you, too." I show him with my hands and then my mouth. His arms come around me as he slides his hands up and down my body. He pulls me closer, giving in to feelings he had tried for weeks to push away. He holds on with a deep longing. His kisses become harder, his need for me taking over.

"I'll never hurt you again," I say. "No more secrets."

Sheepishly, he responds, "I'm sorry, too. I contributed to what happened. I pushed you. My jealousy was unwarranted. I know you, Emma. I know you better than anyone. In a perfect world, it would've never happened, but it did, and I know in some way it makes you who you are and explains why I feel for you the way I do." Then he lifts me up and carries me through the door to our bedroom.

He lays me down across our bed and comes down on top of me. His breath is warm against my cheek, and the whiskers on his skin tickle my neck and face. It sends a thrill down my legs, spreading them apart to let him in.

It feels as though I'm giving myself to him for the first time. I'm not sure if it's because I'm different, or because he sees me differently. It's unclear. But in that moment, we are one.

Afterward, we are on our sides staring into each other's eyes when he says, "I'm going to make it up to Zoe. And to you."

I'm tracing his lips with my finger. "You already made it up to me."

"Making Zoe testify is a mistake," he says. "You were right."

I pop up, the covers falling around me. "Can you repeat that?"

"I'm sorry it's taken me so long to figure it out."

"You have no idea what this will mean to her."

"Yes, I do, Em. I know, because I know what this is doing to her. And I heard the kind of kid she's growing up to be." He stops and sits up. He rests against the headboard, and I lie in his arms. He strokes my hair.

"I'm going to e-mail Rodriguez. We're scheduled to meet Monday. I'm going to ask her if the Hudsons can join . . . and the Howards."

I'm curled into him when I ask, "Do you think she'll listen? Jo Jo says it's a crime no matter what. With or without the kids' testimony."

"I know. But it's worth a shot."

My fingers run up and down his chest. He rolls over on top of me and tells me he doesn't want to talk about Grace Howard anymore. Then he touches me again, in the places he just left, and we have sex for the second time, something we haven't done since we were newlyweds.

CHAPTER 30

The sun drifts off the horizon, and its glow stirs us from sleep. Bobby's first words are "Good morning, beautiful," as if it's my name.

"None of that was a dream, was it?" I ask.

He gathers me in his arms. "Not even close."

"Did you hear from Rodriguez?"

He reaches for his phone. "We have a meeting Monday morning. All of us. And Jo Jo. Don't tell the girls. It's a long shot, but I want to do this for Zoe. Let's hope the Howards show up."

I take a moment to call Monica Hudson about our plan. The relief in her voice is the validation I need. They're on board, eager to put this behind them. We all are.

We spend the rest of the day with Kinsley and Elle and most of the staff. Arrangements are made for a memorial service, and Elle cries on my shoulder. "We're starting our life together with so much sadness."

I tell her otherwise. "Maybe your worst days are behind you. Look at it as things can only get better." I'm reminded of our first few months of marriage and how lost Bobby was without his parents.

He overhears the young couple's worry. "She'll always be with you. You'll never be alone."

Jonny pulls me aside. "I tried, Emma. He was hell-bent on his decision."

I smile at him. "It's okay. If there's anything I learned from all of this, it's that we're merely people just trying to do our best. Sometimes we mess up."

"It'll be hard to leave this girl behind," he says.

I let this buffer me. "I know," I say, but I'm surprisingly okay with the circumstances we find ourselves in. As long as we're on the same side, I know we can tackle anything.

We observe the girls admiring Elle's dress, with its plunging lace neckline and thick layers of tulle. They look like sisters discussing flowers and vows and fairy-tale dreams. Jonny's face is filled with pride, and he squeezes my shoulder. It's a bittersweet afternoon marked by joy and sadness, and we put aside our problems to be there for our family. It's no wonder we all fall asleep early.

Monday arrives, and we rouse the girls awake. The groans are loud. Their blankets come up over their faces. I sit on Zoe's bed and press my lips into her cheek. Her eyes are puffy from sleep.

"Rise and shine, little ladies," Bobby says. "We have to be at the State Attorney's office in an hour."

"Said no normal parent ever," grunts Lily. "Do I have to go, too?"

"You're going . . . we're all going," he says, nudging her to get out of bed. "We're a family; we're in this together."

"I can't do this." Zoe's words echo across the room as she pushes her covers aside and abandons her bed.

Bobby grabs her hand. "It's going to be okay, Zoe. I promise."

She's skeptical. She pulls away and storms off to the bathroom.

Perhaps it's misleading not to let her know what's about to happen. It would ease her reluctance, give her some hope, but we don't want to let her down either.

In the car, Lily is playing Trivia Crack and screaming out questions for us to answer. Zoe is quiet. Bobby is flipping through the talk-radio stations, preoccupied. One hand grips the wheel with intention, the other settles on CNBC, and then my waiting palm.

I squeeze his hand. He briefly turns to me, away from the highway in front of us. His eyes are covered by dark glasses, but his lips turn up in a faint smile. I love him. I love having him back.

Stepping out of the car at the courthouse, Zoe makes one last attempt. "Daddy, please. It's not going to change anything . . ."

Lily concedes, "She's right, Dad."

They're dressed in their uniform khakis and the same orange top with Thatcher's emblem. Whether it was by accident or choice that they chose the same color, their bond doesn't come as a surprise.

Bobby sidles up to the girls and places an arm across their shoulders. "Zoe, trust me. I know what I'm doing."

Her sullen face does anything but trust, and her pace slows. Lily, tough and insistent, pulls away, running ahead. Her long hair fights with the brisk wind, and soon she disappears behind the doors of the courthouse.

Carla Rodriguez ushers us inside her office, where the Howards and Hudsons sit.

"What are they doing here?" Zoe asks, staring at Grace.

Lisa and I avoid eye contact, though I feel the energy burning off her body and smacking against my skin. Grace is pale and withdrawn, her hair a true dirty blonde. Tears have turned her nose red, and she stares at something near the window. She doesn't look up when we take our seats.

"I didn't know they were going to be here," Zoe whispers. Her eyes are frozen in question. Their silvery blue hits my cheek. Monica gives me a nervous smile. Price seems equally afraid.

"Thank you all for coming," Rodriguez begins, "and on such short notice. Under normal circumstances we would never subject the families to this type of meeting, but nothing about this case has been normal."

Jo Jo arrives, taking a seat behind us. "Sorry I'm late." She's lugging her bulky briefcase and bumps into me when she passes.

Lisa's hands are twisted together in tight fists. Her hair is down and unkempt, giving the impression she has given up. Today her sunglasses are large and dark, hiding her eyes and most of her face. Drew is pressed against his wife. One move and he might tip over. He appears less assured, and the uneasiness shrinks him in size.

Rodriguez shuffles papers on her desk. "Mr. Ross, I believe you have something you want to discuss."

Bobby stands while I watch Zoe squirm. *Hang on, baby doll.*

"Forgive me, Ms. Rodriguez," he begins, "for disturbing you at home . . . and thank you for contacting everyone and asking them to join us this morning." He clears his throat. "None of this has been easy. We've all had our share of pain and shock, and certainly, time to reflect. But we've learned. I have. I've learned that we all have the capacity to do things that change us. My daughter taught me that each of us has a pivotal moment that breaks us or shapes us. We are human. And none of us, not one of us in here, is entitled to judge." He searches the eyes of those surrounding him. "Our actions can teach us, but one mistake shouldn't define us. It's not who Zoe is. It's not Grace." My hand lands on Zoe's thigh. I burst inside, knowing this story is nearing its end. "I thought love meant protecting your family at any cost, going after anyone who tried to hurt them. And I justified my actions with laws and retribution and countless other things.

"I was wrong," he says.

His eyes meet mine. A single tear slides down my cheek.

He looks at Zoe and Price. And then he turns to Grace. "What you did was wrong, Grace. And what Zoe and Price did has implications, too. But you're young, and I know you'll learn from this experience. I think we've all had enough." He pauses before starting again. "It took me some time to understand this. We need to accept the mistakes in

287

ourselves and others. And we need to move forward. Without spite. Without anger. Without regret."

The silence is different than when we first sat down; it is the kind that means everything has changed. Zoe's face beams like a summer day. "Does he really mean that?" she asks the room.

I smile and find her fingers. "Yes, he does."

He turns to Carla Rodriguez and says, "My wife and I understand the State has a case with or without Zoe, but she won't be testifying. We realize there's plenty of evidence against Grace, but we're asking you, with all due respect, to please consider dropping the case, to show some leniency to a family we know is hurting, to a young girl who made a mistake."

Grace is sobbing. Lisa is comforting her. She removes her glasses and wipes her eyes. She mouths to me, "Thank you," and I feel a door open inside me that was so recently closed.

Rodriguez looks momentarily annoyed. "That's very righteous of you, Mr. Ross," she says, sitting up taller, "and I was beginning to forgive you for the weekend interruption. The State's unlikely to back down on this type of crime, however. There's a lot of evidence implicating Ms. Howard. Without recourse, these virtual lapses continue."

Bobby's eyes are determined. "Ms. Rodriguez, we've known the Howards for years. Grace has paid. We all have. Some punishments no court can hand down. The public scrutiny. The humiliation. None of them have ever gotten into trouble before. These kids . . . their lives are forever changed. They're forever marked. Let's have them move on from this and learn from it. They can turn it around. Let's give them a chance."

Lisa is openly crying. Drew's eyes are rimmed with similar gratefulness. I am hugging Zoe.

Bobby continues, "We've watched our daughter suffer, Ms. Rodriguez. We've watched her pick herself up off the floor and get back up again." He turns to look at Zoe. "She's made us so proud . . .

and her sister . . . she stood by her, never once turning her back." He pauses while the room quiets. Even the unflappable Rodriguez appears touched. "My daughter begged me to step away from this case . . . to let it go. She didn't want to hurt Grace any more than she's already hurting. I ask you, Ms. Rodriguez, isn't that what we need to teach our kids? Compassion? Forgiveness?"

Zoe gets up and takes the few steps to her father. He grabs her in his arms and hugs her hard. She buries her head in his chest, and he kisses the top of her forehead. And then both cheeks. "I couldn't love you more than I love you right now, Zoe. You make me so proud to be your father."

Lily slides over and whispers in my ear, "Dad just nailed it."

Rodriguez doesn't come out and say they'll be dropping the charges, but it's understood what's happening next. "I'm impressed, Mr. Ross. I don't typically let emotion get in the way of the law, but your arguments are compelling. I'm wondering if Mr. and Mrs. Hudson concur."

Price is nodding and nudging his parents to agree. Monica and I look at each other in kindred forgiveness.

Mr. Hudson answers, "We agree with Mr. and Mrs. Ross. These kids have been through enough."

Rodriguez stands from behind her desk, walks around, and rests her backside against the wood. I'm having trouble sitting still waiting for her response. Jo Jo squeezes my shoulder. "We've all been teenagers," she begins. "Unfortunately, the world is a lot harder on today's youth. In cases like this, with the relationship between the girls, there's a possibility the prosecution might back down. Perhaps the girls would be willing to speak about their experience—to safeguard other kids—and Grace can perform applicable community service. It might be beneficial to everyone involved."

Zoe and Grace meet each other's eyes and nod. "We can do that," says Zoe.

"I can't make any guarantees," Rodriguez adds. "Give me a few days."

Relief descends upon the room, and we file out of the office. Lisa approaches us. "I don't know what to say," she says, careful not to touch.

I look into my friend's eyes. "This was Zoe's doing."

Grace walks over, and her arms come around me. "I'm so sorry, Mrs. Ross." I don't push her away, but I don't do anything else either. Zoe is nearby and keeps a safe distance. I don't know if the girls will ever regain what they've lost, but like the rest of us, they will have a chance to try.

Bobby comes up beside me, and I find the space in his arms where I comfortably fit.

"Don't start celebrating just yet," Rodriguez interrupts as she passes us by.

Jo Jo whispers, "Ignore her. I saw her wiping her eyes."

The girls go to school late, and when they return, their moods are lighter. Their burdens have slipped off their shoulders. We are cautiously optimistic, and every time the phone rings, we ask ourselves if it's finally over. That same night, our family begins to mend. Zoe and Bobby go for a walk along the beach, and I spot them on the shore holding hands. When she looks up at him and he hugs her, I understand the power of love.

"Did you know Daddy was going to do that?" Zoe asks me before bed.

"I had an idea," I say. "But it was because of you, Zoe. He heard you."

"Maybe it was you," she says.

The memorial service for Kinsley's mom is lovely. A few of us walk out to the beach behind the hotel, and Kinsley says a few words before scattering her ashes into the crystal blue water. Elle stands sadly by his side. Leaving his mother here means she'll be at the upcoming wedding, but more than that, always surrounding them with her love.

"You doing all right?" Bobby asks, as we stare out at the water.

"Are you?" The gentle breeze caresses my face. "I know how hard this is for you."

He pulls me near. "You never get used to them being gone. I think about them every single day. It won't be easy to leave here. A lot's about to change."

I'm sad to think that our days here are numbered. I'm sad to think this is the one thing we couldn't fix. But if I had to choose between saving Zoe or the hotel, it's no contest. I'd gotten used to the idea of a house and our privacy.

We'll have a good life. Just a different life.

CHAPTER 31

It's a glorious day for a Thanksgiving wedding.

The sky is painted in a beautiful blue, and a pinch of crisp air blankets the sand. The sea is quiet and clear, and I take a moment to breathe it all in. Lily and Zoe waltz down the sanded aisle. Their dresses are long and flowing, outlining their tiny waists. Lily's is strapless with a pale lilac blended through the coral train. Zoe's is off the shoulder with the same soft accents. They each carry a miniature version of Elle's flowers: a tight bouquet of classic white peonies.

The ceremony is simple, with a slight breeze that spreads wishes along the sand. The happiness I feel while witnessing the man I love preside over the people I love multiplies. Kinsley and Elle exchange heartfelt vows beneath a gleaming sun, and their promises to each other erase, for a short time, the endings that are woven into a beginning.

"I love you," Kinsley says to his blushing bride. Her long hair falls loosely down her shoulders, brushing the fine lace of the ivory gown. "I've loved you since the first day I saw you, when you were cleaning under the bed in room 732 and got yourself stuck on one of the metal coils. We had to lift the bed up to get you out." Elle is smiling, her turquoise eyes shining with love. "You're the perfect mix of beautiful. Eyes like the ocean, and your mouth . . ." He rubs a finger along her bottom lip. "You tell me things without words. You do that to me. Even now. Especially now. Knowing you're about to be my wife, my forever . . .

"This is my promise to you, Elle, and to the family we're going to have. Years will pass . . . time will go on . . . and it'll feel like we want to give up . . . the promises we made to each other will sound old and stupid. Impossible to live up to. But I'll love you through it. I'll take the spoiled parts of us and make them shine again. I won't ever give up. Not ever."

I'm no longer listening to Kinsley. I'm focused on Bobby, handsome in his white linen suit, hearing those words as though he's speaking them to me. Again. Out here. Along our beach. His eyes are filled with joy, and our love connects us deeper and stronger than before.

Kinsley touches Elle's face and tells her with his wide smile that the rest of their life is going to be as happy as this day. "I love you. How do you put that into words?" Then he kisses her—for a really long time.

Lily breathes to Zoe, and I overhear, "Oh my God, I'm in love with him."

Bobby finds us, and we collectively gush over his performance. "Marry someone who loves you like that," he tells them, "or like this," and he takes me in his arms and warms me with his lips. The girls smile and blush. Perhaps it's recent events that have changed them, but their faces reflect a maturity that wasn't there before. I admire the wreaths capping their long, flowing hair. Luz sewed them, using petals from the hotel gardens. Bougainvillea petals. Bobby is admiring the girls, too, and our shared pride laces us back together again.

We follow the stream of guests and family beneath the private tent our staff erected. Jonny catches the bouquet, but passes it off to Sandra, who blushes from ear to ear. A Thanksgiving spread adorns the perimeter wall, and friends are nibbling on buttery turkey sandwiches and cranberry cocktails. Kinsley and Elle slow dance. There's our wonderful hotel staff: Heather. Sandra. Tara. Tabitha. Chef Mirielle is gushing over her culinary skills. Bobby is at the piano. It's Van Morrison's "Sweet Thing," and he doesn't look at the keys while he plays. He stares into my eyes. And I fall in love even deeper than the first time.

The laughter at the table highlights the shift in our lives. By letting go of mistakes and vengeance, we are free to move forward. I am mostly quiet, observing, as I've always loved to do. The girls are giggling with Uncle Jonny, and Alberto is telling them jokes about their father from back in the day. Bobby sneaks up on me with a glass of champagne.

"We've missed a lot of these. Can I make a toast to my wife?"

I don't hesitate. We click glasses, and I bring the bubbles to my lips, savoring all that it represents. The *Gratitude* book sits open on one of the tables. Each year on Thanksgiving, we fill out what we're most grateful for and leave it on display in the hotel for guests to add to or read through. It's a gentle reminder of our blessings, and I know what I'll be writing this year. Before long, the girls are barefoot, skipping along the water's edge, sinking their toes into the wet sand, chasing the seagulls, and racing from the rushing waves. I want to freeze the moment, though I had one rule for the day: no cell phones.

He rests his hands on my shoulders, and I bow my head to let him kiss my neck. Years may pass, but Bobby on this beach kissing me . . . the sensation never gets old. He pulls out the chair beside me, and we watch the girls from afar.

"There's so much tied to this place," I say. "I don't know how to leave her."

He grabs something from his jacket pocket. Folded papers. I begin to deflate. And before he can reply, the shape of a blonde is coming into view. As she gets closer, we say together, "Jo Jo."

"You two are hard to reach," she says, out of breath, but not because of her asthma. "I have my opinion about this and about the law. Yet, I've never met a family quite like yours. The State decided not to prosecute. The call came in last night. It's officially over. You can fire me."

Endings and beginnings. Bobby hugs Jo Jo first, lifting her up into the air and twirling her like Reese in *Sweet Home Alabama*. Then he grabs me, his bride, and his lips come down hard on my mouth. I let the joy and excitement lift me higher.

"They're at it again," shouts Lily from across the way, covering her eyes with her hands.

We insist Jo Jo stay and have some lunch, but she can't. She has her own family she's on her way to see. The young woman smiles, and when she turns to leave, she stops and says, "You're good people, Mr. and Mrs. Ross. You're doing right by your girls." Her smile is sincere, and she waves goodbye.

Jo Jo's departure feels a little like losing a friend. I sit back down.

Bobby slips the papers on the table.

"Is that what I think it is?" I ask.

He nods. "I've been sitting on it for days. Couldn't bring myself to open it."

"We're having such a good day. Let's not ruin it."

"Go on," he says, urging me to take a look.

The papers rustle in the breeze, and I finger them one by one. They're worn and yellowed with age, the handwriting as familiar as his gaze.

He begins to explain. "The first and last time I saw the deed to the Ross was when Mom and Dad died. It was a terrible time. I wasn't thinking long-term, just getting through the day. The deed was in an envelope I never thought about opening. I stuffed it in the vault and moved on." He is staring at the table while he says all this. His lips hardly move, the words a hush slipping out his mouth.

"I had no idea there was a letter in the envelope. I opened it this morning. It was from my parents."

The discovery sends a line of sensations down my legs. What it must mean to him to have those precious words from all those years ago. I feel my eyes glisten, knowing they found a way to reach him.

"Go on," he says. "Read it."

My darling boys,

If you're reading this, few words will ease your pain. In life, we all experience loss. It's what we do with it that dictates survival. Please be strong. And please be wise. You're holding in your hand one of the most precious gifts bestowed upon our family. She has given us more than most experience in a lifetime. And she has taught us just as much. Your father and I have prided ourselves in raising you boys not under the cloak of finer things, but rather beneath the veil of a life lived with exquisite meaning. While this paper gives you power and financial security, it holds something far more valuable.

We're telling you this because there will come a time in your life when you are faced with adversity. Your judgment will be skewed by emotions. It won't be easy to make the right or best decisions. Sometimes they are not the same. There will be changes. Some big, some small. The key is recognizing when things are worth saving. Or letting go.

Our lives have been enriched by the joy we shared in the Ross's belly. She gave off more shine and more meaning than any gems. Of course, she gave us you. We know the memories she has provided, and the gentle ways in which she has nurtured you and your brother through life will guide you through any difficult time. We know you'll steer her through transition when destiny speaks and you are forced to make your own decisions.

Whatever you decide to do with the papers you now hold in your hand, know that your father and I are watching over you, and we are so very proud. We hope the Ross has given you a fraction of the happiness she's given us.

We love you, boys.

With all our hearts. Until eternity. And forevermore.

Mom and Dad

My eyes brim with tears. Some escape, sliding down my cheeks. Bobby's fingers cross the table to softly wipe them off. When he speaks, his voice cracks.

"What do you think?" he asks.

"What do I think? I think you have proof that your parents are with you. I think they're watching. I think they're speaking to you. Do you hear what they're saying?"

"I do. I've been a fool," he says, "about everything."

"You were confused," I remind him. "The Ross is one of your girls. Just because she doesn't have a physical heart doesn't mean you don't love her and judge her the same way."

"I've loved her for as many years as I can count," he says. "Sure, she's let me down, she's crumbled when I needed her to be tough, but she's part of us."

"Bobby . . ."

"This is our home. This is our life. All the good, the bad, and the new. I wasn't seeing any of you clearly. Or myself. I didn't know how to manage the different parts." And then he takes me in his arms. "I'll have to sell another property to get her out of debt."

"I don't care about other properties," I say, lingering on his face. "As long as we keep the Ross."

The girls are there. They're laughing and out of breath from running up and down the shore. They are shivering, drying their damp feet with a large, green Ross towel. The neatly embroidered phrase along the trim of this one reads *Seas the Day*.

"Do you want to tell them, or should I?" I ask.

"I have a better idea." He passes the letter off to a puzzled Jonny and heads toward the band. He whispers something in the ear of one of the band members.

"Girls," he says, waving them over. They follow him on the dance floor. He positions Zoe first. The song begins to play.

She knows exactly what to do. She stands on his feet and takes his hands in hers. After a few chords, Zoe steps down and Lily tries. He's whispering to each of them, and they're smiling. By the time the song ends, they're hugging and running over for me to join them.

"We're staying!" they shout together.

He nods. "We're staying."

Forgetting that they're too-cool teenagers, they jump up and down, shrieking like schoolgirls. "Thank God," Lily announces. "Now that all this craziness is behind us, can we at least get our permits?" Bobby swats her on the backside and says he'll take them this week. Then he tells them to share the news with Alberto and Kinsley and the rest of our family.

He wraps me in his arms and whispers in my ear, "Excuse me, do I know you?" I smile up at him, and he leads me toward the dance floor, where I rest my head against his chest. "Play it again," he says to the band. I collapse into him, whole and full and at peace. I remember dancing with Bobby all those years ago. *Yes. I know you.*

And soon the sun begins to fall, and I take Bobby's hand. "Let's go home," I say, breathing him in with a swirl of ocean breeze. The girls race toward the building, their laughter floating up to the sky. We follow close behind, taking each step with renewed spirit. Up ahead, the Ross never looked more beautiful. We cross the patio toward her double doors and gaze up at her towering presence. She's growing up, shifting, pushing through boundaries. Imperfect. She is surrounded by love and those who will guide her through the next stage. My heart couldn't be any fuller.

Until I spot Zoe up ahead.

She's keeping in step with her sister, though her feet appear not to touch the ground. She is radiant and light, and guests appraise her with their eyes. *That's my daughter,* I say to myself. *That girl. That amazing, beautiful girl. She's smart. She's silly. She makes mistakes, and she hurts. She struggles. She picks herself up. She changes everything inside us, testing and tormenting, loving and loyal. That girl. That daughter of mine.*

And it happened like that. One day she said, "You don't know me." She was becoming someone else. A bigger, scarier version of my little girl. And I begin to understand the depths and the challenges of unconditional love. A heart seemingly filled to capacity, needing to find and somehow finding more room.

I thought it could never happen to us. Until it did. We entered that place where little made sense. I held on. Hard. Because there's nothing more gratifying than watching all the different parts of the people you love come together. To hold your child's hand knowing *You're mine.* We got this.

The path stretches out ahead of us. What happened to Zoe happened to all of us. When you love someone, it's difficult to experience their suffering without remembering your own. When they make a mistake, you remember yours. I foolishly judged my past and carried it forward.

Our children carry magical parts of us inside them. The parts are magical because we don't always know they're there. Then one day their magic breaks through and captures us, changes us, makes us see everything in a different light.

My daughter gave me the gift of tolerance and self-love I didn't know I had. She gave me the courage to accept my actions with love in my heart and to never let fear turn me into someone I'm not.

It is through her bravery and resiliency that I am complete.

She's not somebody's daughter.

She's my daughter.

EPILOGUE

"Turn on your blinker, Zoe," Bobby chimes from the front seat of the car as we approach the Ross's circular drive. I'm hunkered down in the back with Lily beside me; my fingers jut into the leather. *It'll get easier,* I tell myself.

"You're doing great," Bobby comments. I'm just happy they prefer to practice with him. They tell me I'm too nervous and reactive. I won't apologize for it. Motherhood is a bumpy ride. I've learned to hold on tight.

Alberto greets us on the swale. He smiles at Zoe as he opens the door. "This is a sight I don't think I'll ever get used to. The smile? Yes. Seeing you behind the wheel? Not so much." He addresses Bobby and me when he says, "Special delivery at the front desk."

We file into the brightly lit lobby. Bobby's arms stretch around the girls' shoulders. Zoe's color has returned to her face. Her eyes are clear and shiny. Lily hums to herself. Their matching long hair slides down their backs.

The stack of magazines rests on the marble top of the front desk. Our faces stare out at us with the Ross in the background. "Miami's First Family."

"And we're the first family ever featured on the cover of *Ocean Drive*," Bobby remarks, fingering the glossy magazine. The girls ooh and aah, and I take it all in. The memory of that afternoon and the healing since then is a tender reminder. We've come a long way. One would never know the pain we were experiencing. Makes you think twice about judging a book by its cover.

There will be readers flipping the pages of our story who will be wholly unaware of the struggles that played out behind the Ross's doors. They won't see the scaffolds and the dust during the renovation. They won't know of the secrets and lies, or the scandal that threatened to tear our family apart.

I open to the article and begin reading. Our history. Jonny. The girls frolicking in the ocean. And that's when I see it.

"I called Lana," Bobby says, and his dark eyes flicker. "It was time to be honest about us . . . about the hotel."

"'. . . and we've had our share of problems,'" I read. "'Nothing's ever what it seems. You know that. But it made us stronger—less perfect—more human, and the Ross shares the same qualities. Her understated charm. Her blemishes. She's going through a major renovation in the coming weeks—floors, balconies. Change is inevitable. The real draw is in the imperfections—the broken parts that require our deepest love and attention.'

"You really did this." I'm not sure my words capture the depth of my gratitude.

"I did."

I roll the magazine under my arm, and we walk hand in hand with the girls' laughter guiding us to the elevator.

My phone dings, and it's a text from Monica Hudson. Did you hear? A photo's going around. This time it's a seventh grader at Zweig Middle. Hurts my heart for those families.

I shudder, remembering that day. How everything changed. Then I formulate my response: This makes me sad. I'm praying for the families, and I'm grateful I've learned not to judge.

I put the phone away and step inside the elevator. I watch the girls watching themselves in the mirror, their youthful, innocent faces that don't quite match their budding bodies. They still have so much more growing to do. I may not sleep for the next couple of years. I'll worry, I'll wonder, but I'll do my best to give them my best. And I'll never ever give up.

Because I'm their mom.

And that's what we do.

AUTHOR'S NOTE

If you or someone you love is a victim of revenge porn or sexual cyber-harassment, you are not alone. Organizations such as the Cyber Civil Rights Legal Project (cyberrightsproject.com), the Cyber Civil Rights Initiative (cybercivilrights.org), and Without My Consent (withoutmyconsent.org) are available to help you restore your safety and get you back in control.

ACKNOWLEDGMENTS

Just like raising children, writing a book takes a village. Here's to my village. Thank you to my agent, Kim Lionetti, for being a fierce champion of my work. I'm looking forward to accomplishing great things together. Danielle Marshall, Gabrielle Dumpit, Dennelle Catlett, Nicole Pomeroy, and the team at Lake Union, I'm so grateful to have such a faithful group of supporters who have made this ride extra fun. Tiffany Yates Martin, this book almost died a slow, painful death, but you faithfully brought it back to life. Collaborating with you is always a dream, and I so admire your ability to mold and shape a story until it's living, breathing, and magical. Lindsay Guzzardo, Laura Whittemore, Phyllis DeBlanche, and Andrea Chapin, thank you for the additional strengthening of this important story.

Kathleen Carter Zrelak and Jeff Umbro, this token of gratitude is belated for your work on *Where We Fall*, which went to print before I had a chance to edit. I felt very fortunate to have you in my corner, and I wish great things for you both.

Thank you to the book bloggers and influencers who have welcomed me into your generous fold. There are so many of you out there supporting books and readers. My sincere gratitude for your kindness and generosity not just to me, but to readers and writers everywhere. Jenny O'Regan, Kristy Barrett, Lauren Margolin, Chelsea Humphrey, Bethany Lynne, Annie JC, Andrea Bates, Crystal Brutlag, Melissa

Bartell, Emily Lewis, Barbara Bos, Judith D. Collins, Ann-Marie Nieves, Melissa Amster, She Reads, Cyrus Webb, Elyse Walters, all the TLC Book Tour Bloggers, Readers Coffeehouse, the Tall Poppies, Great Thoughts' Great Readers, my pals at FB Book Club US, and anyone I might have missed. An extra-special thank-you to Andrea Katz for your friendship and vowing to trip me should we pass on a busy street. To my Lake Union sisters and gents, my deepest gratitude for providing an endless supply of support and guidance. Special love and appreciation for Emily Bleeker, Camille Di Maio, Marilyn Rothstein, Dina Silver, Barbara Claypole White, and Allison Winn.

Thank you to the readers who have supported my work, reached out, and given me the courage and inspiration to keep writing.

Elisa D'Amico, cofounder of the Cyber Civil Rights Legal Project, thank you for your tireless efforts on behalf of revenge-porn victims nationwide. Elisa's pro bono work makes her the leader in this field, and without her, this book would not exist. To Annmarie Chiarini and Anisha Vora of the Cyber Civil Rights Initiative (CCRI), thank you for advocating for victims and sharing your experience with me. Stacey Honowitz, your legal expertise is invaluable. Keep fighting for our children and our children's children. The world needs more of you. Dara Clarke, thank you for the intro to Stacey. Heartfelt appreciation to my father-in-law, Alan Weinstein, for providing additional legal expertise. Any mistakes from a legal perspective are my own and not the fault of the experts who shared their knowledge with me.

My appreciation to Susanne and Steven Hurowitz and Eric Feder for sharing their wisdom on hotel living and South Florida real estate, and Jeff Herman for fine-tuning a plot point in the middle of a JAFCO event. Amy Siskind, for depicting the intimacy factor in such a moving way. Felix Martinez, I have owed you for years, and you know why. Thank you.

To my early readers—Amy Berger, Don Blackwell, Jill Coleman, Sandi Cooper, Merle Saferstein, and Lauren Schneider—thank you for the thoughtful feedback. Your time, enthusiasm, and suggestions are always appreciated.

I have wonderful friends near and far, from all facets of my life. Thank you to each and every one of you for encouraging me over the years, for sharing life with me, and touching me in the deepest, most meaningful ways. I hold you close to my heart.

Thank you to my family for providing great love and no shortage of interesting stories, and especially my siblings, Randi, Robert, and Ron, who are the best friends a person can ask for—my team, my anchors, my childhood, and beyond.

Mom, I feel you every single day, and I know you're watching us from above. Keep flapping your beautiful wings.

Brandon and Jordan, you inspire me daily to do what I do. Your courage and confidence are admirable. Sharing life with you is always an adventure, one I wouldn't change for anything in the world. You have given me so much joy; I hope I have given you as much. There are great things on the horizon for the two of you. Be smart. Be kind. Be true to who you are. And know how much you're loved.

For Steven, the original Bear, my eternal gratitude for giving me the gift of your love and the many blessings of our life together. I'm especially grateful for our walks and talks and your ability to provide plot points with patience, enthusiasm, and insight. You always find the right words when I'm at a loss; you're the biggest cheerleader, and I could never thank you enough. I love you with all my heart.

QUESTIONS FOR DISCUSSION

1. How much is too much when sharing with our children? How honest do we, as parents, need to be?

2. Technology is here to stay. How can we teach our children boundaries and parameters to ensure online and cell phone safety? What are the rules in your own home?

3. Have you ever searched through your teenager's phone or computer? Where do you stand on privacy versus protection?

4. What are the ways in which you prepare your sons and/or daughters to respect themselves and others?

5. Have you ever experienced being judged by other parents for your children's behavior/actions? How did you handle that situation?

6. Emma kept a long-held secret from her husband. What are your thoughts on the sin of omission versus lying?

7. Nature versus nurture often comes into play in our lives. As parents, we do our very best in teaching our children life lessons, but sometimes our children's destiny is predetermined. What's your opinion on the debate?

8. While *Somebody's Daughter* highlights a negative side to social media, can social media be effective and positive for teens?

9. Our kids are quick to let us know how different our lives are from theirs. What are the greatest differences from when you grew up to today's teens? What is the one thing you wish they could experience? And what are the biggest challenges facing teens today?

10. In a case such as this, which do you believe goes further: forgiveness or retribution?

ABOUT THE AUTHOR

Photo © 2015 hester

Rochelle B. Weinstein is the *USA Today* bestselling author of *Where We Fall*, *The Mourning After*, and *What We Leave Behind*. Weinstein lives in South Florida with her husband and twin sons. She is currently writing her fifth novel, a love story based in the Florida Keys. Please visit her at www.rochelleweinstein.com.